She **came** to this party
for one reason. Him.

"I came to find you," Samantha told him and thought about kissing him.

"And I looked for you."

Now she was surprised.

"When you approached me in the bar, you didn't know who the hell I was, did you?"

She hadn't exactly been concentrating on her surroundings when he took her home. Sam had been busy yanking off his clothes...

"I don't care that you're rich. I don't want forever."

His fingers freed her wrist and he wrapped his arm around her waist. "What do you want?"

She pushed her hand between their bodies, and let her fingers rest over his racing heart. "I told you...*more.*" Sex. Passion.

She felt a distinctly mechanical vibration. Her phone!

Her fingers trembled as she read the text. *Get back to scene in Melborne ASAP. New body.* The message was from Agent Dante.

"I-I have to go," she told Max and saw his eyes widen.

"The hell you do."

Also by Cynthia Eden

Deadly Fear
Deadly Heat

DEADLY
LIES

CYNTHIA EDEN

FOREVER

NEW YORK   BOSTON

Book design by Giorgetta Bell McRee

Forever
Hachette Book Group
237 Park Avenue
New York, NY 10017
Visit our website at www.HachetteBookGroup.com.

Forever is an imprint of Grand Central Publishing. The Forever name and logo is a trademark of Hachette Book Group, Inc.

The publisher is not responsible for websites (or their content) that are not owned by the publisher.

Printed in the United States of America

First Printing: March 2011

10 9 8 7 6 5 4 3 2

This one is for you, Joan.
Thanks for loving suspense stories
and for being a great friend!

ACKNOWLEDGMENTS

I want to thank my wonderful editor, Alex Logan, for her insight and support. Thanks for believing in my SSD characters and giving me the opportunity to write my Deadly books.

For my friends—oh, so many friends who have helped me! Thanks to Manda for talking shop with me. Thanks to Joan for pushing me. Thanks to Ashley for always "getting" me. Thanks to Saundra for inspiring me. Thanks to Dr. Laura P. for advising me (and for being one of my best supporters!). Ladies, I couldn't have done it without you.

For my husband Nick—thanks for understanding that when I disappear into my own mind, well, I'm not ignoring you. Really. And when you have to say the same thing over and over again to me, it's not because I'm not listening to you. The characters that are talking to me are just louder right then, so I hear them better.

For my son Jack, my future writer, keep dreaming, love, and keep coming up with your stories. Dream on!

DEADLY
LIES

Prologue

I thought you'd be worth more." The voice came to him, low and taunting. "After all of your blustering and bullshit, I really thought you'd be worth *more*."

Jeremy Briar jerked in the chair, but there was nowhere for him to go. His hands were bound to the armrests, the duct tape far too tight, cutting into his wrists, and his legs were taped to the legs of the chair. A blindfold covered his eyes, casting him in darkness, and the scent of cigarettes burned his nose.

"L-let me go…" His voice rasped out. They hadn't given him anything to drink or to eat in, Christ, how many hours? "M-my family…th-they'll pay any-anything…." *Just to get me back.*

Laughter. Dark and mean. "No, they won't pay a fucking dime."

The ice in his chest froze his heart. "No!" The tape bit into him. "M-my father, I told you, he is—"

"An idiot." The voice was still low, drifting through the

darkness. "I gave him instructions, but the thing is, Jeremy boy, the asshole just couldn't follow them."

Bile rose in his throat. "N-no..."

"Not like I asked for that much. Just four million for you. Four damn million." The shuffle of footsteps. More than one set. *Someone else was here.*

"The bastard has that much in change." Anger simmered in that tense whisper.

Jeremy licked his lips and knew that the voice was right. His father owned half the city. He had that much money in the bank, easy. *What the fuck?* Jeremy's mouth was so dry. He'd screamed and he'd screamed before, but no one had come for him.

No one had helped him.

"Your father thinks it's a joke." Jeremy flinched when he felt a touch on his shoulder. Sharp. Light. *Fingernail?*

The point pressed into his flesh.

Jesus. *A knife.* A whimper broke from his lips. "L-let me talk to him.... I'll make him see—"

No fucking joke. That blade was too *real.*

"*I* told him what to do," the whisper blew against his ear, and Jeremy shuddered. "Told him when to make the drop. Told him where to put the money. Told him *everything*, and if he'd just followed my instructions, you would've been home by now."

The blade sliced into his shoulder.

Jeremy pissed his pants. "*Pl-please...*"

"Rich boy, is this the first time you've begged?"

His head jerked in a nod. He knew tears streamed from beneath the blindfold. He couldn't stop them. Fear ate at his gut, and he knew, he *knew* that his father had left him to die.

Always disappointing me, boy. Not going to dig your ass out of another mess. You're on your own.

Those had been the last words that his father spoke to him. So he'd screwed up and gotten busted with pot. Did he deserve this?

Don't let me die.

"Beg some more." The blade sank into his shoulder.

And Jeremy begged. Begged and pleaded and promised *anything* because he wanted the fire in his shoulder to ease. He wanted the pain to stop. He wanted to go home.

Bad dream. Just a bad dream. I'll wake up, I'll—

The knife pulled from his flesh with a thick *slush* of sound. Jeremy cried out, sagging back, but the blade followed him. The tip grazed over his jaw, traveled up his cheek, and then slipped right under the edge of the blindfold.

"You're going to send your old man a message for me."

Hope shot through him. *Yes, yes!* If he could just talk to his dad, he could make him understand. Not a joke. Hell, no. His dad would *understand*. The bastards would get their money, and Jeremy would be free. "I'll tell him *anything;* I'll say—"

The blade sliced the blindfold away.

He blinked against the flood of light. So bright.

"You don't have to say a damn thing."

The voice, not a whisper anymore, stopped his heart.

The man crouched over him with the weapon. Jeremy could see the others, too, as they came forward into the light.

Jeremy shook his head. "Don't—"

The knife sank into his upper arm. It sliced down, and the bastard wrenched the blade, cutting through flesh and muscle in one long stroke as he opened the arm from shoulder to wrist.

Jeremy screamed.

"Let's send him a message." The figure moved around him and stared down with a smile that twisted his lips and never touched his eyes. "Let's see what the asshole has to say when he finds what's left of you."

CHAPTER *One*

FBI Special Agent Samantha Kennedy had seen hell. She'd looked into the devil's eyes and heard his laughter. She'd died, but fate had brought her back.

Fate wouldn't be letting Jeremy Briar come back.

Taking a deep breath, tasting decay and blood, Samantha stared at the body laying spread-eagle on the asphalt right in front of the big, black wrought-iron gates.

Jeremy's eyes were open. They had to be. Some asshole had cut off his eyelids. His body was sliced open, each arm cut from shoulder to wrist. A red smile split his throat and his stomach—

She yanked her gaze away. *Don't think. Don't feel.*

Sam spun away from poor dead Jeremy and nearly stumbled right into her boss, Keith Hyde.

His eyes weren't on the body. They were on her. "You up for this?" he asked as his dark gaze searched her face. His deep voice seemed to echo around her, and goose bumps rose on her arms.

Sam knew that he was waiting for her to fail. They

were *all* waiting. All the other agents in her unit. None of them thought that she could do the job anymore.

Maybe I can't.

Sam swallowed. She belonged to the Serial Services Division, an elite unit in the FBI that most agents would gladly sell their souls to join. A team specifically designed to track and apprehend serials. The SSD had nearly unlimited resources. And Hyde answered to no one.

His team. His domain.

And she was the freaking weak link.

"I'm up for anything." Her voice came out soft, and she'd meant to sound hard. Christ. The guy was looking at her like she'd shatter any minute. Hadn't she already proved to him over the last six months that she wasn't going to fall apart? What did he want from her?

The sunlight seemed to darken the rich coffee cream of his skin. His mouth tightened, and she knew that he didn't believe her.

What else was new?

"I've gotten the all-clear." Okay, her voice came stronger now because she was pissed. A dead body waited behind her, and Hyde was wasting time grilling her.

"I know the shrinks said you could work the cases." His arms crossed over his chest. Beside them, a uniform bent over and retched into the bushes. Great. So much for the preservation of the crime scene. Hyde's gaze measured her as he continued, "But working them and *surviving* them are two different things."

He's waiting for me to break.

"Don't worry about me." Sam jerked her thumb over her shoulder even as she felt a trickle of sweat slide between her shoulder blades. "Worry about that poor man's family." The scent of death clogged her nostrils. *Move.* Oh, she wanted to get away. Wanted to run.

But she knew it wasn't possible to run from death. Death could follow a person anywhere. He followed her even in her dreams.

"He fits the established pattern," Sam said as she noticed that the crime scene guys were there, finally. Sam eased away, with Hyde shadowing her steps, as the techs came through to start working on the body. *Hurry.* Because she knew the poor man's parents were inside. She'd seen the shift of the curtains, and she knew they were peeking out, staring at the remains of their son and blaming themselves.

"Jeremy Briar," she murmured, "Twenty-two years old, the only son of Kathleen and Morgan Briar. Jeremy was last seen three days ago, in a dive right outside of the university, a place called The Core." And then he'd just vanished.

"His father got the ransom call," Hyde said, voice cool. "Twenty-four hours after Jeremy went missing."

Samantha didn't look back at the body. Bodies had never been her strong suit. She preferred to stay in the office and track her prey on the Net. But it wasn't about staying safe anymore. Now, she had to prove she *could* handle the job. The shrink in charge of her case had understood when Sam explained that she didn't want to hide behind a desk. So thanks to him, she was out here, shaking apart on the inside and realizing that Jeremy wasn't that much younger than she was.

Your age doesn't matter, not when death comes calling.

"Why didn't the father pay?" Sam asked and shielded

her eyes as she turned to look back up at the house. Freaking huge. Four houses could fit inside that one. The guy would've had the money to ransom his son.

"Seems Jeremy got in trouble with the law a few times, and he had a history of run-ins with bookies." Hyde paused, then said, "Mr. Briar thought his son was trying to scam him."

Oh, damn. The father hadn't believed the call, and Jeremy had paid. "Do you think the vic went fast?" The question came out before she could bite it back. But she knew what it was like when a sadistic freak took his time with you and made you beg for death. "W-were most of the injuries postmortem?"

"No." His answer was immediate.

Her eyes fell closed, just for a moment.

"I don't want you working this case, Kennedy," Hyde's words snapped out.

Her eyes flew back open. "Sir, I can—"

But his dark stare glinted. "I don't want you in the field, and I don't really give a shit what the prick in psych said." He closed in on her. "*You're not ready.* You think I can't see you shaking?"

Her breath caught. "I *can* do this." Desperation edged the words.

"Maybe." Hyde shook his head. "But I want you back in the office. Dante has point on this one. If he wants to use you, well—"

"Don't do this," Sam managed, choking back the lump in her throat. She'd been busting her ass to make sure that she still could work the detail. "I know my job. I *know*—"

"I know my people." No expression crossed his dark

face. He towered over her, cold and unfeeling. "And I know you aren't ready."

She wouldn't crumble. Not here. Not in front of him. *Not him.* "You're the one who sent me out on the Phoenix case." The Phoenix investigation had been the last big case she'd worked, and Hyde had been the one to send her out on that arson case as backup. "If you didn't think I was ready, you shouldn't have sent me."

"You don't belong in the field, Agent Kennedy."

She stumbled back and felt the jab right in her heart. "You don't think I'm strong enough, do you?" It had always been there, right from the beginning. She wasn't like the other agents. Sam knew that she didn't have their experience or their hard edge. She'd just skated past her twenty-fourth birthday so yes, she was younger, but she'd passed the same exams, done the drills, and proven herself, dammit.

"I *know* you're strong."

His words had her blinking.

"The problem is that you don't know that."

Her lips parted but she didn't speak.

"And you're scared. So scared that if you came face-to-face with a perp, I don't know what you'd do, Kennedy."

Neither did she.

"We both know you haven't worked best in the field."

No, she'd always been better back at the office, surrounded by her computers. But she couldn't stay with them forever, and there were times—like with the Watchman case—when she'd had to go into the field.

And the results hadn't been pretty.

Her breath barely fluttered out. *I can do this.*

"Go back to the office," he said again. "If Dante needs you..."

With an effort, she managed a slow nod. She'd been called to the scene today because the other SSD agents were working other cases. *Proximity and availability.* But Sam had also been called in because she *knew* this case. This case and the others like it that had occurred just weeks before Jeremy Briar's disappearance.

She'd been the one to first notice the pattern. She *always* noticed the patterns.

Sam forced her back to straighten. "I'm not going to fail, Hyde." That was all that she'd say because she wouldn't beg. Not yet.

His dark eyes just watched her.

Forcing out a hard breath, refusing to let the stench get to her, she shouldered past him. She kept her chin up and didn't so much as blink, not until she was back at her car.

Sam climbed in and slammed the door closed. She curled her raw palms around the steering wheel and blinked.

Two tears slid down her cheeks.

Dammit.

Didn't he see? Without the job, she had *nothing.*

Sam wasn't normally the type for casual sex. She was the kind of woman who went for commitment, romance, and candlelight.

No, she *had* been that kind of woman. Now she was different, and she *needed.* Needed to forget who she was and just feel.

Can't work the cases. Can't sleep at night. Can't even close my eyes without remembering...

Sam took a deep breath.

Forget.

Right then, she'd do just about anything to forget.

Sam had left the crime scene hours before. When she'd gotten back to her place, the invitation to this expensive party had been waiting on her porch, courtesy of her meddling mother. The woman thought Sam might find a potential mate at one of these boring society gigs.

Sam didn't want a mate. She just wanted a screw. Hot sex. Hard and wild. And she knew the perfect man to give her everything she needed.

Her perfect man stood across the room from her, separated by the crush of bodies. The party was too hot and too noisy by far with the fake laughter and high voices and the people who were pretending to be interested in each other.

Pretending. She was so sick of pretending.

Sam snagged a drink off a waiter's tray. She downed the champagne in two gulps and pushed her way toward her target.

He'd know who she was. Sam didn't doubt that. Well, he'd *better* know.

They'd had sex two weeks ago. Sex that had left her sore and aching and satisfied. Satisfied—for a time.

Until she'd wanted more.

She really hoped that the guy remembered her.

She sure remembered him.

Max Ridgeway. Tall, dark, and sexy. The man who'd made her come in two minutes. The man who'd made her scream.

The man who'd turned her on to casual sex.

Max was lover number three in her lifetime, not that

he knew that. She'd been sure to play the game. After all, she could pretend, too. She'd acted cool and confident and made sure that she didn't screw things up.

"*You.*" His voice, deep and rumbling, caught her, and she looked up to see him striding toward her.

Game face, girl. Get it on. Sam lifted her chin and let her lips curl into a smile that was as fake as all the others in the room. *Forget. Forget everything but him.*

Why try to pick up someone else when he was there? He'd be all she needed. He'd be . . .

Hot enough to banish the chill from her body.

Max caught her wrist and pulled her close. All around them, men stood in their perfect tuxedos and women smiled in their designer dresses. A high-end party. One packed with people who had too much money and too much alcohol.

His face—really not handsome, but sexy, so *sexy*—leaned in close to hers. At six foot three, Max was big and muscled with skin tanned a light brown. His midnight black hair curled just a little too long over the back of his collar.

The first time she'd seen him, she'd known that he would be the one for her. She'd gone into the bar, taken one look, and picked the strongest man in the place.

"You left without a damn word."

Huh. Anger hummed in his words. She wet the lips that she'd carefully painted for tonight. Part of the mask. Normally, she didn't give a damn about makeup.

She'd come to this party for one reason. Him. She wanted more.

"I'm here now." She rose onto her toes and whispered the words close to his mouth.

A muscle flexed in his jaw. "Baby, your timing is shit."

Sam almost smiled. Would have, if she'd been a different woman. Instead, she blinked at him, not just because she was trying to appear cool but because the contacts in her eyes were driving her crazy.

"I came to find you," she told him and thought about kissing him. But no, not yet.

"And I fucking looked for you."

Now she *was* surprised. She'd figured that the guy would just move on to the next woman on his list.

"Come with me." His grip on her wrist was almost bruising. Almost, because Max knew his strength. When he started walking, shouldering through the crowd, she followed because she wanted out of there.

A few moments later, his left hand slammed against the glass door, sending it swinging open, and then they were outside on the balcony. The crisp air of late autumn cooled her body. Max kicked the door shut behind them and finally, *finally*, the noise was gone.

It was just them.

"When you approached me in the bar, you didn't know who the hell I was, did you?" A lamp shone down on him and revealed the faint lines near his blue eyes. The light cast a dark shadow behind him, making him seem even bigger.

Anger had thickened in his voice. What, couldn't the guy just enjoy the sex like she had? What was the big deal? Sam forced a shrug, letting one shoulder rise and fall. Max still had her wrist, and she could feel the rough calluses on his fingertips. Not born into money, not this man. And when she'd seen him the first night in that bar, wearing his faded jeans and beat-up jacket, she hadn't thought—

"You ran when you woke up and realized just whose bed you were in."

She hadn't exactly been concentrating on her surroundings when he took her home. Sam had been busy yanking off his clothes. But with the harsh light of morning, she'd seen...

The picture of his stepfather on the mantle. A man she'd met before. A man her own mother had dated once upon a time.

"You just introduced yourself as Max." Her voice came out husky. Not deliberate that. But his eyes—such a bright blue—narrowed, and she heard the rasp of his breath.

"And you're Samantha," he said.

First names—that was all you were supposed to need for casual sex, right? "I am."

"What do you want from me?" he demanded as he trapped her against the brick wall to the right of the door. So warm, oh, his flesh seemed to burn hers. She could feel the thick length of his arousal pressing against the front of her dress. A short, skimpy dress that she'd found buried in the back of her closet.

"I want more." The truth. She could give him that much.

A growl rumbled in his throat.

"I don't care that you're rich." *Yes, let's just put that out there.* She hadn't run because of his money. Hadn't gone to him for that and hadn't run away because of it. She'd left because the night was over. "I don't want forever." The fake promises of happily-ever-after wouldn't suit her.

His fingers freed her wrist and wrapped around her waist. "What do you want?"

My life back.

She pushed her hand between their bodies and let her fingers rest over his racing heart. "I told you....*more.*" Sex. Passion.

Anything to hold back the shadows. Anything to let her pretend that she was normal. Not some freak. Not someone who couldn't even do her job anymore.

A woman this man wanted.

His left hand slid down her body. His fingers pressed just below the bottom of her dress.

Her breath caught. *Yes. Here.* Right here. So what if others were just a door away? She wanted this.

His rough fingertips smoothed up her thigh. Edged higher, higher, a few more inches.

"Fuck. You're not wearing underwear." Max's words came out, gravel-rough, and his eyes narrowed.

She smiled at him and ignored the surge of her heart. "Problem?"

His fingers slipped between her legs. She was already wet for him. Eager and ready.

His breath blew out on a ragged sigh. Two fingers, big and long, pushed through her folds and found her sex. His fingers drove inside, knuckles-deep.

Sam shot up on her toes. Her hands flew up to his shoulders, and she held on tight as electricity whipped through her body. Her nails dug into his tux jacket. Perfectly pressed. Screw that. She tightened the muscles of her sex around him, wanting a fast release, needing that hard pop of pleasure as—

His fingers withdrew.

Max leaned in close, and his lips feathered over her ear as he whispered, "You want to use me for sex?" Those fingers were tauntingly close to the center of her need as he stroked lightly. Petting and teasing.

Sam squeezed her eyes shut.

"Another fast screw and you walk away?" he asked softly, as his arousal rubbed against her thigh. Long and ready, and he could take her right then. Shove her skirt up, slide inside, and they'd both come. "I could be anybody, couldn't I?" His fingers thrust deep once more, and the stab of pleasure stole her breath. "Doesn't matter who I am."

Max's lips went to her throat and pressed right over the pulse that throbbed too fast. Licked. Sucked.

Yes, yes . . .

Did it matter who he was? Did it?

"Who am I, baby?" Now it was harder to understand the words as he growled against her flesh.

His fingers continued to drive inside her. His thumb rubbed the nub of her desire. A little more, just a little . . . Her climax was so close that her body trembled. *More.*

"M-Max . . ." She breathed his name. The night air felt good on her flesh because suddenly she was hot, burning up, right there, burning so fast.

And she kept her eyes closed because she didn't want to see *him.*

She only wanted to feel. Pleasure. Life. Not the cold touch of death.

The door squeaked, providing a bare second's warning. "Hey, Max!" A male voice called out. "There's someone I want you to—"

Max's fingers pushed deep.

Sam choked back a moan as a rush of pleasure flooded through her body on a hot tide of release.

"*Not now*," Max snarled.

"Ah, shit, s-sorry, m-man . . ." The door slammed shut. Her breath panted out.

Max raised his head and stared down at her. "He couldn't see you."

No. The man would have just seen Max, wrapped around some faceless woman. *Not her.*

Because she wasn't the type for casual sex. Wasn't the kind of woman who tracked a man to a party, ditching her panties and asking him to take her on the balcony. She was the good girl. The quiet one. Always had been.

Her hip vibrated. Not from him, though she could almost expect to—

Christ, her phone!

She slapped her hands against Max's chest and shoved him back.

His fingers slipped down her thighs. "Samantha? He didn't—"

Her fingers trembled as she yanked out the phone and read the text. *Get back to scene in Melborne ASAP. New body.* The message was from Agent Dante. Oh, hell, from Dante.

"I-I have to go," she told Max and saw his eyes widen.

"The hell you do." He shook his head grimly and didn't move an inch. Solid muscle. Angry, aroused male. "You're not running this time. We're not finished."

No, they'd just been getting started, but she couldn't turn down Dante, not if he was willing to give her a chance on the team. "Max, I—"

He kissed her. He'd made her come without once

kissing her, and the touch of his lips seemed shocking. Too intimate. *After what he'd just done?* But, yes, too—

His tongue pushed past her lips. Tasted her. Took and claimed hers, and she met him head-on.

Sam liked the way he tasted. There was wine in his kiss. Just as there must be champagne on her tongue. Tangy, but sweet.

The man knew how to use his tongue. Knew how to thrust and lick and have her straining to meet him.

Her fingers clenched around the phone. Her nipples ached, and her sex quivered.

More. More. They couldn't have all night, but they could have a few moments. Right there.

Sam tore her mouth away. "I-I'm sorry…I've got—work."

He stared at her with his jaw clenched and his strong chin angled down as he studied her. "What kind of work would call you in this late at night?"

He didn't want to know. Sam let her lips curve. Being fake was becoming so easy. "I work with…" Oh, jeez, but she needed her voice to stop sounding so breathy and weak. "C-computers. I-I have a tech emergency."

Half-truth. Half-lie.

He blinked. "You—"

"I have to go." She'd have to change. No way could the others see her in this outfit. It would take an hour to drive out to Melbourne from D.C. Why did Dante want her? And—

Another body? That didn't fit the pattern. No way. She eased away from Max and reached for the door.

"You're running again." Arousal still rumbled in his words. The rough timbre of a man who hadn't gotten his pleasure.

"No, I'm just walking away." She didn't look back. *Say something.* She knew that she should. Leaving the guy like this—

The old Sam would never have done that.

Then again, the old Sam was dead. She'd died in the water months before when a serial killer had left her broken body in a lake. And these days, it felt like her ghost was all that remained.

Her spine straightened. "Sam Kennedy." The words came out softer than she'd intended. "My name's...Sam Kennedy." She waited, wondering if he'd make the connection to her mother, but there was no flicker of recognition on his face. As far as she knew, Max and her mother had never met face-to-face, and since her mother was in Europe right then, she doubted their paths would be crossing soon.

But her heart still beat a little too fast. By giving him her last name, she'd given herself one less shield from him.

"Samantha Kennedy," Max said softly as if tasting the name. But, no, he was wrong.

Max kept calling her Samantha when she was just plain old Sam. Despite her mother's hopes, she'd never been fancy enough for Samantha. Her fingers curled around the door knob, and she began to pull it open.

"How do I find you, Samantha?"

He *wanted* to find her?

Well, duh, Sam, you left the man with a hard-on. Of course he wants to find you.

But she didn't want him to see her world. Not ever. In this fake life, she and Max could touch here. Nowhere else.

Not on the streets. Not in the shadows where she worked. Not with the killers. He didn't need to see them.

"You don't, Max," Sam said with a sigh, and she finally glanced back now. "But I can find you, and I will." Unless he told her to screw off. Unless—

"Sounds like a promise."

It was.

She gave a quick nod and opened the door. A man stood nearby, young and handsome, close to her age, and he eyed her with a knowing smile on his lips.

Sam walked right past him, her mind already on the case.

On the dead body that waited for her.

Samantha Kennedy.

So he had a full name. A name and a face and a hard-on that was really damn painful.

Max Ridgeway stalked to the edge of the balcony. His hands gripped the thick metal railing, and he sucked in a deep breath.

And still tasted her.

Samantha.

She'd come against his hand. He hadn't missed the hard clench of her sex or the soft cream that coated his fingers. She'd come, she'd kissed him, then she'd walked away.

Using him for sex.

Jesus Christ—women usually used him for money. For power.

Sex?

Probably shouldn't complain. He was supposed to like that, right?

But he didn't. Max yanked at his bow tie, loosening the knot, hating the damn thing, hating the stupid party he'd been forced to attend. Five years ago, he never would've been caught in this scene, but these days, he knew he had to play the game in order to keep his business in the black.

His business. The minute he'd seen Samantha, he'd forgotten all about the deals that he'd been working on at the party. As a rule, Max didn't go for one-night stands. He was long past the stranger pickup. Well, he had been. Until Samantha had touched him, and he'd gotten lost in her dark, turbulent eyes.

Walking away from her that night hadn't been possible, not after he'd tasted her. He'd taken her lips and known he'd take *her*.

The beginning. For him, that's what it had been.

Max wanted more from Samantha Kennedy than just a few hot hours in the dark.

Down on the street below him, she ran from the building, hurriedly dodging in and out of the lights. The lamps caught the red of her hair, flickering almost like fire in the heavy curls.

Samantha.

When she'd come up to him at that bar, her heart-shaped face had been so pale. Her brown eyes so wide. Her mouth—slick and red—had trembled.

She'd been afraid, and he'd wanted her.

A fast fuck.

No.

Max knew when a woman had secrets, and Samantha carried those secrets like a cloak around her sensual little body.

Samantha jumped into a small red VW Bug. He almost smiled at that. Hadn't been expecting her to—

She shot out of the lot with a roar of the car's engine, and he watched until the red taillights vanished.

It would be easy to find her. He had connections in D.C. His, his stepfather's. He could track her and discover everything that there was to know about Samantha Kennedy in a matter of hours.

If that was what he wanted.

Secrets.

He had them, too. In spades.

I'll find you. She'd better. Because Samantha Kennedy had made a mistake. She'd given him a taste, and now Max found that he wanted more.

Being a greedy bastard was part of his nature. When he wanted something, he took it.

He wanted Samantha.

"Thought you didn't go for the society ladies." His stepbrother's mocking voice drifted in the air to him.

Max didn't glance back. He'd heard the door open, just as he'd heard it earlier when Quinlan came outside. *At a piss-poor time.*

"Sorry for the interruption." The soft tread of Quinlan's shoes padded over the tile. "Didn't expect you to be ... occupied out here."

Max forced himself to release the railing.

Quinlan's rough laugh filled the night, only to end with a nervous edge. "Didn't know you went for sex in public places, man."

"I don't." *Normally.* "And whatever you thought you saw out here, *forget it*." Kissing and telling wasn't his style either. Slowly, Max turned around and stared at his younger brother. Hell, his stepbrother was probably a lot closer to Samantha's age than Max was at thirty-three.

Quinlan gulped and looked away. His left hand lifted to rub against his neck, and his golden horseshoe ring—his so-called lucky charm, a gift from Quinlan's father—glinted.

His stepbrother always seemed to have trouble look-ing him in the eye. Since his mother's death, so did their "father."

Max headed for the door. He was done with this scene. He didn't need to schmooze and party. What he needed—well, she'd driven away.

I'll find you. She'd better.

Find me, or I'll find you, baby.

CHAPTER *Two*

Sweat was slick on Sam's palms as fear settled heavily in her belly. She slammed the car door, rubbed her hands on the black pants she'd changed into at her place, and stared up at the looming mansion.

Two police cruisers were parked near the gate. A crime scene investigation team fanned over the area.

She sucked in a deep breath, then shoved back her shoulders and marched forward as she pulled out her ID. "I'm with the FBI—where's Agent Dante?" Dante, not Hyde. She didn't want to see him just then.

A uniform pointed toward the big house. "With the body."

Another kill didn't make any sense. The Briars only had one son so no one else at the residence fit the kidnappers' profile. The vics were rich males in their early twenties. Party boys who had parents with too much money and too little time for them.

The first kidnapping had occurred three months ago. The ransom demand had come twenty-four hours after the college student disappeared. The father paid, and the next day the son was back and able to provide absolutely no description of his abductors.

Next a man had been taken from Virginia, then one from D.C. Poor Jeremy Briar had been abducted from Maryland.

All of the men disappeared from college campuses, or rather, from bars located near the campuses.

Two men had come back alive.

Two hadn't been so lucky.

The serial kidnappers were smart, very good at covering their tracks, and too good at picking targets.

When it came to knowing the identity of the abductors, the SSD had nothing. *Nothing.*

She hurried down an elaborate walkway and eased past a fountain that sprayed water high into the air. Voices rose and fell, drifting out of the house through the open doorway. She stepped off the path and found herself on a mosaic that reproduced a Rembrandt painting.

Too much money. Maybe too much time, too.

Sam eased past the uniforms stationed near the door, keeping her ID out. "I need to find Agent Dante." She still didn't know why he'd called her in, but she wouldn't look a gift horse in the mouth.

"He's in the study," the nearest cop told her.

Sam's brows rose. That was supposed to tell her what, exactly?

The cop flushed a deep red—a red that matched his hair. "Down the hallway, second door. The room with the body."

Right, the body. This family had sure been through hell.

Her shoes whispered against the tile. First they'd lost their only child and now—

Sam skidded to a halt just outside the study. The techs were bagging the victim, an older guy with gray-streaked hair, tanned skin, and half his skull missing.

"Morgan Briar," Luke Dante murmured, looking up from his notes and giving her a cool nod. He stood near the large window to the right. "He's been dead about five hours now." Luke's green eyes held hers.

Morgan Briar. The father. Oh, Jesus. "What happened? Why—"

"No, I don't need a damn lawyer!" A woman's shrill cry tore through the air. Sam glanced over her shoulder and saw a tall, icily beautiful blonde being led down the stairs. The woman wore slim black pants and what looked like a white cashmere sweater. The sweater was stained with blood.

"That'd be Mrs. Kathleen Briar," Luke murmured.

Kathleen's hair had come loose from one of those fancy twists that Sam had never been able to manage.

Cops flanked the woman on either side. One, an older guy with graying hair at his temples, was reading the woman her rights. "If you can't afford—"

"I can afford a fucking attorney. I just don't want one right now!" Kathleen's voice rose to a screech.

"She called it in about an hour ago," Luke said quietly, and Sam heard the hint of a drawl beneath his words. He strode forward and came to her side.

Luke was still the newest agent in the SSD. He'd transferred up from Atlanta and had immediately paired up with the unit's top profiler, Monica Davenport. "From the looks of things," he continued, motioning toward the bar, "Mrs. Briar had a gin before making that call."

"She killed him?" Sam shook her head. Okay, she hadn't expected that.

The cop kept reading the Miranda rights to his perp. *"Anything you say or do can be held..."*

"She told the 9-1-1 operator that she shot her husband." Luke crossed his arms and watched the procession. Kathleen and her guards were almost at the study door now. Almost...

Kathleen stopped to glare at Sam and Luke. "I'm not sorry."

Luke lifted one shoulder. "Never said you were, ma'am." His voice was cool. Odd, because of all the agents, he was the one who always seemed the most intense. The one who seemed to care too much.

Maybe he'd been hanging around with Monica and Hyde too long.

Kathleen's eyes were bone dry. No tears for her. "Jeremy was *mine*. That asshole should have told me about the call. He should have—" She broke off and shook her head. "Jeremy would be alive. *Alive.*"

Now her husband and son were both dead, and there was fury glittering in her green eyes.

"He cheated on me," Kathleen admitted in a stark voice. The cops beside her were silent, their own eyes wide. "He bought houses for those sluts that cost more than my son's ransom." She swallowed. "He let Jeremy die. I can still see him, cut up. My baby..." Her eyes closed.

Luke watched her with a somber stare, then he caught the gaze of the older cop. "Take her outside."

This kill would be the local PD's show, not a case for the SSD, but the cops were still looking to Luke for guidance.

The cop nodded and reached for the cuffs on his hip.

"No." Luke shook his head. "Just put her in the back of the squad car."

Kathleen's lashes lifted, and the fury had vanished. That fast. She blinked and just looked ... lost. "Jeremy's gone."

Sam swallowed. *So was Morgan.* "Mrs. Briar, I really think you should reconsider that attorney."

Another slow, almost confused blink. *"My baby ..."*

The cops took Kathleen's arms and guided her down the long, winding hallway. Her heels clicked on the tiles.

"I never expected her to react like this," Luke said.

Sam's gaze shot to Luke. He ran a fast hand through his hair. "Shit. She seemed so *controlled* earlier today."

Because the woman had been in shock.

"I should have brought Monica to the scene." He eased into the hallway. "She would have seen the signs. *I* should have seen them."

Monica could look at a killer and see the darkest parts of his mind, but when it came to the victims ... "She might not have seen it either." The words came out harder than she'd intended.

One of Luke's blond brows shot up.

Sam cleared her throat. Yes, that had sounded wrong, but lately, Monica made her nervous. *Very* nervous. She was worried that Monica might look too close and see—

Broken.

"Why am I here?" Sam asked him, leaving the study and the body and finally feeling like she could breathe again. "Hyde said—"

"I'm lead on this case." Authority pushed through the flat words.

She inclined her head in agreement. "But we both know that when it comes to the SSD, Hyde calls the shots." Sam really didn't think Luke wanted to get into a pissing match with the big boss. "Hyde said for me to stay away."

They walked down the hallway. No staff members appeared. In a place this big, she'd expected a maid or— *someone.* But maybe Kathleen Briar had sent the help away, right before she shot her husband in the head at point-blank range.

"Hyde said to stay away, but here you are," Luke pointed out. "Guess you couldn't stay away from the case, could you?"

She glanced over and found his eyes on her, weighing her. "*You* called me." And she'd jumped at his call.

"Monica wants me to use you on this case."

Sam couldn't have been more surprised if he'd punched her. Monica and Hyde usually agreed on everything.

"She says you need the case."

Her chin lifted. "I do." She *could* work this case.

"But tell me, Sam, what will you do when the danger is right in front of you?"

Her tongue swiped across her lips. *Are you ready to die? Beg…go on, beg…* That bastard's voice always seemed to be in her head.

"Hyde thinks you'll crack," Luke said bluntly. "He let

you out on a test run before, but he doesn't believe you're ready."

Luke had led her away from the other investigators. Maybe he was trying to save her pride by talking to her in private. Like she had a lot of pride left.

"I'm ready." She injected steel in her voice.

"Maybe."

Sam held his stare and refused to back down.

He exhaled on a sigh. "I like you, Sam. You got one messed-up deal on the Watchman case."

Don't flinch. Don't.

"But I can't have you screwing up *my* case." Soft but brutal.

And not unexpected. For the SSD, the case came first.

Luke waited a beat and then said, "I have to be able to trust that you can do your job."

In their division, trust was key. You trusted your teammates. You knew that they had your back.

His lips tightened, and then Luke said, "I know about the panic attack in Virginia."

She flinched. *What?* No, no, she'd retreated to an abandoned office. No one had—

"Two uniforms saw you. They reported to Hyde and that's why he yanked you off field work as soon as you returned to D.C."

Her breath came too fast, too hard. "I haven't had another attack in weeks. The department shrink gave me the all clear." Didn't that fact matter to anyone?

"And I'm giving you a chance." His head cocked to the right. "Prove Hyde wrong. Show him the steel inside, the steel that kept you alive when the Watchman wanted you to break."

I did break. I broke, and I begged.

"But if there are signs you're starting to falter, if I don't think you're strong enough to handle the work..."

He didn't have to finish. She knew. "You'll pull me off the case." Then it would be two failures for her, and she could kiss her career at the SSD good-bye.

Luke's head inclined in a grim nod.

Well, at least she knew where she stood with him. And she knew that she owed Monica a hell of a lot.

"Now go and take over the scanning of all the computer equipment the techs confiscated," he ordered. "As of now, you are officially on the case. Hell, no one can hack into a system like you can. The guys Hyde had running the systems can't even hope to compete with you."

No, they couldn't, but when the big boss gave an order, people listened. He'd wanted her to back off and only provide support to the new tech guys, so she had. But now...

"I want to find out every detail there is to know about Jeremy Briar's life and his family," Luke said, "Every damn detail."

Once she got back to the office, she'd dig deep into their financials and make sure that there wasn't anyone in the family who would benefit from that ransom money. Maybe there was a relative desperate for cash. Maybe a cousin had hit rock bottom. When money was involved, family members often turned on each other—and they could be vicious.

Sometimes, these crimes could hit too close to home.

Getting access to the bank records was easy. Impersonal. Going into the family's private e-mails and wading through their Internet sites would be much more intimate.

"The media will go crazy with this one," Luke warned. "The Briars are always big news in this part of the country, but with both the son and the husband dead, it's going to be a circus."

So far, the media hadn't made the full connection between the kidnappings. The two men who'd been returned alive had been ushered out of the country by their parents. And then any suspicions from the press—well, they had been hushed up by the power of old money.

As for the other man, Peter Hollings, the one who'd been sent back to his parents in pieces after they used marked bills to pay his ransom...

His family had all but erased their son's life. The rest of the world believed Peter had died in a car accident. Money had a way of re-writing history.

"What will the kidnappers do when they make the news?" Sam asked. Some killers craved attention. The pyro that the SSD had tracked in Virginia had been desperate for his fifteen minutes of fame.

Luke's gaze met hers. "At first, it sure looked like they wanted their kidnappings kept quiet." *They*—Hyde was convinced they were looking for a team of abductors. "But the way Jeremy Briar's body was spread out, I think these perps want some attention now."

So the press would soon be fueling the flames for them.

"They were sending a message," she said, rubbing the back of her neck.

"To the next family." Luke agreed grimly. "Telling them that this is what happens when you don't pay."

• • •

Max wasn't asleep when the knock sounded at his door. It was close to three a.m., but he wasn't asleep.

He was thinking about *her*. Still feeling Samantha against his skin, and when the knock reached his ears, he immediately headed for the door.

I'll find you.

Max pulled open the door without bothering to look out the peephole.

Samantha.

She stood in the well-lit hallway, but she wasn't the femme fatale of hours before. No sexy dress. No flash of cleavage.

Instead she wore simple black pants and a black shirt. The color just made her skin look paler. And she looked lost.

"You should really have better security in a place like this," she said, in that smooth voice he loved. No accent, just softness and sex. "It was too easy to get inside."

"I left orders that the doorman was to let you up." He'd spent ten minutes giving Charlie a description of her.

When her eyes widened a bit, Max knew that he'd caught her by surprise. Good. She'd sure surprised him that first night.

I don't want love. I don't want promises of forever. I just want you. Now.

How was he supposed to turn that down?

Samantha rocked back on her heels. "There should be an electronic security system in place. You should see everyone before they—" She stopped and shook her head.

There were shadows under her eyes. Dark circles that

hadn't been there earlier on the balcony. "Samantha?" They were little better than strangers, but something was *there* between them. Connecting them.

She hesitated then said, "I don't want to be alone tonight."

Didn't get more stark or brutally honest than that. His cock swelled as arousal spiked through him. He could still taste her.

Her lashes lifted. "Do you want to be alone?" Her eyes widened. "Wait—you might not be—*are you alone?*"

Max took her hand and hauled her inside. "Not anymore." He slammed the door shut, and his mouth crashed down on hers.

Samantha's lush lips parted immediately for him. Her tongue swept against his, rubbing, teasing, and the light strokes seemed to go straight to his cock.

Her hands were on him, feathering over his bare chest. So hot and soft. He loved her hands. Loved them more when they were wrapped around his cock and pumping hard and fast.

Screw everything but . . . her. *No, screw her. Take her.*

She sucked his lower lip. Drew it into her mouth and sucked, and Max's heart ripped through his chest. Why? *Why* did she affect him so much?

He'd been with his share of lovers. He shouldn't—

Samantha shoved away from him.

"What are you—"

She lowered to her knees before him. "My turn." Her hands jerked down his jogging pants, and her mouth, sweet fuck, her mouth closed over the tip of his erection.

"*Samantha.*"

Her palm curled around the base of his shaft, and she

leaned in toward him, taking a few more inches of erect flesh, sucking strong and tight with her mouth.

His hands sank into her hair.

She swallowed. Took more.

Her mouth moved faster. Sliding along his skin, taking him deeper as her tongue licked and learned his flesh. Deeper. *More.*

Max positioned her head and thrust against that hot mouth. His balls tightened, his spine tingled, and his climax bore down on him. Building, building, so close that his balls ached.

Her hands flew up, and she pulled free of his grasp in an instant. Her breath panted out. "Not yet," she whispered.

Staring up at him, licking her lips, she yanked off her shirt and tossed it on the floor. She had on a plain white bra, but her breasts pushed against the cups, and she made the garment look *damn* sexy.

She kicked off her shoes and shimmied out of her pants. Then Samantha pulled out a small packet from her back pocket.

The woman was prepared. Her fingers tore open the foil, and she smoothed the condom over his throbbing flesh.

Samantha rose before him, her body brushing against his, every smooth inch driving him insane.

Her fingers caught the waistband of her panties, then shoved them down. "Now," she told him, that voice enveloping him.

Like he had to be told twice.

Max lifted her against him. Her legs wrapped around him. Long, supple legs. Her sex, creamy and plump, brushed against his cock.

He took two steps and pushed her back against the wall. Max braced her and thrust deep into her sex.

Christ, he was so close to exploding. His climax bore down on him, and he thrust fast, deep, hard, driving into her as the fury rode him.

Her hips were tilted down, and every glide of his cock swept over her clit. She moaned, thrashing beneath him, and arching her hips as she fought for her release.

Faster. *Faster. Deeper.* Her whispered demands.

Her nails dug into his ass as she urged him on. *There, there* was the woman from the first night. The woman who liked the sex wild and who didn't stop until she'd come.

Over and over.

Her sex convulsed around him. Hard, gripping contractions that worked his erection so damn well. *Yes.*

Max eased out of her, then plunged balls-deep. He came, growling her name, and holding her in a grip that he knew had to bruise.

Holding her. Keeping her locked tightly to him, because this time, he wouldn't let her get away.

The scream woke Max later. A sound of terror so absolute that Max awoke with fear squeezing his own heart. He jerked up in bed and shoved the covers back.

Samantha thrashed in the bed, her pale skin gleaming in the moonlight. Her hands were up in the air, pushing out, fighting nothing, and she was choking, gasping, struggling to breathe.

"D-don't...p-put me b-back...in..."

What the fuck?

He hit the lamp switch hard, and light flooded the room. "*Samantha.*"

Her back arched but her eyes stayed closed. *"D-don't…"*

Max grabbed her arms and pulled her up against his chest. *"Samantha!"*

Her lashes flew open. *"Kill…me."*

His eyes widened. *What?*

And he realized that her eyes were blank. The pupils were dilated and fixed and staring at a nightmare that he couldn't see.

Her breath rattled in her chest. Holy shit, she seemed to be suffocating!

Max pressed his lips tightly against hers. Then he breathed into her mouth. A long, deep expulsion of air.

Her hands came up against his shoulders, and she shoved him back, once again surprising him with her strength.

"Wh-what's happening?" Not the frightened voice from before.

Samantha. She was back.

But her eyes were still blank. So was her face.

He didn't let her go. His grip grew even tighter. *Hold her. Keep her safe.*

Max expelled a slow breath. "Everything's okay, Samantha."

The sound of her swallow was too loud in the quiet room. "What did I do?" She asked, her voice stronger now.

He tried to smile, a hard feat when his heart shoved against his ribs and tension ate at his gut. "I think you just had a bad dream. We all have them."

Her skin was cool beneath his hands, and her muscles were tense. Samantha blinked at him, then narrowed her eyes a bit. "We all have them." Her echo was toneless.

His right hand rose and cupped her shoulder. "Want to talk about it?" It was so hard to keep his voice light and calm. *Want to tell me why you dream about begging someone not to kill you?*

"I don't remember anything." Her lips twisted. "I never remember my nightmares." A pause. "That's a good thing, right?"

He stared down at her, noting the soft curves of her cheeks and the light dusting of freckles across the bridge of her nose. Her jaw was set, that slightly pointed chin up, and her thick hair was a tousled mane around her face.

Sexy.

She'd been that way from the beginning.

But now, there was something different. A tension around her full lips. Shadows in her eyes.

And her nails dug into his shoulders. Not with passion this time. With fear.

"For a minute there, you seemed to stop breathing." As far as he was concerned, that qualified as being way past just a nightmare. "You looked like you were fighting to get air."

Silence. One beat of time. Two, then... "Well, I guess it's a good thing you were here." Her lips curved but the shadows never left her eyes. Her fingers skimmed over his chest. "I'm glad you could give me mouth to mouth."

She was shutting him out. His jaw clenched.

"Let me freshen up a bit, and then..." She kissed him. A light, biting nip. "You can make me forget all about my bad dream." Samantha eased away from him. She rose and walked toward the bathroom, completely naked, with her head held up high and her hips swaying.

He watched her, keeping silent. His damn cock was up, but with her around, there was no real way to stop the lust.

The door closed behind her with a soft click.

The sound of rushing water filtered through the room.

And he realized that his hands were clenched into fists. *That's what she looks like when she lies.*

Sam stared at the image in the mirror. Her hands were wrapped around the faucet, holding on too tightly. The better to stop the trembling in her fingers.

It had been six weeks since she'd had a flashback, and yes, that's what it was. No nightmare. No freaking bad dream.

A flashback.

She was supposed to be *better*.

Max had seen her when she was weak. No, no, he shouldn't have seen her like that. She was with him for sex and pleasure. To push the ghosts away.

She wasn't there so that he could see her get tangled in the past.

"You looked like you were fighting to get air."

Dammit. Just...dammit.

Sam grabbed a handful of water and splashed it on her face. But the warm water didn't thaw the ice in her cheeks.

She couldn't do this, couldn't let the past come back and control her. Luke would be watching her every move. All the agents would. She had to hold things together.

A knock rattled at the door. "Samantha? Are you okay?"

"Fine!" She called and stared back into the mirror. *Liar, liar.*

The knob rattled. Max was trying to get in, but the attempt wouldn't do him much good. She'd locked the door. "Give me just a minute!"

Get out. Run. The tension had her body tight again. She couldn't stay with Max. She should not have made the mistake of falling asleep in his bed. Her defenses came down when she slept.

Water dripped down her face and splashed into the granite sink.

"Samantha, open the door." Quiet. Firm.

Don't show fear. Don't ever show fear. She turned off the water. Slowly, taking her time, she opened the door. A smile was already on her lips, the water drying on her skin, when she faced him. "Sorry, Max, I think I'm going to have to take a rain—"

"Stop it." His gaze raked her face.

Sam let her brows rise. "Uh, stop what?" He didn't know how fast her heart was beating. Didn't know that her muscles were locked.

Max grabbed her hand and tugged her toward him. "We don't have to fuck."

Blunt. But then, she was fast realizing that was his way. He said what he thought and to hell with everyone else.

Must be nice to be able to live like that. She worried too much about others.

Only with him can I let myself go and just feel pleasure. But there wouldn't be any more pleasure tonight, and she couldn't risk letting the memories come back.

"Get in bed, baby." The words were soft but his hold,

the grip that pulled her forward toward the bed, was unbreakable.

The back of her knees bumped into the mattress. "I have to go. I've got an early meeting tomorrow. I forgot—"

"Bullshit." He pushed her onto the bed. She scrambled back, sliding against the cool sheets. Max came in after her, crowding her, and she caught sight of his cock. Big and long and more than ready.

Sam shook her head. "I thought we weren't—"

He wrapped his arms around her and pulled her close. The embrace wasn't sexual. Max was just...holding her.

And that scared her.

"Go to sleep, Samantha."

In his arms. Her body stiffened even more.

"If the dreams come back, I'll wake you up." Max stretched, snapped off the lamp, and turned his head back toward her. "You're not the only one with nightmares."

He didn't understand.

Max pulled her closer. "Sleep."

No, he didn't understand, but—but she didn't want to be alone. Wasn't that why she'd gone to that bar in the first place? To find someone else? To feel skin against hers? To know someone wanted her? That someone didn't see her as twisted and broken?

Moonlight fell on her, pouring through the glass windowpanes. She turned her head away from Max because she didn't want him to see her face.

Sam licked her lips, felt the comfort of his embrace, and finally, Christ, finally, almost believed she was safe.

Safe, in the arms of a stranger.

She was so screwed up.

• • •

The stench of bleach burned his nose when he entered the house on the end of Sycamore Lane.

He'd cleaned the shack himself, every inch, because he wanted to make sure that the job had been done right. There'd be no mistakes on his watch. This was too important.

The chair sat waiting in the back bedroom. The wooden chair was the only piece of furniture in the ten-by-thirteen-foot space. The oak gleamed now, but it had been stained red earlier. The blood had dripped onto the hardwood floor.

Jeremy Briar hadn't died easily. He'd slit Jeremy's throat, not enough to sever the jugular but enough to stop the asshole's screams. He hadn't sliced the guy's throat because he'd been afraid someone might hear Jeremy. No chance of that out here. He just hadn't wanted to hear the desperate cries and the begging anymore.

Begging didn't work with him.

Only money stopped his hand. If Briar's father had just paid the ransom...

Then Morgan Briar wouldn't have been forced to scrape his only son's flesh and blood off the driveway.

A car's engine sounded outside. A soft purr. He glanced over at the window. Right on time.

He turned away from the chair. It wouldn't be empty for long.

Once the news had time to run Jeremy's sad story, he'd take a new mark. This time, the bastards would *know* to pay. No one would screw him over now.

He walked back down the hallway and moments later, he opened the front door and saw the first rays of dawn creeping out against the darkness.

His partner came toward him, hurrying in her heels, her breath fogging in the cold. "I think I've got the next one."

He smiled. "No, *I* do." Time to move to the next level.

He'd already picked their next victim. Actually, he'd picked them all, months ago. He'd planned out every move, and he wasn't going to stop. Not until his list was finished, and he'd gotten everything he deserved.

The bastards can pay or they can bleed.

CHAPTER *Three*

I need money."

The steady rap of pounding hammers filled the air around Max. Electric saws cut through metal, sending sparks shooting into the air. It took a second for the demand to penetrate the layers of noise, and when it did, Max shoved back his hardhat, wiped the sweat out of his eyes, and blinked. "Quinlan? Shit, what are you doin' here?"

His stepbrother never bothered with his construction business. As far as Max could tell, the guy wasn't much for getting his hands dirty. The fancy parties, yeah; that was his scene.

But a site like this was all Max really knew. Construction had been his life for over a decade. Long before his mother had hooked up with her prince not-so-charming, he'd chosen this path and busted ass to make his business a success.

Quinlan ducked his dark head and came inside what would eventually be a world-class kitchen. One day real soon, if Max could just get the rest of his damn supplies in on time.

"You heard me, man." Quinlan glanced around, eyeing the workers nervously, but they weren't even looking his way. "I need money."

It wasn't the first time that Quinlan had come to him. "How much?" His construction company had managed to survive and finally thrive through the years, despite the dive the economy had taken. He wasn't in the same category as his stepfather, didn't want to be, but he was doing well enough that the invitations to those fancy parties kept finding their way to his door.

Quinlan shook his head. "No, I want *my* money."

Ah, now here was the rub.

His brother's hands were clenched. "My grandfather left me that trust. The money is *mine*," Quinlan snapped.

And it was one hell of a lot of money. Enough money to make a man do some damn stupid things. Max sighed. "You only have two more years, then the trust's yours."

"I don't want to fucking wait!"

Now *that* snarl did have the guys looking their way because they knew Max didn't take shit like that from anyone, not even his brother.

"Sorry, I think you're gonna have to fucking wait." Max shrugged and reached for the blueprints once more.

"*Talk to him.* Tell my dad I need more. I need it now—"

"Why?" Max shook his head, aware that his brother was sweating when there was no reason to sweat. "Why do you need the cash?"

Quinlan's lips firmed into a thin line.

Ah, shit. Max dropped the prints and closed the

distance between them, fast. He grabbed his brother's arms, jerked them out so he could shove up the sleeves of his shirt and *see* Quinlan's arms. "You using again?" Quinlan had already been through four rehab programs. *Four*. The docs would say he was clean, then just a few weeks later Quinlan would be using again.

His brother tried to snatch his arms back. *Not going to happen*. Max just tightened his grip. "Are you?" The guy wanted money to support his habit. Great, just—

"*No!*"

There weren't any needle marks on his arms. But then maybe Quinlan was just snorting coke up his nose again.

"I-I only used the last time because of what happened to—"

"*Don't* say her name." Max didn't want Quinlan talking about his mom or about the tragedy that had happened to her.

"She said we were brothers," Quinlan swallowed. "Th-that I could count on you."

Max dropped his brother's hands. "You can." He was the one who'd tossed Quinlan's ass into rehab. Not the old man. Quinlan's father hadn't seemed to care about getting him clean.

"Talk to him, Max. Get me the money. I *need* it."

Try earning it. He bit the words back. They'd had that fight already. Quinlan didn't know what it was like to fight your way up from nothing. To work eighteen-hour days over and over until you thought that you'd collapse.

No, Quinlan didn't know anything but wealth.

And a prick of a father.

Max had worked until his entire body ached, worked night after night as he struggled to get his life on track.

Yeah, he could be in an office now, running things from some plush suite, but...

My projects, my job.

"Please, man, I don't have anyone else to turn to."

Max gave a curt nod. Fine. He'd talk, for all the good it would do him—and that was *none*.

"Thanks, Max!" A broad grin split Quinlan's face, making his dimples flash. "I knew you'd help me!"

Right.

Quinlan spun around and took a few fast steps away. "Oh!" He glanced over his shoulder. "Should have told you last night. That new girlfriend is hot."

Max stared back at him. Girlfriend? Not quite.

"How'd you two meet?" Quinlan asked.

In a bar. She picked me up. Offered me no-strings sex.

But the strings had come from nowhere last night as he'd just held her and ignored the hard-on that had kept him up until dawn. "Around." He tilted his head and studied his brother. Were the guy's hands shaking? Yeah, they were.

Using.

Quinlan gulped. "R-right....see you, man, okay?"

Yeah, he'd be seeing him again. Max's lips tightened.

He'd promised his mother that he'd look after Quinlan. A brother, not by blood, but by a mother's command. He'd promised....

And Max kept his promises. Even the ones he wanted to break.

"Every major newspaper in the area headlined with the Jeremy Briar kidnapping and murder." Monica Davenport's cool voice carried easily through the conference room.

Sam shifted in her chair. Yes, she'd seen the headlines. *WHO KILLED THE PLAYBOY?* Big, bold, in-your-face headlines. But playboy? No, he'd been—

"Some rag even managed to get a picture of Briar's mutilated body. A shot that looked like one of *our* crime scene photos." Monica's lips tightened, the only change in her expression, but that small flicker was enough to tell Sam that the woman was pissed. Monica, or *Ice* as she'd been nicknamed back in her Academy days, wasn't one for much emotion.

The team Luke had assembled for the serial kidnappings case had gathered in the conference room to hear Monica's update and to find out just what they could expect in the coming days.

"The kidnappings are out in the open now. The families know exactly what will happen if they don't pay for their sons' release."

Sons. So far, only men had been taken. Strong, fit men in their twenties. All had been abducted within a two-hundred-mile radius of D.C.

"Can we expect copycat crimes?" This came from Agent Jon Ramirez. Since he'd recently finished up a serial rapist case in Denver, Dante had pulled Jon onto the team. Jon lounged back in his seat, black eyes watchful, as he tapped a pen against the edge of the long conference table. "Rich boys vanishing...maybe it will tempt others."

"It might." Monica crossed her hands over her chest and gave a slow nod. "Expect them."

Great. More drama to cloud the case.

"And expect the real kidnappers to strike soon. *Very* soon."

Sam shook her head. "But there's usually at least two weeks between—"

"The kidnappers didn't get their paycheck for the last victim. They'll make another snatch."

Snatch. Such a cold way to talk about a person's life.

"The last four victims all disappeared from bars near college campuses...those are the hunting grounds," Monica said. "So far, the kidnappers haven't visited the same place twice."

That they knew of.

"We've canvassed the bars where our vics were," Luke's much warmer voice cut through. "We couldn't find anyone who remembered seeing the men leave."

Sam cleared her throat. "I tapped into the traffic camera that's located right down the street from The Core. I was able to retrieve license plate numbers for over a hundred vehicles."

Luke raised a brow.

"I cross-referenced those tags with the vehicles that we saw from the traffic cameras at the other scenes. There were no matches." But she wasn't ready to give up yet. "I've got the names and addresses of the people who owned the cars. We can interview those folks; maybe someone remembers seeing Jeremy."

Now Luke nodded. "Good work, Sam." He pointed at Ramirez. "Why don't you and Kim take the witness list? See if anyone was sober enough to remember our vic and the person who took him out of the bar."

"The perps are smart," Monica murmured. "I counted at least three exits at The Core. A bouncer is usually stationed at the front, but the other doors would have been clear. If they went out the back way—"

"Then they could have taken the East Benedict Road and not gotten caught on the traffic camera," Sam finished quietly. Yeah, she knew about the alternate route, and if the killers were as organized as they thought they were, they knew, too.

But everyone made mistakes, and just maybe their killers had screwed up.

"We grill every potential witness." Luke's gaze swept the room. "And we focus on finding the perps' next hunting ground." His stare rested on Sam.

And she knew what he wanted. Sam licked dry lips and said, "I've been working on generating a statistical pattern trajectory for possible bars that the perpetrators might hit." *Patterns.* She knew them and had always been able to see them where others couldn't. "Our kidnappers like to hit the most crowded bars, those within a ten-mile radius of college campuses, and they like the bars that stay open until at least 4 a.m."

"How many bars have you found?"

"Within the kill zone?" Sam asked. The kill zone—that two-hundred-mile stretch that the perpetrators used for hunting. "Twenty-three." College kids liked their bars.

Ramirez swore. "We can't cover that much territory."

"We can," Luke said. "We just have to get our asses moving. We'll call in the local police for backup, and we'll make sure the staff at these clubs are alerted."

Sam's shoulders hunched. *Field work.* Okay, she could do this.

Luke's attention was still zeroed in on her. "Sam, I want you to keep searching the family's financials. Dig deeper into their computer systems and see what you can discover."

Sam forced a curt nod. "Consider it done." They hadn't been given access to the other victims' computers. The families had closed ranks with their lawyers as fast as possible. This time, things were different.

That morning, Sam had already started a scan on the laptop—too easy. The password had taken five seconds to bypass. She had a download program retrieving all of Jeremy's deleted e-mails and encrypted files now.

The family's financial records were coming up clean. No major debts. No missing money that couldn't be accounted for.

Luke rattled off several target areas, bars situated around college campuses. They were focusing on the bigger schools, those with students connected to powerful, wealthy families.

Luke assigned search areas to the other agents, leaving Sam grounded.

"Let's move, people," Luke said. "Talk to the bartenders and waitresses, tell them to keep their eyes open—and let's find these bastards before anyone else gets taken."

Or killed.

The music was loud. No, ear-splitting. But this dive on the edge of the Georgetown campus was where Sam needed to be.

She stood just inside the doorway of The Core, letting her gaze sweep across the packed bar. The bouncer at the door, a tall, muscled guy with an ear full of piercings, had waved her inside when she'd flashed her badge. She knew other agents had already talked to the guy. Kevin Milano had been working the door the night Jeremy vanished, but he hadn't remembered seeing the vic leave.

According to the e-mails that she'd read, Jeremy Briar had met his friends here every other Friday night.

And the third victim, Curtis Weatherly, the guy who'd managed to come back home and then get shipped right out to Mexico, had also visited this bar. Sure, a visit to The Core had meant a long drive from his home in Virginia, but he'd come...a week before he'd vanished. Curtis hadn't answered the agents' questions, so she hadn't gotten that detail directly from him.

Luckily, he'd posted it on his Facebook page, and she'd logged his activities.

Two victims, one bar.

Another pattern. And maybe, just maybe, if she dug deep enough into the lives of the other victims, she'd find that they were linked to The Core, too.

It was edging close to midnight. She hadn't told Luke about the link yet, but she'd tell him first thing tomorrow.

And she was there because—

Someone bumped into her, and Sam spun around, her arms coming up.

"S-sorry..." A drunken slur as the man weaved past her.

She exhaled slowly. *Get a grip.* Her weapon was in her bag. She was surrounded by drunken frat boys. Not killers.

But, no, maybe one of them was a killer.

And *that* was why she was here. Why she'd forced herself to come inside the bar after staying in the car for twenty minutes. She was an FBI agent, for Christ's sake! Her job was to follow leads. She *could* do this.

If she'd called someone else to check the bar, Hyde

would've wondered about her. Even more than he already did. A quick sweep, sure, she should be able to handle that.

Right?

Pulling her jacket close, Sam eased her way through the crowd. *Not her scene.* But then, she'd graduated college when she was seventeen, so it hadn't exactly been legal for her to be in a joint like this.

After an eternity, she made it to the bar and slapped her palm down on the gleaming surface. The bartender glanced up, one eyebrow raised. "Whattaya need?"

Sam took a breath. "I'm looking for a man." The profile pointed to a man as the leader of the kidnapping ring.

"Sweetheart..." He motioned to the crowd, "take your pick." The guy looked to be around thirty with a gleaming bald head and tattoos on his hands.

Her back teeth ground together and her spine snapped up. "No, a young guy, probably in his twenties, attractive, smart—"

"Yeah, look, your to-do list is fuckin' fascinating, but—"

"He would have been alone," she continued doggedly, aware that her cheeks were heating and her words coming too fast. "And he would have spent his time staring at the other customers. Maybe focusing on the ones who liked to spend too much money..."

"*Samantha?*" The gravel-rough voice came from behind her. Sam spun around—

And came face-to-face with Max. *What?*

He shook his head. "What are you doing here?"

Oh, crap. She wet her lips. "I—"

"She's looking for a man, bud, same thing as all the others." The bartender's bored drawl rose behind her.

Max's eyes slit. "The hell you are."

Oh, damn. This was not good. "Um, no, I was—" *Working a case.*

He leaned in close. "Looking for more no-strings sex?" Anger glinted in his gaze.

Maybe it was time for an explanation. *Hi, I'm Sam, an FBI agent. I picked you up in a bar, and I don't even know why I did that. I may be having a breakdown but don't tell my boss because he'll fire my ass.*

Sam licked her lips. Not the right time, not the right place, and no way could she get all that information out right then. "It's not what you think," she managed instead.

The steel in his eyes told her that he wasn't buying that one. "Look, I was—"

"Max!" Another man shouldered through the crowd. Younger, familiar. "Max, I didn't think you'd ever get here!"

Dark gray eyes. Pretty-boy face. Ruddy cheeks already flushed from too much beer.

The image clicked instantly. He'd been at the party last night. And that voice—he was the guy who came out on the balcony.

Her gaze flew back to Max. A muscle flexed along his jaw. "Samantha, I want you to meet my brother, Quinlan Malone."

She didn't offer her hand. It would be a little hard to do because Max had both of them in a steely grip.

Quinlan flashed her a smile but seemed to weave on his feet. "Nice to meet you, pretty lady."

Uh, right.

"Did you talk to him?" he asked Max. "What did he say, man, am I—?"

"No money, Quinlan," Max gritted, turning his head a fraction to meet his brother's stare. "No deal."

"*Fuck.*"

Sam glanced between them. "Max..." Okay, this was just awkward. She didn't have experience with the whole family situation. An only child, she'd never dealt with sibling drama.

"Frank says you have enough for now." Max's lips were tight. "No more."

Quinlan spun away and stormed through the crowd. "Hell. Give me a minute, okay?" Max released her and took off after his brother.

But Quinlan slammed into what looked like a football player, a big, thick guy, and chaos erupted.

Fury. Fists. Screams. A ball of men tumbled onto the floor.

Fear pumped through her blood but she raced forward. "S-stop!" She screamed.

Quinlan got slammed into the floor. Hard.

Her fingers moved to her bag and to the gun that was hidden inside it. She pushed forward. "Let him go! That's an or—"

"*Jesus,*" Max growled, shoving other bodies back, "*give it a damn rest!*" His roar seemed to quiet the crowd. He snatched his brother free of the violence.

Sam took a breath.

Quinlan shoved away from Max and took off through the gawking group.

Sam realized that she had her fingers curled around her

gun. Carefully, she eased her hold and let the weapon sink back into her purse.

Then Max stalked back toward her. He held out his hand. "Let's get out of here."

He never hits the same bar twice.

Sam put her fingers in his.

Quinlan watched them leave. *Sonofabitch.* He'd known, deep down, that the old man wouldn't give him the money.

"That jerk shouldn't have hit you." A woman's soft, sexy voice murmured. She sidled up to him, tall and slim, dressed in a slip of a black dress that barely skimmed her thighs.

He took another long pull from his beer. "A sore jaw's the least of my damn worries." His horseshoe ring gleamed, mocking him.

She sat next to him. Didn't wait for an invitation. Just sat and that skirt hiked up a little more.

No panties.

"I'm a good listener," she murmured, and her fingers skimmed down his arm. "I bet talking will make you feel better."

"No, the only thing that would make me feel better is if my tight-ass father gives me *my money.*" But his father wasn't going to *give* him anything. How many times had he asked only to get fucking shot down?

He'd hoped his father might change his mind, so he'd gone to Max to run interference. *One last chance.*

No deal.

And no more.

Her lashes lowered. "Parents can be hell." She leaned

forward, and her long, blond hair brushed against his arm.

"I just want what's mine!" Was that so wrong? No, no, he wasn't the one who'd made the mistakes. That had been the old bastard.

She took his beer from him. Enjoyed a long, slow drink. "I know you do...." Her index finger traced around the rim of the beer bottle. "I know, Quinlan, I know...." Her fingers rubbed over the rim once more. "Finish this one," she said, "and the next one will be on me."

"Where's your car?" Max demanded, fury still heating his blood.

Samantha blinked at him with her wide, dark eyes.

Picking up another man? Shit, I should have known that I was just one in a line for her. Should have known.

When she didn't answer, he spun around and found the red VW at the end of the street. "You're packing it in. *You're done for the night.*"

"I wasn't there to pick up a lover." Halting, soft.

He turned back to find her frowning at him, a faint furrow between her brows.

"If I need sex," she told him quietly, "I know I can come to you."

What? Jesus, who went around saying things like that? Well, other than her?

"You meet my needs. I don't see why—"

Sometimes, the woman seemed too damn clinical. "How old are you, Samantha?" He'd thought she was in her mid-twenties—*please, don't be younger*—but she'd been at the bar, and if she was a student at Georgetown, she could be—

"Twenty-four."

Okay. Still too young but, "I'm thirty-three."

She just nodded.

"You're in college. I'm—"

Now she laughed. "I've been out of college for a long time. I finished up my doctorate three years ago."

What?

She stroked his cheek. "You don't really know me, Max. I'm not the woman you think I am."

Yeah, serious understatement.

"Trust me on this. I wasn't shopping for a new lover."

And why should it matter? She was right. He didn't know her. They'd had sex, not long, deep conversations. He shouldn't give a flying fuck who she wanted to screw. He'd had his fun, and now—

I want more of her. Haven't had enough yet.

Samantha stood on her toes, bringing that unpainted, plump mouth close to his. "I like having sex with you."

His cock jerked. *Down, boy.*

"You're giving me what I need now. *Exactly* what I need."

In another two seconds, he'd be giving her what she needed, what she was asking for with those big eyes and that husky voice.

Her tongue snaked out and licked his bottom lip.

Dammit.

He caught her arms and held tight. His mouth took hers, and his tongue plunged deep. She didn't taste like wine or beer. Sweet, tangy.

Just woman.

Her breasts stabbed against his chest, the nipples already tight, and his hand pushed between their bodies. He cupped her breast through her thin shirt, squeezing and stroking and wanting that tight nipple on his tongue.

"*Max!*"

She wanted him, just as much as he wanted her. *Just as much.*

Quinlan shoved away from the bar. "I've got to get out of here."

The blonde smiled at him. "Want some company?"

Yes. He kissed her, took those dark red lips, and the room seemed to spin around him.

He pulled away, real slow, and took her hand as he headed for the front door.

"No," she said, tugging back. "This way," and she pointed to the back.

Whatever. Right then, he'd go anyplace she wanted to lead.

Any damn place.

They made it back to Max's place. Barely. He'd followed behind Samantha, tailing that Bug and cursing the hard need in his dick.

He hadn't been this bad off since he was eighteen. What was it about Samantha? Why couldn't he seem to get enough of her?

They stumbled through the lobby. When the elevator doors closed behind them, he couldn't wait any longer. She slipped back against the mirrored walls, and he yanked up her shirt. Pale blue bra...

He shoved aside the lace, found her nipple, dark red like a tight, sweet cherry. His mouth closed around her breast, sucking, taking that nipple against his tongue. Licking, stroking, using his teeth to score her flesh.

Her moan filled his ears even as her hips bucked against him. His cock was so swollen that he hurt, and if the elevator didn't move faster...

He'd take her there.

Ding.

Her hands shoved against him. "Max, someone..."

He had her shirt off in two seconds. Her face flushed, her eyes gleamed with lust, and when she glanced down, well, hell, Max knew there was no missing the tent in his pants.

But no one was there. His floor. They hurried down the hall. He nearly knocked down his door before he got the key in the lock and the door finally swung open.

Bed, bed, make it to the bed.

Their clothes littered the floor. Her shirt. His.

The hallway. They'd made it that far.

She lost her shoes.

His followed.

Her pants came down.

Fuck.

She stumbled into his bedroom. Stripped off her bra. The panties...

Samantha fell back onto the bed, spreading her pale thighs, and he caught her silken flesh, opening her up more. His turn to taste.

He found her wet. Ready. Her flavor was richer, sharper below. He licked her clit, loving the way that she pressed up against him, and her breath hissed out. But this time...

"Say my name, Samantha." He nearly growled the order.

They were using each other.

Sex. Pleasure. Fair enough, but he wanted no confusion when it came to who was fucking her.

His tongue drove inside her.

"Max!"

One more lick. One more. Damn, not enough. He tasted her, and he wanted more. *Like a damn addiction.*

Her hips arched. Her climax was close, so close that he felt the quiver in her sex.

Max reared back and yanked out a condom from the nightstand drawer. He sheathed his cock, positioned, and drove deep.

Samantha came with the first thrust. A hard explosion that shook her whole body and had her sex clamping fist-tight around him.

He rode out her pleasure. Plunged into her, again and again, and the tension built. Higher. Sharper. Stronger.

Sweat coated his shoulders. Her moans filled the air. The bed started to squeak.

Her legs wrapped around him. Her ankles dug into his ass. Her eyes were open, on him.

Seeing me.

He erupted inside of her.

Max dozed, not long, and woke to the sound of the bedroom door creaking open.

Awareness came instantly. He shot up in bed. "Running away again?"

Clad in her bra and panties, Samantha glanced back at him. "I can't stay the night."

Can't. *Won't.* Right. Just sex.

If he wanted a woman to stay the night, he had a drawer

full of numbers he could call. Maybe he would. His jaw clenched, and he gritted, "You know the way out. Just go and—"

The phone on the nightstand rang. Who the hell was calling him this late? Shit, if there was a problem at one of his sites...Swearing, Max grabbed the phone. "Ridgeway."

Samantha backed out the door. He wasn't going after her. Wouldn't stop her. Maybe it was time for the madness to end. This was going nowhere; it was—

"*I have something of yours*...." A gruff whisper.

"What?" Max blinked and then ran a hand down his face. "Who is this?"

"If you want him back, you'll make sure I get my payment."

"Listen, buddy, I don't know who you are, but this conversation is *over*." Too late for this shit.

Samantha stilled in the hallway. He caught the flash of her hip, the curve of her sweet ass.

"Don't call again, got me?" Max started to drop the phone.

"How much is your brother's life worth?" That same damn whisper taunted.

It took a moment for understanding to sink in. *Brother.* His spine snapped straight. "What are you talking about?" he barked.

Laughter. Mocking. Chilling his blood. "I have your brother, and if his old man doesn't pay, I'll send him back to you in pieces."

No, no, this wasn't happening. This was bullshit. Some sick joke. "You've got Quinlan?"

The door squeaked. Not closing this time; opening.

Samantha slipped back inside. His gaze shot to her, and Max found her watching him with wide eyes and a pale face.

"If you want Quinlan to keep the blood inside his body, you'll do what I say."

Hell. "Let me talk to him, *now!*"

"You don't give the orders."

That drumming in his ears—nearly drowning out the bastard's words—was that his heart? "You don't have him," he said with sudden certainty. Sick freak. "You don't even know—"

"If you hadn't been so busy trying to screw the pretty whore on the street, you might have even seen me take him from The Core. You were right there. You could have saved him."

His fingers nearly smashed the phone. *Watching.* "Put my brother on the line!"

"No." Again that twisted laughter. "Just be a good errand boy and do what you're told. I'll be sending the old man a message—and you're going to damn well make sure he pays."

Joke, had to be a joke—

"You go to the cops, you try to mark the bills, and the ME will be piecing your brother back together for weeks. Got me? *Weeks.*"

Then the phone went dead.

CHAPTER *Four*

M ax?" Samantha stepped toward him. "Max, what's going on?"

Very carefully, he set the phone back on the cradle. "You need to leave now." *Quinlan. Shit, how had this happened?*

He'd read an article in the paper about that guy, Briar. The poor bastard had been nearly sliced apart and then left outside his parents' house. But Jesus, that had been over in Maryland. Not in D.C., not—

Max jumped from the bed and started yanking on his clothes. "*Leave, Samantha.*" She couldn't be here for this. He didn't want her anywhere near the nightmare that was about to come calling on him.

Taken.

He had to get to Frank's place. *Hold on, Quinlan. Just hold on.*

Max spun around and nearly slammed into Samantha. Her hands reached up and locked around his shoulders. "Tell me what's happening."

"Family issue. That's all." Max pulled away from her. He hurried into the hall and scooped up her shirt, then he tossed it back to her. "Playtime's over."

Her eyes narrowed at that, and he knew he was being a bastard, but he had to get away from her. *Can't let this touch her.* "The next time you're looking for a fast fuck, baby, give me a call, but—"

"*Stop it!*" Red stained her cheeks. "I heard you. You know I did!" She took a step toward him, a furrow between her brows. Her voice lowered as she asked, "Someone has your brother? Someone has kidnapped Quinlan?"

He just stared back at her.

"What do they want?" Whispered now. Afraid.

That same fear was in his heart, twisting and turning along with a fury that flamed too hot. "I don't know yet." His mouth had gone bone dry.

Samantha pulled the shirt over her head. Her soft curls tangled around her face. "They'll call you again, right? If we stay here, they'll call..." She hurriedly finished dressing.

He shook his head. *Wasting time.* "I have to get to my stepfather's." He swung away from her. "The asshole on the phone said there'd be a message...." But when would it come? And just what would he want?

Money, obviously, but how much? Frank Malone was worth so damn much money. Malone's first wife had been one of those rich, old-money types, and when she died all of her fortune had gone straight to Frank.

No matter how much the bastard wanted, Max would make sure that Frank paid. Max wasn't going to let his brother wind up like Briar. "I think it's the same ones," he muttered, not looking back. "Like that guy in the paper."

"You don't know that for certain," her voice came with a fast, hard snap, and he stopped in surprise.

Samantha circled him, forcing him to stare at her. "You don't know anything about these people. This could just be a hoax, a trick, somebody who saw the story in the papers and who wants to screw with you."

If only. "The guy on the phone—he saw us at The Core."

Her lips parted in surprise.

"He was *there*, baby. He saw you, he saw me, and he took my brother while I was so distracted by you I could hardly breathe." He stared into her deep eyes, eyes so wide and open, and for a second, a dark suspicion twisted in his soul.

They'd met so suddenly. She'd come on so strong.

Then she'd just appeared at the D.C. party. *With me and Quinlan.*

And she'd been at The Core, *with me and Quinlan.*

Samantha had been there last night, and tonight…

Frank Malone would pay nothing if Max disappeared. Max wasn't real flesh and blood, so the old man wouldn't give a shit about him. The money—the family money— was all tied to Quinlan.

"The guy said he'd been following you?" Real surprise flashed over her delicate features.

He grabbed his keys. "Go home. I don't have time for—"

"I'm coming with you!" Fast, tumbling words. "Wherever you're going, whatever you're doing, I'm coming."

He glanced up in time to see Samantha snatch up her shoes. "I'm not letting you do this alone," she told him.

Max shook his head. "You don't know what—"

Her fingers wrapped around his. "You don't know what's coming either. But you *don't* need to be alone."

His jaw clenched.

"Either you let me come with you or I'll follow you, so just accept—"

"*They could still be watching.* Shit, they *are* watching. That asshole on the phone, he told me if I went to the cops, I'd get my brother back in pieces!"

She flinched. "Max, you should—"

"Did you read the headlines? Did you *see* what they did to that other poor bastard?" The guy had suffered for a long time. "They'll do it." His eyes squeezed shut for an instant. Worry and guilt ate at him. "I was right there, and I didn't even see them take him."

"This isn't your fault!"

"I'm getting Quinlan back. I don't care what I have to do, but I'm getting my brother back." His gaze met hers.

Samantha just stared at him, her expression worried. *She doesn't think I'll ever see him again.*

And deep down, he was afraid of the same damn thing.

Max drove fast. Too fast. The seatbelt cut into Sam's shoulder as he rounded a too-sharp curve, and her breath hissed out. Her fingers were shoved in her purse, and she was sending the text on her phone as quickly as she could.

And she was hoping like hell that Max was so focused on the road and so distracted by his brother's abduction that he wouldn't notice what she was doing.

Hurry, hurry. Her fingers tapped quickly even as her stomach twisted.

He told me if I went to the cops, I'd get my brother back in pieces! Max's words wouldn't stop playing through her head.

If he knew who she really was...If he knew what she was doing...

No choice. This was her job.

And Quinlan's life.

Sam sent the message and knew that she'd lost her lover.

Luke Dante's phone beeped, a slow, deep tone that told him a message had come through for him. It was piss late, and he was comfortable, satiated, and in bed with the woman he loved.

Not just in bed with her. Three weeks ago, he'd moved in with her. *Next step is marriage, baby. Get ready.* Before Monica realized it, he'd have her bound to him for life.

And he wasn't going to be satisfied with anything less.

For an instant, he thought about ignoring the text for a few hours, just until the sun slipped into the sky. He wanted to see the sun rise with Monica. The woman had a killer view from her bedroom. Much better than he'd had at his apartment. Not that he'd spent many mornings there.

Prefer to be with her.

"You want me to look..." Monica asked, her voice husky from sex and sleep, "or are you getting it?"

Shit. They didn't have the luxury of ignoring calls. Not with their life.

Even damn doctors got more sleep than they did.

Luke rolled over and turned on the lamp. The soft glow spilled over the bed. "You think they've already taken another one?" Fully awake now, Luke growled the question as he reached for the phone. *They.* The kidnappers who were hunting rich prey.

Monica didn't speak, but then that was an answer, wasn't it? Hell.

He touched the screen on the phone. *Sam.* No, that didn't make sense. If someone else had been taken, the call would've come from Hyde, not her.

"Luke? What is it?"

He scrolled over the screen and pulled up the message. *K has another. Stand by.*

"What the fuck?" K—that had to be the kidnappers. They had another victim and that was all Sam was telling him? What was this shit?

Soft fingers pressed on his shoulder. A light breath eased against his ear. "What's she doing?" Monica asked as she leaned in close to read the message.

"Hell if I know." And that scared him. "This isn't procedure. Sam knows—". *Sam knows better than to screw with FBI protocol.*

The bed squeaked as Monica eased back. "She does know. Sam knows a *lot* that most people don't realize. Take a breath," she ordered, "and figure out why she contacted you this way. She knows you're here, so she could have just called the house line."

He glanced over his shoulder and found Monica watching him with her bright eyes, glinting in the dark. "She... couldn't talk." So she'd texted him.

"Because maybe she's not alone."

Not again. Not to her. His left hand knotted in the bed sheets. "You think they've got—"

"No, Sam's not the kidnappers' type," she immediately reassured him.

But Luke shook his head. "She's from money, baby. We both know that. Old Boston money. If the perps found out about her, if they know what she's worth..." Sam had turned her back on that rich life to take the job with the Bureau, but that life was still there, reaching out to her. *What if the kidnapper had found the link? It wouldn't be the first time the perps watched the hunters. Not the first, not the last.*

"They take men," she said quietly, and not a flicker of worry showed on her face. "Sam's not the target. If she'd been taken, they never would have let her text you."

He sucked in a deep breath. "Her phone." If he wanted to find Sam or if Sam wanted *him* to find *her*, it would be easy enough.

Monica raised a brow and nodded. "Hyde put those handy tracers in all our phones after the Watchman case. To find her, you know all you have to do is activate the trace." Whether the phone was on or off, the tracer would still work.

Damn straight. He punched in the number for the SSD. While he waited for an agent to answer, Luke's left hand reached for Monica's. His fingers curled around hers.

The elaborate house rose before them, huge and stark, as it waited on the hill just beyond the black, electronic gates. Max braked hard, making the car squeal, and he punched in the security code for the gate with hard stabs of his fingers.

"Maybe you should have called first," Sam said quietly as her gaze scanned the perimeter. A big wall, yes, but no guards, no one actually outside to protect anything. There were two security cameras that she could see perched up on the entrance gates, but those would be easy enough to bypass.

"He wouldn't have answered." Hollow. Cold.

Sam frowned. That didn't sound like Max. Not at all.

The gates opened with a low groan. The Jeep lurched forward, narrowly missing a slash on each side from the gates' long poles. Somewhere in the distance, dogs snarled and growled.

The vehicle shuddered to a stop in front of an ornate entranceway. Max jumped out and she was right behind him, hurrying up the marble steps as he pounded on the door. "Beth! Jesus, open the door!" he yelled.

Lights flashed on inside the house. Sam eased back so she could look above them.

Max's fist crashed into the door. "*Now!*"

But the door didn't budge.

Sam licked her lips and tightened her hold on her bag. Her ID was in there, her phone—her only way to be traced. "Max, we should—"

The door opened. A tall woman wearing a gauzy blue robe glared at them. "What the hell, Max? Do you know what time it is?"

His gaze raked her. "Wake him up."

"You know what he takes at night." A long sigh filled the air as the woman stepped back. "That's just not gonna happen."

Max strode over the threshold. Sam followed close behind.

"Brought...company, did you?" The woman asked softly. "Well, isn't this just—"

Max was already on the stairs.

"Wait, no, you can't—"

He paused halfway up the steps. "I got a call thirty minutes ago, Beth. Quinlan's been taken. Some asshole wants Frank to ransom him."

Beth's eyes widened, and she staggered a bit. "T-taken?"

Max raced up the rest of the stairs.

Sam hesitated. "Who exactly are you?" She needed to figure out all the players in this game.

The blonde swallowed. "B-Beth Dunlap. F-Frank's... personal assistant." Light blue eyes narrowed. "And who are you? The latest girlfriend?"

"Uh..."

An older man with stooped shoulders walked from the shadows. "Beth, what's happening here?" The man asked in a quiet voice.

Beth belted her robe. "Max is here, Donnelley. He says—he says Quinlan is missing."

No, he'd said that Quinlan had been *taken.*

"I think—" Sam began.

There was a roar from the floor above them, loud and enraged.

Sam ran for the stairs with Beth right on her heels. "Frank!" The other woman screamed. "*Frank!*"

They reached the landing. Sam spun to the left, then the right. *There.* Broken wood in the hallway. She ran forward, racing under the giant chandeliers and darting around the wood. Max was in the room, shaking another man, a man with silver-streaked black hair. A man whose body was slack and whose eyes were closed.

Still closed?

You know what he takes at night.

"Wake up!" Max shouted. "*Wake the fuck up! Your son*

is gone, do you hear me? Gone!" He shook him, sending the guy's head flopping back.

Sam lunged and grabbed Max's arm, stilling the rough movements. "Don't..."

His head whipped toward her, and there was agony in his eyes. "I didn't want to come back to this damn house," he muttered. "Didn't want to see—"

"M-Max?" Bleary eyes opened.

"What's he on?" Sam demanded. The older man from downstairs had come into the room. He was watching everything, but staying back.

"Sleeping pills," he told her in that same quiet, calm voice. "He always takes some at night."

That's why the kidnapper called Max and not this Malone. He knew what Malone did every night. Knew that he couldn't talk with them.

That meant the kidnappers had to possess an intimate connection to the family, one that had allowed them access to this knowledge.

"You're his damn doctor, Donnelley," Max fired at him. "Get Frank up!"

Donnelley swallowed. "I-I'll do what I can."

Sam kept her hold on Max. His stepfather's eyes had already closed. She pulled Max back from the bed, tugging hard and curling her fingers around him. His body was tense against her.

A small chime sounded from her purse, a faint vibration of sound.

Her breath caught. *Oh, hell.*

Max shook his head. "Beth, has anyone been by tonight? Did you—"

Beth's hands were balled into fists. "I don't think so. I was here, but asleep. I didn't—"

"What did he say when he called, Max?" Sam cut in. *A message.* He'd mentioned something about getting another message.

The phone on the nightstand began to ring. Long, hard warbles of sound.

Frank flinched, and his eyes opened again, but everyone else froze.

Max exhaled on a hard breath. His gaze was on the phone. "He said they'd be contacting Frank."

The phone rang again.

"They wanted you to get him up," Sam breathed the words. "They knew, and they wanted—"

Beth sprang forward and grabbed the phone.

Max locked his fingers over hers. "No."

Another ring.

"Answer it!" Beth cried.

Max glared at his stepfather. "Bastard. He *needs* you." He shook off Beth's hold and picked up the phone.

"We've got her location," the cool voice said in Luke's ear. "She's at 1000 Rightmont Lane. It's the home of Frank Malone, the guy who—"

"I know him." Everyone knew about Fuck 'em Frank Malone. The guy had made his fortune by leveling the small business district just outside of D.C. Luke huffed out a breath. "Frank has a son, right?"

"Right," Ramirez told him, seeming way too awake for a guy who was still in the office at three a.m. "His son is Quinlan Malone, age twenty-three. Until pretty recently, Quinlan was a student at Georgetown."

Now they were talking the kidnappers' type. "Pull up everything you can on the Malones, got me? Everything." Luke didn't know how Sam had found out about this guy. Usually the SSD found out too late. With the two survivors, they'd only discovered the kidnappings *after* the young men were back home.

But for this case, if he was right, if *she* was right, and they were on this thing from the start—

We could take the kidnappers down.

Max's hands were sweating when he lifted the receiver. "Hello." Max didn't identify himself this time. Maybe he was wrong; maybe it wasn't—

"You moved fast, Ridgeway," the same low whisper rasped in his ear. "You moved fast, but you can't get the bastard to wake up, can you?"

"How the hell—"

"*This is my game,*" the man grated. "*My show.* I've known everything about your family for weeks now. *Weeks.*"

Max's gaze lifted. Donnelley had Frank sitting up on the bed, and his stepfather blinked owlishly as he struggled through the drugs and layers of sleep.

"If you knew," Max snapped back, his rage bubbling over, "then why send me here? Why—"

"Because I had to see if you could follow instructions. You're the one who's gonna make the drop, Ridgeway. You're the one that's gonna save your brother, and I had to be sure I could trust you."

A *test.*

"Didn't want you goin' to the cops. Didn't want you making any phone calls you shouldn't have made."

Max's shoulders were so tight that they hurt. "I followed your rules."

Samantha pressed close. "Ask to talk to Quinlan." He glanced up at her. She barely mouthed the words as she said, "Make him put your brother on the line." Dark shadows lurked beneath her eyes.

"How much do you think your brother is worth?" The voice rasped over the line.

Samantha's eyes bored into his. Max took a deep breath, and instead of answering, he ordered, "Put my brother on the phone."

That damn twisted laughter broke across the line. "Quinlan isn't quite up to talking right now."

"*Fuck—is he alive?*" How long had Briar been held before the bastard had started cutting him?

"Quinlan is alive. And if you want him to stay that way, you're gonna get five million dollars ready by ten a.m."

"What? I can't get that much cash ready by—"

"I know *you* can't, but when the old man finally rolls those fat eyelids open, *he* can."

Five million dollars. "We pay, you give us back Quinlan? Is that how this works?"

"You pay..." No more laughter now, just that dark rasp. "You don't try to trick me, and yeah, you'll get him back...mostly all in one piece."

"I want proof!" Max ordered as his heart slammed into his chest. "Before I do anything, I want proof. I want—"

Click.

"Proof," he whispered and tossed the cell phone into the closest garbage dump. They always wanted proof. He hurried back to his car, air puffing out in front of him. As he reached for the door, his gaze shot to the black gloves covering his fingers.

Proof.

He smiled.

He knew just what piece he'd send to the big brother asshole. Just the proof the guy wanted.

"Call return," Samantha said, and Max blinked at her. "Do star sixty-nine now," she ordered. "You can get his number."

He glanced over at the caller ID. "Unidentified number, there's no way for me to—"

Sam spun away from him. "He could have blocked before he called, but I bet he's probably calling from a disposable cell."

Max frowned. His temples throbbed as he stared at her. Her shoulders were back, her strides tight and quick, and the way she was talking—

"Only on the phone for forty-two seconds." Her gaze was on her watch. "He's timing this thing, working it so that—"

"Wh-where's...Quin?" Groggy, slurred. *Frank was awake.*

Max loomed over his stepfather. "Not here. Look, he's been—"

But Frank's eyes weren't on him. They were on Samantha. "K-Katie? I-is...that—"

Max's hands curled into fists. *"It's not her!"*

"He always asks for her when he wakes," Donnelley said, shrugging his rounded shoulders. "Give him some time, let him adjust, and then you can tell him—"

That his only son was gone and might soon be dead.

Max shook his head. *Five million dollars.* "Beth, come with me. We need to get downstairs, and we need to call the bank." As his father's assistant, she'd have access to Frank's accounts.

"We need to call the cops!" Beth fired at him, backing up fast. "Are you kidding me? We can't handle this! We need the police. They can find Quin! They can—"

Get him killed. "We're telling no one." Max let his stare drift around the room, touching on each face, even locking with Frank's bleary eyes. "Not a soul, do you understand me?"

Beth would be the weak link. She was standing there shuddering, as fear raked her body. He'd need to watch her carefully. "This story isn't winding up on the news because if it does, we won't see Quinlan alive again."

"You believe...them." Donnelley's hesitant voice. "You're sure it's not a trick?" His green eyes were steady but the lines on his face looked deeper, harder.

"They have to give you proof," Samantha's hands were on her hips. "If they can't prove that he's—"

"They were at The Core. They saw us, and they took Quinlan." This wasn't some bullshit scam. He knew it.

Samantha shook her head. "You don't know what happened after they left the club." She paused, then said, "Your brother could have tried to get away. They could have used too much force to subdue him...."

No, Jesus, *no.*

"Quin...lan?" Frank pushed up against the covers. "Wh-what's h-hap...pening?"

Samantha never looked away from Max. "Before you give them the money, you have to get proof that Quinlan is still alive."

Because she thought his brother was dead.

And he was afraid she might be right.

Forty minutes later, Luke received the next text from Sam. His phone beeped, and the screen lightened. Then…

K called. Unidentified number.

"Dammit." He'd expected as much based on the other cases, but they'd still be contacting the phone company. Maybe, just maybe they'd find a link back to the killer.

"When we get the records, it's gonna be like the others," Ramirez warned. "Just a disposable, we're not—"

Luke whistled as he read the last of the message.

Cops = dead.

He dragged a hand over his face. "I need a way in." His gaze met Ramirez's. "Find me a way in, Jon." A hard trick because he'd bet a month's salary that the kidnappers were watching the house. They'd be making sure no cops came. No new faces.

I have to get in.

"Get him a cover," Monica said. She sat nearby, watching. "He has to be doing a job that won't set off any alarms, but one that'll give him access to the house."

"Give me some time," Ramirez promised, "and I'll have you walking right through the front door without raising any suspicion."

Luke knew Ramirez could do it. No doubt.

But…

What about Sam? What cover was she using in that house? And she had to be using a cover. Because if the kidnappers knew that she was an FBI agent, then the vic was already dead.

• • •

Quinlan Malone screamed when the knife sliced into his skin. Blood flowed over his hand, wet, warm.

"This'll convince them." Whispered. *"A piece…"*

Quinlan's breath hissed out. The pain blasted him like the touch of fire, and bile rose in his throat.

"He'll pay." The words were gritted. *"He'll…f-fucking… pay…"*

Quinlan's heart thundered in his ears, nearly drowning out the words. His hand throbbed and burned and, *oh, shit…*

Tears leaked down his cheeks.

"He'll pay." So quiet, then, "He'd better."

"We're not paying the kidnappers a dime." Sam's eyes widened at his words. The speaker's voice wasn't slurred any longer. No, now the voice was strong and fierce and very, very pissed.

Sunlight flickered through the windowpane in the study as dawn cut through the last of the night. Frank Malone stood by the window and stared out into the distance. Dressed now, completely aware, he was no longer the drugged man desperate to understand.

Max paced in the room, tension evident in the taut lines of his body. At Frank's words, Max stilled. "You're not serious."

"I damn well am." Frank spun toward him. "I'm not going to bow to pressure, boy. I'm not going to—"

"He's your son," Sam said, stunned. "If you don't do something, he'll die." Didn't the guy get it?

Steel gray eyes raked her. "I don't know you, sweetheart, and I'd advise you to keep your nose out of family business."

Right. Sam swallowed and lifted her chin. Once upon a time, she would have backed down at that, dropped her head and hunched her shoulders. But she wasn't the same woman any longer, and staring into Frank's gaze, she realized that this guy—with his power, his money, and his arrogance—didn't scare her. *When you've already faced the devil, a pompous jerk is nothing.*

"Haven't you read the papers? Didn't you see what happened to Jeremy Briar when he was taken? This—this seems like the same kind of—"

Frank waved his fat fingers in the air. "It's a copycat. Some assholes read about the crime, and they thought they'd get rich off it, off *me*."

Yes, the SSD had been worried about a copy, but...

"This could even be Quin's doing." Frank's eyes, if possible, narrowed more. "Little bastard just hit me up for cash. Maybe he thinks this'll be the way to—"

"What if it's not Quinlan?" Max demanded, and Sam's gaze flew to him. "Do we just sit with our thumbs up our asses and wait for Quinlan to die?"

"That Briar shit wasn't even in D.C., Max!" Frank paced toward him. "Come on, you're smarter than this. At least, I thought you were."

Sam almost preferred the guy drugged.

"This isn't the same bunch." Frank was adamant. "They wouldn't come to D.C. when they're hunting in Maryland—"

"Yes," Sam said quietly, "they would." The certainty in her voice was obvious, and Max's head cocked at her words. His gaze bore into hers.

Her heart pounded way too fast. Her hands were sweating. *Tell him. Have to tell him.*

Frank wasn't going to pay. She could see it in his eyes. Feel it in the thick tension in the room.

So maybe Quinlan Malone was an immature asshole who liked to burn his way through his father's money. She'd sure met enough of that type in her lifetime.

But this was a different game, not some spoiled-boy routine, and she had to make sure that they all knew that.

The silence in the room stretched too long. Then...

The floor creaked softly as Max stalked toward her. "Samantha..."

She'd loved the way he said her name. Never Sam, not with him. He stroked the word out, tasted it each time. Made it sound sexy. Strong.

But this time, there was something different in his voice. Suspicion. The heat was gone, and now a chill had caressed her name.

"You know more than you're saying, don't you?" Max pressed.

Sam wouldn't lie to him. Not then. She gave a slow nod and saw his eyes narrow. A muscle flexed along his jaw.

"Who is she, Max?" Frank demanded. "You don't ever bring women here. You don't—"

"She didn't really give me a choice," Max murmured, drawing closer. His eyes seemed to burn through her. "She was with me when the call came in, and she was with me when I saw Quinlan for the last time at The Core."

She sucked in a sharp breath. Oh, no, she *knew* where this was going. "You don't understand—"

"The Core?" Frank's voice dripped disgust. "I told Quin to stop hanging out at that shithole. After he got clean, I told him to—"

The back of Max's hand brushed down Sam's cheek. "I don't really know you, do I?"

She could only shake her head. He had no idea.

His fingers curled around her chin. Max leaned close and whispered, *"Who the fuck are you?"*

The rage in his eyes was new, and dammit, a flicker of fear ignited inside her.

What else is new?

"Max?" Confusion came from his stepfather. "What's—"

"Quinlan was taken from The Core." Max's hold tightened. "*She* was at The Core. She was at the Lenwoods' party the night before…*when Quinlan was there.* She comes from nowhere, right before my brother vanishes, and I can't tell you *who she really is.*"

Sam struck out with her left arm and shoved him back.

"And there's that," he said. "Baby, you're a whole lot stronger than you should be."

If only.

"It's not what you think." Sam's eyes darted from Max to Frank. "I-I'm not working with the kidnappers. That's not it!" She took a breath. "Look, I haven't been completely honest with you, okay?"

But Max just waited and watched and she knew—*he's going to freak.*

"What I tell you can't leave this room, do you understand?" Her voice dropped, hardened. "You can't tell Beth. You can't tell Donnelley. You can't tell *anyone* else."

Max's eyes had never seemed so cold. "Tell them what?"

She held his stare. "I'm with the FBI."

CHAPTER *Five*

Bullshit," Frank's automatic response.

But Samantha just shook her head and her eyes—stark and sad—held Max's. "I work with the SSD—"

"What the hell is that?" Frank demanded.

Samantha never looked Frank's way. "It's the Serial Services Division, a fairly new unit in the FBI that was formed specifically to track and apprehend serials."

Rage churned in Max, and a film of red coated his vision. "You've killed him," Max growled, the words rising up from his gut. *I'll get my brother back in pieces.*

Samantha blinked, and for a second, it seemed like tears glittered in her eyes. But, no, nothing was there now. Just darkness.

"You're too damn young." Frank moved to Max's side. "You're not—"

"I'm twenty-four years old," came her cool voice. "And I've been working for the Bureau since I completed my Ph.D. at MIT."

What? No, wait, computers, she'd said she worked with—

"My specialty is information retrieval." Still so cool and calm. "I also work on pattern detections through a careful analysis of—"

"They said no cops," Max gritted. "I told you. You *knew*."

"By then it was too late," she whispered. And what, was that pain in her voice? No damn way. This woman had been playing him from the first minute they'd met.

An FBI agent. A genius from the sound of things. She'd come on to him for hot, dirty sex. Was that the way it worked for the Bureau folks? Did they—

"*No!*" She burst out, and Max realized he'd been barking his words at her the entire time.

Samantha caught his arms and held tight. "*You don't realize...the SSD has been working this case for so long.*"

His heart raced in his chest.

"That bar...the night we met," she wet her lips. "I was there because that place fit the kidnappers' hunting profile. The kidnappers take men from bars near campuses. I wasn't there because I was looking to hook up, I was canvassing the place. Then...then I saw you."

The fucking FBI?

"When you got the call...your brother..." Her lips trembled. "Your brother, *my* case. I couldn't walk away, not when this was my chance to—"

Max pulled free. *Her chance.* "This isn't your chance for any damned thing. This is my brother's life we're talking about here! This isn't time for you to get some media coverage 'cause you're working a case. *This is my brother.*" Didn't she get it?

Her lashes lowered, and she blinked. Once, twice. He

could almost see her processing, like some kind of freaking robot.

Robot.

Where was the woman who'd gone molten in his arms? This—this wasn't her.

Max rubbed his grainy eyes. *Think.* "They don't know who you are." Oh, Jesus, he hoped they didn't. "You haven't called in to your boss, so the—the—" What had she called it? "SD—"

"SSD. The Serial Services—"

He dropped his hand. "Do I look like I give a shit right now?"

Her lips tightened.

"They don't know," he fired on, aware that Frank was now watching Samantha with assessing eyes. Different eyes. "And you're not going to tell them. We're not going to so much as breathe a word to your FBI boss until this is over, and Quinlan is home." *We can do this. We can....*

"She's already contacted them," Frank said, tilting his head as he studied her. "Haven't you?"

What? No! Max had been with her nearly every moment—

Nearly.

Samantha nodded. "I'm sorry...but it's my job." A quiet admission.

Anger shot through Max's body, heating his flesh, boiling him from the inside out, and he spun away from her.

And slammed his fist into the nearest wall.

Blood pooled on the floor. Dark, dark red. Not bright. Why did people always think blood was bright? It wasn't.

It was dark and really, after the first few moments, it was so cold and—

"We've got a problem."

The kidnapper stared at the token in his hand. "No, we've got proof." He held it up and heard the swift inhalation of air from behind him.

"What did you do? Are you fuckin' crazy? What did you—"

Slowly, he turned to fully face his lover. Her beautiful face looked so pale, almost stark white, beside the golden rain of her hair. Not that the pallor hurt her looks any. No, the ivory skin just made her look softer. Like she was weak.

But she wasn't.

He'd never made that mistake about her.

A smile curved his lips as he stared at her. She'd been such a good lure. It was so easy to take the victims when they were willing. "The asshole wanted proof." He shrugged. "I got him proof."

Her gaze darted to his hand, then away. "Y-you could have just—"

"Let the guy talk to his brother on the phone?" He finished and shook his head. "No, we couldn't risk that." He smiled. "Besides, this way was so much more fun, love."

She swallowed.

He touched her neck. His hand stroked that soft column, and he left his bloody fingerprints on her flesh.

He'd have to clean the blood up soon.

All of it.

She glanced at the chair behind him, almost helplessly. "You...like this too much."

His fingers tightened around her throat until he cut off

her air. Fear flickered in her gaze. Smart—because she was right to fear him.

His grin grew. "So do you." He crushed his mouth to hers and eased his grip, just enough to let her wheeze in some air.

A whimper hung between them.

He took his time with her mouth. Enjoyed it, but this wasn't the right place. Not for what he had in mind.

And there was more work to do.

His head lifted slowly. "Are we working on the next target?" Because the plan he had—oh, it was going to be good.

So damn good.

The media had his story now. The Feds were watching. He'd give them something special to watch.

She nodded, but wet her lips with a flash of her pink tongue. They'd use that tongue later. "Are you—are you sure this will work?" she asked.

His smile was gone. Really, she shouldn't have any doubt. "Two for the price of one, love. You can't beat that deal."

Do the unexpected. Always keep the enemy off-guard. Lessons he'd learned so long ago.

Do the unexpected.

They'd be profiling him. Planning and plotting and trying to track his next move, but they'd be wrong. Dead wrong.

He tossed his prize into her hands. Her horrified yelp made him laugh. "Have that delivered, will you?"

He had another victim to meet.

Veronica James was shaking as she prepared the package. She hadn't signed up for this deal. No damn way.

Blood was on her hands.

Shit. She hurried to the sink and turned on the water. The icy cold blasted her as she scrubbed and scrubbed.

He was going too far, he was—

"It's almost over, love," his voice whispered from behind her, and Veronica stiffened. The pink water poured down the drain.

The old floor creaked beneath his feet. "A few more days," he told her, his voice rumbling, "and we'll be free and clear."

Her hands were clean now. Blood was surprisingly easy to wash away. If you did it fast enough, there was never any stain. She turned off the water and faced him, her heart pounding too fast in her chest. When she'd first seen him at The Core, she'd thought he would be the perfect target.

Now she knew that she hadn't been the only one hunting that night.

"Just one more?" she asked him. She couldn't think about all the things they'd done. All they would do.

She had to focus on survival. Hers. Theirs.

Surival and money. All of that wonderful money would be waiting for her.

He smiled, and it was the same crooked grin that had first caught her attention. "We've almost got enough cash for the group. We'll ditch this fucking town and start over."

Money. That was what it was all about for her. To finally have enough that she could do whatever she wanted.

His lips skimmed her jaw. Sometimes, he could be so gentle.

And sometimes...

Veronica swallowed and leaned toward him. Her eyes drifted closed.

"You're with me until the end, aren't you, love?" He whispered.

She nodded against him.

"I can trust you," his fingers caught her chin and tipped back her head, "and you can trust me."

Veronica's eyes opened.

"You do trust me?" he pressed.

"Yes." Veronica knew just how dangerous he was, but...*not to me.* He wouldn't hurt her. He loved her. He wanted to marry her.

And they were going to be so fucking rich.

She licked her lips. *The blood washes away.* "I love you," she told him. He was right. They'd start over again, free and clear, with a shitload of cash. No one would know about the past, and there'd be no blood on her hands ever again.

The phone call didn't come at ten o'clock. Max stared at the phone on his stepfather's desk, willing it to ring.

Samantha sat in the chair across from him. Frank was in the den, drinking, having a breakdown—who the hell knew what he was really doing?

"What did you tell them?" Max asked Samantha, forcing his gaze to her.

Her chin lifted. "I let the agent in charge know a victim had been taken, *who* he was."

"How."

"I sent him a text on the way here."

Ballsy.

"Then I sent him another when we were upstairs, right after the call came."

And right under his nose. Talk about being a blind idiot. *Why wouldn't the phone ring? Why?* He'd been a piss-poor brother, he knew that. He and Quinlan had never gotten along like they should have, but—

But his mom's last words to him had been, *"Watch him."* A week before she'd died, she'd given him her order, and she'd never spoken to him again. Never opened her blue eyes again.

One thing. All she'd ever asked him to do. To watch over the brother that blood hadn't given him.

And he'd screwed that up. Max exhaled on a long sigh. "I had you wrong, didn't I?"

"I don't...know what you mean," Samantha said hesitantly.

Ten-oh-three a.m.

His gaze sharpened on her. "I thought you were weak. That you were running scared." The nightmare flashed in his mind. He'd actually wanted to protect her that night. What an idiot. "But I guess it was just some game to you." His fingers curled around the edge of the desk. "How many men?"

Her brows lifted. "What?"

"How many men have you picked up in bars? How many men have you asked for sex, but not forever? I mean, is that some line you like to use?" Pretty effective.

She leapt out of the chair. "You don't know me. *Do not say*—"

"The truth? It can hurt, can't it?" Why had he been so addicted to her? Why was he *still* so addicted? He looked, and even in the middle of this twisted hell, he wanted her. He could still taste her on his tongue and smell her on his skin.

You don't know her.

Sex. That was all they'd had. Sex and lies.

A knock rapped at the door.

Max rose and stormed around the edge of the desk. "Come in!"

Samantha stepped in front of him. She lifted to her tiptoes and kissed him.

His hands came up automatically and clamped down on her arms. The kiss was angry, fierce. Her mouth was closed. His was—

No.

Her lips opened. Softened. Her tongue snaked out, licked across his, and the growl in his throat burst out as he dragged her closer. The furious tension that had been riding him snapped, and for just that moment, he wanted her in his arms, her mouth on his, her breasts against him as—

Samantha's mouth tore from his. She kissed his jaw, pressing her lips against the line of stubble that he knew would be rough. Her lips feathered over him, and then her breath blew lightly at his ear.

"Whatever you feel..." Her soft whisper slid right through him. "Whatever you think about me...to everyone else, we have to be lovers."

Because everyone was watching.

His head lifted. His hands still held her, but his control was back. Razor thin, but fueled by the fire of understanding.

She didn't touch me, didn't kiss me because she wanted me.

Business. Before, it had just been pleasure.

"Ah...excuse me..." A deep voice he'd never heard before interrupted.

Samantha turned, and Max's eyes zeroed in on the

doorway. A man stood there. He was clad in dusty jeans and a loose white t-shirt. His blond hair was mussed, and he held a stack of files in his hand. "I've got those guest house designs you needed, boss..."

Boss?

The guy began to close the door. "Yeah, I told Mr. Johnson we could get started today, but he said—"

The door shut with a click.

The man tossed the files onto the nearest chair. He crossed his arms and his green gaze shot to Samantha. "Are you okay?"

She nodded slowly.

Max's gut clenched as the guy's stare jumped between them. "Who..." Max began, stepping forward, "are you?" Just after ten o'clock... maybe they weren't getting a phone call. Maybe they were just getting a visit.

Since it was the weekend, most of the staff weren't working. Only Beth and Donnelley and one security guard were there. Hell, he should've had more security. He should've—

"He's Special Agent Luke Dante," Samantha said into the silence. "He's the lead agent currently working the serial kidnappings."

Max's hands clenched. "Was one agent in the house not enough? Why don't you just start slicing Quinlan up your damn selves?" This dick had strolled right in the front door, when he *knew* they were supposed to stay away from the cops and—

"No one knows who I am," Luke Dante drawled. "To anyone watching, I'm just another crewman on your team. You *did* have plans to start work on a guesthouse for Tyler Johnson this week, didn't you?"

What? How had he—

"As far as the rest of the world is concerned, I'm part of the crew you scheduled for that site. And when I leave here, I'm going to make damn sure no one follows me, so that's all anyone will ever know."

"I don't want you here," Max told him bluntly. Everything was out of control. And the phone wasn't ringing.

A fast nod from Dante. "Understood. Hell, I'd feel the same way in your position."

"You don't know my position," Max said, voice tight.

"Sure I do." He shrugged. "You're the stepbrother, the one Quinlan wants to be like, the one your mother doted on. You're the one the victim would turn to for help, probably the only one around here that he counts on, and right now, you're feeling like shit because you think you signed your brother's death warrant."

"Pretty good," Samantha murmured. "That from you or Monica?"

But Max snapped, "You're the assholes signing the death warrant. They said *no cops!*"

"They don't know I'm here." Luke's gaze was on Samantha. "And I'm guessing they have no clue who you are."

She shook her head.

"Girlfriend?"

She blushed. *Blushed.*

The agent whistled quietly. "I wondered how you fit in. That's one lucky break, Sam."

Sam. Too familiar. Just who was this guy to Samantha? There was something there, warmth and affection, in his eyes. If she'd wanted a lover, why not him?

Why had she gone trolling at the bar?

"You know what Hyde says..." Dante began.

Who was Hyde?

"There aren't any coincidences," she finished. "He's right. I met Max while I was canvassing possible target bars in the area."

The male agent hesitated. "You sure you weren't made?"

"No one knows." Samantha glanced over at Max with a flicker of her dark eyes. "Even he didn't—" She swallowed. "Max just found out."

Another whistle. "Bet that's a real bitch, huh?"

Who was this asshole?

"We don't have much time, so I need you to listen carefully..." Dante's stare pinned Max. "What did the kidnappers tell you?"

Max rocked back on his heels. "That I'd be getting another phone call. One I should have gotten ten minutes ago."

"It's a scare tactic," Dante dismissed with a wave of his hand. "Same way, every time. You won't hear back from them for at least two more hours. They want you to sweat. They want you to worry."

Max was doing both. "How many have been taken?"

"Quinlan makes five." Samantha's instant answer.

"And how many came back alive?"

No instant answer. Not from either of them. "Samantha?"

A soft sigh slipped from her lips. "Two." She shoved back the hair that had fallen over her forehead. "You know about Briar. His father refused to pay."

"And they sliced up his son. Yeah, heard that." Tension had his gut clenching. "What happened to the other guy? Why didn't he make it back? Why—"

"The ransom drop was made with marked bills," Dante told him quietly. "The kidnappers had been watching the house. They knew the cops were involved. They knew the bills weren't clean. So they gave the man back but..." his shoulders rolled as if he were shaking off a bad memory, "not in one piece."

"Max..." Samantha's husky voice.

Max held up his hand. "You know the way they operate." *The kidnappers had been watching the house.* His thundering heartbeat filled his ears. "You *know*... and you've both put my brother's life on the line?" His eyes narrowed on Dante. "Get the hell out of this house."

Agent Dante didn't move. "We know the way they operate, and we're trying to stop them and *save* lives."

Max could only shake his head. The guy didn't get it. And Samantha—*Sam*—he didn't want to think about her.

"You're going to stay with him," Dante said to Samantha, and it seemed like an order. Wait, he was the lead agent, so it *was* an order.

"No way." Max could give orders too. "She leaves with you." Because he was done with whatever game she was playing. The FBI could go screw off.

Dante crossed his arms over his chest. "I understand this is a difficult time for you, Mr. Ridgeway, but you need our help."

Not from where he was standing. He needed them to get lost.

Dante's attention shifted back to Samantha. "You've already got a cover here, Sam. Use it. Stay close and keep your eyes and ears open. When you learn something, you let us know." Now his sharp gaze swung back to Max.

"Mr. Ridgeway, I assure you that the kidnappers will not know about the SSD's involvement. You're in the clear."

He'd better be.

"But this is the best chance we have to stop these perps. We can't force your compliance, but..."

But the guy would really like to. Yeah, he could see that.

"But we can put you under a protective detail. And that *is* something we could force." A nod toward Samantha. "Either way, Agent Kennedy isn't leaving your side."

Not a threat. Not blackmail. Just a fact.

Dammit. "Does it matter to you? If this gets my brother killed, *does it matter to you?*"

Samantha flinched but Dante didn't bat an eyelash. "All the victims matter to me. That's why I'm in this business. You might not like the way we work—"

"I fucking don't." *Protective detail.* Right. He could always just have them both thrown out—*he* could throw them out. But if someone was watching, that person would see what was happening, and Max didn't want to risk that exposure.

"Just play it cool," Dante advised him. "Listen to Sam. She won't steer you wrong."

What? He was supposed to trust her? When she'd already lied to him?

"Report when they make contact," Dante told Sam. "We'll set up surveillance for the drop."

Max's mouth opened to protest.

"They won't know." Dante rushed to assure him. "You'll get your brother back, Mr. Ridgeway, and we'll get the men who took him."

Promises, promises.

"Can you handle this?"

Max blinked. "Don't worry about me, I can—"

"Sam?" The agent cut through his words.

Her chin lifted a notch. "I've got it."

Dante grabbed the files. "Are you in, Ridgeway?"

Samantha touched his arm. "There's no other option now. I'm here."

Because she'd tricked him. He wouldn't forget that.

But now Frank would have to act. They'd get the money, and they'd damn well get Quinlan back.

Get him back in pieces. The bastard's voice seemed to whisper through Max's mind as he stepped away from Sam. "If Quinlan dies, I'll destroy the SSD."

Samantha flinched. "I want to get him back for you."

But she wasn't promising that she *would* get him back.

"Trust us to do our jobs," Dante said. "We'll have eyes on you from now on. When you go to make the exchange, we will be there."

"And if they see you?" Max demanded. "What then?"

"They won't." Certainty from Dante. "We know what we're doing, and believe me, we have agents who specialize in not being seen."

"Ramirez," Samantha murmured.

Dante nodded. "Our agents will follow the kidnappers after the drop. They'll track them back to their hole, and they *will* recover your brother."

The guy was obviously confident, but then, it wasn't Dante's brother on the line.

Dante's gaze searched his face. "Now do we have your cooperation on this?"

Not like Max had any other options. He inclined his head in a grim nod.

Samantha's hand fell away from his arm. "Thank you," she whispered.

His jaw locked.

"You made the right decision." Dante turned toward the door. "Be careful, you two. I'll be watching."

"Luke, you need to know, Quinlan was taken from The Core," Samantha said.

That stopped the other agent, and he glanced back at her. "You sure about that?"

"*I'm* sure," Max answered.

"I was at The Core right before he vanished. If we'd stayed just a little longer..." She shook her head. "We need to get agents in that bar. Curtis Weatherly also visited that place shortly before he vanished. The Core is a link."

Dante nodded. "I'll get Ramirez and Daniels to talk to the staff again. We interviewed them all before and ran background checks, but everyone turned up clean." His head inclined. "So we'll just look deeper, and we'll make sure we keep our eyes on that place."

Shouldn't have left Quinlan. Guilt ate at Max's gut. If he hadn't left his brother in The Core...

"I can get some plainclothes cops in there ASAP," Dante continued. "We'll keep a surveillance team in The Core from now on."

A little too late to help Quinlan.

Dante rolled his shoulders and yanked open the door. "S-sorry, boss. Didn't realize you were...occupied." His southern drawl was thicker, his posture a bit weaker. "I'll come back later."

"You do that," Max called out, voice tight.

And then the guy was gone.

• • •

Sam slipped upstairs when Max and Frank were on the telephone again with the bank. She moved as quickly and quietly as she could. Her gaze darted into the rooms, scanning, searching—

There.

The closed door. The one at the end of the long hallway. Quinlan Malone still had a room at his father's house.

She twisted the knob, and the door opened silently. Sam didn't turn on the lights. No need. The computer sat waiting for her, right in the middle of Quinlan's gleaming glass desk.

Sam closed the door behind her. The bedroom was huge, more of a suite than just one room, but... there was nothing personal there. No pictures. No ball caps. No books or magazines. No intimate touches.

A bed with a black bedspread. A chest of drawers. The desk—so neat and organized.

And the laptop. Just waiting.

Like a hotel room. Ready for any guest, not a particular person. Shaking her head, Sam eased into the chair and booted up the computer. Time to get to work. She'd start with Quinlan's laptop and use a batch script to crack the network encryption. Once she had enabled remote access to the systems in the house, the computers would be hers. Then she'd access all the e-mail accounts and scan the drives to see just what sort of information the Malones and their staff might be hiding.

The computer beeped as the system came online. Then the password screen came up.

For the first time that day, Sam smiled. This was her favorite part of the job.

• • •

"Sir, are you sure you want to make a f-five million dollar cash withdrawal?" The banker's voice quivered over the speaker phone.

Frank's stare held Max's. "Yes."

"I'll draw up the paperwork," John Adams said, "but this is going to take some time, sir. I can't have the money ready for at least forty-eight hours."

"*Now*," Max mouthed.

"I need the money now," Frank ordered. "Cut the paperwork bullshit, John, and get my money ready, understand?"

"There's no way I can get that amount ready before—"

"Get it ready. I'm taking it today." No discussion, just a flat demand.

And that's why he was called Fuck 'em Frank.

John's sigh drifted over the line. "Sir, you don't seem to realize just how—"

An ear-splitting scream ripped through the house.

Samantha.

Max leapt from the chair and ran for the door. Frank followed right on his heels. The banker's voice droned behind them.

Max's feet pounded over the tiles. "*Samantha!*"

The scream echoed again. Even louder now and then . . .

Retching.

He spun, sliding around the corner, and saw Beth curled on the floor, her long blond hair streaming around her face.

Not Samantha.

"Beth?" Frank demanded. "Woman, what the hell were you screaming—"

Her head lifted. She shoved back her hair, and her eyes
fixed on them. "B-box..."

Footsteps thudded behind them. "Max!" Samantha's
voice now. Fierce.

He didn't look back. He'd seen the box. Small and
brown, lying on the floor with the top torn open.

Beth pushed back, crawling like a crab away from
the box.

A fist squeezed Max's heart. "Where did it come
from?"

"I-it was on the steps. The guard put it there, I-I
thought..." Beth sucked in a sharp breath. "I thought
one...of the m-messengers had brought it from the
office."

Max bent down and reached for the box. *Jesus.*

Beth whimpered.

Samantha grabbed his hand. "Don't." Her soft skin
pressed against his. Her mouth came close to his ear as
she whispered, "Not bare skin...we have to check for
fingerprints."

His hand fisted.

"Use this." She dug a pen out of her pocket.

He took it, his fingers rock steady. He shoved the top
off the box with the tip of the pen. *Fuck me.*

A bloody finger lay nestled inside.

Beth started crying.

A ring finger, one still adorned with his brother's lucky
horseshoe ring.

Sonofabitch.

"Max?" Frank's voice wasn't so tough now. "What's in
the box?"

Proof. "They've got Quinlan." And he'd just gotten a

piece of his brother. His head turned, and he met Samantha's worried stare. *The first piece.*

Max surged to his feet. Samantha rose right with him, her hand gripping his wrist. "He's still alive, Max," she said urgently.

Max tried to shake her off. Her grip just tightened. "*He's still alive.* This is just to screw with you, to make you desperate."

"*It's his f-finger!*" Beth cried out.

Samantha didn't look away from Max. "It's a message. You wanted proof, so they gave you proof. Your brother is out there. He's alive, and we're going to get him back."

Proof sent.

Luke scanned the text. *Victim's finger delivered in box. Fingerprint and DNA testing needed ASAP.*

"Fuck."

His head lifted, and he stared at the team assembled in the SSD's conference room. "The kidnappers just made contact again." The first time that they'd done this. Changing the MO.

Hyde straightened in his chair. "They called already?"

"No." His gaze found Monica's. She'd been working on the profile for the kidnappers. "They sent a finger to the Malone house in a damn box."

No change of expression crossed her perfect face.

"Why change the plan, Monica?" Luke pressed because she would know. When it came to the killers, she always knew.

"Because the kills are changing *him*," she said.

Yeah, that's what he'd feared but he'd wanted her take on the situation.

"The leader was much more violent with Briar's body than he was with Peter Hollings'," Monica continued. "He kept Briar alive longer. He inflicted the wounds not to kill, but to *hurt.*"

Yeah, and that worried him.

Monica confirmed his fear when she said, "Seems to me that our perp might have found something he likes."

"Or maybe we're not dealing with the same kidnappers," Jon Ramirez offered from his position on the far right of the table. "Maybe this is some wannabe who read about Briar in the paper, and he thinks he needs to slice and dice to make his point."

Monica gave a slight negative shake of her head. "There are too many similarities that weren't released to the press. No one knew the men disappeared from college bars, and no one knew the initial calls came within three hours of the disappearances. And no one knew a ten o'clock call was promised, but never delivered." Her hands flattened on the table. "It's the same leader. The same group."

"And just how many folks are we talking in this group?" Hyde asked from the head of the table, his gaze sweeping all of their faces.

"Kidnappers are rarely solo workers," Luke said. "You're talking a unit here, one that follows an alpha..."

"Like a pack of dogs," came the quiet rumble from Special Agent Kim Daniels. Her eyes glinted but her face was as blank as Monica's.

"Someone has to stay with the vic, to guard him at all times." Luke lifted his hand as he began to count off the possible abduction team members. "Someone has to go for the drop. And someone has to cover the leader's ass." Because the leader would never leave himself vulnerable.

"And someone is the constant watcher who keeps an eye on the victim's family."

They needed to identify that watcher. In case it was someone *in* the household, Sam would continue to communicate through texts for secrecy. They weren't taking any chances with this case.

"At a minimum," Luke told them, "we're looking at four people. At most, six—no more than that, though. That would mean too many hands in the pie."

"We need that box," Hyde stated flatly. "The sooner we dust and run a fingerprint check, the better."

Hell, yeah. They were all on the same page there. Luke grunted. "We need to talk to those other victims." Luke wanted to meet with them, one on one. And actually get them to answer *all* of his questions. But money and power—those got in the way of sit-downs. "I want them back in the country."

Hyde nodded. "I'm working on it."

If Hyde couldn't get them back, no one could.

Luke considered his options. *Not many.* "In the meantime, let's get them on the phone. Get a conference call set up ASAP because I *need* to talk to them."

The vics were scared shitless. He got that. They wanted to pretend the nightmare that they'd lived through wasn't real. But another man's life was hanging in the balance.

And Luke wasn't in this business to stop the killers after the fact—after the blood had flowed and the dead had been hauled away. He was there to save lives, dammit, and that's what he was going to do.

Sam went to the bank with Max and Frank. She smiled at the other customers. She kept her face all nice and bland. After a few moments of small talk, the bank manager, John Adams, led them into his office, and the money was brought out to them.

Five million dollars. The price of a life. Quinlan Malone's life.

The bank manager was sweating. So was Frank.

Not Max.

Max kept a strong hold on her hand. Almost too tight. His fingers threaded with hers, keeping her close.

He had his job to do. She had hers. "Excuse me, gentlemen," she murmured. "Could you please direct me to the ladies room?"

The bank manager pointed to the left.

She offered him a wan smile, then she stood and walked down the narrow hallway and toward the restroom. The dress she'd borrowed from Beth shifted easily as she walked. Within moments, her hand pushed open the women's restroom door.

As she headed toward the sink, a woman turned around, reaching for a hand towel. They bumped into each other.

The purse Sam had borrowed slipped to the floor.

"Sorry," the woman said, her blue eyes wide. She bent, her curtain of black hair sliding around her face as she picked up the purse. "Didn't see you there." Her grip on the bag was firm.

Sam inclined her head. Special Agent Monica Davenport always had perfect timing. "No harm done." The finger and the box were inside that purse, covered by a plastic bag.

The exchange was made in less than ten seconds.

When Sam walked back out, her head was up, the bag

was hanging on her arm, and Max waited for her, a duffel bag gripped in each of his hands.

Her gaze darted to the bags.

"Let's get out of here," Frank said.

A guard stepped forward and led them to the door. Sam's borrowed heels—way too tight—clicked on the floor. It seemed like every eye was on them.

Frank had his personal guard with him. Jared Kinney doubled as his driver and his bodyguard. Sam had learned that Jared lived at the Malone house, in an apartment above the garage.

Jared pushed open the door. Bright sunlight hit Sam in the eyes. In another hour, the sun would be setting. It had taken so long for the bank manager to get that money ready. Too much daylight had already been lost.

But another phone call *had* to come that day. If the kidnappers followed their established routine, they would contact Max again soon.

They walked down the steps, slow and steady, not saying a word. Jared opened the door of the Cadillac for Frank. When the older man was inside, Max handed off the duffel bags. Max's Jeep waited on the other side of the road. He turned away.

But Frank grabbed his hand. "You're coming back to the house?"

Max stared down at him.

"I *need* you. You have to stay 'til this mess is over."

"I'll be back." Max eased away. Jared slammed the door. She and Max watched as the long car pulled away.

When the light changed, she and Max began to walk across the street. A slow, direct stride as—

A car's engine roared to life.

Sam's head whipped to the right. A small, black BMW headed straight for them, coming fast, so fast...

What the hell? Her heart slammed into her ribs in a split-second of understanding. "*Run!*" The damn car was aiming right for them. Coming closer, faster, turning to follow them as they rushed across the nearly deserted street.

No, not them. The car wasn't aiming at *them*.

She shoved Max forward and felt the rush of air behind her as she launched after him. Sam slammed into Max, and they crashed onto the cement. The smell of burnt rubber and blood filled her nose. She pushed upright as quickly as she could and turned back to see the tail-lights on the car vanish as the BMW took a hard right and disappeared.

"*What the hell?*"

Sam glanced at Max. He was up on his knees and brushing off hands that dripped blood.

Just like hers did. The cement could be a real bitch. "We need to get off this street. *Now.*"

"Because some asshole ran the light?"

"No." She grabbed his arm and all but jerked him toward the Jeep. "Because I'm pretty sure some asshole just tried to kill you."

CHAPTER *Six*

The angel in the red dress came up to him in a cloud of perfume and sex. Adam Warrant blinked at her, took another long look, and enjoyed the view. "Baby, where have you been all my life?"

She smiled at him and reached for his beer bottle. Pretty fingers. Long and pale. Blood-red fingertips traced the mouth of his beer. "You wouldn't believe me if I told you." Those fingers circled the mouth of the beer again. "But I'm here now, Adam."

His brows furrowed. The music was so damn loud. He could barely hear her. He leaned in closer and caught more of her scent. *Just like sex*. His cock throbbed. The top of her dress nearly showed her nipples. "Who are you?"

One more slow slide of her fingers around the top of the beer bottle, then down the neck, a caress, almost a pump.

He gulped. *Jesus*.

She handed him the beer, and her fingers pressed against his chest. "I'm the woman who's going to give you a night you'll never forget."

Adam smiled at that, then he drained his beer. "Promises, promises..."

Near hit and run. Almost took Max out. New game?

Luke shook his head as he read Sam's text. "Kim, we've got a problem" A big problem. A hit and run wasn't part of the MO.

"Hey!" Her voice came, high and tense, from right beside him. She had her phone pressed to her ear. "Ramirez is on the line. He says a BMW nearly clipped Sam and Ridgeway at the bank on Pines!"

Ramirez. Their shadow guy on this case. He was watching Sam and Ridgeway, and he'd make sure no one saw him. "Yeah, I know."

Her eyes narrowed. "Did you know that Ramirez got the guy's license plate?" Her fingers tapped on the nearest keyboard.

Luke stared over her shoulder as she pulled up the DMV access and typed in the numbers. It took less than five seconds for the results to pop up. "I'll be damned..." He muttered. The tag number matched the BMW registered to one Jeremy Briar. A car that had been reported missing by his mother right before she'd been booked for killing her husband.

Jeremy's car. A car that his killers had just tried to use to run down another man.

But...why? Sure wasn't good business sense. Dead men couldn't pay ransoms.

"We need to talk about this," Sam said when it became obvious that Max was just going to ignore the near hit-

and-run. *Ignore it.* Was the guy crazy? He'd almost been killed, and he hadn't said a word.

They'd gone to his place and picked up fresh clothes and an overnight bag. They were nearly back at his step-father's, and they *were* going to discuss the attack.

Sam saw his jaw clench. She swallowed back her own fear and fury and tried to sound calm. "Max . . . *someone aimed at you.*" Okay, not so calm. Forget calm.

"Why the hell would they want to hit me?" he demanded. The Jeep accelerated with a growl of sound.

That's what she wanted to know. She didn't like this situation. Not at all. The kidnappers had never made an attack like this. Breaking the MO would mean trouble.

"You shouldn't have pushed me out of the way," he told her, his deep voice rumbling.

She fiddled with the seatbelt. "Well, if you moved faster, I wouldn't have needed to push."

His fingers curled around the steering wheel. "You made yourself a target out there. You should have hauled ass and gotten out of the way, not worried about me."

"Worrying about you is my job." For now.

"That all it is?"

Sam blinked. "Wh-what?"

But he was turning the wheel and pulling into the long, winding drive that led up to the Malone house. A guard stood at the gate, and when he saw Max he waved them through with a roll of his hand.

"I don't get you," Max said, easing the Jeep toward the house. "The FBI? Hell, no, I never would have pegged that for you."

Why? Because she was weak? "It's all I've ever done." All she'd ever wanted to do.

He braked the vehicle and turned to face her. "And what? You get off on it? On tracking the killers? On seeing the bodies?"

Her breath sucked in. "*No.*"

"Why do it?"

"Because I know that some monsters are real." God, how she knew that was true. When she closed her eyes, she saw her own monster. "And they belong in cages, far away from innocent people." Or they belonged in the ground. But she wasn't supposed to say that. Think it, yes, but the badge wouldn't let her say it.

Max's hand reached out, and his fingers caught a lock of her hair. "You think every killer belongs in a cage." A darker tone hardened his voice.

"My job is to stop killers. That's what I do." Sam unclipped the seatbelt but didn't pull away from him. The sad truth was that she liked the touch of his hand against her cheek.

But his hand fell away and his mouth tightened. "Everything's black and white for you. You don't have room for gray in your world, huh?"

"Do you?" She fired back. "I saw your face when you found out I was with the FBI. You were pissed, Max." No masking that look of fury.

"I *am* pissed. You shouldn't be here. You should be so damn far away from here..."

Way to make a girl feel wanted. "I'm not going anywhere." The SSD wouldn't let her, and besides, she wasn't leaving him.

This was her time to be strong. *I can do this.* Hyde would be monitoring her every move. If she screwed up...

Well, Quinlan would be dead. Max would hate her. And she'd find her ass on the street.

No pressure.

"They'll call tonight," she said. The kidnappers always made contact again twenty-four hours after they took the vic. "They'll give you instructions for making the drop."

"And you'll tell your agents." He killed the engine.

"Trust me, okay?" Yes, there was desperation creeping into her words. "The SSD won't blow this. The agents will be far enough away that no one will see them, but they'll see everything. They'll be able to track the kidnappers after the drop. They'll stop this. No one else will get hurt."

"I want to believe you, baby." His fingers closed around the keys, forming a strong fist. A fist with bruised knuckles courtesy of that punch into the wall earlier. "But the thing is, I seem to have trouble trusting you."

Sam kept her chin up. "Then don't trust me, but listen to me. This isn't my first case. This isn't the SSD's first case. We bring down killers, and we bring victims back alive." They'd brought her back.

His head cocked, and his eyes glittered. "Now why do I think you're not being all that truthful with me? Some of the victims, they don't come back, do they?"

She turned away from him and shoved open the door. Cold air hit her like a slap, but it was what she needed. Sam hurried forward, determined to get inside the house.

"*Samantha*."

She froze at Max's voice. Gravel crunched beneath his feet as he followed behind her. Then he was there, catching her fingers, and curling his own around them. "You never know who's watching, baby." A sensual reminder, one with an edge of steel.

She glanced over, her eyes slanted toward him.

"I don't really know you." His head leaned down, and his lips brushed against hers. A lover's caress. "But then, you don't really know me, either." A warning.

His mouth pressed tight against her lips. Hard, insistent.

She opened her mouth for him. Not because someone might be watching, but because she wanted to kiss him, and screw anyone out there. Let them watch. Their tongues met. They tasted. And the cold seemed to fade away.

Back with him. In his arms. Her heart beat faster, and her sex began to moisten. In his bed, she hadn't needed to pretend. She didn't have to lie about being strong. In bed, it was just bodies, needs.

Man.

Woman.

Rain began to fall on them, softly at first. Little drops that tapped on her skin, then harder, steadier as the storm that had threatened all day finally came calling.

Max's head rose, and he stared down at her with water on his eyelashes and drops sliding down his cheeks. She tasted the rain on her tongue, and she still tasted him.

"Max!" A woman's cry. High and frantic.

Sam's head turned. Beth stood in the entranceway, waving. "The phone!" Beth shouted, "It's—"

They ran for her.

Max beat Sam inside, and Beth pointed down the hallway. "Frank—he's in his study. They called his cell. I-I know it's them..."

Sam's shoes squeaked and the water dripped onto the expensive tile as she raced for the study.

"Yes, I damn well got your *proof*," Frank shouted into

the phone, and Sam shut the study door, securing them inside. "Now you listen, and you listen good—"

He broke off, and Sam saw his eyes narrow. His thick Adam's apple bobbed as he swallowed. "I thought you wanted...five million." His gaze darted to Max. Another hard swallow. "No, I *don't* need another delivery. I'll pay, you bastard, just don't hurt him anymore!" Frank ran a shaking hand through his hair.

A victim. That's what Fuck 'em Frank had become. Afraid. Desperate. He didn't like being this way. She could see the fight in his eyes, but he didn't have a choice, and he didn't know what to do.

Sam looked away. She didn't like seeing the victims. Couldn't seem to deal with them anymore. Luke was great with them. He could always put them at ease and get every bit of witness testimony from them. The victims just made her feel...*weak. Because I'm one of them?*

"When." The word snapped out from Frank like a command, but broke like a plea. The age spots on the back of his hand stood out in stark contrast to his white-knuckled grip on the phone. "I-I'll have to go to the bank again. I'll go and..." He broke off, listening. "Yes, he's here."

They want you. Frank mouthed the words to Max.

"We'll make the delivery." Frank's gray eyes darted to her face. "Just the two of us, you have my-my word." His shoulders slumped, and he ended the call.

Sam advanced on him. She took his phone and used caller ID to find the kidnapper's number. The number was listed this time. The guy hadn't blocked the number for this call. Damn odd. Their kidnappers seemed too smart for a slip like this.

But everyone screws up....

Sam took out her phone and immediately texted the number to Luke.

"They want ten million now." Frank sounded lost. "*Ten* million. Bastard said the price went up because it took us so long to get to the bank."

"He's playing you." Sam typed fast. *10 million.* "The ransom was always going to be ten million."

"Then why didn't he say so from the beginning?" Frank yelled, turning on her, and really, it was only to be expected. That much rage, bubbling up, had to go somewhere.

Sam knew she was just a convenient target. She inhaled slowly before she answered. "Because this guy likes to jerk people around. He knows you'll be frantic tonight, making calls to the banker at home, calling your lawyer, and busting ass to get the rest of his money. You'll be weak and controllable. Exactly what he wants."

Frank blinked.

"He's upped the ransom before. He didn't demand more with the first victim. I don't know, maybe he thought after the deal that he could have gotten more." The kidnapper wasn't making that mistake again. "It's the way he plays now."

"*Plays?*" Max repeated. "We're not playing. This is my brother's life."

"I know, and I need you to trust me. I can help bring Quinlan home." Her gaze held his. "Tell me the location of the drop site."

But Frank hesitated. "He said only me and Max."

Sam's hold on her phone tightened. *Not the perps' MO.* One person always made the drop. Just one. "The SSD will monitor from a distance." It was the same thing that she'd told Max. "The kidnappers will never know the agents are there, but we'll be able to track them after the drop-off. We'll find Quinlan—"

Frank shook his head. "They said they'd send him to me. One hour after the drop, they said they'd send him."

Didn't he get it? "And then they'll take someone else. And maybe they'll cut him. Maybe they'll let him live. Or maybe they'll toss his body on his parents' driveway like they did with Jeremy Briar."

She took another deep breath, aware that her voice had started to rise. "Tell me the drop point." They needed this. The SSD had to break up the kidnapping ring.

"Wyham Park."

Big, public. So many entrances. So many trees. All those places to hide. A person could vanish in thirty seconds if he wanted to. *Great.*

"Noon," Frank said.

The busiest time of the day. The lunch break.

Smart.

Her fingers raced over the touchpad screen on her phone as a soft knock tapped at the door.

"Beth." Max exhaled her name on a sigh. "She told us about the call." He strode to the door and twisted the knob as he opened the door.

Beth stood on the threshold, her eyes big, her face pale. "I-is he . . . ?"

"They want to make an exchange," Frank said. "Bastards want ten million now or they're going to kill him."

"Frank . . ." Beth whispered his name as she hurried across the room to his side. "I'm so sorry." She reached for him.

His hand flew up. "Not now, Beth." He knocked her hand away and then marched toward the bar. Frank poured a tall glass of whiskey. "*Not now.*"

Sam saw the other woman's flinch. Interesting.

Very interesting.

Sam remembered the e-mails that she'd read on Quinlan's laptop last night. She couldn't help but wonder if Frank knew his younger lover was also sleeping with his son. Sometimes it was so easy to hide an affair, especially with one lover dead to the world every night. *So easy.*

Sam shoved her phone back into her bag. Beth turned around and headed for the door. But Sam had caught a glimpse of Beth's eyes before she'd whirled away. Tears hadn't been filling that blue gaze. Rage had burned in Beth's stare.

Sam typed one more note. *Want background checks ASAP.* That would have been routine, of course. As soon as the SSD learned of the disappearance, they would have started working every angle.

She'd been doing her own checks while she was in the house. When she'd used Quinlan's laptop, she'd gotten access to his complete social networking system. She'd backtracked through his wall to follow his activity for the last few weeks, and she'd sent his list of "friends" to the SSD office so that they could cross-reference those with the other kidnap victims.

She'd also entered Donnelley's system. The good doctor apparently liked his porn, and he'd been trying to hook up online at a dating site. None of his e-mails had raised a red flag with her, but she still planned to search his financial records the instant that she had access to the SSD's computer system.

When she'd tapped into Frank's online accounts, she'd seen that he had far more than a healthy balance in the bank. As with the previous kidnap victims, their perps had picked a target that could easily pay them.

But she wanted more information than what she was retrieving through the house network. After the drop tomorrow, she'd have full access again. Then she'd take an hour on her equipment at the office, and she'd be able to find out every secret the Malones possessed.

"I want Jon on point in the park tomorrow." Luke gave the order to his team and knew it would come as no surprise. An ex-sniper, Jon was by far the best when it came to observing from a distance. "Keep a weapon on them, Jon. This thing…" His shoulders rolled. "I don't want it blowing up in our faces."

"No," Hyde's deep voice cut from the doorway. "We sure as hell don't."

Luke inclined his head. "Sir, this is our best chance. Sam is serving this case to us on a platter." The pieces still didn't fit for him, but he wasn't about to look a gift horse in the mouth. If they could break this case…take down these killers…

"We need to talk with Kathleen Briar," Monica said, nodding her head. "I want to know exactly what her husband said about the ransom drop demands." A soft sigh escaped her lips. "As far as I know, two people have never been asked to come to the drop site. Either they're changing their MO now or they changed up the plan with Briar…"

"It would be easier to find out if she hadn't blown the guy's head off," Kim murmured, tapping her pencil against the edge of the table. "Then we could've just asked him directly. So much easier."

"If you wanted easy," Hyde drawled, "you wouldn't be in the Bureau."

"Guess not." Kim flashed a wide smile, one that faded quickly when she said, "There's something you all should know." Kim flipped open the file in front of her and pushed some pages toward them. "The fingerprint check on the box turned up a hit on an ex-con. A woman named Kailey Elizabeth Gentry, a prostitute from Boston."

Shit, this might be it. The break they needed. The one—

"I pulled up a picture of Kailey." Her lips twisted into a humorless grin. "Funny thing. She looks just like Beth Dunlap, only about ten years younger."

Well damn. "Sam texted that Dunlap was the one to pick up the box."

"Yeah, and I'm guessing the lady didn't know just what she was giving away when she did." Kim shook her head. "So far, Beth has been coming up clean on the check."

Not so much for Kailey.

"But I did more digging after I got the hit," Kim said. "I'm not as fast or as good as Sam on a computer, but I did find some info. Seems Ms. Kailey married a man named Gunther Dunlap when she was twenty. An older guy, with a little money. When he died a year later in a car crash, she kept the cash and got a new name."

So her current last name had come courtesy of the dead husband. And now Kailey was living with another older, richer man.

"Kailey isn't the only one in that house with a record," Kim told them as she leaned forward, her face intent. "And I think we need to get this info to Sam right away."

Luke's eyes narrowed. "Who else?" The security

guard? He'd had the look of a man who'd been around the block and seen the dark streets, but...

"Maxwell Ridgeway isn't quite the clean-cut man that the business papers would have you believe."

Luke's gaze dropped to the paper that she'd shoved his way. He scanned the lines, his heart pumping faster. *Shit.*

"Had to unseal some records." Kim gave a careless shrug but he knew that the job hadn't been easy. "Seems that once Max's mother married Frank Malone, well, Max's past vanished."

Not completely. Nothing and no one ever vanished completely.

"Manslaughter," Luke said, and felt a throb begin in his temples. Did Sam know about his past?

No, no, she couldn't know.

"What is it?" Monica asked, craning her neck to read the paper in his hand.

Kim handed her a copy of the file then passed other copies to the rest of the team as she said, "When he was fourteen, Maxwell Ridgeway beat a man to death with a baseball bat."

Damn.

Kim waited a beat. "And that's the man that Sam is currently protecting, 24–7, with no backup in sight."

Sam answered her phone on the first ring. "Hello." She was careful to sound like a civilian and not provide her usual, automatic agent identification.

"Get to a secure room," Luke barked in her ear. "Get in there, alone, and get there *now.*"

She turned away from Max and automatically shut the

door. "I'm secure." But not alone. Frank had gone after Beth. And she wasn't leaving Max right then.

"He's got a record, Sam. One that his old man worked damn hard to keep hidden."

Her shoulders hunched. "Quinlan?" She'd wondered about that. Two of the other kidnapped men had been arrested for drug possession.

"No, Max."

She blinked. "You sure?"

"Samantha?" Max questioned. The thick carpet muffled his steps "Who is it? What's going on?"

She glanced over her shoulder. Had Luke heard Max's voice? She shook her head but kept her eyes on his.

"He killed a man," Luke told her. "Do you hear me? He *killed* a man."

Her lips felt numb so it was hard to ask. "When?"

"Hell…years ago. He was fourteen. Ridgeway used a bat to hit some guy named John Dean. The courts tried Ridgeway as a minor, and he got kicked out of the system when he was eighteen. Then when his mom hooked up with Malone, well, some judge magically sealed his files."

But the SSD knew how to unseal any file.

"Watch your ass with him, got me?" Luke pressed.

Max's blue gaze bored into her.

"And Beth Dunlap isn't who she says, either," Luke continued. "Her real name's Kailey Elizabeth Gentry. She was busted for soliciting when she was eighteen."

No one was ever who they seemed to be. *Not even me.*

Her breath choked out.

"Samantha?" Max's brows shot up. "What is it?" Worry darkened his eyes. "Is it Quinlan? Has something happened to him?"

She shook her head.

"*He's there,*" Luke growled in her ear.

Yes, Max stood right in front of her now and crowded her against the wall. She still had her weapon, but it was in the purse on the desk and no use to her.

You don't need a weapon. He hasn't hurt you. He's not even touching you.

Luke's sigh carried easily over the phone. "Stay on guard, every minute. Don't trust this guy. Don't trust anyone there."

Once upon a time, trust had come easily for her. Those days were gone. She didn't need Luke's warning.

Screwing a killer. Is that how messed up her life had become?

She'd thought Max was the toughest-looking guy in the bar. The strongest. The sexiest.

But had there been more? Had she been drawn to him because he was dark inside? Dark, just like she was?

Her stomach clenched. "I can take care of myself," she told Luke.

"If you need me, you call me," Luke ordered. "Fuck the case. *Call me.*"

Sam pressed the screen and ended the call.

Max reached for her, and she flinched—an instinctive reaction.

His expression hardened. "You know." A wealth of understanding and a simmer of rage filled the simple words.

Then Max stepped even closer, and her back rammed against the wall.

Be strong. Don't do this. Stop backing down.

"Guess that was your Special Agent on the phone."

Max's lips twisted into a mirthless smile. "And let me guess; he's been digging around in my past."

"I-it's procedure." It was. "Family members and close acquaintances always have to be-be investigated." *Killer.*

Max? No, he wasn't a cold-blooded killer. He'd held her when she woke up screaming in the night.

His hands rose and trapped her against the wall. "Big tough agent," he murmured. "But you're so scared right now, you're shaking." His eyes held hers. "Does it make you afraid, knowing how close you are to a killer?"

"St-stop it."

His lips grazed her jaw. "You said killers all belong in cages, right? But you let me touch you. Let me taste every part of you."

She brought her hands up and pressed them against his chest. He didn't move.

"You had sex with a killer," Max continued.

Sam shoved him back. "Get away from me!" The order came as nearly a scream when it should have been a controlled order. But she was shattering from the inside out. Max didn't know, couldn't know. Her secrets were *hers.* No one had dug them up.

"You wanted me closer before." How could blue eyes look so dark? "You all but *begged* me to get closer."

She attacked. Her hands balled into fists. Sam slammed her shoulder into his mid-section even as she struck out with her right hand. *Take him down. Take him out.*

They crashed to the floor. Max grunted at the impact and his hands came up.

Fight back, fight—

He grabbed her wrists, rolled and twisted so that she was under him. Sam head-butted him and bucked, kicking out with her feet. No, not done yet, not out. She was strong. *Stronger.*

"*You won't hurt me anymore!*" The words burst from her as the past tangled with the present. "*I won't beg. I won't—*"

"Shit, Samantha, for Christ's sake, *stop!*"

A fist pounded on the door. "What the hell is happening in there?" Frank roared.

The doorknob rattled. She'd locked the door automatically to secure the room.

Max's breath panted out as he stared down at her. No fury glittered in his gaze. Worry. A touch of fear. For her. *Broken.* Oh, no, oh God, no—if Hyde found out what she'd just done—

"We're fine," Max yelled, but his hold on her didn't loosen. "Just leave us alone!"

She could feel Frank's hesitation, but after a few beats of silence, she heard the thuds of his fading footsteps.

Her eyes squeezed shut, and her head fell back against the carpet. What had she done? And *why?*

"You're not what you pretend to be," Max said, voice rumbling as the fingers holding her began to stroke her in long, slow glides. Trying to soothe. "You're not the tough agent, are you?"

She wanted to be.

He lowered her hands to the carpet, but kept his caressing hold. "Someone hurt you," he said with certainty and, finally, with the anger that she'd expected.

Her lashes lifted. "Let me go." They'd make it through tonight. Somehow, some way, they'd make it through. After the exchange tomorrow, she'd tell Hyde what happened. She couldn't protect Max—not when she was the one attacking him.

And Hyde would see that he'd been right. She shouldn't be back on duty. She wasn't ready. Not even close.

"Were you raped?" he asked with his body flush against hers, strong muscles tight.

Sam jerked beneath him. *I-I'll do any-anything! Just d-don't...* "No," she whispered. The truth. That bastard hadn't been interested in sex. Just fear. "Let me up."

"You're crying," Max told her, and his voice was...odd.

She couldn't stop the tears. They just trickled down. Why couldn't she be like Monica? Monica would never cry. She'd look at the killers, she'd rip them apart, and then she'd go right about her business.

Max released her wrists, and his callused fingertips brushed away her tears. Her breath seemed to burn in her lungs.

Slowly, he rose off her and stood. Max reached a hand down for her, and she took it, noticing the tremble in her own fingers. "After the drop-off, a new agent will be assigned to your case." The words were wooden but she just had nothing left right then. She stood on legs that felt too weak. "I-I'm sorry. There's no excuse for what I did."

She exhaled and realized that he still he held her hand. "I'll report the incident immediately and..." And what? What would she do?

"I was a dick," Max said, and her gaze snapped up to snag his. "I was furious, and I struck out first." He inclined his head toward her. "There's nothing to report."

She'd attacked him. In her book, that counted as something.

"You didn't hurt me, baby, and something tells me, if an FBI agent really wanted to take someone down, she could."

A bitter laugh slipped from her lips. "Maybe she couldn't." Because she hadn't been able to get away before. And she sure hadn't been smart enough to see the devil coming for her.

Her gaze dropped again.

"Look at me."

But she didn't want to. She saw herself reflected in his eyes, and she couldn't stand that image. Sam pulled her hand away. She grabbed her purse and kept her back straight as she headed for the door.

"I killed him." His confession fell heavily into the room.

She didn't look back.

"I picked up that bat and I swung, and Dean went down, and there was blood all over the floor."

Won't look back. The door was close. Just a few more feet.

"Before I swung, I told him to get away from her. I told that bastard to stop hurting her, but he wouldn't listen."

Her fingers flipped the lock.

"She was bruised and bloody and begging him to stop."

Her hand curled over the doorknob. Hesitated. Sam looked back. His stare pinned her.

"I wasn't going to let that bastard rape my mother," Max said, "so I took the bat I'd brought home from baseball practice, and I swung." Echoes of fury and pain slipped into his voice. "One hit and he went down, and he didn't get up again."

Fourteen.

"They locked me up." His shoulders straightened. "I did my time, and when I was eighteen, they pulled me up in front of a roomful of folks and asked me if I was sorry I'd killed John Dean." The strained half-smile that tilted his lips was a touch cruel, a touch cold. "I told them 'hell, no.' You see, Samantha, if I had the chance, I'd do it again. I'd take that swing, and I wouldn't hesitate." He shrugged. "That's who I am."

Not perfect. Dark. Dangerous.

"But I want to know," the faint lines near his eyes seemed to deepen, "just who are you?"

I don't know. Sad and true. "I-I have to…" *Run.* She swiped a hand over her cheeks and felt the wet stains from her tears. "I need to finish checking the other computers here. There's not much time left." Sam turned away from him. *Tell him you're sorry. Tell him you don't think he's like the perps you chase.*

Say something. The order was a scream in her head, but this time, the words didn't come out. She opened the door and walked away.

"You can't run forever," his whisper followed her, and she knew he was right.

CHAPTER *Seven*

I have something of yours, Mr. Warrant." The kidnapper glanced at the watch on his wrist. The lamp light shone down on him, letting him see perfectly. One-thirteen a.m. They'd taken Warrant's son two hours before, right in front of the cops who'd been stationed in The Core. Thanks to his inside man at the club, he'd known all about the cops... and how to avoid them.

Getting his guy hired at The Core had been a stroke of luck. No more hunting down the prey they wanted. Now, well, he just waited for the fools to come looking for him. When they came in The Core, his man gave him a call.

Then playtime started... as Adam had found out.

Adam. Dumbass Adam. Since Adam had left willingly— just like all the others—the cops hadn't noticed a thing out of the ordinary.

"Wh-what?" Warrant's voice was groggy, but then, that figured. He'd awakened Slayton Warrant from his mistress's bed.

The same routine. The old bastards were so predictable.

It made the game so easy. "I have Adam," he told the guy, keeping his voice a whisper, "and if you don't pay, I'll send him back to you in pieces." *That* always got their attention.

"What? Who the fuck is this?"

Now Slayton was awake. Good. "I'm the man who has dear dumbass Adam, and I'm the man who'll kill him if you cross me." He began to walk. The street was deserted, always was, but he knew better than to stay in the light too long.

"This is crap. You don't have—"

No one ever believed what they were told. Sad. Why were the folks in this world so untrusting? "I can send you proof." He rather liked that part now. And it would only be fair. If he was doing a favor for one family, he should provide the same courtesy to them all.

"Adam's at school! He's not—"

"He was at The Core, drinking like a good frat boy." The cops and the FBI agents would face hell in the papers after this one. *Took him while you watched.* Adam had been so eager for a piece of ass, there'd been no need to drug him. When the sexy blonde had left, Adam had gone racing after her, alone. His mistake.

"I've got Adam," he said, "and he's tied up and begging for his life." Or Adam would be begging, if he didn't have duct tape over his mouth.

"No, you're lying, you—"

"How much is he worth to you?" He cut across the yell. "You'd better figure it out, old man, and figure it out fast." Adam would be his last mark. He'd have enough money then—*they'd* have enough money—to get the hell out of that area. No, out of the country. That was supposed to be the plan, right? And everyone on his team knew the plan.

Silence hummed on the phone.

"You go to the cops, I'll start cutting and your boy *will* die." He gave warnings, so it wasn't like the deaths were his fault. If people couldn't follow simple instructions... well, they hurt themselves—and the ones they loved.

"Wh-what should I do?" Slayton asked, the fear breaking his voice.

"Wait for my call, and start getting your money ready." He disconnected and grinned down at the phone. So easy. He strolled over the bridge ahead, hunching his shoulders against the cold swipe of the wind. When he was dead center on the bridge, he tossed the cell into the murky water and never stopped walking.

The watcher would keep an eye on Warrant. Usually he had two watchers per prey, but this time, he'd split his resources.

Now it was nearly time for the big finish.

The faint glow from the computer screen lit Samantha's face. Max walked into the room, deliberately making his steps loud so she'd know he was coming. She was in the bedroom that they'd been assigned. *His* bedroom, not that he ever stayed there.

Frank was down the hallway, not dosing on sleeping pills tonight, but, from the sound of things, fucking Beth.

Max closed the door, locked it, and stared at her. "Find anything?" He knew that she'd gotten access to every computer in the place as he'd shielded her from prying eyes. She had Quinlan's laptop again, and he wondered what she'd found on his brother's system.

She looked up at him, and he saw the hesitation in her stare.

"What?" He stripped off his shirt and tossed it toward the chair. Almost two-thirty in the morning, and he was still wired. Christ, he'd never get to sleep at this rate.

How can I sleep when I don't know what the hell is happening to Quinlan?

"You know Beth is your brother's lover, too, don't you?" Samantha asked.

His arms crossed over his chest. "I didn't." He didn't move closer. He didn't want to scare her. Not again. "But I'm not surprised. He's the one who introduced her to Frank." If Frank had thought his son was sleeping with Beth, then, yeah, in his mind, that was all the more reason to screw her.

Frank was a real dick.

But not nearly the worst guy that his mother had picked in her life. She'd sure been good at choosing losers.

Don't go there.

"Your brother gambles." Samantha's fingers curled around the laptop screen. Her legs were stretched out on the bed with the computer nestled on her thighs. "It took me a while to find it, but there's a code system in here." A quick swipe of her tongue made her lower lip slick and kissable. "He gambles a lot, Max."

Her admission had him blinking, then shaking his head. "Gambling?" Drugs—yes, he knew about them. But gambling?

"He deleted the e-mails. But they were easy to recover," she added under her breath. "The gambling has been going on for a while. And he seems to bet on everything. Playoffs, horses, fights."

"No wonder he wanted me to hit Frank up for an advance on his trust." Max huffed out a breath and paced toward the window. A million-dollar view that was worth nothing. "How deep is he in?"

Silence. Then... "He asked for money before he disappeared?" A soft click as the laptop closed.

Stars glittered over the lake. The first time his mother had seen the lake, she'd been blown away. She'd called him, talking about how beautiful it was as it reflected the stars. But now, when he looked at it, all Max saw was just black water. "Yeah, Quinlan needed money, and he wanted me to do the asking. He never could stand up to Frank." Tension had an ache building in the back of his neck. "Like it was gonna make a difference that I was the one coming with my hand out."

He glanced over his shoulder and found Samantha watching him, a faint line between her brows. "How much?" he asked. "How deep was he in?"

"About two hundred grand."

Fuck. "I'll pay it." Quinlan should have just come to him. "When we get him back, I'll clear it up. I'll make sure he stays out of that mess. Everything will be fine." If he said it enough, it might make it true. *When we get him back.*

She eased to the edge of the bed and stood slowly. "Does Quinlan have a lot of problems that you have to help him with?"

She still wore that borrowed dress, one that was a little too loose across the top of her chest. One that gave him a tempting glimpse of flesh when she leaned forward. He took a breath and could almost taste her. "You already know about the drugs, don't you?" he asked. The woman seemed to know everything.

She knows about me. Knows and can't stand for me to touch her.

Max glanced back at the lake. His fingers pressed against the cold pane of glass.

"When I saw him before…" She cleared her throat. "Uh…Max, is he using now?" Worry thickened her voice.

Hell, probably. "He's been in a half-dozen rehab centers. He got hooked after—after my mother became sick." *All I'll say now about her.* He'd laid his soul bare enough for one night. "Just when I think he's clean, the drugs pull him right back." And it didn't help that Frank didn't seem to really give a shit what Quinlan was doing.

"It's hard to watch someone you love fight an addiction." Her words were so quiet—and it sure sounded like she was talking from experience.

"You can't fight it for them," she said, and the hardwood creaked beneath her feet as she came closer to him. "No matter how much you might want to."

He squared his shoulders as he faced her once more. "Who was it for you?" He asked.

"My mother. It took a long time, one *hell* of a long time, for her to drag her way out of the bottle." Samantha gave a sad shake of her head. "Her friends weren't any help. She was just partying, right? What was wrong with that?"

Samantha pushed back her hair. "But they didn't live with her. They didn't see her drinking at breakfast. Didn't see her stumbling in after midnight, all but crawling up the stairs, and they weren't there the day—" She broke off, sucking in a deep breath of air. The smile that covered her lips then was grim. "It's hard," she said again. "Very hard."

He just stared at her. "They weren't there the day—what?"

Such darkness in her eyes. "They weren't there the day I fell into the lake, and she didn't even notice because she was so drunk."

His hands clenched into fists.

"She's been clean for years, but it was a long, hard fight. My dad didn't stay around for it. She lost most of her friends...I guess she wasn't as fun to them anymore."

The day I fell into the lake...

"You can't control other people," she said after a moment. "You can't make them do the things you want, even if it's for their own good."

She'd been brutally honest with him. He could give her the same benefit. *Guess I am going back to hell tonight, for her.* "My mother was diagnosed with cancer two years ago. She went through the rounds of surgery and chemo, but nothing worked."

He'd watched her wither away right in front of him. Every day, she'd just grown paler, weaker. "Quinlan...his own mother abandoned him and I don't think he could handle watching someone else disappear before his eyes." *I sure couldn't take it.*

Quinlan had always been in his mother's room. Watching her and talking to her as she slipped away.

"At first, no one even noticed what Quinlan was doing." They'd all been so busy mourning his mother that it had taken them a while to see the shape Quinlan was in. "I think the drugs must have numbed the pain for him, at first anyway. Then..." Then Quinlan had just gotten to where he liked the rush.

Their gazes held.

"I'm not giving up on him. I won't." But he knew that she was right. He could send his brother to every program, but if Quinlan just planned to start using the minute he walked out...Max ran a hand over the back of his neck, trying to push away that knot. "I'll get him home, and I'll do anything I can to help him get clean." What else was there to do?

"It's all *you*," she whispered. "What *you'll* do for him. What about Frank? What's he doing?"

Frank seemed shaken now, like his world had spiraled away from him—and it had. Maybe he'd step up now and finally *see* his son.

Her head tilted. "How would you say Quinlan feels about his father?"

"He hates the old man." And that's what Quinlan always called him. "Frank is screwing his lover, so how do you think he feels?"

"I'd say there is animosity there."

Yeah, too damn tame a word. But then Max understood. He advanced on her. "No, hell, *no*. Don't even think it." His back teeth clenched. "My brother is the victim here." Had the woman been playing him just then? Trying to make him feel close to her, trying to get him to let down his guard?

One of her shoulders lifted in what was probably supposed to be a careless shrug. "I never said he wasn't." Her stare didn't waver.

But for a minute, when he'd first gotten the call, *he'd* doubted. He wondered. Quinlan had wanted that money so badly and then just disappeared...

The doubt hadn't lasted long, though, not with that prick on the line promising to hurt Quinlan. Then that damn package had arrived.

His brother *was* the victim. "Get to sleep," he ordered,

tired of the doubt and the worry. "It's late, and we're both going to be sharing the bed."

Her eyes widened as she glanced at the bed.

"Part of our cover, remember?" Screw the cover. The grim truth was that he still wanted her. And the sick truth was that she didn't want him touching her.

You could run from your past. You could spend a dozen years trying to change, but there would always be people who looked at you and saw the blood and guts of who you were.

A killer. When Samantha looked at him, he knew what she saw.

She exhaled on a breathy little sigh. "I'm not here right now because I need a cover, Max." Her hair looked soft and silky, and her lips, bare of color, were plump and just inches away. "I'm here because I want to be. I told you about my past because I wanted you to know *me.*"

What?

"You scare me," she admitted.

Just great. *You scare me, too, baby.*

"And I—I'm sorry about what happened to your mother. The cancer...and before. With her attack."

She might as well have hit him again. He tried to hold on to his anger, but with her, it kept sliding away. "Got the story verified, did you?" She must have called her agents when she was alone. He didn't buy that she'd taken him at his word.

"Max..."

He brushed past her. "I'm going to bed. Do whatever the hell you want." He ditched his pants. No boxers. Like she hadn't already seen him naked. "Stay up all night." He probably would. Every time he closed his eyes, he saw that severed finger and wondered where his brother was. "But don't worry about me. I'm not going to jump you."

If only. Frank had the right of it. Hard, driving sex was the way to shove the demons away.

The way to hold onto sanity until dawn came.

Hold on, Quinlan. Just hold on.

Max climbed into the bed, closed his eyes, and tried to shut her out. But he could hear her. Every soft move. Every rustle.

The bed dipped when Samantha eased in beside him. He caught her scent, light, flowery, and wanted more.

No. You couldn't always have what you wanted. He knew that better than others.

Silence.

In bed with him. Close. If he reached out, he could touch her.

He wouldn't reach out. But, dammit, he had to ask. "Is he alive?" His eyes opened to darkness. "You know these bastards. Do you think he's alive somewhere, hurting and scared, or have they already cut him up?" His eyes struggled to adjust to the dark as he waited for her answer. Not a bullshit response, *the truth.*

Her fingers brushed his arm. Heat shot through him. "He's alive."

Max could almost believe her. Almost.

Her hand slipped over his chest, stopping just over his heart, and he knew that she had to feel the desperate drumming. "Wouldn't do that," he warned. This was the only warning he'd give. "Not unless you want me to finish what you're starting."

Between them, there could be no innocent touches now. No comfort in the darkness. In the middle of hell, he still wanted her. Fuck, *had* wanted her, every moment, even when rage bubbled in his chest.

His cock was hard, ready, because she was near. The temptation to reach out to her was strong because he knew she would make him forget, for just a few moments, the nightmare he was living.

"I'm afraid of the way you make me feel." Her words came again. In the dark, his Samantha was being honest. A surprise. But, no, maybe she'd always been honest in the dark. Honest when their bodies touched and the need exploded.

The real her?

"I know I shouldn't," she said, her voice husky and seeming to stroke right over his cock, "but I still want you." Samantha rose a bit, turning on her side, and her breath blew over his cheek.

And he wanted her. If she didn't pull back...

No more warnings.

"It's wrong," she told him softly, her voice sin in the dark. "The case, us. But...but I need to be with you one more time."

He grabbed her and pulled her toward him. Her skin slid against his, and he wanted more. He'd have more.

"You don't trust me," she whispered, and her lips were less than an inch away.

And you don't trust me. But he didn't say that. No need. They both knew it.

"You don't—"

Max kissed her. He tangled his fingers in her hair, pulled her head down, and pressed his lips to hers. She moaned into his mouth and arched toward him. Still wearing that damn dress when he wanted to feel her bare skin.

His hands snaked down her body. No preliminaries. No caresses. This was sex. Wild. Raw. Pleasure and climax, that's what he'd take.

She straddled him, placing one soft thigh on either side of his legs. The dress pooled around them. He caught the fabric and shoved it up to her hips. One tug and he ripped her panties away.

Her mouth broke from his as she gasped.

Condom. Christ, he needed the—

Hot, creamy flesh brushed against his cock. Ready for him, just as he was ready for her. No, he was damn near exploding for her. His hand shot out and fumbled with the night stand. He hit the lamp switch, and light spilled onto the bed. He'd stashed his wallet in the nightstand drawer earlier. One condom left. *One.*

She leaned over him and opened the drawer. "Got it." So soft. Her fingers tore open the wrapper. She took out the condom. She touched him, and he shuddered. No, no, too close. When her hands were on him...

He rolled, pushing her back against the bed, leaving her legs spread, and the dress bunched at her waist. *Just sex.*

That was all it had ever been.

The condom covered him. *Wanted flesh to flesh. Wanted that hot core, squeezing around me, nothing separating us.*

His erection pushed against the entrance of her sex. She reached out to touch him again, but he caught her hands and pushed them back against the mattress.

Just sex.

Her gaze seemed to burn right through him.

Fuck, *lost.* One look and he was... Max kissed her. The kiss should have been hard and angry, but it was more.

Desperate. Like he was starving for her, and maybe he was. Starving, addicted, so hungry for *her*.

His cock thrust deep. She made that moan in the back of her throat, the moan that made him crazy, and he thrust faster, stronger, and he kissed his way down her neck. Soft skin. So soft. He bit her flesh even as he thrust balls-deep.

She bucked beneath him, then whispered, "Harder."

His cock stretched even more, and he gave the woman what she wanted.

Her hands were free. She'd pulled them from his grasp, and now her fingers were on him. Her nails dug into his shoulders.

He wanted her breasts. Wanted her nipples in his mouth.

She pushed against him, angled up, then swiped that small pink tongue over his nipple.

He groaned. And she laughed. *Laughed*. Her head tilted back, and she stared up at him. No fear in her gaze, just blind need.

A killer. She knew what he was, but she gazed at him and seemed to see just a man.

Faster, deeper. The bed squeaked beneath them, and he didn't give a shit who heard. The climax bore down on him, but he didn't want the pleasure yet. He didn't want to stop. Her delicate inner muscles squeezed so tight. *Too good. Don't end*.

His thumb pressed over her clit. She had to enjoy it. Had to need the sex as much as he did. More. He caressed her and felt her sex tighten even more around him as he drove into her.

She came, and he saw the pleasure wash over her face and darken her eyes.

Just sex. Just—

"Samantha!" He fought the release. Longer. *More*. Her sex contracted around him in a sweet ripple that had his body tightening. So close. He could feel her pleasure. Feel her. Inside, out. Everywhere, *her*.

He exploded inside her, the release a red-hot firestorm of pleasure that heated his blood and burned its way through his body.

Dammit, more. *More*.

So much more than he'd bargained for.

"*Some people can't follow simple fucking instructions*." He stared down at the bound man, and rage pumped through him. "I mean, really, how hard is it to understand?"

The guy jerked at his ropes and grunted something behind the duct tape.

"Guess you're gonna get a real piss-poor deal on this one." He gave a long sigh and let his fingers tighten around the hilt of the knife he held. "And just so you know…it's gonna hurt."

Moving fast, he ripped off the blindfold. Wide, desperate eyes stared back at him, and the guy shook his head, fast, over and over.

But he just shrugged as he stared down at the helpless bastard. "Blame the family, man. They're the ones who are doing this to you. They are the ones who turned their backs on you."

More muffled grunts came from behind the gray line of duct tape. He raised the knife and stepped closer to his prey. He caught a flicker of movement behind him and knew that she'd come to watch. Just like before.

He liked it when she watched him work.

The blade traced down the guy's face. A slow, careful trek. That bastard Briar had pissed him off, but this one? He almost...liked him.

But he'd still slice the prick apart. "They should have just paid." He shrugged. *Not my fault.* "I showed everyone what happens when you don't pay." *They knew the rules.*

He'd left his message for the world to see. But still, they tried to screw him. Thought that they could outmaneuver him.

A last sigh slipped from his lips. "You *should* have been worth more."

Sam didn't wake screaming that night, but only because she didn't sleep. She lay in bed next to Max, her heart still thudding too fast, his arm across her stomach, and she wondered what she was doing.

Not really a new question.

She should move. Get up. Not feel so comfortable in bed with him. Not feel like his body fit against hers.

The darkness surrounded them. She didn't have to worry about her emotions flashing on her face. Sometimes it was so hard to hide what she felt. How many times had her mother told her, "*I know what you're thinking, Samantha Jane! I can see it...right there on your face.*" Acting had never been her gift, but she was trying, as hard as she could.

Her fingers caressed his shoulder. He'd rolled onto his stomach, and his face was positioned toward her. She could hear his breathing, deep, even, but she knew he wasn't sleeping.

Together, but so far apart.

A soft chime pealed in the room, and she tensed. *Oh, no, not now, please.*

But Max was already moving. He rolled away from her in a flash and stalked, naked, to pick up her phone. The dim light from her screen lit his face as he read the message.

Not Quinlan. Don't say they've found a body. Max's head lifted but shadows hid most of his face. "New development," he said, voice rumbling. "'*Problem.* Stay on guard.'"

She pulled the covers up, too aware of her nudity when she hadn't cared before. "Max..."

But he'd spun away and lunged toward a tall cabinet near the balcony. He wrenched open the cabinet doors, revealing a large flat-screen television. "Dante said to turn on the damn TV."

That drove her from the bed. *Oh, shit, they'd found a body.* She grabbed Max's hand before he could press the button on the remote to activate the TV. "Don't, Max. You don't need to see—"

His thumb pressed POWER. The screen burst to life. Max flew through the channels, shooting past infomercials and old black-and-white films to find a local station.

Newscasters—faces tense as they sat at their desks, their hair perfect, their clothes pressed—stared back at her. "Shocking news out of D.C. this morning," the dark-haired anchor said. "A well-known man has recently been kidnapped, and his family turns to *you* for help."

"Oh, shit," she breathed the words. No, no, this couldn't be happening. She'd been with Max every moment. He hadn't gone to the press. Had Frank? Was he the one who'd leaked the story to the world? Beth?

In the next instant, the reporters vanished, and a live action shot filled the screen. An older man with dark gray hair and fierce eyes glared at the camera. "I want my son back. Someone took Adam. The bastards have him, and I *want him back*." An image of the missing young man appeared in the lower left-hand side of the screen. A smiling guy with curly blond hair and a dimple in his right cheek.

"They want me to pay to get him back. Well, I'm not playing their games," the man on screen continued, staring hard out of the television set. "I'll pay *you* to tell me where he is. I'm offering a fifty-thousand-dollar reward for any information about my son, Adam Warrant. He's twenty-two, he's five foot nine, about one hundred and seventy pounds. Blond hair, blue eyes. He was out last night..." His words came fast. "At a bar near Georgetown. He was at The Core, and I *know* someone saw something."

This wasn't the right thing to do. Didn't he understand? Her hands clenched. Oh, God.

"Call me." He barked out a number, one that instantly appeared on the screen below him. "Tell me where my boy is, and tell me who these freaks are that took him."

Sam's eyes squeezed shut.

"That's Slayton Warrant," Max said quietly.

She knew who he was. Most of D.C. did. She also knew that he had a whole big chunk of money sunk into this particular television channel. No wonder he'd gotten an instant broadcast. Not that the news station would have passed up a story like this one, but...

But he doesn't realize what he's done. She opened her eyes, swallowed, and almost swore she tasted blood.

"The SSD will be on their way to his house." To try and stop him, too late. The damage would have already been done.

Max tossed the remote down as the broadcast continued to blast in front of them. "He's right. Somebody *did* see something."

And a lot of people had seen nothing. All those people would be calling in too.

He raked a rough hand through his hair. "Adam and Quinlan both disappeared from the same place.... *Dammit!* This shouldn't have happened!"

"No," her voice came so much softer than his. "It shouldn't." Another break in pattern. Two men gone at the same time. Two taken from the same bar. The SSD had interviewed the employees at the bar—*twice*— and they'd even put undercover agents inside The Core as a precaution. Oh, hell, Hyde was going to flip over this. No way should another vic have vanished from that place.

And why another victim so soon? This was rapid acceleration. Usually, the kidnappers only took someone else if the ransom had been paid or if—

She slanted a quick glance at Max.

If the other vic was dead.

"What's going to happen?" He turned toward her, pinning her with his gaze, and Sam hoped the fear didn't show in her eyes. "When they find out what Warrant's done, what will the kidnappers do?"

Kill.

"Maybe Slayton will get the right tip," Max said. "Maybe they'll find Adam and Quinlan."

If he wanted to believe that, why shatter his hope?

• • •

He walked down the street, taking his time as he rounded the curve and headed into the park. His hood was pulled up, concealing his face, and the thick jogging suit hid the shape of his body.

His gaze didn't meet that of any of the other runners or walkers. When he was sure no one was watching, he ducked into the woods and pulled out his phone.

The call was answered on the second ring.

"Slayton Warrant."

But, of course, it wasn't him. The voice belonged to some flunky. Some idiot Warrant had slapped with the job because the asshole was all fake bullshit on the air.

"I've got a tip." He kept his voice a whisper because he figured they were recording the calls. Recording, tracing, doing whatever they could. The cops would be at Warrant's place by now. The cops, maybe even the FBI. He knew the FBI was following him as best they could.

Not good enough.

He'd taken Adam right under their noses. So much for the big, bad FBI and their cop flunkies.

Taking Adam in front of them had been such a big damn rush. *No one can stop me*.

"Sir," the voice on the phone chirped in his ear, "Sir, I need you to speak louder. We have a bad connection—"

"He fucked up." He didn't raise his voice. "Warrant knew the rules, and he fucked up." And he'd known instantly. As soon as that news van pulled up, the watcher had alerted him.

And Adam had been dead.

"Uh...sir?" A hint of fear there. Good. The idiot should be afraid.

"It's his fault. Tell him that." Simple damn rules. "But I gave the guy his son back." *Just not the way he wanted.* A soft laugh. "Warrant has so many fucking properties in this town. Too many. If he wants Adam, he has to start cleaning house." *Oh, yeah.*

"Wh-who is this? We have a reward, sir, if you'll just—"

He could almost see the cop next to the jerk, probably rolling his hand and telling the guy to keep him on the line. Not going to happen. "I didn't ask for 50K." That small change wouldn't have even been worth the effort. "Adam was worth more."

Sighing, he ended the call. He had his gloves on so he'd blend in with the other joggers—it really was a bitch of a cold morning—so he didn't have to worry about leaving prints as he dropped the phone. The cell fell into the bushes near his feet. Then he took a deep breath and ran forward, knowing the path picked up again in about thirty feet. His heart began to pump, faster, faster...

He shot out onto the path and kept running. Blending with the others would be so easy now. Blending—he'd always been good at that. A smile could get you anywhere.

But money could get you everywhere.

He gave a little wave as he passed a sexy blonde. *Everywhere.*

How long would it be before they found the body? Hopefully not too long. Even in the cold, Adam would really start to reek.

If he'd timed things right—and he was so good at

planning—the cops would be tearing apart those build-
ings looking for Adam just as the exchange was made for
good old Quinlan.

Diversion. So simple. So perfect.

Damn, but this was easy.

CHAPTER *Eight*

W e divide the team," Luke said, hunching his shoulders against the biting cold and talking fast to Kim Daniels as the Warrant residence swarmed with activity around him. They'd pulled up a listing of every piece of property that Warrant owned. Turned out the guy owned nearly half the town. "Kim, we need to start with the most secluded properties first." Because the kidnappers wouldn't want an audience when they dumped their victim.

His finger tapped on the list of addresses. "These three businesses are closed down." A fabric shop. A gym. An old garage.

"No eyes, no ears," Kim murmured. "Sounds like prime dumping stops."

Kim wasn't sugar coating. She wasn't the type. When she'd first heard about the news story, she'd turned to him and said two words: "He's dead."

Special Agent Kim Daniels wasn't what most folks would call an optimistic kind of person. But then, with this case, it was hard for anyone to be.

"We need Monica," she said quietly, her breath forming a small cloud before her face.

She was right. Of course she was. He and Monica couldn't work as direct partners, but he could use her. "Take her to the properties with you." He knew Monica was already on her way. Nothing would keep her away from a scene like this.

To keep working the profile, Monica would need to see the crime scene. When she saw the layout of the body and its placement by the killer, maybe something would click for her.

"Talk to Hyde," Luke advised. "See who else we can spare for pairing with the local PD on searches." *Why did Slayton Warrant have to go to the media? Why?*

"You're sending Ramirez with Ridgeway and Frank Malone for the drop?" Kim asked.

"Yeah, he's going, and I'll be backup." Because he *had* to be there. "Hyde's calling in Kenton. He wants him to manage the media when this shit hits the fan." And it would, soon. Especially once the media learned that Adam Warrant had been taken while two FBI agents were on the premises of The Core.

Kim stepped forward and grabbed his arm. "This isn't your fault." Her tight whisper. "Warrant went to the media on his own. He was warned, just like the others—"

"Like Ridgeway was warned?" He bit out the words and knew that up in that big freaking mansion on Rightmont Lane, Sam was having the same thought. "When you break the rules, people die with these assholes, right? We broke the rules, too."

Her gaze held his. "They don't know that."

None of them could be sure about what the kidnappers

knew or didn't know. "Once the exchange is made, I'll feel a hell of a lot better."

Luke understood the job. He realized that risks were there, every damn second, but acid had eaten away at his gut from the minute that he'd found out about Sam's connection—and known that he'd use her. "I don't want Sam caught in the crossfire." He'd never forget the look in her eyes when he'd found her in the water...

Luke clenched his jaw. Seeing Sam, he knew what Monica must have been like, years before, when the nightmare first came to her life.

There were too damn many nightmares in the world.

"Sam's stronger than you're giving her credit for," Kim said flatly. "Than we all are. She survived once, and she'll do it again."

But Kim hadn't been there. She hadn't *seen* Sam. Or heard Sam's first choked whisper when they'd forced her to breathe again.

"Men." Kim shook her head. "Don't you know, what doesn't break us just makes us more dangerous?" A wide smile flashed now, one with a vicious edge. "That's sure as hell what happened for me."

Such a small, delicate woman. Exotic face. Slender build. But if the stories about Kim were true, and the things he'd seen in the SSD certainly made him believe they were, the woman was a perfect killer. Just one who happened to work on the side with the good guys.

"This is damn bullshit! Get out of my way!" Slayton Warrant appeared in the doorway, his face blotched red, his eyes glittering. "You assholes don't know anything! I want someone in charge. I want—"

"Us," Kim said, her hands rising to her slim hips and

balling into tight fists. "If you want the people in charge, you're looking at them."

Warrant's eyes narrowed. "You two with the FBI?"

"Special Agent Luke Dante," he told the older man, offering his hand. Warrant frowned, but took it in a quick, hard shake. "This is Special Agent Kim Daniels." She didn't offer her hand. Kim didn't exactly have the best people skills.

"All the local PD on scene will be reporting to us from here on out." Luke kept his voice cool. Monica would have been proud. "We're going to start canvassing your properties to see what we can——"

"That's bullshit." A Texas drawl rolled beneath Slayton's words. "He's not——"

"The kidnapper told you to 'clean house,'" Luke said, keeping his voice flat. "That word choice was deliberate. He was telling us where to find your son."

But Slayton Warrant adamantly shook his head. "No, that jerkoff on the phone was just trying to rattle me. He needs to understand, I *don't* get rattled."

Kim's gaze once again met his. He couldn't miss the disgust in her stare. Luke cleared his throat and said, "Mr. Warrant, you do understand that recently a kidnapping victim was found murdered, just outside of his parents' estate."

Warrant's eyes narrowed. "You tryin' to tell me it's the same kidnappers?"

Too early to know for certain. But... "While the teams prepare, I'll need to ask you some questions."

Warrant shook his head. "No, no questions. I'm going on the air again. I'm raising the stakes. One hundred thousand. That will get the snakes to crawl out and turn on each other. I'll have Adam back here in an hour's time."

The guy just didn't get it.

"A man will do anything for money." Warrant's thick brows pulled low. "Learned that a long time ago."

"Then you should know," came Kim's smooth voice, "that these kidnappers are going to be very, very angry if they think they aren't getting their money."

Warrant blinked at her.

Jesus—had that thought not even occurred to the guy? "Sir, I'd advise against going on the air right now." Luke crossed his arms over his chest. "How did the kidnappers first contact you?"

Warrant tried to step around him. Luke just moved with him. "Sorry, maybe I wasn't clear." He let the steel flow in his words. Not so cool anymore. "*How did the kidnappers first contact you?*" They were losing time, and he wasn't going to dick around.

If there was a chance, any chance, that Adam Warrant was still alive, Luke was jumping on it. "I need to know every detail," Luke demanded, "and I need to know it now."

He'd already ordered cadaver dogs, but, dammit, he wanted to be wrong. He wanted to have hope. And he wanted to find Adam Warrant *alive*.

"Be careful," Sam said, the words tumbling out. She hugged Max, letting her arms hold him a bit too long and a bit too tight. She'd given him her gun. The butt of the holster scraped against her arm when she held him. Knowing that he had the weapon didn't make her feel better.

It made her more afraid.

Frank waited near the doorway with thick, black duffel bags in each hand and sweat beading his brow.

"It's gonna be just fine," Beth said, leaning in close to Frank, a wobbly smile on her lips. "You'll get him back." Her fingers shook a bit as she skimmed her hand down his chest. "In less than an hour, this will all be over."

Frank didn't smile back at her. A light coating of gray stubble lined his jaw. Right then, he looked older, weaker. After a silent moment, he turned away from Beth and said, "Max! Dammit, *come on.*"

Max stared down at Sam, then he leaned in close and whispered against her ear. "If your team messes this up, I'll crucify them."

"Don't worry, love," she told him, and let her eyes squeeze shut. "This will go down like clockwork," she whispered back, hoping it was true. "Make the drop and bring your brother back."

He kissed her. *Last time.* Then he was gone, hurrying with Frank to the car that waited just outside.

Sam didn't follow him. Not part of her role. Her role was to pretend to be the supportive girlfriend so she didn't make anyone out there nervous.

No one wanted the kidnappers nervous. Nervous men were dangerous.

"I think I need a drink," Beth muttered. "One big, heavy drink." She headed toward Frank's office. Sam waited until the other woman disappeared then she pulled out her phone and typed in one quick message.

Body?

The cadaver dogs didn't turn up anything at the first two locations, but the instant Monica walked into the old garage on Murrows Road, she knew the ending for Adam Warrant wasn't going to be a good one.

The dogs stood just inside the entrance, sunlight streaming down on them. Their handlers held them back, but the dogs' tension was evident in the tight lines of their bodies. "Him." Monica pointed to the smaller dog, the one with his nostrils flaring and his front paws braced apart. "Keep him tight, but let's see where he leads us."

Kim was at her back. "This place has been closed for the past three months, but there were fresh tire tracks outside," Kim said. After the search, they'd photograph and make molds of them, if this scene went down the way the knot in Monica's stomach told her it would.

They trekked through the dust-filled lobby and went past the wall of heavy machinery. Turned to the left, the right. A tight hallway snaked down the middle of the building. The place was just like a maze.

And then the smell hit her, slapping her right in the face. It was a smell that Monica knew all too well. Her shoulders stiffened. "Pull the dog back." There was no need for him to go inside that room in the back. *Keep the scene clear.* She understood exactly how to work the area, but…

But for a moment, she hesitated before that door. *So much damn death.* Sometimes, it felt like she was always surrounded by death. *Except when I'm with Luke.* Luke brought her back to life.

As she stood before the door the scent choked her, but she knew she had to keep her game face on. Keep the image up. Over the years, Monica had gotten plenty of practice at masking her emotions. *Ice.* Yes, she knew the nickname was still whispered about her, but the folks who whispered were wrong. She might look like nothing cracked her shell, but Luke had slipped right past and gotten to her.

Monica lifted her hand, motioned to the others to stay

back, and pulled out her gun. Her gloved fingers curled around the butt and her left hand pushed against the door. One, two . . .

Monica went in low and fast, with Kim coming up behind her. The other woman's gun was out and up, too. A quick sweep of the room and—

"Clear," Monica whispered, and pity had her heart slowing.

Slayton Warrant *would* be getting his son back today.

Adam's body lay on the floor, spreadeagled just like the last victim. Long, deep slices covered his face and arms, and his throat had been slit from ear to ear.

Beside him, a small, brown box sat, just waiting.

Kim clicked on the safety and shoved the gun back into her holster. "This is one sick, twisted bastard."

Monica's eyes raked the room as she secured her own weapon. There was no blood spatter anywhere. No marks in the dust on the floor. Just a perfectly dropped—and dead—body.

And a box. Monica knelt next to the box and carefully opened it with gloved fingers.

Kim crept forward and peered over Monica's shoulder. *A finger.*

She'd noticed that Adam was missing his left ring finger.

Kim exhaled on a heavy sigh. "Guess the asshole is showing off his new signature."

Proof of life. That's what it had been for Quinlan Malone. For Adam Warrant, it just looked like more proof of death.

"It appears that way." Monica put the box back down, right in the exact spot. "He's linking them all. Briar's body position and wounds were nearly identical to this scene. It's all so close."

"From the looks of the wound," Kim cut in, "it looks like the perp cut it off before Warrant died."

Monica suspected most of the wounds had been administered before death. Their killer enjoyed the pain he caused his victims. "We know the leader is highly organized," Monica murmured.

"Right." Kim pushed out a hard breath. "So what's the asshole got planned for his next trick?"

Monica knew Luke would be finding out very soon, and she couldn't help the kick of fear that made her heart race. Luke was a good agent. No, better than good. He could handle himself. But...

She worried because she cared more about him than she'd ever cared about anyone or anything.

And if she were to lose him...

Be careful, Luke.

Wyham Park was full of people. Joggers. Mothers who pushed bundled babies in giant strollers. Couples snagging a quick lunch.

Max walked past them all. His gaze swept the park. Left to right, back again, over and over.

Frank kept perfect pace with him, not saying a word, just walking fast with his duffel bags. They'd make the drop in less than two minutes.

And they'd damn well better get Quinlan back right after that.

They rounded the corner, and the crowd began to thin. Max hadn't seen any sign of the agents yet, and he hoped he didn't.

Samantha's face flashed in his mind. Wide eyes. Soft lips. The gun she'd given to Max pressed into his back.

"Th-there." Frank's shaking voice. No longer hard or arrogant. Max hadn't heard the guy sound this way since he'd gotten the phone call from Frank almost a year ago. The call that had come in the middle of the night. The one that had told Max that his mother had died.

Max's hold on the duffel bags tightened. Ten million dollars. A hell of a lot of cash. Two large bags for him, two for Frank.

"He said...behind the broken oak," Frank murmured.

The broken oak tree waited, split straight in the middle by a blast of lightning long ago. Max glanced around. He couldn't see any more joggers. No more women pushing their kids. Hell, they were just going to dump the money? Here? What if someone else came along? What if—

Two men came toward them from the woods. Had to be men. Tall, nearly his height, with thick shoulders. They had on black jogging suits, and ski masks covered their faces.

They also had guns equipped with silencers. The better for killing when others were around.

"Drop the bags and back away." This came from the guy slightly in front. The one with his weapon pointed straight at Max. The other guy, about an inch shorter, had his gun trained on Frank.

Frank dropped the bags. So did Max. The bags thudded onto the ground. Max and Frank stepped back, their hands up. "We're not armed," Frank said, raising his voice.

Bullshit. Max knew Frank had a gun tucked under his jacket. Frank always kept a gun in the main house, locked in his bedroom safe. Frank had taken the weapon out before they left for the drop.

"*Turn around and walk away!*" The order was barked at them. "If either one of you looks back, I'll put a bullet in *both* of you."

Max's body tensed. "What about Quinlan? When do we get him back? *When?*"

"When the money's counted," the man taunted. Max saw the jerk's finger tighten around the trigger. "Now *move* or I'll tell my friend here to shoot the old man in the head."

Max believed that he'd do it. Slowly, carefully, he turned around.

"Keep your damn arms up, every minute! You got me? Keep 'em up!"

Max kept his arms up and started walking away with Frank by his side. And with guns pointed at their backs.

"Two with guns," Jon Ramirez's low voice drifted through the earpiece Luke wore. Luke bent down, pretending to tie his shoe near the entrance of the park. "Drop's been made. Ridgeway and Malone are walking away."

"Stay with the perps," Luke ordered quietly, speaking into the mouthpiece that was hidden just inside the hood of his jogging suit. Two men. Figured. They'd separate as soon as they left the park to make tracking harder. Smart. Not smart enough.

"You and Hyde break off, each taking a perp," because the big boss was out there watching too, "and let's see where they're gonna take us," he ordered.

"They've got the money. They're moving."

Luke rose and made a show of stretching. Every muscle in his body was tight with tension. One dead vic already today. *Not another.*

"No visual on Ridgeway and Malone. Perps are in sight. Out."

Ridgeway and Malone should be rounding the corner any minute and coming back out of the thick forest path. They'd be clear in just a few more moments. *Hurry up.*

Max's hands were still up. The thud of footsteps disappeared into the distance. The assholes, running away with their money.

But they wouldn't get far. And right then, Max was real glad the SSD was hiding in those woods.

"Are we clear?" Frank asked, and Max saw him begin to lower his arms.

Then he heard the twig snap behind them. Too damn close.

If either of you looks back, I'll put a bullet in both of you.

He let his hands lower. Slow. Easy. Frank had flinched. He'd heard the snap, too.

Not gonna wait until we look back, are you? Max sucked in a breath and slammed into Frank. Fire ripped along his left arm, a blast of pain accompanied by no sound. *Sonofabitch.* As his blood spilled onto the ground, Max yanked out Samantha's gun.

Another man—no, one from before? He couldn't tell for sure. Max just saw a man in a black jogging suit with a black ski mask, his gun up and aiming—

Max lifted his own weapon. No cover. Shit. *"Get to the trees."* He fired at the bastard.

The bullet thudded into the man's shoulder. *Can't kill him. He knows where Quinlan is.*

The man screamed. A loud, long shriek of pain and rage.

Max lunged for the trees and fired again as the asshole lifted his gun and shot back at him.

"Gunfire!" Luke took off running, aware that the woman with the short blond hair and bright pink jogging suit was right with him. Moving fast, faster...Running toward the thunder of gunshots even as everyone else streaked away in a mass of confusion and fear.

The woman was Sam in disguise, because he'd ordered her in right after Malone and Ridgeway left the house. She kept perfect pace with him as they rushed for the line of trees. They rounded the corner and went in low, sticking to the tree line as much as possible, and Luke saw...

Blood, staining the ground. Ridgeway and Malone weren't there. No one was there and—

"Here!" A deep, booming voice called from the brush.

"Max," Sam whispered and raced forward in a flash, snaking through the trees as Luke stuck tight to her tail.

"Secure the area," Luke snapped into his mike. "We've got men down in the first quadrant. The perps are armed. Use extreme caution."

"Max?" Sam fell beside him.

He blinked at her, shaking his head. "What the hell? You aren't supposed to be here!"

"She's an agent with the SSD." Luke kept his gun up. "She's wherever we need her to be."

Blood dripped down Max's arm in thick, dark rivulets. Sam clamped her hands over his wound. "How bad?"

"Went right through." Sweat beaded his upper lip. "Just hurts like a bitch."

"Malone?" Luke questioned the other man. He was kneeling on the ground and hunched forward.

"I'm all right." Gruff. "Bastard shot at me and would have blasted a hole in my head if Max hadn't been here."

Luke noticed both men still had guns in their hands. Holding 'em tight.

"Who are we looking for?" Sam asked as she worked to staunch the blood from Max's wound. "Who did this?"

"Don't...ah...didn't see much...a guy from the looks of things. Maybe six two, two hundred pounds, black jogging suit—"

"Two men wearing all black," Frank muttered, his knuckles white around the gun. "We gave them the money and they tried to kill us."

Not part of the MO. What was going down here?

"Get the EMTs here," Luke ordered, knowing they were already on standby.

Max shook his head. "No, they could still be watching. They'll see—"

"*They know, Max.*" Sam's voice. Tighter and harder than Luke had ever heard before. "When the shots were fired, we ran right over, anyone watching—*they know.*" Her breath heaved out. "You're bleeding too much, and it's not stopping. We have to get you to a hospital."

"Quinlan—"

"Our priority is *you.*" She nearly shouted at him. "We don't have Quinlan here; we've got you!"

"I'm all right." A muscle flexed along his jaw, and Max caught her hands. "I'm not going to be hauled away from here, not while Quinlan is still out there."

Luke's gaze swept the ground. *Too much blood*. Shit. Sam was right. The bullet must have clipped an artery. "*EMT, now.*"

The park would be insane. Luke knew it. Those gunshots would have sent folks right into panic mode. Chaos would reign as everyone ran.

That would be just what the kidnappers needed. So easy to disappear in the madness.

"Ramirez, tell me you've got him!" Luke said. Ramirez wouldn't have lost his mark. No way. Ramirez never missed his man.

Static crackled in his ear. Then… "I got him." But those words didn't come from the earpiece.

They came straight from Ramirez as the agent shoved through the brush. Oh, hell.

"The perp circled back. I stayed clear at first, to see what he was doing…" His dark eyes narrowed. "I had to fire. He had a clear shot at Ridgeway. There was no choice."

Sam's breath hissed out. "Where is he?"

"On the ground, about fifteen feet back." Cold.

"We're not gonna be tailing him anywhere," Luke said and cursed beneath his breath.

"Fuck," Ridgeway growled, and Luke didn't know if it was because of the pain he was in or because they'd lost a lead.

"The second man—where is he? *Where is he?*" Luke wrenched the tiny microphone as he fired out his question. Hyde was there. He'd—

"Moving," came Hyde's cool voice. "The suspect is driving fast, in a blue pickup truck, heading west."

Hell, yeah. Calmer, Luke spun away as the EMTs

burst on the scene. "I want chopper coverage on this asshole," he instructed, knowing the command center was monitoring the line. "Keep him in sight, but *stay back*. Give me the tag number and let's track this rat back to his hole."

"What about Quinlan?" Frank demanded. "Where's my son? Dammit, is he even still alive? What happened to that other boy? Where is he—"

In pieces. Monica had called to go give Luke the news. He lowered the mike, just for a moment. "Sir, stay with the agents," he said to Malone. Luke threw a quick glance at Ramirez and Sam. Ramirez nodded but Sam didn't look away from Ridgeway.

Luke sucked in a quick breath and turned his attention to the civilians. "Until this is over, you're both remaining in protective custody." He wasn't losing either man.

Hyde rattled off the license plate number in his left ear. The techs would have heard it, too, and the APB would be hitting the airwaves—but with the order to stand down. Follow the perp, but no confrontations. Not yet.

"What happened to the other young man?" Frank demanded, voice shaking.

Luke holstered his gun. Malone and Ridgeway deserved honesty. He always tried to give the victims honesty when he could. Even when the truth hurt. "They killed him." With the way this drop had gone down, Quinlan Malone would be the next to go. If he wasn't already dead.

But that part he didn't tell them, because he knew Malone was already close to breaking.

"I'm coming with you," Ridgeway's cold voice stopped Luke as he turned away.

Luke slanted a fast glance over his shoulder. Bloody,

but on his feet now, Ridgeway stared back at him. Sam stood right beside him.

"You're not shoving me to the side," Ridgeway said. "*I'm coming.*"

Luke could understand the man's determination. This was about family. Didn't even matter that it wasn't by blood. Family was family.

"I played by your damn rules," Ridgeway snarled, "and look at the shit that's happened."

Luke squared his shoulders. Did the guy really know what he was asking? "You understand what we might find." Once they'd tracked the kidnappers back to their base, there might not be a happy ending. Just more blood and another body.

"You all think he's already dead." Ridgeway's gaze darted to Sam. She didn't speak. Just stared right back at him. Once, Luke knew she would have tried to give him hope. Not now.

"Either way," Ridgeway said, not even flinching when two EMTs grabbed for his arm. "I'm coming."

It would be so easy to put the man down. To lock him up until this hell was over. But that just wasn't Luke's way. "Stitch him up," he ordered the EMTs. "He's bleeding all over our scene." If they could stop the bleeding, if an artery hadn't been nicked...

Then he'd give the guy what he wanted. Luke just hoped Ridgeway knew what he was asking for.

"Stay with him," he ordered Sam. Then he inclined his head toward Ridgeway. "You'll stay with the team for as long as we can let you."

The two EMTs got to work on Ridgeway. His jaw was clenched tight, blood covering his shirt. His right hand was locked around Sam's. Luke couldn't tell if Sam was holding him, trying to give her lover support, or if Ridgeway was trying to chain her to him.

Maybe it was both.

The blue pickup swept into the parking garage, driving nice and slow, and circled down to rest on the second level, near the side entrance. The level without a security camera. The level half-concealed by darkness thanks to the lights he'd broken earlier.

The driver hopped out, now clad in a white t-shirt and blue jeans. "*We've got it. Hot damn, we got it.*" Sweat coated his black hair, making it stick hard to his head.

The guy hurried toward him as he waited near the old sedan. They wouldn't have long for the transfer, maybe a minute. Less. "Throw the bags in the trunk," he told the driver.

His trunk was already open. *Ten seconds.* The first two bags were tossed inside. *Thirteen seconds.* The other bags landed with a thud.

Sixteen seconds for the exchange. Perfect.

"Mike went back to finish them off, just like you said." A wide grin split the truck driver's face. "Bet it was like shooting ducks to take out those two bastards."

But Mike hadn't called in. Maybe it hadn't been so easy.

No Mike meant...even less time. "You used gloves in the truck?" The stolen pickup that they'd had for three hours. They'd swapped plates and been good to go.

"The whole time." The guy slammed the truck's driver side door closed. "Now let's get out of—"

The knife caught him right between the ribs. The blade

dug in deep, then twisted. Blood bubbled up from the driver's lips.

"The plans have changed." *Not really.* This had been *his* plan all along. Why split the money? Splitting didn't make sense. Not when it could all be his.

"Sorry, Jim, but I guess you won't be getting out of here." He pulled back the blade in a long, slow glide.

Jim fell to his knees. His head sagged back as he stared up with big, dumb, what-did-you-do eyes. Stupid sonofabitch. Had he really not seen this coming?

No time to waste.

He slashed Jim's throat open from ear to ear. One down...

By the time Jim's head smacked into the cement, he was already in the sedan.

Then he just backed out, adjusted his mirror, saw the dead man on the ground—and kept going.

Hyde stared down at the body, careful to keep his distance from the pool of blood already settling on the cement. Different clothes, same build, and the guy was positioned right behind the damn truck that Hyde had been following.

Hyde's jaw clenched. He'd known the instant the truck turned into the garage that trouble was coming. He'd gotten in as fast as he could, but it had taken two minutes to get inside, thanks to a traffic slowdown on the street. Two minutes.

Plenty of time for someone to die.

His gaze rose and swept the perimeter. No security cameras. Figured. He pulled out his radio. "Seal the place up," he ordered. Too late, though; he knew it. The kidnappers had been so smooth. "No cars in and no cars out." Not until they'd checked every inch of the place.

"Sir?"

"Get Dante on the line. Tell him we've got another body." He shook his head. *And tell him to get ready for more.*

Because he knew how criminals operated, and it sure looked like someone was tying up loose ends.

CHAPTER *Nine*

Max had never been in FBI headquarters before. He paced the small room, his hands knotted and his shoulder aching.

Samantha had herded him there after they'd left the park. They'd swept away from that chaotic scene right before the reporters swarmed. She hadn't talked to him much, but he'd caught her glancing at him, eyes wide but shadowed.

The door squeaked open behind him. He didn't turn around. It was about time someone came in, though he knew that he'd been watched every moment since he'd arrived. That long mirror to the left had to be a two-way.

"There's been a new development." Samantha's quiet voice filled the small room, and he couldn't help but tense. "Hyde trailed the second kidnapper to a parking garage near the train station."

Max looked over his shoulder.

"By the time Hyde got inside—"

"Who the hell is Hyde?"

Her shoulders squared. "Keith Hyde created this unit. Hyde *is* the Serial Services Division." She'd ditched the eye-hurting pink jogging suit and now wore a simple black blouse and pants. The black made her skin look paler. Her hair tumbled across her shoulders.

So they'd sent in their big dog on this case. "And?" Because there was more that he wasn't going to like. But what had he liked so far? Christ, sitting there doing nothing was killing him. For almost two days now, he'd done *nothing*.

Not the kind of guy he was.

"By the time Hyde got inside the garage," she said, "it was too late."

His heart slowed, then immediately began racing too fast as he faced her.

She exhaled. "The perpetrator he'd followed was dead, and the money was gone."

What? "What about Quinlan? Is he alive?" He wanted the brutal truth.

Max got it.

"I don't know," she said softly and he realized that Samantha feared his brother was dead.

The kidnapper knew the authorities were involved. He had his money. Why bother keeping Quinlan alive?

"They planned to kill you and Malone all along," Samantha told him. "You realize that, don't you? That's why they attempted the hit in the park."

His shoulder throbbed.

"Special Agent Monica Davenport wants to talk with you. She has some questions about your family—"

Max grabbed her, clasping her shoulders and drawing her close, even as he ignored the burst of pain from his wound. "I'm a suspect? Is that what you're telling me?"

Samantha shook her head. "Monica's our best profiler. She's trying to figure out why things are going differently with your family. These perps—they've never gone after any of the other families at the drops. But they came gunning for you."

If he hadn't heard that twig snap...

Samantha's brows lowered and a faint furrow appeared on her forehead. "If you'd walked in there unarmed, you would have been a sitting duck. Even with weapons, if it hadn't been for Ramirez, you'd probably be dead." Her voice seemed wooden, so at odds with the dark fire in her eyes.

Max stared at Samantha, caught by her burning gaze. "You didn't tell me you were going to be there." If he'd known...hell, what would he have done? No way to stop her.

"I couldn't let you walk in there without me. And when I heard the shots..." Her breath rushed out. "You scared me, Max."

Honesty. Real emotion plain to see on her face and to hear in her voice.

This was the woman he'd needed to see. The one who'd been hiding from him. Maybe from herself. Christ, this was the woman he wanted.

"Max?"

He took her lips, crushing his mouth against hers, and he just tasted her. *Not over.* She couldn't slip away from him yet.

A low moan rumbled in her throat, and a shudder worked the length of her body. Then her hands were on him, tightening around his shoulders and—

He wrenched back from her. *"Fuck!"*

"I'm sorry. I forgot—"

Max caught her hands and pushed Samantha back against the wall. Screw the pain. He had her, right then, right there, and he wasn't going to lose her.

His tongue plunged deep even as his cock shoved against the front of his jeans. Wrong time, wrong place. He couldn't have her here, but he'd take his taste.

And it would have to sustain him when she walked away.

Her breasts stabbed against his chest. Tight nipples, eager, aroused. She wanted him just as much as he wanted her. They touched and ignited.

"Why?" The question was torn from him as his mouth tasted the slender column of her throat. "Why do I need you so damn much?" Like an addiction. The more he had, the more he craved.

Was it the same for her? Did the hunger just keep growing?

Her pulse thudded beneath his mouth, so fast, but she didn't answer him.

And he heard the squeak of the door again. *Fuck them.* He tightened his hold on Samantha.

"Ah...should I come back?" Quiet, cool, a woman's voice questioned.

Samantha stiffened against him. Her hands jerked beneath his. Strong again. Why did he keep forgetting that strength?

Max eased away from Samantha and turned his stare on the new agent.

"Is everything okay in here?" Now the guy was there. Dante. He crowded in behind the dark-haired woman, and Max didn't miss the way the guy's hand moved to the small of her back.

"Everything's fine," Samantha said, and she really, really needed to get better at keeping her voice level.

Max flashed a cold smile at the agents in the doorway. "You interrupted." So they could come grill him. *Tired of this shit.* He could play the bastard, and he was getting ready for his role. "I thought you were going to keep me in the loop from now on, Agent Dante."

The woman strolled inside with careful tap-tap-taps from her high heels. She pulled out a chair next to the small wooden table. Yeah, he knew that he was in an interrogation room. These rooms all looked the same, and he hadn't forgotten his last visit inside one.

He'd been alone then. No lawyer. No family beside him. His mom had been hysterical. They'd shoved her into the back of an ambulance, and then they'd taken him away. He'd confessed fast enough. After all, why lie?

I swung. I hit the bastard. I'd do it again.

"Why don't you have a seat, Mr. Ridgeway?" The female agent suggested.

"Call me Max."

Her lips curled but her bright blue eyes didn't warm, not even a little. "Max, I'm Agent Monica Davenport."

Right. The profiler.

Dante walked around and positioned himself near the window. A window Max was sure was reinforced, but since they were several floors up, he figured perps didn't jump much.

Max pulled the chair out with his foot. He sat down and stretched his legs out before him. Samantha hadn't moved yet.

Had these two been watching them from behind that mirror? If so, then they knew his weak spot. *Her.*

"So I heard your team screwed up again, and the other asshole is dead," Max said, ready to cut right through the bullshit.

"I'm afraid the perpetrator was dead before our agents could arrive on scene," Monica said cooly, not so much as a line appearing on her face. "But I assure you, we are doing everything possible—"

"Not good enough." Max turned his stare to Dante. "I told you, I want to know everything. No more shutting me out. Good, bad, I want to *know*."

Dante nodded. "We just need you to answer a few questions first." The guy's voice was so calm, almost friendly. "Then we'll move ahead and share everything we have with you."

Max laughed. "Really; what is this? Are you supposed to be the good one?" His gaze returned to the woman. Good cop, bad cop. Stupid game. "You don't look bad," he told her.

"You have no idea," she murmured back, and the arctic in her gaze nearly froze him.

"Do you know," Dante's voice with its hint of a southern drawl cut through the room, "why your family was targeted?"

He leaned back in the chair. "Because my stepfather is rich. Pretty easy one to figure."

"Your stepbrother fit the victim profile," Samantha said. His gaze slanted toward her. She stepped forward with that chin up. "I told you, he was victim number five."

"He didn't fit the profile perfectly. Quinlan wasn't attending college," Monica pointed out.

"No." Max shook his head, aware that Samantha was coming closer. "He dropped out of Georgetown last semester." Just a year away from getting his degree. Quinlan had said that he'd go back. Now would he have the chance?

"Does your stepfather have any enemies?" Dante asked.

Max laughed. "Yeah, dozens. Every business owner he's ever screwed." And there'd been a lot of them. "But for names, you're going to need to ask him."

"We are." Monica tucked a strand of dark hair behind her left ear. Her right shoulder moved in a small shrug. "Do *you* have enemies, Max?"

A hand came to rest on his uninjured shoulder. Soft and smooth, a light touch. Samantha stood by his side. Enemies? He straightened a bit. "No one who hates me enough to do this."

Monica opened a folder and pushed a series of photos across the table toward him. "Do you know any of these men?"

His gaze scanned the color photographs. He touched the picture of the blond with the winking grin. He would have recognized the guy even if his picture hadn't been splashed on the news. "Adam Warrant. He and Quinlan hung out a few years back."

He felt the sudden tension in the room. "Anyone else?" Dante asked.

Max stared down at the photos. The redhead with the broken nose looked familiar. "I...might have seen him with Quinlan once, but I can't be sure."

"Do you know his name?" Dante's voice was still easy.

"No, no, I'm not even sure I saw him but I think—" He frowned, remembering a rain-soaked day when he'd gone to Quinlan's dorm room. "I think I saw him when Quinlan was at Georgetown." His fingers tapped on the photo. "He another vic?" Another one who knew Quinlan? What were the odds...?

"No, he's not a victim." Monica pulled the photo away. "He's the perp we found with his throat slashed in the parking garage."

His gaze flew up to catch hers.

Monica's head inclined toward him. "Sam ran his prints and turned up a hit in our system. That's where we got the picture. His name's James Hackley. He's an ex-con, and as far as we can tell, he's never been a student at Georgetown or any other college."

Max's eyes narrowed.

"And this is the other man." A photo slid toward him, and this time, it was obvious that the guy was dead. Close-cropped black hair. Closed eyes. A bullet's entrance wound in his forehead. "Do you know him?"

Had to be the guy who'd tried to kill him. "No. Never seen him." At least, not without a black ski mask.

"He's not in the system," Samantha said, "but I'm running a facial recognition program right now. I'm comparing his image to the video we took from the traffic cameras outside the bars. If we can tag his image and link him to a car, I can trace the plate." She exhaled slowly. "And the plate will give us a name."

Monica pulled all the photos back. "We're going to connect all these men, and we *will* find your brother."

"*Pieces* of him?" The question burst out.

And Monica didn't answer.

"We'll find him," Samantha's soft voice reassured. "Don't give up hope yet."

He saw Dante's gaze jump to her.

"You've given us a link," Monica said. "Two victims knew each other. Maybe they *all* knew each other."

"Or maybe they all knew the wrong person." Samantha. said.

James Hackley.

Monica straightened her files. "We start with Hackley and work our way out from there. He's going to lead us to the others."

Max's hands flattened on the table. "You sure about that? My brother is out there, *dying.*"

Monica's stare drifted to Samantha. "I understand." And she actually sounded like she did. "Believe me, we are doing everything that we can. Stay here, okay? We might have some more photos for you to ID soon." She rose, shoving her chair back.

Max jumped to his feet, too. "That's it? That's all I get to do? Look at some damn photos?"

Dante stepped forward. "Easy. We know this is a tense situation—"

"You don't know what it's like to have someone you care about in a killer's hands! You don't know what it's like for time to trickle away while you *know* he's going to die. You don't *know.*"

Silence.

"I know." Whispered from Samantha. His head whipped to the left, and Max found himself caught in her gaze. "And they know too. Believe me, they do." Her hand lifted, and her fingertips pressed against his cheek. "We're working 24–7. Don't give up on us yet. You *can't* give up."

There was so much pain in her voice. "Samantha?"

"We're getting out of here," Samantha told him, and her voice was stronger, firmer. She fired a glance at Monica. "I read the files. I know that you talked to the bartender, Nic, at The Core. He said—he said he saw a woman with Quinlan right after Max and I left."

"A blonde." Monica's gaze slid back and forth between them. "Maybe twenty-one or twenty-two. He said she had long legs and a small knife tattoo on her left shoulder."

"He remembered her only because he remembered *you*." Dante's head was cocked as he watched them. "He said a redhead came up asking him questions, and some man with her got into a fight."

"You all left quite an impression on him," Monica murmured.

"After you left..." From Dante, "the bartender saw a blonde approach Quinlan."

"We haven't been able to find her yet, but we've got plainclothes officers at The Core looking for her." Monica eased away from the table. "Thanks to Kim, we know a blonde matching her description was also seen with Adam Warrant right before he vanished." One dark brow arched. "The same bartender remembered her."

Too damn big of a coincidence. "She's part of the ring?"

"We think she was the bait." Monica curled her hands around her files. "We wondered how the men were lured out—we know roofies were used. The two men who were ransomed couldn't remember anything about even *being* in the bars."

"Memory loss is common after Rohypnol ingestion," Dante explained. "But because of the drug, the guys couldn't tell us who led them out."

"Now we have a suspect, one we're looking for and one we *will* find." Ah, finally some heat in Monica's voice.

"Yes, we will," agreed Samantha. "Max and I are going to hit the bars tonight. You promised him that he'd be part of the investigation, and he will be."

Well, damn.

"No more sitting on our asses. We're in this thing." Samantha gave the agents a curt nod. "If you need us, you can text me, but we're not waiting anymore." She grabbed Max's arm and headed for the door.

"The waiting's hard, isn't it, Sam?" Monica questioned quietly. "It reminds you too much."

Samantha flinched. "I don't need reminding. Forgetting—that never happened. No matter what I did, I just couldn't forget."

And what the hell was she talking about?

"Let's get out of here," Samantha muttered. "Sometimes I feel like I can't *breathe* here."

Max knew the feeling. He pulled open the door.

"Wait!" Monica called out. "Sam...do you—do you trust him?"

Ah, shit, there it was. His past. Sure they had all the gory details in their nice, neat files, and they just needed to throw it in his face one more time.

"Doesn't matter," Samantha said. "I'm with him either way."

Not the answer that he'd wanted, but one he'd take. He stepped forward and nearly slammed into another agent. A woman. Small, delicate, with fierce green eyes.

"Come on, Max," Samantha said, grabbing his arm. "We don't have time to waste."

No, they sure as hell didn't.

• • •

Monica took a shaky breath as she watched Sam and Ridgeway hurry away.

Sometimes I feel like I can't breathe here.

She'd caught Sam's words, and she'd understood. Once upon a time, Monica had felt like the world was closing in on her, too, and it had been a struggle to push back the fear.

But she'd pushed and she'd pushed and she'd walled herself off from everyone else until...

"You okay, baby?" Luke's voice whispered from right behind her. She felt his fingers skim down her arm.

Monica turned her head, just a bit. They were in the hallway, and too many eyes were on them.

But screw the other agents. All that they would see was two agents discussing an active case. So if she wanted to spend a moment with the man she loved, then she would. "I was worried about you." Her confession was stark.

Luke blinked, and his expression softened.

She held up her hand, stopping him before he could speak. "Since you've moved in with me, things are—" *More intense. Deeper.* "Good," she said instead, because it was the truth. "Better than good." She was the happiest that she could ever remember being.

He caught her hand and pressed a quick kiss to her knuckles. "For me, too."

"I'm afraid." Her admission was hushed.

He shifted closer to her. "Of what?"

With him, she could always be honest. "Good things don't always last long for me. My life isn't about picket fences and happy endings. It's not—"

"It can be," he said, voice firm, as he cut across her words. "Your life, *our* life, can be anything we want." His gaze burned with intensity. "I was going to wait on this but... *dammit,* I love you, Monica, and I don't just want to live with you. I want to marry you."

And she lost her breath.

"Dante!" Hyde's voice cut through the hallway. "I need you to prep for the press conference. We've got to explain how the cops let Adam Warrant walk out of that bar. Dammit, we need Kenton Lake in here for this shit."

But Luke didn't move. "You don't have to be afraid," he told her softly. "You won't lose me."

And that was her fear. Ever since the Watchman case, she'd known that Luke was her weakness. When she thought about something happening to him, dark terror washed through her.

"Dante!"

She swallowed. "Go. We'll talk—"

"Soon," Luke promised, eyes glittering, then he walked away.

I want to marry you.

"Yes," Monica whispered and knew that when the time was right, she'd tell Luke.

No more fear.

Frank Malone wasn't used to being kept in the dark. And he sure as shit wasn't used to being stuck in some eight-by-ten room while agents asked him the same damn questions over and over again.

Sweat beaded his brow, and he glared at the door. Five more minutes, *five more,* and he was getting out of there. The agents had been gone too long. They had already fucked things up, and if he didn't get his son back—

The phone on his hip vibrated. He hauled it up to his ear. "Look, I can't talk now—"

"You'd better." A soft whisper. Familiar.

Frank's gaze flew to the mirror on the left-hand side of the wall.

"*I know where you are, Frank.*" Anger there, throbbing in that whisper. "And that makes me very, very *pissed off.*"

Frank swallowed. "Wh-wher—"

"Don't talk, asshole. Just listen. I don't want them hearing what you say."

Frank shut up.

"You gave me your money, every dime I wanted, but you screwed me over."

Fear nearly choked him.

"Guess who's going to pay for that?"

"*Not—*"

"*Told you to shut up!*"

His lips clamped together, and he turned away from the mirror, hunching his shoulders.

"Quinlan told me about you." Low, grating.

Frank clenched his teeth.

"A real dick of a father, huh? Screwed around on his mom, his stepmom, and even screwed *his* girlfriend."

Frank swiped a hand over his forehead.

"He thinks you're gonna let him die."

No, no, Quinlan was the only thing that he had in this world. His blood.

"I started cutting him."

Bile rose in Frank's throat. "D-don't—" He bit back the word.

"He screamed, and he begged me to stop." A soft laugh. "Your boy's a bleeder, but you know that, don't you?"

An image of red flashed through his mind, and his whole body shuddered. *Quinlan.*

"A couple more slashes with my knife, and he'll be gone."

"*No.*" Frank couldn't hold back the whisper.

"Doesn't seem right. I mean, you were the one who messed up the trade, not that piece of crap son you have."

"Then take me," he rasped.

More laughter. "You just can't shut the hell up, can you?"

Frank's eyes darted around the room. He had to get out of there. Had to go—

"I'll take you. You for him, old man. A sweet trade." Silence, then, "Is he worth that much? Is he worth your life?"

Frank turned and stared into the mirror. He saw the lines and the white hair, the age spots that dotted his skin. What did he have? After all these years, what did he have? Money, hell *yes,* and he'd enjoyed the shit out of his fortune, but...

Alone.

Ever since Katie had died, he'd been so alone. Even the pills couldn't ease the ache inside him.

The only thing I have...

Quinlan.

So the answer, the *only* answer he had was, "Yes."

"Then get out of there, bastard. Get away from those agents, and I'll trade your son for your life."

A soft click sounded in his ear. He stared in the mirror. *Had they seen?* They couldn't know. *They couldn't.*

He lifted his chin. He was Fuck 'em Frank. He could do anything that he wanted.

Frank shoved out of his chair and marched to the door.

He grabbed the knob and yanked the door open. Not a prisoner. No one could hold him, never could. Once outside, phones rang. Voices buzzed. His shoes slapped against the tiled floor.

"Wait, Mr. Malone!" The agent, Kim Daniels, called his name. "There's something I need to tell—"

He glanced over his shoulder, barely sparing her a glance. "I'm getting some air." He hurried his steps, all too aware of the slight weight of his phone in his front pocket.

"Then I'll come with you." Ramirez appeared at the corner. That agent could move so quietly.

Frank glared at him. "The hell you are. Get out of my way. I want *out* of here."

"Frank?" Max's voice. His stepson hurried toward him. "What's going on?"

Damn but that man favored his mother. Looking at him *hurt*. Because he could stare into Katie's eyes. He'd let her down. When she'd found him in bed with Beth... *didn't mean anything to me. Shit, why, why had I done it?* He still couldn't remember why he'd crawled into her bed the first time. Couldn't *remember* crawling there because he'd been so drunk. He just remembered waking and realizing that he'd screwed up.

Then the cancer had started eating away at Katie. It had touched her, and she'd never let him touch her again.

Gone.

Everything, gone.

Not Quinlan. Not yet.

"These assholes have messed up the case." Frank jerked his thumb toward the agents. "I'm getting out of here. Going back home. Maybe—maybe Quinlan will contact me there." *Fuck 'em. You can do this. Don't let them see…*

"Sir, it's not safe for you to—" Kim began.

"*I wasn't asking.*"

"They tried to kill you," Ramirez said, his voice flat. "Until this is over, you're not safe."

"I'll have a dozen guards at my house. *My* guards." But he wouldn't be calling the guards. This time, he'd do everything the kidnapper wanted. "I'll be fine."

But Max was still watching and staring with eyes like Katie's. Max knew what he'd done. He knew, and Max had hated him for breaking Katie's heart.

Sweet Katie. She'd loved him, not the money.

Always about the money.

Not for her.

"Frank…" Max stepped closer. "Is everything all right?"

No, and life hadn't been, not for years. "You're like her." It slipped out. Dammit. But… "That's good." Too many people were twisted up, with crap for priorities.

He'd been the one to twist Quinlan. He'd shoved that boy aside when he was younger and left him alone for too long.

Not anymore. Time for atonement. "I'm getting out of here."

Max grabbed his arm. "We *will* find him."

Always hopeful. Katie had been like that, too. Until those last few days. Then she'd just given up.

Frank nodded grimly. "Right." He *would* find his son.

They went back to Max's place first. Sam knew he wanted to ditch his bloody clothes. She felt the battle-ready energy in him as the elevator rose. He didn't speak. Neither did she.

I almost lost him.

The elevator doors opened. They walked down the hallway. He opened the door; she went inside—

And found her back pushed against the wall as Max pinned her and took her lips in a long, deep kiss.

Her hands lifted, then hesitated as she remembered the bullet wound. She didn't want to hurt him.

"Fuck it," Max growled as his mouth rose. "*Touch me.*" His hands were sliding under her shirt. Such warm, strong hands. Need tightened her body as his fingers curled around her breasts. Just a touch, and she ignited.

With him, Sam suspected that would always be the case.

"I want you." His gaze was stark.

And she wanted him.

But Sam's hands pushed against his body. "Easy." Her whisper.

Jaw clenched, Max stepped back. "Fine, we don't have to—"

Oh, yes, they did. But they had to be fast, and she had to take *him*.

"Get on the sofa," Sam's voice trembled when she gave the order. Max's eyes narrowed a bit, but then he moved back and sprawled on the wide sofa.

Sam swallowed and began to strip. She heard the low growl that built in Max's throat as her shirt and pants hit the carpet with a soft rustle.

Want him. Need him. She unhooked her bra and let the lace drift to the floor. The only garment she wore now was her panties. She walked toward him, and his gaze seemed to drink in her body.

She could see the thick bulge of his arousal, and she wanted his cock inside her. Driving deep. She wanted wild and hot but...

But this time it would be different.

Sam knelt on the soft carpet. Her fingers were steady as she undid his pants and lowered the zipper. His erection spilled into her hands, and she stroked him, enjoying the hiss of her name from his lips.

She leaned forward. She licked his cock, enjoying the taste. And then Sam took him into her mouth.

His hands locked on her shoulders. Not to push her away, but to bring her closer. She licked, and she sucked, and her sex moistened as she savored him.

Her hand eased down her body, and her fingers pressed between her legs, right over the tight ache that had her quivering.

"*Now.*" Max pushed her back. "I can't wait, baby. I need you *now.*"

Sam glanced up, swiping her tongue over her lips as she enjoyed that last taste.

A muscle flexed along his jaw, and he pulled her up onto the couch. Then his fingers were pushing her panties to the side and driving knuckles-deep into her body.

Her knees pushed into the couch cushions. "*Yes.* That feels so good..."

"It's about to be better." And one hand yanked out his wallet. She caught sight of the foil packet. Sam took it from him and opened the condom.

She rolled the protection over his straining length. Sam braced her hands on Max's chest, being careful not to touch his shoulder, then slowly, so slowly, she eased down.

His cock stretched her, filled her, and...*perfect.*

She began to move. Up. Down. Not too fast. Not too rough.

"*Not . . . easy.*" Max's hands locked around her waist. He lifted her, taking over the rhythm. Making it faster, driving ever harder into her.

She forgot about his shoulder. She felt only . . . him.

Sam arched forward. His cock slid along her clit, and the rush of sensation jolted through her.

Again.

Another thrust. One that had her sex clamping around him.

Sam stared into Max's eyes and saw the same desperate desire she felt.

She kissed him. Their tongues met as he thrust into her once more. She came, gasping against his lips. His hips lifted, pushed, again, again . . .

When he came, she held him tight. So tight because she didn't want to let him go.

Unfortunately, she knew that was exactly what she'd have to do.

There was no time for soft touches after sex. No tender words. They dressed. She checked her weapon, and they left—all in silence.

Silence . . . when Sam had so much to say.

I need you. Don't leave me. Trust me again. I won't let you down. We will get Quinlan back.

But she didn't speak then because Sam didn't want to make a promise she might not be able to keep.

Sam didn't take Max to The Core. No real point in that. Other FBI agents would already have staked out that bar, waiting, hoping to see the blonde.

So she and Max went to the other bars she'd mapped that fit the profile. One after the other. They questioned waitresses and bartenders and tried to find out if anyone else had seen the blonde with the knife tattoo.

The problem was that there were too many young blondes in the city. And when people were drinking, they didn't exactly pay close attention to the folks around them.

Their sixth stop was a club called Express. Loud. Smokey. A band shrieked onstage, and dancers crammed the small floor. Sam made her way to the bar and did her usual routine of slapping the counter and leaning forward to talk to the bartender. "We're looking for a woman," she said, raising her voice to be heard above the roar of music.

When Sam flashed her badge, the redhead with the pierced nose and eyebrow stared back at her with vague interest. Tattoos lined the woman's arm. Snakes. Blades.

"She's blonde." Max crowded in beside her. "Around twenty-one—"

"And she's got a tattoo on her right shoulder. A small knife," Sam said and hoped the tat would click, because from the looks of things, this woman knew her tats.

The bartender didn't blink. "Don't know her." Her voice rose a bit.

"It's important we find her." Sam slid her card across the bar.

"Why? She in trouble?" Asked too fast.

Sam held her wary stare. "She could be. We need to find her so that we can help her."

The card wasn't touched. "Well, good luck with that." The bartender spun away and grabbed a thick beer mug.

"Fuck. Another one." Frustration boiled in Max's voice. "Should we talk to the waitresses? Go to the next bar?"

Sam grabbed his arm. She rose onto her toes and whispered in his ear, "No. We find a dark corner, and we wait." Then she led him away from the bar. He followed her as she pushed through the crowd. *There.* The booth to the left. The one that let them see the front door and the back exit.

She pushed him down first, then sidled close to him, real close. "This is it."

Max stiffened against her. "What?"

"The bartender knows her." There had been worry in the woman's voice. A tremor that she hadn't been able to hide. Sam's gaze searched the crowd. So dark, hard to see... "If she's here now, the bartender will tell her about us, and she'll try to slip out the back." Her eyes tracked to the front door. "Not that way." Sam's nails drummed on the table. "We just have to wait."

His hand curved into a fist near hers. "I'm not so good at waiting."

"Not like we have much choice." She wouldn't take her gaze off that back door because it would only take a split second of missed concentration, and the woman could disappear. "We can just—"

A slim blonde shoved open the rear exit door. She glanced back over her shoulder, her eyes sweeping the room. The woman wore a black leather jacket, so no seeing the tattoo, but...

"Is that her?" Max asked, his entire body tensing.

Sam was already on her feet. "Only one way to find out." She stepped forward, her holster a steady weight at her side.

He rose beside her. They were less than ten feet from the door.

The blonde's gaze slid right past Sam, but then she saw Max. In that instant, fear flashed across the woman's pretty face, and she spun away, rushing out into the night.

"She knows you." The blonde had recognized Max, and she'd run. As a rule, the innocent didn't usually run.

As a rule.

Sam took off after her. She raced forward, intent on the door—and slammed into the bartender. The woman had rushed out in front of Sam and knocked her down. Drinks tumbled onto the ground and broken glass bit into Sam's arm.

"Oh, didn't see you…" The bartender murmured, fake innocence in her voice but a grim smile on her lips. Sam cursed and shoved the woman to the side.

Max grabbed Sam's arm, pulling her to her feet. Seconds later, she and Max tore through the back door. The cool night air hit her, and she heard the fast rapping of high heels on the pavement. With no time to call for backup, Sam sucked in a deep breath and chased her prey.

Fuck, fuck, fuck.

The FBI was after her. The FBI and *him*. If Gina hadn't given her that warning…

Veronica James threw a glance over her shoulder. How had they found her? She was supposed to be safe. Untouchable. He'd promised her. *Promised.*

Veronica had to get out of there. Her car was parked three blocks up from Express. She could cut back around, sneak down the alley, and get away. Gina had agreed to buy her some time, so she should damn well be able to make it.

Veronica's heart slammed into her ribs as she ran. She hated running. Already her side stung and her breath choked out. Damn asthma, soon she'd be choking, trying to gulp in air.

Footsteps thudded behind her. Close, closing in.

No.

They couldn't catch her. That wasn't the way things were going to end. She wasn't going to jail. She was going to an island. She'd be a rich bitch and drink piña coladas on a beach for the rest of her days. No more poor white trash. No more rich frat boys looking down their stuck-up noses at her.

She'd earned her new life, and no one was taking it away from her.

"*Stop!*" A woman's voice. The redhead who'd been with him. "I'm with the FBI, and I'm ordering you—*stop!*"

Veronica threw a quick glance over her shoulder. Her right foot stumbled. She almost went down. Almost. But this wasn't the first time that she'd had to run like hell through the night. She ditched her shoes and ran faster.

She snaked into the alley. Her breath wheezed out. She'd make it. Veronica knew there was no choice. *Not going down for murder.*

Mike was already dead. She'd seen the story on the news. The drop had been screwed, and those agents had shot him. They wouldn't be able to identify him, though, not for a while. Mike had always skated right past the cops. *Not this time.*

Mike was gone, but Kevin was still out there, and she'd

always been able to count on Kevin. She'd meet him at the warehouse, and they'd lay low until some of the heat cooled off.

Someone grabbed her. A hand slapped over Veronica's mouth and closed off the ragged gasp of her breath.

"Don't move." At his familiar whispered voice, she sagged. He shouldn't have been there. They weren't supposed to meet—but, oh, damn, she was glad to have him with her in the dark.

He pulled her deeper into the alley and shoved her behind the garbage bin. He kept one hand around her mouth while he locked one hand around her waist.

Tears leaked from her eyes. Her lungs hurt. But he was there. He'd take care of her. He'd promised.

The footsteps grew louder, pounding hard. Or was it her heart?

His?

Don't look in the alley. Don't look.

She saw the redhead. Caught a flash of her hair under the streetlight. The woman ran forward. *Heading for the parking lot.* Exactly where Veronica had been going.

Max Ridgeway thundered past with her. He never once glanced Veronica's way.

Her lips pressed harder against the soft glove on her lover's hand. He kissed her cheek and whispered, "They're gone."

She was safe.

His hand eased away from her waist, and a white-hot pain sliced her heart.

His hand pressed harder over her mouth, choking back the scream that built, the scream she didn't even have enough breath to voice.

"They're gone, but they'll be back soon. So I have to hurry, love." The knife twisted. Burned.

A numbing cold swept into her blood.

"Did you really think I'd let you have the money?" His voice was still a whisper. *"You're such a dumb bitch, but a perfect whore."*

He pulled the knife out of her heart. Her blood splattered upon the ground. Her body began to sag. She tried to grab for the garbage bin but her hands slipped on the side. The metal lid crashed down as she struggled to stand.

And he melted into the black night.

Sam skidded to a halt. She'd heard something. A clang, a hollow echo—like a metal door slamming shut. She spun back around.

"Samantha?"

"The alley—" Her gun was up, and she gasped out the words as she ran.

Ten feet. Five. The mouth of the alley that she'd passed earlier yawned before her. Sam hurried inside.

A cat screeched and shot past her legs.

Dammit, dammit, dammit!

"She's gone." Max's disgusted voice, and he didn't even sound winded from the run. He stalked farther into the alley. "Shit, this connects to the main road. She probably went through here and back to her car."

Sam's nostrils flared as she caught the harsh scent of garbage, cigarettes, and crap that she didn't even want to think about. A big garbage bin slumped to the right, its lid half closed.

A metal screech.

She took a few more steps forward. Another scent filled her nostrils. Heavier. Fresher.

"That bartender knows her," Max said. "We need to go back inside and make her tell us where that woman lives!"

Sam's eyes narrowed as she struggled to see in the thick darkness.

A car engine revved in the distance. Tires squealed. And a heavy ache lodged in her chest. "I know where she is."

Max whirled back around to face her.

Shaking her head, Sam leaned forward. She knew the scent of blood. A sliver of light trickled down from a second story window. Light that fell on strands of blond hair.

Sam pulled out her phone and called Dante. When he answered, she said, "I've got a body."

The killer's foot pressed hard against the accelerator. Damn, but that had been close. He rolled down the window and let the cool air blast against his face.

Too close.

He'd planned to kill Veronica. Just not then, not there. But he'd been following that dick Ridgeway, and when the guy had gone in Express—*time's up.*

Veronica was weak; he knew it. He'd used that weakness. If the Feds had gotten hold of her, she would have confessed and ruined everything.

He'd known that he had to move. And then sweet Veronica had run right to him. Good thing he'd been prepared for her.

The Feds were closing in faster than he'd anticipated. He had to be ready for them.

He stopped at the streetlight. He looked down and saw

the blood staining his shirt. Veronica had died easily. No long, pain-filled death. Just a quick kill, with minimal pain. He figured she'd deserved that.

Poor Veronica. All her life she'd never been worth much.

But she'd sure been one fine piece of ass.

He fished out his phone, dialed the number, and when old Fuck 'em Frank answered with his trembling voice, he told him, "It's time."

CHAPTER *Ten*

Spotlights shone down on the body. Max stood behind the yellow police tape, but he could see the woman, see the red that bloomed from her chest. The blood that mixed with the trash and the mud beneath her.

"Let him through!" Dante's order broke the air, and suddenly, Max was pulled under the tape and led closer to the scene.

"You know what's happening," Dante said.

No, he didn't have a clue. He just knew dead bodies were turning up and that *wasn't* good.

"The lead kidnapper's covering his tracks. Taking out his team and eliminating anyone who can ID him."

"What about Quinlan?"

A muscle worked in Dante's jaw. "At this point…" Dante ran a hand over the back of his neck. "I'm sorry, Ridgeway, but the odds of his survival are slim."

Max took that hit, and his hands fisted.

"*We were so damn close to her.*" He could still see her face. Wide eyes, staring at him with *recognition* before she'd run into the night. "If she'd just talked to us…"

"Then she might not have wound up with her heart nearly carved out." Brutal.

The agent wasn't pulling any punches.

"You're seeing this!"

Max turned at the voice. Samantha's voice. Angry, fierce, and splitting with emotion.

She was at the south side entrance to the alley. Her hand was clamped around another woman's arm—the redheaded bartender who'd alerted the blonde and who'd tripped Samantha when they gave chase.

Those few moments…if they'd just had…

"Uh, Sam?" Dante rushed toward her, even as he motioned for Max to stay back. "Sam, what are you—"

She ducked under the police tape and hauled the woman after her.

The bartender screamed, *"No, fuck, no, I don't want to—"*

"I don't give a damn what you want." Samantha jerked to a halt and glared at her. "Your *friend* is dead, and you are going to see her."

The woman shook her head and tried to back away.

Samantha didn't let her budge.

"Sam…" Dante closed in on her. *"Crime scene*, remember? You can't just—"

"I'm out of time." And just like that, the heat was gone from her voice. She sounded flat. Sad.

Max stepped toward her. Instantly a cop was there, putting a hand against his chest and stopping him. Making sure he didn't contaminate the scene. Right. Like he probably hadn't screwed the scene when he'd trampled through the alley the first time.

"I'm out of time," Samantha said, "and so is Quinlan Malone."

The bartender wasn't looking at the body on the ground. "I-I don't know any—"

"My brother," Max snapped. "His name's Quinlan Malone, and he's missing."

Samantha glanced his way. Their eyes held for a beat of time. Then she dropped her hold and stepped to the side. The redhead got a full view of the dead woman. "*No!*" The bartender whirled away, shaking.

Samantha stared at the woman's back. "You were friends, Gina."

Gina gave a fast nod.

"You warned her to get out of the bar, but you should have listened to me. I *told* you I could help her."

Gina's shoulders shook as she cried—loud, gulping sobs.

"I need to find the man who did this," Samantha said.

Gina glanced back at her and did *not* let her gaze drop to the body again.

"I need to find him because if I don't..." Samantha shook her head. "More people are going to die."

"Cover the body," Dante ordered the tech who'd just finished photographing the scene. "*Now.*"

Gina's lips trembled. "I-I don't...know any-anything—"

"You knew her." A jerk of Samantha's thumb over her shoulder toward the body. "And now we need to know her. We need to know *everything* about her."

A white cloth was pulled over the body.

The redhead's eyes dropped, and she stared at the cloth.

"He left her with the garbage," Samantha said. "Is that what she deserved?"

"N-no..."

"Then help me find the bastard who killed her."

A tear trickled down Gina's cheek, and she nodded.

"Good, *good*." Samantha caught Gina's shoulder. "Let's start with her name. What was her name, Gina?"

"V-Veronica. Veronica J-James."

"And where did she live?" Samantha asked as she guided her away from the crime scene.

"Seventeen-oh-nine Belmont..."

"Near Georgetown?"

"Y-yeah."

They disappeared, turning right at the edge of the alley.

"Get the body out of here," Dante ordered the team around him. "And I want a unit to head with me to Belmont." He fired a glance at Max. "You in for this, Ridgeway?"

Try to keep me out.

Sam went with the uniforms to 1709 Belmont. The officers immediately went to work searching the one-bedroom apartment. Max came with them, but Luke ordered him to remain outside until they'd secured the scene.

Ignoring the team around her, Sam sat at Veronica's keyboard, tapping quickly. The password was eliminated in five seconds. Veronica's favorite band. Luckily, Veronica had left a stack of their CDs near her desk.

She scrolled through the files. Nothing. *Nothing.* E-mails flew past her, names, dates. She checked as fast as she could, looking for something that would tie Veronica to the kidnappings.

"Anything?" Kim asked from behind her.

Sam shook her head and went deeper into Veronica's search history on the computer. Wait…*driving directions.*

She pulled up the archived file. Directions to 2917 Kyler Boulevard in Fairfax, Virginia. Directions that Veronica had looked up the day before the first victim went missing. *The day before.*

Fairfax was right in the middle of the kill zone. They'd mapped out a geographic zone for the kidnapper, and that area of Fairfax was within driving distance to every disappearance. She glanced back at Kim, who already had her cell out.

"Pull up this address," Kim said into the phone. "Two nine one seven Kyler Boulevard. In Fairfax, Virginia. Yeah, yeah, that's right. Now tell me who owns that property." After a few moments, Kim's eyes widened. "No shit."

Sam's heart thudded against her ribs. *Hurry, hurry.* Kim whistled softly. "Guess who owns an old warehouse in Fairfax?"

Sam wasn't in the mood to guess.

"Frank Malone."

What?

"Seems he bought some property over there about five years ago. Bought it, used it, then forgot it. The warehouse has been boarded up for the last six months." A brief pause. "Interesting, don't you think?"

Sam jumped out of the chair. "I think we need to get to

that warehouse." Because Jeremy Briar had been left in his father's driveway. Because Adam Warrant's body had been found in a garage owned by *his* father.

No, Christ, no.

Fairfax would be a perfect kill site.

Frank had taken Beth's car and slipped away without the guards. Frank had his gun—he wasn't stupid—but he was scared.

The warehouse waited at the end of the street. Darkened windows, tall walls. Abandoned.

He reached for his phone. Hesitated. *Call Max.* The whisper in his head. He should let Max know where he was. What was happening.

Would you trade your life for his? Is he worth that much?

His hands curled into fists, and Frank sucked in a sharp breath. No, he wouldn't call Max. *Time for me to do something right.*

He shoved open the car door and climbed out slowly. "*Hello!*" His voice echoed back to him. There were no cars here, no lights. Nothing but the night and that damn warehouse.

Was this a trick? Another sick, twisted joke to pull him in and leave him with nothing?

But then a low moan filled the air and he froze. No, not a moan. The slow grind of a door scraping over old wood. The front entrance to the warehouse...the door had opened.

He couldn't see anyone, but *someone* was there and inviting him in. "*Who's there?* Dammit, come out here! Bring Quinlan out!*"

"Come in..." Was the taunt he got in return.

His jaw clenched, and he loped forward. If he had to, he'd kill every sonofabitch in there, but he *was* getting his son.

His hand closed around the old door handle, and he wrenched it all the way open. As soon as he stepped over the threshold, the scent of blood and bleach burned his nose.

Quinlan?

Please, son, be alive.

"What's going on?" Max demanded. They were in the back of a government SUV, racing behind two other units toward Fairfax. "What do you mean, we're going to one of Malone's properties? Why?"

Sam glanced at him, knowing that she had to be careful. "We found the address on Veronica James's computer."

"Malone's warehouse?" He shook his dark head. "That doesn't make sense!"

"By all accounts, it's an abandoned building. No other businesses close by. It seems like..." She wet her lips. "Like it might be the perfect place to keep someone locked up." *Or to dump a body.*

Max's eyes narrowed, and she knew that he under-stood the unspoken words. "*Faster,*" Max barked at Luke. "Can't you drive this damn thing *faster?*"

They were already flying past the speed limit.

"We're going in silent," Luke said, and she knew that he was talking into his phone, giving orders to the locals on scene. "We're not giving these bastards any warning."

"*Samantha.*" Max's fingers brushed hers.

She held his gaze.

"Is he alive?"

Her breath came on a slow rush. "We'll know soon."

"That last guy...Adam...they found him on his father's property, too, didn't they? That was where they dumped the body."

She curled her fingers around his. She wanted to give him hope. "Quinlan could be alive."

He squeezed her hand, but didn't speak again. And neither did she—Sam didn't like lying to him.

"Quinlan? Are you here?" The scent of blood was so strong, filling Frank's nose and making bile rise in his throat. He fumbled and drew out his gun. The Feds had confiscated the Glock that he'd had earlier. But lucky for him, there'd been plenty of other guns waiting at home for him.

His feet shuffled forward. The warehouse was too damn dark. He should have leveled the place months ago. "Are you here?"

Frank's right foot kicked something. Something big and soft. His breath heaved out. *"Quinlan?"* He slipped and fell to his knees. "Quinlan!"

A flash of light hit him right in the face. The bright light blinded him. "Not your boy, old man," a hard, male voice rumbled from behind the light.

Frank lurched forward but froze when a gun barrel pressed against his forehead. No mistaking that, not even in this black pit.

"Wanna see him one more time?"

Frank was on his knees before the bastard holding the gun. His body shook, but he wouldn't back down. "Let him go."

"Shouldn't have brought the FBI in." That voice rumbled.

"Dad!" Quinlan's scream had his heart slamming into his chest.

Still alive. *Quinlan's still alive.*

Frank's right hand was behind him, his fingers curled around the gun. The bastard hadn't seen it yet. He'd have to move fast. "I-I want to see him."

The barrel eased back. "And he wants to see you. One more time."

The flashlight beam bounced. Frank lurched up. He didn't take time to aim, just fired. Again. Again. Two fast booms. A scream.

The flashlight hit the ground. So did the bastard. "Fuck you," Frank snarled and followed the sound of his son's screams.

"You have to stay here." Sam stared up at Max's tense face. They were about fifty feet away from the warehouse, in the safe perimeter that the agents had just set up. "Stay with the uniforms until we come back."

His eyes were on the building as he strained to see. "It's so damn dark." Why weren't there any streetlights?

"Stay here." Sam squeezed his hand. "And don't give up." She wanted to say more, to do more, but too many eyes were on them.

Sam turned and fell into line behind Luke and Ramirez. They'd be the first team in. They'd tried to leave her out, but hell *no*. She wasn't being left out anymore.

Luke lowered his hand, giving the order to move. The officers behind them were silent as they waited. Tension filled the air, so thick it seemed to weigh her down.

The SSD had gotten a warrant. Fast. They'd tried to reach Malone for permission to go in, but he had been unavailable. More pills, according to Beth. He'd dosed up and gone down for the night.

When she got the signal, Sam's feet seemed to fly over the gravel driveway. Her breath blew out in cold puffs of foggy air. Her heart thudded in her chest. Was this what it had been like for Monica and Luke? When she'd been taken and they'd been desperate to find her, had this icy fear filled them?

Hurry. Can't be too late. Hurry.

Now that they were so close, she was afraid of what she'd find. Jeremy's mutilated body flashed in her mind's eye.

Hurry.

Ramirez kicked the door open. Sam went in behind him, staying low, her gun up. Her left hand held a flashlight above her weapon. The place was pitch black.

And it smelled of death. A heavy, deep odor of blood and bleach. Someone had been killing and trying to clean up the mess.

Sam found the wall. She stuck to it like glue and started moving quickly.

The second that the kidnappers heard them—*if they were there*—they'd run. Or kill Quinlan. Probably both.

Quiet.

Luke was in the lead now, slipping around the corner. She followed. Her light swept the ground.

And landed on the body.

A man lay slumped on the ground. Dark black liquid pooled near his body. No, not black. The blood just looked black in the darkness.

She bent and pressed her fingers to his throat. Nothing, noth—

A jerk of his pulse beneath her fingers. *Jesus, still alive.*

She stared at his face, then her eyes darted to his left ear and the line of piercings. She knew him. Recognition clicked instantly. Kevin Milano, the bouncer at The Core.

Well, damn. The kidnappers had been using an inside man there, someone who could contact them when their prey came by for a drink.

"We've got a man down," she whispered into her mike. "Get the EMTs ready. We're clearing the scene and—"

A shout echoed in the warehouse. A deep, guttural cry of fury, and Sam rushed into the gaping darkness.

Max paced the lot, his gaze sweeping from the left to the right.

"Easy," Agent Kim Daniels told him. "I know it's hard, but in just a few minutes, this will be over."

That was what scared him.

His gaze raked to the left once more. There was one car parked in the shadows near the edge of the street. One lone car. He frowned, staring at it. A BMW that looked so out of place. Nothing else was there. No one. But that car . . .

He squinted, struggling to see a bit better. No street-lights, but there was a reflective decal on the back of it. Kinda looked like a dolphin. Beth had a decal like that. She'd gotten it when she and Frank went to Orlando for a business trip last fall.

What were the odds?

"That car . . . it's Beth's." Same model. Same damn decal. Same position on the far left of the bumper. Dammit. *Dammit.* He whirled away from the car and raced for the warehouse.

But Kim jumped in front of him and slammed her hand onto his chest. "What are you talking about?"

"That car!" He pointed back to the BMW. "It belongs to Frank's assistant, Beth Dunlap."

But why would she be here?

Pitch black. The only light spilled from their flashlights. Sam rushed into the darkness, twisting and turning as she followed the beam.

A soft *squish* of sound. Ragged breathing. Groans.

Her flashlight revealed an open door before them.

Luke went inside first. "FBI! Freeze. Stand down, it's—*fuck.*" Horror there, and Luke wasn't a man to be horrified.

Sam sped in after him, the glow from her light joining his on the floor. *Quinlan.* Quinlan was there, covered in blood. Slashes on his arms, his bare chest. Deep, oozing wounds.

He had a knife in his hand. A bloody knife. His tight fist gripped the hilt of the knife that he'd shoved into another man's neck.

The man gasped, and it was a choking, watery gurgle of pain. Her flashlight fell on the man's face. Not the kidnapper. *Not him.*

Frank.

Tears leaked from Frank Malone's eyes. The knife had plunged, hilt-deep, into his throat. Blood poured from the wound, soaking Quinlan's hand and staining Frank's shirt.

"D-Dad?" Quinlan's broken whisper rasped out as he

stared at his father, now illuminated in the pool of light. "*Dad!*" Quinlan started shaking, hard, his whole body trembling.

Luke grabbed Quinlan's arms and heaved him back. "*Get the paramedics in here, now!*" The order was yelled into his mike. He put his hand over the knife and held it in place. Removing the blade would just make the wound bleed faster. "Secure the scene," he barked to Sam and Ramirez. "Check every damned room. Find them!"

But she couldn't move. Quinlan was still in that small bubble of light. He lifted his hands, torn, bloody hands. "The b-bastard told me…s-said…I'd hear the gunshots…s-said…said…my dad would be d-dead…." He lurched forward and grabbed his father's hand. "*Dad! No!*"

"Get more units in here," Sam spoke quietly into her mike. "We've got three victims." Her voice grew stronger. "We need uniforms searching every room. *Move!*"

Ramirez was already moving. He headed back into the dark hole of a hallway.

Malone's eyes were on his son. Wide. Desperate. His lips trembled but only groans and gurgles came out of his mouth.

Sam fell to her knees beside him. "Malone, *Malone*, stay with me. Focus. You're going to be all right." *Lie, lie.* He wouldn't make it. His skin had already started to turn ashen. So much blood.

A gun lay on the ground at his side.

Quinlan began to rock back and forth. He had on a pair of jeans, nothing else. Sobs shook his shoulders.

Attacked his father.

Another watery gurgle tore from Malone's lips.

"What was he doing here?" Luke demanded, putting pressure on the wound, but the blood wasn't slowing.

"*S-sorry...*" Quinlan's wild cry. "So...fucking... sorry, Dad!"

Frank's lips moved. *Max.*

"He's here," she told him. "Just hold on, okay? He's here."

"*Dad, don't die!*"

But he was dying. She knew it. Luke knew it. There was too much blood. The wound was too deep.

Her fingers curled around Frank's. His lips moved, trying to soundlessly form the words that he couldn't speak.

Footsteps thundered outside. The EMTs. Coming to try and save Malone.

"*Frank?*" Not the EMT. That was Max's desperate voice. No, no, he couldn't be there.

"*I-I did it!*" Quinlan's scream. "Oh, God, *me!*"

Frank spasmed. The EMTs pushed through the doorway and shoved Sam away. She grabbed Max, holding onto him, smearing his stepfather's blood on his shirt. "You can't be here." Crime scene. Evidence. But more... *You can't see this.*

"*Quinlan?*" Max whispered his name.

His brother's head wrenched up at the sound of Max's voice. Quinlan tried to stand, but his legs gave way, and he hit the floor again.

The EMTs swarmed around him.

"*M-my fault...*"

Max shook his head and lunged for his brother.

"Get him out of here!" Luke ordered.

And Sam had to do it. She grabbed Max and held tight

when he fought her. "*Come on.*" He couldn't be there now, couldn't see—

Frank die.

Two officers helped drag him outside. Outside, into the air that was already too chilly for the fall but didn't reek of blood and death. But it wasn't so dark outside now. Lights spilled from the cop cars that had swarmed the scene. Spotlights had been brought from some of the vehicles to illuminate the area as they searched for evidence and secured the perimeter.

"He's alive." Max's hands were clenched into fists. "Sam, he's *alive.*"

Quinlan was.

"Frank." He said the name and shook his head. "I-I saw him. H-he's going to be okay, right?"

He hadn't seen, not in the darkness.

"He was hurt, Max. Badly." She tried to pull him away, needing to shield him from what was coming. But his shoulders just stiffened in a move she'd seen him make so many times now.

"He tried to save Quinlan." Certainty there, in his voice and eyes. "When I saw Beth's car; I *knew* it was him. The way he acted at headquarters, trying to get out so fast…" Max broke off, shaking his head.

The front door burst open, and two EMTs ran out, pushing a gurney. Their patient was the man from the hallway. His eyes were closed, and his dirty blond hair was matted with blood.

A gun had been on the floor next to Frank. Had he shot Kevin? Kevin fit Monica's profile…early twenties, definitely strong build. And he'd been at The Core, so he sure would have had plenty of opportunity to commit the crimes.

Another gurney emerged from the warehouse. This one carried Frank's still body. *Too still.*

The lights from the cars hit him and revealed too much.

"*What the fuck?*" Max's startled cry. "Frank!"

The EMTs pushed the gurney into the back of the ambulance. The lights flashed on as the siren screamed.

Frank Malone wouldn't have long.

"Go with him," Sam whispered. Quinlan would be out next. Max shouldn't have to choose between them. "Go." She pressed her hand against his back.

Quinlan would make it. He'd better. But Frank...

Max hurried forward and jumped into the back of the ambulance. Before the doors closed, his eyes met hers. Held.

Sam didn't blink. Not until the doors slammed closed. Then her eyes squeezed shut, and a shudder shook her body.

When Quinlan was wheeled out moments later, he was calling for his father, a broken, weak cry because he knew what he'd done.

"Take him," Luke said from behind her. "We've got the scene."

Sam climbed into the ambulance. Quinlan's chest looked like hell. The flesh was red and criss-crossed with knife marks. His left arm had been slashed from shoulder to elbow. And his left hand...bandages had been looped around his knuckles, but the EMT was cutting them away and revealing the small stump that used to be his ring finger.

"I killed him." His hollow confession.

Her gaze rose to his tear-stained face. "Frank's on his way to the hospital. We don't know..."

"*Jesus Christ*!" The EMTs had cut away Quinlan's jeans. Deep slashes lined his legs and cut across his thighs. It had been so dark that she hadn't even noticed those wounds. "What did he do to you, man?" the EMT asked.

The siren wailed. Luke slammed the doors closed behind them.

"He wanted me to beg," Quinlan whispered sadly.

Beg, bitch. Beg me. The memory slipped through her mind. Another time, another killer—only he'd wanted *her* to beg.

She grabbed Quinlan's hand and held tight.

"I did." Quinlan's voice was as broken as his body. "But he didn't stop, he just—just—" His eyes rolled back in his head as his lashes fluttered. "K-kept...cutting..."

Her fingers clenched around his. "You're safe now."

CHAPTER *Eleven*

I'm sorry, sir, but there was nothing we could do." Cold, inadequate words.

Max blinked and stared at the doctor. The guy's green scrubs were stained red with Frank's blood.

"By the time your stepfather arrived at the hospital," a helpless shrug, "it was already too late."

The doc's face was lined, his gray eyes bloodshot. Max knew that he should probably say *something* but he just felt so numb.

"Your stepbrother…" The doctor swallowed. "He's still in surgery, but it looks like he'll be all right. As soon as he's in recovery, I-I'll let you know."

"Thank you, doctor," Samantha said. She stood beside Max, quiet and calm. She'd been there just moments after he'd arrived. She'd come in right after the doctors had run down the hallway, screaming orders, and he'd seen Frank's pale hand fall off the gurney.

He'd known then. *Dead.*

Max stared in silence as the seconds ticked by. After a

while, his breath heaved out, and he turned away, stalking for the door.

"Max!"

He didn't stop at Samantha's call. What was he supposed to be feeling? Frank—dead. And Quinlan. Oh, damn, Quinlan.

His palms slapped against the emergency room doors. He hurried out as the security beep sounded behind him.

"Max, stop!" Samantha caught his arm and swung him back to face her. "Max, *I'm sorry.*"

So was he. Sorry he'd trusted the FBI. "Why was he there, Samantha?"

She shook her head. Her curls bounced against her shoulders. "I don't know. Ramirez is working on that. We think—we think Frank must have gotten a call from the kidnapper, telling him where to go."

And he would have gone. The bastard would have walked right in there without telling him.

"We'll pull his phone records, see what we can find—"

He stepped away from her, breaking her hold. *Can't let her touch me, not now.* "And what about Quinlan? What's going to happen to him? Samantha, *he killed Frank!*"

A man standing in the hallway shot him a wide-eyed look and hurried off. His footsteps rapped against the floor.

"Quinlan's going to survive, that's what he's going to do."

So easy to say. "You ever killed someone?" With her job, yeah, maybe, but...

"No."

"There's not really any coming back from that." He knew. Some things you could never forget.

He could still feel that baseball bat in his hands. The

smooth wood. The hard strength. He could see that bat swinging through the air, hear the faint whistle of sound, and see the bastard's eyes as he realized what was going to happen to him.

What had Frank realized in those last few moments? Max closed his eyes, not wanting to see the line of cars buzzing outside. Life going on, while his family lay shattered. "He just wanted to save Quinlan."

"Frank did. Quinlan's—"

"They tortured him."

"He survived. Give him a chance. Your stepbrother can get past—"

Max's control snapped, and he whirled to face her. "*You don't know!* You forced your way in here. You forced yourself into my life, and now Frank's dead!" *Tell the cops, and you'll get him back in pieces.* Rage churned in him and exploded on the closest victim—her. "They'd already gone to work on Quinlan. They were cutting him up. Know why, baby? You know why they were cutting my brother apart?"

Because of you.

It hung between them, stark and painful. The kidnappers had changed their plans because they'd known that the FBI was involved. Samantha and her team had broken those stupid rules.

She swallowed and eased toward him. "Yes, I know why." A brief pause, then, "Because they were freaking psychopaths who got off on hurting other people, that's why."

Red stained her cheeks, and her chin lifted. "There was escalation from these guys, right after the initial abduction. The first guy came back unharmed, but the second vic—they made sure he suffered. They sliced his chest. Carved his back. Yes, he came back alive, but they had fun with him first, and they got a *taste*."

What? "You never said—"

"Because I was trying to protect you. What? Did you want me to tell you that the bastards who'd took your brother liked to torture? That they got off on pain? Well, they did."

Frank's face, eyes wide, lips dripping blood.

"They killed the third victim. The parents broke their rules, sure, but, like I said, the kidnappers were already escalating. The fourth victim went down, too. They could have given the Briars more time. They didn't *want* to. Monica's profile showed the attacks weren't just about the money. Based on the way the bodies were carved, the killer enjoyed hurting the victims."

Max stared at her and struggled to process everything she was admitting to him.

"I couldn't tell you," Samantha said, her voice softer, sadder. "You already had enough on your mind. And Frank—what? Was I supposed to tell a father that the bastards who had his son were slowly slicing him apart?" She gave a slow, negative shake of her head. "I couldn't do that."

His shoulders fell. "Leave me alone."

Her hand lifted, reached for him.

He stepped back. "Just—*go*, now, okay?" His hand raked through his hair. Too much. It was all too much. "You've done enough. Just…go."

Her eyes didn't waver, but her hand dropped. "I'll give you some time alone."

A ragged laugh broke from his lips. "Yeah, yeah, you do that."

"But I'm not leaving you. If you need me, I'm here."

Didn't she get it? The rage inside was so strong. He wanted to strike out, and she was too close.

"*Go.*" Before he said something that he couldn't take back.

Sam paced along the hospital corridor. Kevin Milano was still alive. He hung by the barest of threads while Frank's body was already cold one floor down.

It didn't seem fair. But then, life had a way of twisting and turning on you. Sometimes, the good guys didn't win.

The doctor came out of surgery, her lips tight and her gaze steady. "He's still with us," Dr. Joyce Bradshaw said, "but I can't say for how much longer."

Sam sucked in a sharp breath. "Is he conscious?"

"Barely."

Good enough. "Then I want to talk to him, now." Because there wasn't any time to lose.

The doctor's blue eyes widened. "Uh—excuse me?"

Sam edged nearer to the closed operating room door. "I need to talk to the suspect." While she still could.

"I don't think you understand." The doctor shook her head. "The man has sustained massive internal injuries. He's not—"

"He's my prime suspect in at least four murders." Sam crossed her arms. This was her job. She'd do it. "Before he goes and talks to God about the shit he did, he'll be talking to me." Her eyes burned as she stared at the doctor.

"I-I don't know—"

"I do." She'd pinned her ID to her belt. She knew the

doc could see it. "I know that I've got a pile of dead bodies, and I'm about to add one more."

The lines around the doctor's eyes deepened. "He might not even be able to answer you."

Sam forced a shrug. "I'm still asking my questions." She took another step toward the recovery room.

The doctor moved aside and shoved open the door. "Fine."

The hiss and beep of machines greeted Sam as soon as she stepped inside. The suspect lay on the bed, his face ashen, his breath rasping.

A groan broke from his lips, and her gaze lifted to his face. A young face. Handsome, or it had been. High brow. Strong cheekbones. A dimple in his chin.

Sam leaned over the bed and touched his cheek. "Can you hear me?"

Kevin flinched. His skin was ice cold beneath her touch. The machines beeped louder, faster.

"*Special Agent Kennedy*," Dr. Bradshaw began.

"Open your eyes," Sam sharpened her voice, "and *look* at me."

His eyelids twitched, but didn't open. His breath rasped out. The nurse on the left-hand side of the bed looked up from the chart, her eyes wide.

Sam leaned in closer. "Why did you do it?" she demanded. "Why did you take those men?" But she knew, of course: money. Everyone had a price.

His head moved in the faintest of negative shakes.

Her eyes narrowed.

Chalky lips moved, but no sound emerged.

"Kevin, why did you kill them?"

Nothing.

And that beeping...it wasn't so fast now. Slow, slowing down.

His breath eased in. Out.

"*Why did you kill them?*"

His mouth moved again. She couldn't read his lips because the movement was too faint so she put her head right next to his mouth as she tried to hear the words. "*Why?*" She demanded again.

"Not...m-me..." Kevin's whisper ended on a sigh.

A long, constant shriek pierced the room.

"He's coding!" The nurse yelled, lunging for her patient.

The doctor grabbed Sam's arm and hauled her back. "You have to leave, *now!*"

Blood gurgled from Kevin's mouth. Red bloomed across the bandages on his chest. His breath wheezed out.

Sam backed up, but didn't leave.

Two more nurses ran into the room. Another doctor. They huddled over the bed.

"*Clear!*"

She couldn't even see Kevin anymore. Just a jumble of green scrubs.

"No pulse!"

Sam stared at the mass of bodies.

"*Again!*" Dr. Bradshaw's order.

Kevin was someone's son. Maybe someone's lover.

And a killer.

The whine of the machines continued to blast, and the doctors kept working. Sam stayed there, watching.

They worked on their patient, voices tense. The minutes ticked past.

She watched, and when the nurses and the doctors stepped back, their gloves covered in blood, Sam was still there.

"Calling it," Bradshaw said, yanking off her gloves. "Time of death, one fifty-eight a.m." She stormed toward the door but stopped to glare at Sam. "You didn't even get anything from him. His last few moments, and you didn't get a damn thing."

Maybe.

Not...m-me...

Maybe not.

Max stared at Quinlan's still body. The bandages covered him from neck to foot. So many wounds. Some small and light, designed just to tease, to let him know that the pain was coming. Others deep. Meant to hurt. Meant to make Quinlan suffer.

The door behind Max opened with a soft swish, but he didn't glance back.

"I wanted you to know," Samantha said quietly, "the suspect died about five minutes ago."

His eyes were on the thick bandages that covered Quinlan's left hand. "Good."

"Two slugs were pulled out of him. We're going to run a ballistics test and see if they match up with Frank's gun."

Quinlan barely appeared to breathe, but then, the doctors had pumped him so full of drugs that he would seem dead to the world. *Painkillers.* Max had been told Quinlan would be out the rest of the night. "What's going to happen to him?"

Jesus, what a mess. A sick, sad mess.

"The team will run a full investigation of the scene before determining anything."

Max rose from the bed and turned to pin her with his stare. But she wasn't looking at him. Her eyes, narrowed, distant, were on the bed.

He stepped in front of her, blocking her view of Quinlan. Making her see *him*. "He's not going to jail." Jail wasn't for his brother. The guy wouldn't survive there, and dammit, Quinlan didn't *deserve* to be there. "He didn't know what he was doing. He didn't know—" *Not like me.*

"It appears he thought the kidnapper was coming back." Now her eyes were on him. "And he attacked. In the dark, he couldn't see what was happening—or who was coming for him—not until it was too late."

Blood soaking Frank's clothes. The knife embedded in his throat.

Max drew in a long breath. "The press is going to be all over this."

"We're taking care of the press. Agent Kenton Lake is on top of it."

He'd better handle them. "My family has been through enough." With more to come. The funeral. Quinlan's treatment.

"I know."

His gaze traced her face. Damn but she was lovely. Staring at her made him ache.

"He's not going to jail," Max said again, aware that his voice was too rough. Behind him, the machines hooked up to Quinlan steadily hissed and beeped.

Samantha didn't speak. Her stare darted to the bed,

then back to him. "I'm sorry about your stepfather. If there's anything I can do…"

He stiffened at the familiar spiel. The same refrain that everyone always offered.

She swallowed and turned away. "We're going to keep two guards outside of your brother's room."

"What? Why?" All the kidnappers were dead.

Her hand was on the door. "We have to be absolutely certain that the people who took your brother are—"

"*They're dead.* They're all fucking dead."

Samantha wasn't looking at him. "We haven't determined that yet, and until we know *exactly* what we're dealing with, the guards stay." She glanced over her shoulder. "And that's *my* order."

Tension had his temples throbbing. "You really think someone else could still be out there? Someone who might want to hurt Quinlan?"

"I think it's a possibility, and I'm not going to leave your brother unguarded until we know for sure."

"*I'll* get guards. I'll hire some, bring them in—"

"You can do that, but the agents are going to stay on duty until the SSD is satisfied." She pulled open the door.

"That's it?" The words tore out. "You're done now?"

Samantha stopped. "I told you, we're going to finish the case."

He caught a glimpse of a guy with close-cropped black hair and saw the flash of a badge. Screw who heard. "I was talking about us." *Look at me.* She didn't. "You're just walking out."

"Isn't that what you want?" So soft.

And then she was gone before he could tell her that hell, no, that wasn't what he wanted.

You pushed her away. Told her to leave.

Max whirled around and headed back to the chair near Quinlan's bedside. He wasn't leaving, wasn't going to chase her.

Not yet.

Six hours later, Quinlan's eyes opened. His hand moved first, jerking against the sheets, and Max leaned forward at the small movement.

"Quinlan?"

His eyes fluttered and opened in a squint. Quinlan blinked as fear filled his gray gaze. His mouth opened—

"It's okay." Max grabbed his stepbrother's right hand. "You're safe."

Quinlan's head turned toward him. Slowly, carefully. "M-Max?"

"Yeah, yeah, it's me." Max blew out a hard breath and punched the call button for the nurse. "Everything's all right. You're safe."

Quinlan's gaze drifted around the room, tracking to the left, then to the right. "H-hospital?" he rasped.

"You're all stitched up." Max tried to smile but the move just felt awkward. "In a few days, you'll be as good as new." But he'd carry the scars inside and out.

A deep furrow pulled down Quinlan's brows. "Wh-what happened? I don't…" His eyes widened. *"That room."* His left hand flew up as the beeping machines screamed. "They…c-cut off my finger…."

And tried to slice him apart.

"Said—said I wasn't w-worth…anything…" His voice broke. "Said D-dad wouldn't…" He stopped. Didn't seem to breathe. *"Dad!"*

Shit, shit.

Quinlan looked up at Max. "Where's Dad?" The question came softer but was laced with fear.

The door opened behind Max. He looked back and saw a nurse bustle in. "He's awake!" she said, smiling.

Max gave a grim nod. He tried to step away from the bed.

"Dad?" Quinlan's fingers clamped down on his wrist.

Did the guy remember? Max didn't want to tell him this.

Quinlan stared at him, his gaze searching Max's face. "I-I…didn't…" His hand fell away, and he shrunk back against the mattress. "Not a dream…" A hard sob broke from his chest, and he shuddered. "N-not…a-a…" His whole body shook, and his breath heaved out.

"Calm down, sir!" The nurse bustled past Max. "Everything's all right."

But the machines were going crazy.

"It's okay!" she told Quinlan, grabbing for the IV bag. "You're in a hospital. You're—"

"Dead." Such a low whisper.

Max couldn't lie to him. He nodded.

"Wh-what?" The nurse glanced up with surprise.

Quinlan's eyes closed. "Oh, God, *Oh, God, it…was me…*" Tears leaked down his cheeks.

As his brother cried, Max stood there helpless knowing there was nothing he could do.

"I killed him."

• • •

Sam spun away from the hospital room. The sound of Quinlan's sobs tore at her heart.

Dammit, the last thing I expected.

Frank Malone shouldn't have been at that scene. It should have been a rescue mission. Not body recovery. She yanked out her cell and called Luke's number. He answered on the second ring. "Tell me you've got something on Frank's phone," she said.

A rustle of air. No, his sigh. "The number went back to a disposable cell, one we found here, in the same damn room that they kept Quinlan in."

Luke was still at the crime scene. She knew that he was searching the area and going over every inch with the investigation unit.

Her eyes squeezed closed. "Are we missing something?" *Someone.*

Not...m-me.

"Ramirez is at The Core, talking to the manager," Luke said. "He found out that Milano was hired on at that place just four days before Jeremy Briar went missing."

"From then on," Sam said, rubbing her aching temples, "Milano watched every move the cops made." And he'd taken more men, with the authorities right beside him. Damn ballsy.

"And there's something else you should know," he continued. "The money isn't here."

Her eyes opened. "It wasn't at Veronica's."

"Either the perps stashed it somewhere before hell came to town, or—"

Or someone else had the money. And if someone else was out there...

Then the nightmare wasn't over.

• • •

By the time Monica and Luke made it home, the clock was edging past nine a.m.

The door closed with a soft click behind them, and Luke's sigh whispered to her.

She turned and caught his hands, pulling him close. "This isn't your fault." But she'd seen the guilt in his eyes. When it came to the victims, Luke always took things personally.

A muscle flexed along the hard line of his jaw. "We had the perps' location. If we'd just gotten there fifteen minutes sooner, Frank Malone would still be alive." He shook his head. "I don't even know how he got there. He *shouldn't* have been there."

Monica stood on her toes and pressed a light kiss to his cheek. "The perps wanted him there. It was part of their plan." Luke understood that, but right then, Monica knew that emotion ruled him.

It often did.

"Come on, let's get in bed," she said. More questions would come soon. More interviews. More crime scene searches. But for a few hours, it would just be the two of them.

Luke nodded slowly and stepped forward.

Monica didn't move. Her heart drummed faster. This wasn't the perfect time. She'd thought to wait for romance and—*hell.* Her fingers were shaking.

"Monica? Baby, what is it?"

"I love you," but she knew that he already realized that. Now for the hard part. "And I-I…" A deep breath. "Yes, I want to marry you."

And just like that, she was in his arms. The death and

the blood were pushed away, and it was just her and Luke. He was smiling and holding her tight, and in that moment, she was happy.

His mouth took hers in a deep, long kiss.

Sometimes, it wasn't about the killers and victims.

Sometimes, it was just about life.

CHAPTER *Twelve*

Sam wasn't much for funerals. She stood away from the gravesite, hanging back beneath the yawning branches of an oak as she watched the graveside service.

Max was there, dressed in a dark suit, his face grim. Sunglasses hid his eyes, but she knew that he wouldn't be crying.

Quinlan stood beside him. Pale. Weak. No sunglasses for him, and she saw him swiping away tears with the back of his hand.

Beth hovered at Quinlan's side. She'd wrapped her arm tightly around his waist. Beth wore a stylish black dress and a small black hat perched on her blond hair.

No tears from her either. Mascara stains probably wouldn't go so well with that perfect image.

Sam eased back but kept watching.

At least two dozen mourners were gathered around the gleaming coffin. A giant stream of red roses covered the lid. Blood red.

They'd delayed the funeral until Quinlan could be there for the service. And there he was.

Frank Malone would be in the ground soon, and then the family would gather for the reading of the will. Sam would be there for that part, too—courtesy of orders from Hyde.

But for now she watched and waited.

Quinlan shuffled forward, with Beth close to offer help. Did he know about her secrets?

Quinlan bent down and placed a trembling hand on the casket. Sam saw his lips move as if he were talking to Frank. Maybe he was. He could be telling his father that he was sorry. Maybe whispering good-bye. After a moment, Quinlan straightened and walked away, his head down.

One by one, all the other mourners followed suit. Some approached the casket. Some just walked away. Soon they were all gone.

All but Max. His shoulders weren't hunched—they were thrown back, strong, and he wasn't looking at the coffin. No; he'd shifted his position. Even with the sunglasses on, she knew he was looking at her.

Sam just waited. Taking his time, Max came to her. A slow, deliberate stride brought him under those hanging limbs and close to her.

"I thought the SSD was giving us some space," he said. His sunglasses reflected her image back at her.

The SSD *had* been staying back. Not anymore. Hyde wanted the gloves off, and he wanted the interrogations to begin.

"Can't even give us time at the grave, can you?" Anger boiled beneath his carefully controlled surface.

"There have been some...developments," she told him. *Like the fact that the money is gone. Gone.* The SSD had searched every location linked to the crimes and the perpetrators. They'd turned up nothing. "I wanted you and Quinlan to be aware that there is a very strong possibility another suspect was involved in the kidnapping."

He took off his sunglasses. His blue stare locked on her face. "Any agent could have come and told me this."

She knew what he meant. "I requested the assignment." She'd needed to see him.

"I haven't heard from you in six damn days."

Her breath caught. Did that mean he'd *wanted* to hear from her? "You wanted space. You were grieving." One shoulder lifted, fell. *Staying away had ripped me apart.* She kept her voice level, saying only, "Hyde gave orders that the family was to have privacy." But she'd thought about him. No, she'd worried about him.

"Hyde." Max's lips twisted. "Yeah, from the sound of things, he gives a lot of orders." His head inclined toward her. "Why'd you ask for this job?"

"Because I wanted to see you." She couldn't get more honest than that.

He looked away, glancing back over his shoulder at the grave. "When I close my eyes at night, I see you." His gaze slowly came back to her. "What did you do to me?"

She shook her head. "No, Max, I—"

"*Max!*" Quinlan's yell.

She took a quick breath. "The cars are leaving." The black limo waited up at the front with the back door open. "You need to go." She'd see him at the house. This wasn't the end. Not even close. Hyde wanted to know what the will said.

So did she.

Max caught her hand. "We both know you're going for

the will reading." The faint lines around his eyes deepened. "What is it? Your boss thinks maybe I had something to do with all this? That I tortured my brother with some sick idea that he'd attack my—"

"We believe the kidnappers planned to kill Frank." She could reveal that. "Calling him, telling him the location—we think it was a setup. We found the phone records. We have proof that Frank received a call from a cell phone recovered at the scene, so we *know* they lured him there."

His fingers tightened. "You think I set him up? For money?"

"No, I don't." Honest. But Hyde wanted more than her belief. Hyde wanted cold, hard evidence.

"I'm not getting a damn thing from that will." His thumb brushed over her wrist.

"*Max!*" Not Quinlan's cry this time. Beth's. The SSD would be getting to *her* very soon. Kim had already dug deeper into her past. Now it was time for a trip to the SSD and a one-on-one interview.

"I believe you." And Sam meant it. She'd started trusting someone again—him.

"Should have been different," he said. "A different time…"

"Different place." She forced a smile. So much lay between them. Half-truths. Blood. Death. Was there any going back from that? Could they even try?

His left hand lifted, and his knuckles brushed over her cheek. "I wanted you from the minute I saw you."

Her heart jumped.

He dropped her hand and stepped back. "I still do. Probably always will."

• • •

Sam and Jon waited outside the lawyer's office. When the door opened and she saw Max's face, Sam snapped to attention.

"*Why are they here?*" Beth's fierce demand. Her grip on Quinlan was still deathly tight.

Max strolled toward them. The lawyer, Kris Jared, followed right behind him. Max shook his head, and his gaze drifted from her to the ever watchful Ramirez. "I got it all," he said with a tiger's smile.

Not what she'd been expecting.

"*Only* until Mr. Malone turns twenty-five," Jared interjected, wiping a sweaty brow. "Then Frank Malone's estate will revert back to his biological son, Quinlan."

Holding it in trust. Sam gave a nod. Okay, right. The SSD agents had known this outcome was a possibility. Squaring her shoulders, she faced Quinlan. "I know this is a difficult day for you…"

He blinked at her. "You…you're my brother's girlfriend."

She didn't look at Max. Or Ramirez. "I'm Special Agent Samantha Kennedy, and I've been working your case." She kept her voice low. Others were around, too eager to hear and run to the news. Every day, a new story appeared in the papers or on the news about Quinlan.

It was a good thing that Hyde had called Kenton Lake in from the Virginia office to help with the press. So far, the media had an insatiable appetite for the kidnapping case. The more lurid the details, the more they fed.

The fact that the other two surviving victims were back in town and broadcasting their story on every news channel wasn't helping. Those two victims thought they were safe now. They just might be dead wrong.

"I already talked to the other woman." Quinlan's mouth tightened, and he glanced at Jared. "Daven—"

"Monica Davenport," Sam inserted smoothly. Yes, Monica had wanted to talk to him right away. She'd only been able to talk with Quinlan briefly, though, before his lawyer had swooped in and closed them out. They'd had the options of forcing an immediate sit-down with Quinlan—and letting the press make them look like the big, FBI assholes who were attacking the injured victim—or waiting until he was out of the hospital. They'd waited.

Quinlan was out of the hospital now, and although she understood his situation was damn painful, she had to bring him in. The waiting game was over.

"This isn't the time…" Jared began, huffing with indignation.

Max just watched them with inscrutable eyes.

"We've given you time," Ramirez said as he kept his arms loosely at his sides. "Time's up."

Sam held Quinlan's gaze. "Tomorrow morning, we need you to come into the FBI office and answer some questions for us." Deliberately, she let her stare drift to Jared. "You and your lawyer should check in at nine a.m."

"You actually suspect my client of—"

She raised her hand. "Save it, Jared. We have routine questions for him." Questions that the lawyer had blocked in the hospital. And with the press raining down on them, the SSD had allowed the delay.

But they'd kept a constant eye on Quinlan.

An eye that told them that, despite his injuries, Quinlan

had spent last night with his father's mistress. Grieving? Hurting? Yes, undoubtedly.

And screwing.

"We need you in the office tomorrow," Sam said again. Then she turned her attention to Beth. "And we'll need you, too, Ms. Dunlap."

Beth's lips parted in an outraged gasp. "Me? Why would you need—"

"We have some background questions for you," Ramirez said flatly, and Sam caught the woman's slight flinch.

Yes, Beth, we know. A past can be an inconvenient thing.

Beth fired a fast, nervous glance Quinlan's way.

And this was the hard part. Sam turned her attention to Max. She found him staring at her with too-watchful eyes. "And we'll need you there, too," she said.

He didn't blink. Damn but it *hurt* to see his eyes so blank like that.

"I'll be there." He inclined his head.

"Thank you." She wanted to say more, but didn't have the words to offer comfort to him. Sometimes, the job sucked. Ramirez took her elbow, and they both stepped back.

"I don't—your girlfriend's an *agent*?" Quinlan's voice seemed too loud. "*What the hell?*"

She didn't hear Max's response and maybe that was a good thing. Because right then, she wasn't sure that she wanted to know what he had to say.

When someone pounded on her door just after midnight, Sam was awake. Awake, lying in bed, and staring up at the ceiling. Her heart lurched at the hard thumps, and she jumped to her feet. Her hand automatically dove into the nightstand drawer—going for her gun.

This time of night…

She hurried down the stairs of her townhouse. The pounding came again, harder now.

Sam peered through the peephole and saw Max. She wrenched open the door.

He froze with his hand still up. Raindrops glistened in his hair and clung to his wet coat. The chill air slipped inside, raising goose bumps on her arms.

"You think you need that?" he asked, and she followed his gaze to the barrel of her gun.

She kept her hold on the weapon. "What are you doing here, Max?"

"I traced your name. Traced *you*. Should have done it long ago." The words were deeper and darker than she'd heard before.

Understanding hit. "You're drunk."

"I wish."

Lightning streaked across the sky behind him.

"You're a genius." His hands slapped against the wood on either side of her door. "How many degrees did you get from MIT?"

She shook her head. "Why are you here?"

His gaze seemed to burn her.

"*Why?*" she demanded.

"Because I needed to see you." He leaned forward. Max ignored the gun as he caught her chin in his hand and tipped her head back. "I just needed you." His lips crushed hers. His mouth was hard, hungry, wet from the rain, and she wanted him. Her lips parted, and Sam tasted whiskey on his tongue. Whiskey and…him.

Her mouth widened. She needed more of him. Her left hand pressed against his chest, right above his heart that raced so fast beneath her fingers. His tongue thrust into her mouth, and she moaned in her throat, a low rumble, even as her breasts tightened with hunger.

More.

His tongue swiped against hers. His head lifted. Slowly, so slowly. "I figured out something tonight."

She fought to keep her breathing steady. Okay, he was playing it cool. She could do it too. "What's that?"

"*We're not over.*"

She knew her eyes widened.

"Work your case. Do whatever you have to do, but we're not ending, not yet." A pause, then his lips kicked up on one corner in a rough half-smile. "That is, unless you tell me to drag my ass out of here."

She didn't say anything. One hand stayed over his heart and one hand clamped around her gun.

His gaze searched her face. "We started . . . at the wrong place. Too fast. Too hot."

But she shook her head. He didn't understand. "No, we started just right." He'd been what she needed. Sex. Pleasure. No past. No future. And now . . .

A blast of thunder broke the night. Sam inhaled sharply. "Come inside." She turned away and headed toward the desk. The door clicked shut behind him. The snick of the lock seemed a bit too loud.

She opened the drawer and put her weapon inside.

"You trust me, don't you?" he asked.

With her back to him, Sam hesitated.

The wood groaned beneath his feet as he walked toward her, then his hands caught her and wrapped around her shoulders. "You know what I've done."

She stared at the closed drawer of the desk.

"They say everyone's got the capacity to kill..."

If pushed far enough. Yes, she believed that.

"...but we both know I've crossed the line." A stark pause. "And if I had to protect someone I loved, I'd do it again."

The hands that held her had killed. Her gaze shifted to her own hands. Pale. Small. But they held her gun so well.

"I want you to know, though," he said, and his breath blew lightly over her ear, "that I didn't have anything to do with the kidnapping. With any of them. I don't need Malone's money. I don't want it. As soon as Quinlan turns twenty-five—just a year and a half to go— it's his."

Her breath hissed out, and she turned toward him. "Max..."

"I've always tried to protect the people in my life, but no matter what I do, they get hurt." His gaze burned bright. "*They get hurt,* and I can never stop the pain."

She swallowed. "Wh-where is Quinlan?" The FBI still had a team watching him. One phone call, and she'd know instantly where he was.

A muscle twitched in Max's jaw. "He's back at Frank's, with Beth. I hired bodyguards for him. They'll stay with him, 24–7, until we're damn sure he's safe." His hair was slick from the rain. "I just...I had to see you."

Sam leaned toward him. She wouldn't ever forget his eyes in the hospital. All that rage had been directed right at her. "Max, I'm sorry about the way this went down." Because, yes, she felt guilty *as damn hell.*

"You busted ass to find him." He shook his head. "What those bastards did—that was them, not you."

Her eyes watered—stupid contacts, had to be them—and she blinked.

"I tried to sleep, but every time I closed my eyes, I saw you."

Oh, damn. Sam admitted, "I didn't even try." Because he'd been all she could think about.

"Fuck." He pulled her even closer. His clothes were wet, but she didn't care. "*I need you,*" he growled.

When they kissed this time, she was desperate for him.

A thin cotton t-shirt covered her breasts. A pair of old jogging shorts skimmed her thighs, and she wanted them off. Wanted her clothes gone. Wanted his on the floor.

Wanted him on the floor.

No, the bed. Do this right. This was different. Not just sex.

Not. Just. Sex.

"You're wet," she whispered against his lips. "G-get out of those clothes." She licked his lower lip. Nipped him.

A shudder worked over his body.

Her gaze bored into his. "Come to bed with me." Her hands caught the bottom edge of her t-shirt, and she pulled it over her head. She tossed the shirt to the floor, let him look, then walked away—slowly, carefully, knowing that he watched her every move.

Sam climbed the stairs. She heard his footsteps behind her. *He's coming.*

At the top of the stairs, she pushed down her shorts and ditched the panties that would only get in the way. *Look back.* Sam glanced over her shoulder. Max was halfway up the steps. His shirt was gone. That chest—oh, how she loved those sexy muscles.

His stare was like a hot touch on her skin. And he would be touching her soon. Touching every inch of her. Just as she'd touch him.

She went into her bedroom. Dark, so dark. She liked the dark. Always had. Things were softer in the dark. It was easier to hide in the dark.

Sam went to the bed and slid beneath the covers.

His footsteps were muffled by the carpet upstairs, but she could all but feel him. Sam knew the instant he walked into her room.

Closer, closer...

Her eyes had adjusted to the dark, and she could see his silhouette looming near the edge of the bed. Her hand lifted and touched the flat planes of his stomach. Hot flesh. Her fingers slipped down. His pants were gone. His cock was up. Straining, thick, and more than ready. Her hand curled around him. She pumped that hard flesh. Once. Twice.

Max caught her hand and locked his fingers around her wrist. He climbed into the bed and surrounded her with his strength and his scent. His mouth took her breast, closing over the nipple as he sucked.

Her back arched off the bed. Sam bit her lower lip. *Yes.*

"Don't hold back." His breath blew over her tight nipple. "I want to hear you." His hand eased its grip on her wrist. He stretched over her, reaching for the nightstand. The lamp light flickered on, too bright, and she blinked. "And I want to see you," he said. "Every bit of you."

No hiding in the dark. No pretending to be someone else. No pretending at all.

He'd risen over her. His gaze weighed her, and Sam

realized he *knew*. Her secrets. Her fears. He could see everything. Maybe he'd always seen.

"Not just sex between strangers." His whisper had her tensing. His palm slid down her stomach and curled around her hip. "I want more."

She'd give more. This time, to him. Her legs parted and eased open for him. He could thrust inside, could take her and—

"No."

An ache lodged in her heart, like she'd been punched, right there. "Max?"

Another swipe of his tongue over her nipple. The light score of his teeth against her flesh. "I'm going to watch you. I'm going to see everything."

He already did. But his hands were on her—lifting her, turning her, and the covers rustled beneath her body.

Max stretched out on the bed. His eyes glittered, and he waited. His cock glistened, and he waited.

Sam rose above him. She put her knees on either side of his hips, and her sex brushed over his cock, a long, slow, slick glide because she was ready, too. Had been, since that first kiss downstairs.

The light seemed too harsh as it shone on them, but she knew it was just a small glow that barely drifted past the bed. *Too bright.* There was no hiding now, not from him or from herself.

His fingers were warm and strong on her hips, and when she arched up, the broad head of his shaft pushed just inside her sex.

Flesh to flesh. So tempting...

Swallowing, she eased back up. Fumbled. "I-I don't..." She didn't have protection near the bed. She did have a box of condoms in the bathroom, shoved in the back of her linen closet.

"Nightstand." His breath blew over her skin. "I put one down before I got into bed."

Her gaze shot to the left, and she found the foil packet. Her hands trembled when she grabbed it, and Sam knew he saw. She ripped open the packet, pulled out the condom, and eased it down his shaft as quickly as she could.

His body stiffened beneath hers. His muscles were so taut and hard.

Her fingers wrapped around the base of his cock, and she guided his shaft into her, positioning him just right—then she pushed down in one fast glide, taking him deep.

"Samantha!"

He filled her completely, stretching her, and for a moment, she hesitated. Not sexy and sure now. Instead, she was lost, floundering—

And he could see. Her eyes squeezed shut.

His fingers eased down, caressing her abdomen, then pushing between her legs. His thumb pressed against her clit and a shiver worked over her. "Easy." His whisper.

But she didn't want easy. Fast, hard, wild.

"*Easy*," he said again, and her eyes opened so she could meet his stare. *Not just sex.* "Kiss me, Samantha."

She bent toward him. The movement pushed her clit against his stroking fingers, just the right touch. His cock shifted and slid along her sensitive flesh. Her mouth touched his. Lips. Tongue. Her sex squeezed him, and there wasn't any more pain. Only pleasure. Her mouth broke away on a moan.

"Better." His growl. "Slow, just . . . slow."

Her hands flattened on his chest. Her knees dug into the

bed, and she pushed up, the head of his cock still inside her. Then she pushed down, so slowly this time, taking his cock one inch at a time.

Oh, damn.

"Again." His order, hard, gritted.

She rose again. Slid down.

"Again."

A little faster now. His fingers worked her clit. Tugged, pressed. His thick length slid easily now, driving into the cream between her legs.

She drove down—just as he thrust his hips up to meet her. *"Max!"*

His hand left her aching flesh, and she could have screamed. *More!* Too close, she wanted—

Max's palms slammed onto the bed, and he rose up, facing her, chest to chest. His mouth took hers in a deep kiss even as he thrust against her, rocking his hips hard, and she loved it, *loved* it. Sam didn't care about the light. She didn't care what he saw. Everything was finally right. He was right.

Sam's nails dug into his chest as she clung to him. The climax was so close that her sex quivered.

His mouth was against her neck now. Licking. Sucking. His hands buried in her hair and held her tight.

"You're so damn beautiful."

He made her feel that way.

His head lifted. His eyes blazed at her. "Beautiful."

Sam trembled and seemed to break apart. The white-hot stream of her climax swept over her, and heat spiraled through her as she came.

And Max watched her.

Her sex contracted around him. Max kissed her, driving his tongue past her lips, and she shuddered against him. Sam rose higher onto her knees, drove down once more, and he came. No, he seemed to erupt in her. His cock jerked, his body went bow tight, and the pleasure rocked between them. So strong. So hard.

Her heart drummed in her ears. She tightened her inner muscles around him, wanting to steal every drop of pleasure from him.

She wanted to freeze time. To stay with him.

To be safe in his arms.

Even if it was just an illusion.

"My brother's gone." Quinlan's gaze wasn't on the full moon that hung just outside his window. His head was bent, and Beth could see him gazing at his left hand. That hand was still wrapped in white bandages, like most of his body.

Not that the bandages had slowed him down any in bed. They'd just been...careful. She knew the difference between sexual pleasure and pain. Beth had learned that lesson a long time ago.

And those damn agents knew about her past.

After taking a slow, deep breath, Beth crossed to him and pressed a kiss to his bare shoulder. "You know where he is." *With her.* Unspoken, but it hung between them.

His body tightened. "She's an FBI agent?"

That had been news to her. Dammit. All her plans... "I just thought she was his latest screw." Max liked variety in his women, and she'd even thought about making a play for him once or twice.

Quinlan turned toward her. "She is the latest. His lover

and an agent." The moonlight slid over his face. "They told Max no cops. They *told* him, and he broke the rules."

"And your father died," she said softly. Beth figured she should probably feel badly about that. She didn't. No more screwing the old bastard and wearing that stupid smile, the lying smile that said she loved having his small dick inside her.

Quinlan flinched. His uninjured hand balled into a fist. "When I go to sleep, I see my dad. The agents shined their flashlights on us, and I was over him, and his blood was *everywhere*."

Beth swallowed. Okay. She didn't want to hear this. "Don't think about it." Her hand curled around his arm. "Come back to bed." The rumpled bed sheets waited for them. If he gave her the chance, she could make him forget almost anything.

His gaze held hers, and for an instant, anger flashed across his handsome features. Anger and...disgust? "You were in his bed just nights ago," Quinlan muttered. "He's not even cold in his grave, and you're back with me."

If he expected her to blush or feel some kind of shame, he had the wrong woman. "I was with you while he was still breathing." So easy to do—all it took was a quick walk down the hallway. But Quinlan had been able to give her what she needed when Frank hadn't even been able to come close. "Now things are just easier for me."

He shook his head. "I can never tell for certain." A brief pause, and his eyes narrowed. "Are you really as cold a bitch as you pretend to be?"

A smile curled Beth's lips. "Maybe." Her heart pounded too fast. *Maybe not.* "And are you really the lost little rich boy that you pretend to be?"

His lips took hers. Softly at first, then harder, *harder*. Because he knew what she liked. "Maybe," he whispered against her mouth. He moved to face her fully, and his cock, aroused, thick, so ready, pushed against her legs.

Maybe not.

CHAPTER *Thirteen*

A few cases back," Samantha's husky voice floated in the darkness, "something happened to me." She lay in bed next to Max, her hand on his chest and her head turned so that their eyes met. The scent of sex and woman hung in the air, making Max want more.

With her, he always wanted more.

But an echo of pain drifted through her words and Max's body tightened. "What?" Her hand slipped off his chest, and he missed that touch instantly. "Samantha?"

"I was working a case down in Mississippi. The Watchman case."

The name clicked. "That bastard who was killing women?"

"Not just killing them." Still husky and soft. "He tortured them first. He turned their worst fears into reality."

Max didn't like where this was going. He reached for her, curling his hand around her hip and pulling her next to him. "You stopped him?"

A broken laugh. "If only." The click of her swallow was painful to hear.

"My plane had just landed in Jasper, and I was walking through the terminal. Well," she gave that same weak laugh, one that held no humor, "that's what they tell me, anyway. I don't really remember much about the airport. I just remember waking up and being tied to a chair in some cabin."

When she sucked in a sharp breath, Max realized that his fingers had pressed too tightly around her hip. He forced his hold to ease. "What did he do?"

Her lashes swept down. "Does anything scare you, Max?"

You do. "I was scared as hell that I wouldn't get Quinlan back alive. When I got to the hospital and found my mother in a coma because she'd overdosed on her pain pills, yeah, I was scared." Terrified. "I know fear. Everybody does."

"But you're scared for *others*." Her lashes rose. "You're like Monica. Both of you—you're strong."

"So are you." Absolute certainty.

The covers rustled as she shifted against him. "I need to—I have to get up."

He didn't want her to move, but he wouldn't force her to stay with him. So he pulled back his hand and let his fingers graze her silken skin as he released her.

Samantha all but jumped from the bed. She hurried to the vanity and picked up a robe. Her arms shook a bit as she pulled it on and tied the belt. *Protecting herself.*

She paced a bit, and then stopped near the side of the bed. He eased up, sitting, and kept the sheet over his hips as he waited. This moment was important for her, and he wouldn't rush her, even though he was desperate to find out—

"If I'd been stronger, he wouldn't have broken me so quickly." Her arms crossed over her chest. "By the end, I was begging him to let me die."

The nightmare she'd had—*dammit.* Max was out of the bed and on his feet in an instant. So much for holding onto his control. He needed to hold her. His hands closed around her upper arms and he pulled her against him. "What did he do?"

"I told you before. When I was a kid, I-I almost drowned at my parents' lake house."

And she'd said her mother…hell, *she didn't even notice because she was so drunk.* Not like he'd forget that story any time soon.

Her breath heaved out. "I hated the water after that. *Hated* it. My mom—she started working to get sober, and when she was better, she wanted *me* better."

"You? What was wrong—"

"Every time she tried to get me to so much as dip my toes in the pool," she said, cutting across his words, "I started shaking. If I thought I'd have to get in the water, I'd have a panic attack. My mom took me to see some shrinks. About half a dozen of them. They said I had hydrophobia—"

She broke off and shook her head. "Like I needed those guys to tell me that I was afraid of the damn water."

"It's normal to be afraid after an event like that."

"So they said," she murmured. "They also said that I could work my way past the fear." She breathed out a long sigh. "But I just said screw 'em. I didn't like the water, and I sure didn't want to go jumping in it again."

And then the Watchman had come along.

Her gaze darted to his, and Samantha said, "When I woke up, tied in that chair, I heard the water lapping nearby, and I knew what he was going to do." The words were so low that he had to strain to hear them. "I just didn't think...I didn't think he'd bring me back so many times."

He shook his head because he had to be wrong. No way did she mean—

"After the fifth time he killed me in that water, then brought me back—*his mouth on mine, his breath in my lungs*—I stopped counting. And I started begging him to let me die."

He dragged her against his chest and held her close to his heart. *No, no, fuck, no.*

"Do you know what it's like to drown?" Her voice was still whisper quiet, but unfocused now and weak.

"No," he bit out and tightened his arms around her. His hands were in her hair, and her body pressed against his. Soft. Warm. Alive.

"Most people think drowning is fast and easy, but it's *not*. Every second stretches for so long, and your throat closes and your lungs burn, and you want that air *so badly*." The words tumbled out in a quick whirl, gaining strength and getting louder. "Your temples explode, and the pain comes in, hitting in waves just like the water, and then—then you start to sink. Your body won't work. You can't kick anymore, you can't claw the water, you can just sink and the water gets darker and—"

"*Samantha!*" He shook her, and her head whipped back. She blinked and seemed to *see* him.

Her lips pressed together. Silence held for a beat of

time, then she told him, "It's not easier the second time. Or the third or—"

Tears slid down her face. His lips feathered over her cheek and tasted the wet salt. "You survived."

"No."

His head lifted, and he found himself staring into the dark pools of her eyes.

"I died that day," she told him. "And no matter what I did in the months after that, I couldn't come back. I couldn't *live*." She swiped her tongue over her lips. "My control was gone. Fear rode me constantly, and I just wanted to break away. I wanted to pretend I wasn't the damaged agent."

He remembered a beautiful woman walking into a smoke-filled bar. Short skirt, long legs, and a smile made for sin. But eyes flickering with fear.

She'd only wanted sex then. No past, no future, just the two of them in the darkness.

She'd left him after only a few hours. Walked away. But she'd come back and found him at that party...

Then the world had gone to hell around them.

"You were supposed to be a one-time deal for me," she admitted, echoing his thoughts, and her eyes were stark. "A chance for me to take control back, to prove I wasn't some broken doll."

A woman who took what she wanted.

Her head shook slowly. The tears had dried on her cheeks. "But I needed you. Just one time, *but I needed you*, and I had to find you again."

He didn't free her. Wouldn't. "Good," he said bluntly, "because if you hadn't come back, I would have found you."

And some of the shadows seemed to lift from her face. "The others all looked at me like I was going to break apart. They expected me to fail." Her eyes searched his. "You looked at me in that bar, and you just saw a woman."

A woman he'd wanted more than breath. "That's what I see right now." No, he saw that she was *strong*. So much stronger than he'd realized.

"I have to do my job, Max." Her chin tipped up a bit. "I have to prove that I *can* do my job, no matter what comes at me."

Why did those words sound like a warning?

"My job brought me to you. It took me to that bar," her smile held a bitter edge, "but I never expected this. I thought I could be safe, that..."

No one would know. Though she didn't speak, those words hung between them. "Then hell came crashing in," Max said.

A grim nod. "And now we have to pick up the pieces." Her sigh slipped easily from her lips. "So you know. You know it all now."

"And you know my past." A killer and a victim. Christ, talk about two worlds colliding. No wonder she'd been afraid when she first found out about him. The real surprise was that she'd ever let him touch her again knowing what he was.

But she'd taken him into her bed so sweetly and given so much. In bed, she'd never shown fear. Just passion.

"You killed to protect." She shook her head. "You were a kid. You were trying to save your mother."

He was a man now, and he'd do the same damn thing again. If that bastard who'd hurt Samantha was in front of him, he'd destroy the asshole.

Her hands rose up, slowly, and curled around his neck. "I just—I thought you should know. If you want us to be together, you deserved to know."

His lips skimmed the top of her cheek. The light, flowery scent of her shampoo teased his nose.

"We can start fresh now," she said. "No more secrets."

His eyes closed, and he held her. Her heart thudded so fast and hard that he could feel the beat against his chest. She'd bared her soul to him.

He lowered his head and took her lips. Trust. Yeah, he knew how delicate it was.

Hard to give. So very easy to break.

Max waited in Interrogation Room Two. His brother Quinlan sat in Room One. And the two other victims, Curtis Weatherly and Scott Jacobson, were scheduled to arrive any moment. Beth Dunlap hadn't shown yet, but an agent had gone to the Malone house to collect her. Apparently, Beth wasn't that interested in walking down memory lane.

Too bad. The walk wasn't really optional.

Sam took a deep breath, pressed her sweaty hands against the front of her pants, and then knocked on Hyde's office door.

When she heard him bark, "Come in," she twisted the doorknob and poked her head inside.

"Sir," Sam sucked in another deep breath, "I need to talk to you."

His dark brows snapped together. "I thought you were supposed to be in interrogation."

She pushed the door closed behind her. "You know— you know I'm seeing Max Ridgeway." And that's why she hadn't understood when she'd been given her assignment that morning. "I can't do an interrogation with him."

His shoulders rolled back. "I thought that was just the cover."

"No, sir, the relationship," *Is that what they had?* "is real."

Hyde dropped the pen that he'd been gripping in his hand. "Then you're off the case."

What she'd thought he'd say. Some of the tension eased from her shoulders. "I understand."

"*Officially.*"

That one word froze her. "Ah, sir?"

The leather squeaked softly as he rose from his chair. Hyde came around the desk, his steps slow, deliberate, and his eyes never left her face. "We've got a problem. Quite a few problems, actually." His head inclined toward her. "But you already know that, don't you?"

That twist in her stomach said yes, she did.

"I don't like this case, Kennedy. I don't like *any* of these damn kidnapping cases. We got all our perps tied up for us—not just tied up—dead."

Quite a body count.

"That's a little too neat for me," he said. "When everyone is dead, no one's left to point the finger of blame."

With an effort, she kept her hands at her sides and hoped she looked relaxed. *Hoped.*

Hyde's gaze weighed her. "We have questions that we need answered. Those victims who were dodging us for weeks, now their asses have finally been dragged home by their parents."

Because their parents thought they were safe now. Was anyone ever really safe?

"Until I'm satisfied with the resolution of the serial kidnapping case, it stays open."

Sam forced herself to nod. "Of course."

"And I need you." His eyes glittered at her. "I still want you to watch the interrogation with Max."

She was already shaking her head.

His hand rose. "Hear me out."

Her head stopped shaking.

"I want you to watch him, and let me know if you think he's lying."

"Sir, I don't—"

"You're the one who *knows* him." Hyde crossed his arms. "Officially, I can't let you to go into that viewing room…"

But *un*officially, he wanted her to spy on the session and report back to him. "I just told you he was my lover." Her gaze didn't waver from his, and she kept her spine straight.

"And if Ridgeway doesn't have anything to hide, it doesn't matter. There's a lot of money at stake here, Kennedy, and even good people can get tempted by the promise of millions."

But Max didn't care about Frank's money. Max had built his own way in the world.

"If he's hiding something," Hyde continued, "then wouldn't you want to know anyway?"

Damn him. "Max isn't hiding anything." She'd finally found someone she could trust, and she'd be damned if she violated *his* trust now. Even for the job.

"We'll see," Hyde said.

Sam turned away.

"I want you to watch that interrogation," he said again with steel beneath his words. "Do your job, Kennedy."

Fine, but she'd do it her way.

• • •

"Are we going to get started any time soon?" Max flicked a glance at the black watch that circled his wrist. "I've got contractors waiting on me."

"We won't keep you too long, Mr. Ridgeway," Luke Dante murmured as he pulled out his chair. He dropped a fat stack of folders onto the table. "We just have a few questions."

Max's eyes narrowed. "You've already asked me a shit-load of questions."

"And I'm going to ask some more." A sharp smile from his least favorite FBI agent.

"Where's Samantha?" His gaze tracked to the mirror behind him. Was Samantha in there, watching him? He'd left her place before dawn so he didn't know if she was even at the Bureau yet.

"I'm certain that Agent Kennedy is on the premises." Luke flipped open a folder while the other agent, Kim Daniels, leaned near the back wall, her arms crossed over her chest. "Now, if you'll be so good as to answer my questions?"

He threw his hands up. "Go right ahead."

"And you don't want a lawyer?" Daniels pressed.

"Don't need one." Because he hadn't done a damn thing wrong. Not this time.

Quinlan Malone looked like death. Sam stared through the two-way mirror, her eyes on the man as he sat hunched at the small table in Interrogation Room One.

"Mr. Malone," came Monica Davenport's smooth voice, "are you certain you don't want a lawyer present?"

"I'm the victim." He rocked forward a bit in his chair.

His bandaged hand rested on the top of the table, a silent reminder of his hell. "Not a damn criminal. I don't *need* a lawyer in here with me."

"Right." Monica opened one of her files.

Sam adjusted the volume control. The interrogations were being video-recorded—they always were at the FBI office—but she didn't want to watch from the control room. She wanted to watch here, where she could see every move and catch every flicker of expression instantly.

"Please tell me about the night of your abduction," Monica said.

Quinlan drew in a shuddering breath. "I-I was at The Core. My brother was there—"

"Max Ridgeway?"

"Yeah, yeah, he was there...with his new girl." Quinlan's lips twisted. "That agent."

"You're referring to Samantha Kennedy?"

"I'm referring to the redhead with the sexy smile." A shrug of his shoulders. "Didn't get her name then."

Sam stared at him. Both of his hands were flat on the table now, and the bandages appeared a stark white.

Monica didn't bat so much as an eyelash. "I'd like a list of the people you talked to at that bar."

Another shrug. "After my brother left, I hooked up with—with—a woman." Quinlan's brow furrowed, and he shook his head. "Blond hair, I think. And she was... she had on a black dress." His breath huffed out. "I *know* I met a girl but I can't remember her, not really."

"What is the first thing you remember after being at The Core?"

His head rose. For a moment, his gaze flickered toward

the mirror, then back to Monica. He lifted his left hand. "Some asshole cutting off my finger."

It would be hard to forget that.

"I passed out after a while." Rough, gravelly. He cleared his throat. "Woke up a few times, and it was always dark. I think—I think I must have been blindfolded. I never saw anyone, just heard their voices."

"Their?" Monica pounced.

"Yeah, yeah, some guy who always whispered. The bastard kept saying he'd 'see how much I was worth,' and there was a girl with him, a woman. When he went to work on my hand, I think she tried to stop him." Softer, he said, "I *think* she tried to."

"So you heard her voice?"

His eyes narrowed. "I heard a woman. I *know* I did."

"And what did she say?"

He stared back at her. The moments ticked by in tense silence.

Then quietly, "Tell me this, Mr. Malone," Monica leaned toward him. "Did you know Adam Warrant?"

Quinlan reached for his glass of water. The guy nearly drained it dry in two gulps. "You already know I did."

"What about Jeremy Briar?"

"I—"

"Here's his picture." Monica slid a photo across the table at him. "It's a picture of him, with you. Taken last year at a frat party at Melline University."

His gaze was on the photo. "He's dead, too."

"Three dead victims, three survivors." Her nails tapped on the table. "You've read the stories, so I know you're aware of the other two survivors." Monica waited a beat then asked, "Do I need to show you the photos or are you going to admit that you knew them, too?"

His gaze jumped to the mirror once more. Anger tightened his features. "I know what you're doing. *I'm not the fucking criminal!*" He shot to his feet. "*I'm* the one those assholes tied to a chair. I'm the one they tried to cut open! *Look at me!*"

Monica was looking. So was Sam. Looking and seeing rage and fear.

"You knew them all," Monica said softly. "Isn't that a big coincidence?"

The chair fell backward and hit the floor with a clatter. "I don't remember Scott Jacobson." His voice fired out at her. "Yeah, I remember having a class with Greg Tyler my freshman year, but I haven't seen the guy since."

"You're the only link we've found between the victims so far."

"I'm not the one you need for this." His breath expelled in a frustrated rush. "Maybe we all hooked up with the same girl. Maybe we pissed off the same psychotic asshole." He spun away and headed for the door. "It's not just me. There's another link. Do your job and find it."

"I have more questions, Mr. Malone." Monica's voice remained low and calm, and she didn't get out of her chair.

"I'm *done* answering your questions." He tossed back a tight smile. "At least, not unless my lawyer gives the all-clear, and after I tell him about *this* conversation, he won't."

Now she did rise. Slowly. "I want a sample of your DNA. It will help us to clear up—"

"No, no! You're not getting *anything* else from me."

Monica's head tilted to the right. "I thought you didn't have anything to hide."

"Yeah, well, that was before I realized you don't give a shit what I've been through. You're just looking to make your damn case." He wrenched open the door. "You don't get it, do you? I thought I'd *die* in that shit-hole. And when they started working on me, I *wanted* to die."

Then he stormed away. Monica turned around to look at the mirror. *No, to look at me.*

I wanted to die. Quinlan's last words. Words she understood too well.

Sam rushed for the door. She stepped into the hallway and appeared right in Quinlan's path. He stumbled and nearly plowed into her. She threw up her hands, stopping him, and freezing them both. "You're going to get past this." Her words blurted out.

He gave a rough laugh. "Bullshit." Quinlan tried to brush past her.

Sam's right hand curled around his arm. "You survived." She'd been told all of this once, too, but . . .

I didn't understand then.

"I *killed* my father." His eyes glittered at her. "I wake up every night, and you know what I hear? That gurgle he made when I drove the knife into his throat. I hear that sound, and it makes me *sick*."

Monica had left the interrogation room, and she stood back, watching them. Sam ignored her. "You need to see a shrink. Start therapy right away."

"Screw therapy." Quinlan wrenched away from her. "Some things, some people, can't be fixed."

"And some can." She took a deep breath. "You're not

alone, Quinlan. Your brother cares about you. He'll be with you every step of the way."

He threw a glance back over his shoulder at Monica. "What do you care? You got the bad guys. Go slap yourself on the back and leave me alone."

Not that easy. "Don't you want to know why?" she asked. "Why they picked you? Why they did all of this to you?"

"I know why." His lips twisted. "I'm an unlucky asshole. Always have been."

Quinlan walked down the hallway, his wounds slowing his steps, but he kept his head up. Then he was gone.

"Is that what you wonder?" Monica asked softly as she moved up close to Sam. "Do you wonder why the Watchman took you that day?"

Sam met her gaze. "I wonder a lot of things, but not that." Right place, perfect victim. He'd been ready for her, but she definitely hadn't been prepared for him. She glanced at her watch. Max would still be in interrogation. Well, maybe. "Excuse me, I need to—"

"Do you still have nightmares?"

Was that her friend asking? Or was it the senior agent who reported directly to Hyde? Sam swallowed. "This isn't about me."

"You can't get over hell so fast. *You* can't, and Quinlan can't."

True. "I have to go." Sam hurried down the hallway and almost missed the soft—

"*I* can't." The words slipped from Monica's lips.

"Did your brother tell you how he came to be in possession of the knife?" Dante asked.

Max stared back at him. "I didn't ask. The guy hasn't exactly been in a talking mood. He lost his father, and he's grieving." And Quinlan shouldn't be at the station. The press would be out there, waiting like vultures to catch the money shot—a photo of Quinlan's damaged hand to splash in the papers and magazines.

Dante stared down at his notes. "The surviving victims indicated they were tied at all times."

Max rolled his shoulders. "Then I guess they were, but Quinlan must have worked loose." That was the only thing that made sense. "He found the knife they'd been using on him, and he got ready for some payback."

But Quinlan hadn't got his payback. *Frank*. Talk about screwed up timing.

"The only fingerprints on the knife were Quinlan's," Kim Daniels said. "We also found traces of his blood on the knife. Frank's blood, of course, and Quinlan's."

"Because they used it to carve him up, and they were smart enough to wear gloves while they did it." Come on, they *knew* this. The agents weren't idiots.

"Our ME noticed something...odd about the slashes on your brother's chest." Dante slid a picture across the table. A photo of Quinlan's torso that must have been taken at the hospital before the wounds had been bandaged. "Do you see this...?" He pointed to the lower left-hand side of Quinlan's stomach. "The wounds are deepest here, then as the line angles up diagonally, the wounds become shallow."

"So?" Damn, there were at least five long slashes on Quinlan. His brother hadn't complained of the pain. Not once.

"The wounds weren't deep enough to hit any major organs—"

"So either the bastard got lucky or he knew what he was doing," Max snapped and shoved the picture away. He didn't want to look at his brother's torn body.

Dante steepled his fingers together and leveled a hard stare at him. "Based on the entry depth of the wounds and the angle, our ME thinks it's possible the wounds were self-inflicted."

Red coated his vision as Max leapt to his feet. "That's bullshit!"

The door squeaked open behind him. Max spun around and found Samantha standing in the doorway. Her gaze darted from him to Luke.

"Did you know about this?" Max demanded and stabbed a finger at the gory photograph. "Did you know they were going to say Quinlan cut himself? Hell, I guess he kidnapped himself, too, huh?"

Silence from Dante and Kim.

"What are you talking about?" Samantha asked and she stepped toward him. "I haven't heard—"

"Brantley took a look at the photos for us," Kim finally said. "He thinks the wounds could have been self-inflicted."

Could have. Shit. "And they *could* have been made by a sick freak who was torturing him," Max blasted.

Samantha crept closer and stared down at the photo.

"The point of entry is deep on the lower left-hand side." Dante pushed the photo toward her.

"I see it." Her breath eased out. "We need to ask Quinlan exactly where the attacker was standing when he sliced him." She glanced up. "And that's not going to be easy because Quinlan isn't in the mood to cooperate with the FBI anymore."

"And I don't blame him," Max tossed back. "I thought we were here to tie up loose ends." *Self-inflicted, my ass.*

"This *is* a loose end," Dante said.

"Bull. This is you trying to pin some sick crap on my brother." Max pointed at the agent. "Go talk to the other victims. Find out what the hell they know."

"I'm afraid that won't be so easy," said a deep voice from the doorway.

Max glanced over his shoulder and found a tall, dark-skinned man waiting there. "We just received word," the guy said, his voice hard and booming, "that the first kidnap victim, Scott Jacobson, won't be making it in for his interview today." This guy had to be the infamous Hyde that he'd read about in the papers.

"He's not coming in?" Dante repeated. "Why the hell not?"

"Because somebody just killed him," Hyde said. "Jacobson's car exploded on his way to our office."

CHAPTER *Fourteen*

Max rushed out of the FBI building, his phone pressed hard against his ear. He had to find Quinlan. Dammit, if anything happened to him...

"Wait! Max, stop!"

He whirled around and found Samantha running after him, her red hair blazing in the sun. Just then, his brother's voicemail picked up. Shit. "Quinlan, call me. Stay with your guards and *call me,*" Max urged before ending the call. His Jeep sat just a few feet away. He'd parked a couple of blocks from the federal building, and he wanted to rush to his Jeep and chase after his brother.

Get to Quinlan. Because his brother wasn't safe. Not yet. Not with Jacobson dead.

"They thought it was him," Max gritted out. "Your friends, those agents—they thought it was *him.*" They'd thought his brother was a killer.

Samantha narrowed the distance between them until just a few feet remained. "You know every option has to be explored."

"Screw that! He's barely walking! He's the victim!"

"I know." Soft. If anyone knew what it was like to be the victim, it should be her.

Max sucked in a sharp breath. "Baby, I've got to go. I have to go and see about my brother. I—"

"I can't let you go anywhere, Max."

Those words were the last that he'd expected her to say. "What?"

"Members of the bomb squad are already on the scene of the Jacobson attack. Scott's car was rigged to explode." Her gaze darted to Max's vehicle. "Now I want you to step away from your car and come with me."

She wasn't serious. Wait; yeah, she was. Max glanced back at his Jeep. "You think it was the kidnapper? That he rigged Jacobson's car?"

"At this point, we can't afford to think anything else." She lifted her hand. "Come with me, Max."

He stepped toward her. "But I wasn't a victim." No one should be coming after him. He should be safe.

The faint jingle of a cell phone seemed to echo in the sudden tense silence. He glanced down automatically. No, wait, that wasn't him—

"Max!" Samantha screamed.

His head whipped back up, and he saw the terror on her face. She lunged forward and grabbed his hand. Then something slammed into his back, something big and strong and *hot,* and he flew forward.

Seconds later, when he crashed onto the pavement, he brought her down with him.

Max lay on the ground, unmoving, with that FBI bitch sprawled beneath him. The bitch had stopped

Max from getting into the Jeep. Just a few more
seconds...

It was really too easy to make bombs these days. A few
keystrokes, and you could find a how-to guide online. Of
course, she'd remembered the basics for the bomb. Not
like a woman could forget that. Just a little matter of getting her parts together.

Simple.

But cleaning up someone else's mess sure was fucking
hard.

The motor revved as the BMW shot down the street,
zipping right past the billowing clouds of black smoke
and nearly plowing into an old lady who didn't have the
sense to stay on the sidewalk.

Dammit, now Max would be cautious, and that bitch
agent would be guarding him.

But there'd been no choice. *Couldn't risk leaving evidence behind.* The bomb had been set that morning. If the
FBI had gone and found it on the car...

They might have linked it back to me. She couldn't take
that chance. So whether Max had been in the car or not,
the Jeep had to go.

She took a fast turn to the left, and the trail of smoke
vanished. Max was in the way, and he'd have to be taken
out. After everything that had happened, it wasn't going
to end like this—not with Max holding the purse strings
and everyone else screwed.

No way.

Killing Max and taking that Jacobson guy out on
the same morning would have been so perfect. The FBI
would've just thought one of the kidnappers had come

after them. They would have directed their attention back to the cases.

"And not to me," Beth whispered, adjusting her rearview mirror. Sirens wailed, and a fire truck flew past her. Since she was clear of the immediate scene, Beth pulled over to the side of the road and did her good citizen routine. She tried to make sure the fire truck and the two police cars swerving past her had enough room.

She waited a bit, giving them ample time to pass, then she pulled back onto the road. She was driving slowly now, carefully.

And planning. Always planning. She hadn't been that old bastard's fuck toy for nothing. No, she'd earned her money and her happiness—and she was getting both. Nothing would stop her. No one.

If she had to kill to get what she deserved, so be it. Not like it was the first time. She'd made sure her dick of a husband got what he deserved. He'd planned to leave her. *Her.*

Instead the cops had been picking pieces of his body off the interstate. Just like they'd be doing with Jacobson.

She just had to be careful . . . *don't get caught.* Her only rule.

And she hadn't been caught before. She'd used her connections, gotten the bomb, figured out how to place it on the car, and learned to make it go *boom.* Her brief stay in prison for that lame solicitation charge had introduced her to a very useful crowd of friends.

Her grin stretched as she drove through the green light. Maybe she'd get lucky. Maybe Max was dead. Maybe a chunk of metal had slammed into his head, into the bitch's head, and taken them both out. *Maybe.*

She'd never been particularly lucky before. If she had been, then her mother wouldn't have been a lying crack addict who'd overdosed at twenty-three, and her old man wouldn't have been a freak who liked to touch little girls.

But she'd fixed that asshole. He'd been in the car with her husband when she'd called to tell them both just how much she loved them.

"Samantha? *Samantha?*" Fear pounded through Max's blood as he grabbed Samantha and rolled her over. Blood trickled into his eyes, and he swiped his hand over his face as he tried to clear his vision.

She wasn't moving. Her eyes were closed. Scratches covered the right side of her face, and when he smoothed his hand down her cheek, she didn't wake up.

No.

Smoke billowed around them. Voices rose, screaming. No, not voices—sirens.

Max glanced over his shoulder. His Jeep had been blown to hell and back. A damn tire was still rolling down the street. If Samantha hadn't stopped him, it wouldn't just be pieces of his vehicle on the road.

His hands shook as he cupped her head. "I need *help!*" he yelled into the smoke. He'd slammed into her when the blast erupted. Hit her hard and taken her down onto the concrete.

Her lashes began to flutter.

"Samantha?"

Her shoulders shifted a bit on the ground.

"What. The. *Hell.*" That furious voice belonged to the guy from before. Hyde. The head of the SSD.

"I need an EMT!" Max shouted as he held Sam.

"You're hurt?" Hyde burst through the smoke. Ramirez, the agent who'd taken out the perp in the park, was right at the man's heels.

"Not me." The scratch on his head was nothing. "Samantha." The fear and the rage boiling inside seemed to be shaking him apart. *Shouldn't have happened.* This nightmare should have been over.

But some asshole was still out there. An asshole who couldn't let the case go. And now Samantha was hurt. She'd damn well been hurt enough in her life.

Hyde tried to pull Max away from her. "No!" His hold tightened. He wouldn't leave her.

"You want me to help her," Hyde snapped out, "then *move.*"

"Max?" Sam whispered, and nothing would have moved him then. Her lashes lifted. Dark eyes stared up at him. "You...okay?"

Him? The first thing she asked was about him? His head bent, and he pressed a kiss to her lips. "You saved my ass, baby." Then she'd scared ten years off his life.

"Ridgeway, get *back.*" Hyde's bark.

Max's gaze held Samantha's. "Are *you* okay?"

"Hit my head..." A weak smile curved her lips. "Just left you for a minute."

"How about you don't ever leave me again?"

Her eyes widened.

A siren wailed, even louder now, and an ambulance braked to a hard stop about ten feet away.

"Scott Jacobson *and* Ridgeway," Ramirez's voice

carried even over the siren's scream. "Sir, I'd say we have a problem."

"A big damn problem," was Hyde's instant response. "I already have officers en route to the Weatherly house. They're taking Curtis into protective custody before his father ships him out again."

"Or before he winds up dead," Ramirez muttered.

Samantha sucked in a sharp breath. Her eyes stayed on Max. "He came after you."

Max couldn't look away from her. Whoever the asshole was, yeah, the guy had come after him, but he'd almost taken them both out.

"I want this scene canvassed!" Hyde ordered as the EMTs broke through, and Max forced himself to ease back from Samantha. *Need to feel her against me.*

"I want access to every surveillance camera within a ten-block radius. Get the footage and get it *now!*" Hyde demanded.

"On it, sir," Ramirez said and backed away.

Hyde's hand clamped down on Max's shoulder. "We're going to find him. This guy's coming on to my turf, planting a bomb blocks away from the FBI. Damn *bold.*"

"Bold" was one word for it. "Crazy" was another. "Why?" Max just didn't understand. An EMT grabbed his arm but he shook free and said, "I'm not getting on the damn stretcher! Take care of her. She could have a concussion." Her eyes were so dark that it was hard to see her pupils.

If they'd both been a little closer to the Jeep...

A dull throbbing burned in his temples. "It's him, isn't it? The bastard who took Quinlan." And they'd been *questioning* his stepbrother just moments before. Oh, Christ...

"*Quinlan!*" He turned on Hyde. "If the guy came after me and the other victim, he'll go after Quinlan too." Or he could have already gone after him. Two car bombings. Why not three? Just how well had that bastard planned? Ice froze his stomach.

"I'm already on it, son," Hyde told him. "I've got two agents and the bomb squad en route to the Malone residence."

"Puppet master," Samantha muttered and winced when the EMT probed the back of her head.

Max's eyes narrowed. "What?"

"One got away from us." Her breath hissed out. "The one...pulling the strings. Someone in the background who was watching...tying up the loose ends."

Puppet master. Who? Who was he?

And where was the bastard?

Beth ran up the stairs, her heart racing. "Quinlan?" Dammit, he was back earlier than she'd expected. His car had been sitting out front when she pulled into the driveway.

This better not mess up her timeline. She'd targeted the attacks while he was supposed to be in the office with those FBI pricks. She'd given him the perfect alibi. No more suspicion, and no more jerkoff stepbrother standing between Quinlan and her money.

"Quinlan, where are you?" She shoved open his bedroom door. Empty. "Quinlan?" She hurried down the hallway. Where was everybody? Two maids were scheduled to work today but she hadn't seen them.

A *thud* came from Frank's room. The crash of breaking glass. Beth ran forward, grabbed the door handle, and shoved open the door. "What the—"

The room was a wreck. Furniture overturned. Mirrors shattered. Pictures broken on the floor. In the middle of the mess, Quinlan stood with his shoulders bowed.

Beth sucked in a deep breath. "Quinlan, what are you doing?" *Not a breakdown, not now.* That was the last thing she needed. Once they were settled, and she had a ring on her finger, then the guy could go nuts. *Not now.*

He bent and picked up one of the long glass shards from what had once been an antique mirror.

"I have the worst luck," he said, his voice so low that she had to strain to hear him.

"What are you talking about?" If the guy wanted to compare piss luck stories—

No. She'd never told Quinlan about her parents. She'd given him just the briefest of details about her past.

"My mom walked out when I was four. She left me with that prick who didn't give a damn about me, and she never looked back," Quinlan said as he turned the shard of glass over in his hand. The point was sharp, like a knife, and the light hit the gleaming tip. "When I was fifteen, he finally called me home from that prison of a boarding school, and why? To introduce me to *her.* The low budget whore he'd decided to marry!"

At least he didn't shove his hand up your pants every damn day. Her own shoulders straightened, and Beth shut the door behind her with a soft click, suddenly very, very grateful that no one else was around. She couldn't afford to let anyone see him this way.

"Quinlan, you need to calm down, honey." Deliberately, Beth pitched her voice nice and low in an attempt to soothe. "You've been through a lot. You're stressed, but this—this isn't helping." Yeah, that sounded like she cared, right? Poor little rich boy. Cry her a damn river.

A bitter laugh broke from his lips. "He never had a space for me in his life, but he had room for *her*. Her and her ex-con son."

What?

At her quick breath, Quinlan's head lifted, and his gaze settled on her face. "You didn't know, did you? Max killed a man. Beat him to death with a baseball bat." His eyes glittered with a feverish intensity. "And my old man still thought he was the golden child. Always comparing me to him, *always* telling me how good old Max was bustin' ass to make a name for himself—hell, yeah, he was, with *my* father's money."

Max had killed a man? She hadn't seen that one coming.

"And when the whore finally got sick, I found out the truth."

"Have you been drinking?" Beth asked him. This *wasn't* like Quinlan. Sure, he bitched and moaned, but he'd never called Katie a whore.

"Not booze. Pills." He raked a hand over his face. "So sick of seeing his f-face. Took more of the pills that damn shrink gave me."

Her tongue swiped over her lower lip. Ah, drugs. She'd used enough of them to keep Frank in line. "We need to get you in bed. All this—" She motioned to the chaos in the room with a wave of her hand. "You could have hurt yourself." He *had* hurt himself. Blood seeped through the white fabric over his abdomen. He must have broken open some of the stitches.

"You know he wanted to give his money to charity? When she was dying…" Quinlan acted like Beth hadn't spoken, and his gaze fell to the mirror shard one more time. "I found out that he wanted to give all the money to the cancer society. Can you believe that?"

Yes. Because even though Frank had been screwing her, the old bastard had actually seemed to love Katie.

"I stopped that. Stopped him." The fingers of his right hand curled tightly around the glass. Too tightly. A drop of blood fell onto the floor. "*Worst fucking luck.*"

Beth climbed over the broken drawers from Frank's chest. She needed to get that glass away from him. The way he was acting, there was no telling what he'd do. And if the rich boy went and sliced his wrists, what would she do then? And what would she get? *Nothing.*

"Then this kidnapping…" His left hand rose. "My dad, *my dad—I see him…*"

Her hand curled around his. "It's okay."

"No." He pinned her with his wild gaze. "It'll *never* be okay again."

A swirl of red and blue lights lit the scene. While firefighters circled the still smoldering wreckage of the Jeep, cops and FBI agents swarmed the street.

"I think it was a cell phone-activated bomb," Samantha said as she stood beside Max. The EMT had finished checking her out after trying to get her in the ambulance, but she'd refused his order. "I heard the ring, and I-I just knew."

He caught her hand and squeezed her fingers. "Without you, I'd be dead."

Hyde walked toward them. "We have a suspect."

"What? *Who?*" Samantha demanded.

Hyde pointed toward an elderly lady, one standing with her hat slightly askew and talking animatedly with Agent Daniels. The lady's shaking hands rose, and she pointed down the street.

"Mrs. Sarah Ann Douglas was almost the victim of a hit and run today." Hyde's head tilted toward the left. "Just after the explosion that took out your car, a woman driving a blue BMW nearly plowed into Sarah Ann."

A woman? A blue BMW...

Max stiffened. No, there were hundreds of BMWs in the city. Just because Frank had one in his garage didn't mean a damn thing.

"Video surveillance at the red light caught the car and license plate. And we just got a hit in the system." Hyde's gaze cut to Max. "We're heading there now, but I thought you might want to come with us."

"Go with you where?" Samantha asked, shaking her head and narrowing her eyes. "Who owns the car?"

Shit. Max answered, the kick in his gut telling him it had to be..."Frank." And the woman driving the car? Hyde's suspect?

Beth.

"It'll never be okay again," Quinlan spat the words at her, "because I just saw the news. Scott Jacobson is *dead.* He was taken by the same kidnappers who took me, and he's *dead.*"

She let horror wash over her face. It was the reaction

that he'd expect. "What? Oh, God, Quinlan, I'm so sorry!"

His left hand flew out and curled around her wrist. The bandages bit into her flesh as he hauled her closer. "I caught the story on TV right before you got here. Max was also targeted. The bomber went after him, but missed."

Dammit. Not next time, though. She wouldn't miss again.

"I had almost convinced them," he muttered, "I had Max's bitch eating out of my hand. The woman nearly *cried* for me, and then you went off and you fucked up everything for me."

Beth blinked, his words slowly sinking in, too slowly. "Wh-what?"

In a flash, he spun her around, and his right arm looped over her body. Her back pressed against his chest. "You're such a dumb bitch," he whispered. "Did you really think I was going to stay with you? Did you think if the money was all mine today, I'd keep you?" His breath blew against her hair.

Real fear began to settle in Beth's stomach. "Quinlan, l-let me go."

The bandaged hand, the hand that she tried not to look at, had her wrist in a too-tight grip.

"You've fucked things up," he said again. "Now what the hell am I supposed to do with you?"

OhGodOhGod...

"I guess this..." He took the shard of glass and he slit open her left wrist.

"*No!*" The scream ripped from her as blood spattered onto the carpet. She shoved back against him, slamming her head into his. "No! Let me go!"

His hold eased. Her wrist and arm throbbed and burned. *Quinlan?* He'd been the one to bring her into the house. He'd set everything up so that she fit into his world.

He'd even been the one to tell her to screw Frank.

Beth stumbled away from him. He'd cut her deep, a long slash from the base of her palm nearly to her elbow. Her fingers curled in, the tips already numb, and a moan trembled on her lips.

"Did you think I loved you?" he asked softly, and Beth's knees buckled as she fell to the floor. Her blood stained the gleaming wood, coating her fingers as she tried to crawl away from him.

"I loved you," she yelled at him. And she had. From that first day, she'd wanted him. Wanted the life that he'd given her.

But he just stared down at her, and she wondered why she'd never seen the ice in his eyes before. *Get up.* No man would make her crawl. She shoved to her feet, stumbled again, and slipped in the blood. He stood there, watching her with his lips curved in a grin and the bloody glass shard held tight in his hand.

"I killed for you," she threw back at him. Didn't he understand? "Why did you—" The drumming of her heartbeat filled her ears. So loud. So fast.

"I needed you to keep an eye on the old bastard. To make sure there were no more changes to his will." Quinlan glanced down at the bloody glass and his lips twisted. "And then there was the added bonus. Every time he screwed you, my father felt so guilty he could barely look at me." A rough laugh. "I liked for him to squirm. He hated himself, and he didn't pay any damn attention to me or the plans I was making."

Her breath expelled in a hard rush, and the fingers of her right hand pressed over the pulsing wound. Her left hand felt totally numb, and blood was pumping out way too fast. "We can fix this," she said, desperate. *All that money.* She'd worked for that money for so long. Screwed. Lied. Killed. The payoff was so close. "Y-you're upset. You didn't mean to—"

Quinlan laughed at her. "Beth, I *meant* to." He took a step toward her, and Beth couldn't help it; she fell back.

The money. She needed that money. Needed the new life it would give her. Not a whore's daughter, not the girl everyone pitied. A new person.

"I'd always planned to kill you," Quinlan said and took another gliding step toward her. "But I'd planned to wait until the cops weren't watching my every move." He lifted the glass. "Change of plans."

"Bastard!"

He lunged for her. Beth spun away, running for the door and screaming as loud and as long as she could.

Someone had to be there. *Donnelley.* He never left. He'd be there. He'd be—

Quinlan grabbed her hair, but she kept running for the door. Blood droplets flew into the air, spraying from her wound.

"You're making a damn mess," he muttered, "one *I'*ll have to clean up."

She twisted the knob and jerked open the door. Her feet sank into the thick carpet.

"Not so fast, bitch." His fingers closed around her neck.

"*Help me!*"

"No one will," Quinlan told her as he wrapped his

arm around her and wrenched her tightly against him. He pulled her back into the room. She kicked and twisted but he held her too tightly. Why hadn't she ever realized how strong he was?

Or maybe she was just getting weak. Because the room was starting to spin, and her face felt too hot, then too cold and—

A hot slice of pain burned her right wrist.

"Have to make it deep enough," he muttered.

Beth blinked and shook her head. She glanced down at her wrists. Nausea rolled in her stomach at the long, thick slits. This wasn't supposed to happen to her. She was gonna have a big house. A driver. Everyone was gonna envy her.

Beth swung out with her hand. She tried to hit him, but her fingers wouldn't work. The drumming in her ears was so loud. But not so quick now.

"You're a fast bleeder, Beth."

Her legs gave way.

"Wonder how long it will take for you to die."

Tears tracked down her cheeks. "I-I...killed for... you."

His smile broke her heart. "And now you're dead, Beth."

No, not yet. She pulled in a deep breath. *Not yet.* Beth kicked out with her leg, aiming hard for his knee.

The sound of sirens filled Sam's ears. The shrill screams made her head ache even more.

"You all right?" The question came from Hyde. He was right beside her and driving too fast. Max was in the back of the SUV, quiet, tense.

Sam nodded then realized that she should speak. "Fine." She'd had to fight the EMTs for her freedom, but no way was she going to miss this.

A caravan of FBI agents and cops raced toward Frank Malone's residence. Going as fast as they could, shooting through intersections, racing over the streets.

"Why?" Max finally asked. It was the first word that he'd spoken since jumping into the SUV. "Why would Beth try to kill me?"

Money.

"The way I see it," Hyde said, "you're the only person standing between Beth's lover and one hell of a lot of money."

Sam glanced back at him and saw Max's jaw tighten.

"Why'd she go after Scott Jacobson then?" he demanded. "He wasn't standing between her and anything!"

"That's a question I'm going to ask her." The caravan made a sharp right turn. Hyde drove behind the lead car. "As soon as I have your stepfather's assistant in custody."

She'd been a fighter. Quinlan stared down at Beth's still body as he stripped off his clothes. She hadn't gone down easy. Beth had fought for every breath.

Not that he'd given her much time to fight.

Naked, he stalked toward Frank's hidden safe. Still hidden—he'd made sure not to reveal its location as he trashed the room. The safe would make the perfect hiding place for his bloody clothes. No one would get inside for a while. His father had made sure to get a crack-proof safe.

But his father had made the mistake of giving Beth the combination.

Quinlan spun the dial easily and heard the soft snick as the lock opened.

And Beth gave it to me.

He shoved his clothes inside. He'd come back for them later, and he'd burn them. For now, he had to get clean, fast, before the cops showed up.

Thanks to Beth, Quinlan knew they'd be coming. The cops and the dicks from the FBI.

He stepped over Beth's body. She'd fucked things for him, but he could still finish his plan. *Would* finish. Nothing, no one, would stop him.

If anyone tried, they'd die.

"Do you think she was part of it all along?" Max wanted to know. "Was she part of this whole sick plan to kidnap them? To take Quinlan?"

Sam wet her lips. The seatbelt bit into her shoulder, rubbing against the same bruised spot that had crashed into the pavement. "Too early to say."

God, I nearly lost him. She hadn't been able to move fast enough. Hadn't been able to get to him. As soon as she'd found out about Jacobson, she'd been terrified for Max. Then she'd heard that peal of sound. Just a cell phone, just a ring...

But Ramirez had told her about his time in the Middle East: how so many bombs were linked to cell phones. One call and the world exploded, thanks to an electronic trigger.

If Sam hadn't heard that stupid little sound...

I would have lost Max. She'd never forget the sight of

him, his eyes intense as he stared at her and fire exploded behind him.

Sam swallowed. Before, she'd feared for her own life. Feared death would come for her—and then that it wouldn't. But tonight, she'd feared for Max.

Just when she thought that she might be getting a handle on this case, the game changed. *Scott Jacobson. Dead? Christ.* The guy had come back because he thought that it was safe. He'd been coming to talk to them.

It seemed to take forever to reach the house. Traffic blocked them, and they had to take a detour away from the snarled roads. Then, finally, they reached Malone's place with brakes squealing and sirens shrieking. And there was Quinlan, standing outside of the house. He was already surrounded by the other agents that Hyde had sent earlier, as well as the team from the bomb squad.

"Quinlan!" Max jumped out of the SUV even before it had fully stopped. He thundered toward his brother. "Dammit, man, where have you been?"

Quinlan blinked and shook his head. Sam hurried toward them even as Hyde barked orders to his men.

"I-I had to clear my head." Quinlan slammed his car door shut behind him. "After the station…" His gaze swept to Sam. "They thought it was *me*, Max. *Me.* I just had to—to get away, you know?"

Max pulled his brother close in a hard hug. "We got trouble, okay? When you saw me call, you should have answered the damn phone." He stepped back, glaring. "After all that's happened, you should have—"

"My phone's dead." Quinlan shifted from his right foot to his left. "With everything going on, shit, I just forgot to charge it. I saw the shrink this morning. He's putting me on more meds—"

"Mr. Malone." Hyde's voice cut through the ramble of Quinlan's words. "Have you seen Elizabeth Dunlap today?"

"Beth?" His Adam's apple bobbed. "Uh, not since this morning, before I-I went in to your office."

But the BMW was there, sitting in the drive.

"Have you been inside yet?" Sam asked him as she pulled out her gun. Hyde already had his weapon ready in his hand.

Quinlan shook his head.

"We're going in the house to search for her." Hyde was telling Quinlan to stand back.

"I'm coming with you," Max said immediately.

"Son, this isn't—"

"Right now, that house is *mine*."

Quinlan's gaze flickered to Max. Sam saw the slight tightening of his eyes.

"Maybe so, but we've got just cause, and you're both staying out here." Hyde inclined his head toward Max. "We all know what happened the last time a civilian went running into a crime scene."

Quinlan stepped back. "A . . . crime scene?"

Max held Hyde's stare. She could see the fierce anger in his blue gaze.

But Hyde wasn't backing down. This was *his* scene. And after a moment, her boss spun away, shouting out orders as the agents lined up.

Sam turned to follow him. Max snagged her wrist. "Watch your back, baby." A gruff order.

She forced a smile to her lips. "These days, I always

do." She wanted to kiss him right then because fear rode her, too. Fear and rage, and she needed to taste him. They were alive. Nothing was going to come between them. Not now.

But Quinlan was there and watching so closely. And Hyde waited. So she walked away.

When the team went in, she was ready. Her fingers curled tight around the butt of the gun. She kept her weapon up, and her gaze roved the house.

First floor—*clear*.

She crept up the stairs, keeping her back to the wall. Hyde was in front of her. Their steps moved in almost perfect sync. He called out for Beth.

No response. But then, had they really expected one?

The team made a fast trek down the hallway. Sam pointed to Beth's room. She'd go in first this time. One, two, *three*. The door flew open with the force of her kick.

Empty.

The agents spanned out. Searched the rooms. No one appeared to be in the house. Where was everybody? Wasn't Quinlan supposed to have guards?

Too quiet.

The door to Frank's room was closed. Sam stared down at the thick carpet around the door, and her nostrils flared. That scent...oh, dammit, she knew that smell.

"*Hyde*." Just a whisper, but his head immediately turned toward her. He took two fast steps her way, then she saw his nostrils widen. His jaw clenched. Yes, he'd caught that telltale odor too.

Hyde raised his hand, signaling her. He'd go in first.

She'd cover him. Her heart slammed into her ribs. *One. Two. Three.*

Hyde kicked the door open. It bounced back, thudding into the wall. He raced inside, crouched low, and Sam swept right in behind him, her body tense, and her weapon ready. Her gaze searched the room, left to right, and her breath hitched when she saw the body.

"Check the room!" Hyde barked as he knelt beside Beth Dunlap.

Sam pulled her gaze from the body and hurried forward. She checked under the bed. Did a sweep of the closets and bathroom. "Clear!" She hurried back to him, already yanking out her radio and calling for backup— backup and an EMT. Though it didn't look like an EMT would be able to help Beth.

Elizabeth Dunlap lay in the middle of chaos. Shattered furniture. Slashed pictures. A broken mirror littered the floor beside her and her fingertips lay inches away from a long, bloody shard of glass.

Beth's eyes were closed, but the blood from the gaping wounds on both her wrists stained the floor. So *much blood*.

Hyde's dark fingers pressed against Beth's stark white throat. "Dammit." He shook his head and rose, staring down at her with shoulders that hunched just a bit. "This wasn't the way it had to end for her." His hands tightened into fists. "Death isn't the only way out."

Max paced behind the police cruiser. He wanted *in* that house. Wanted to know what the hell was going on.

Quinlan sat on the hood of a patrol car, his gaze on the house. "What's taking them so long?"

They'd only been inside mere moments, but it seemed like for-fucking-ever. Max forced his teeth to unclench.

"They're searching for Beth. They have to go over every inch of the house."

"Man, she really tried to *kill* you?" Quinlan ran a hand over his face. "*Beth?*"

"That's what the Feds say." He hadn't seen the footage, but Hyde had been dead certain.

"Aw, man." Quinlan lowered his head. "What the hell is going on? Nothing seems right anymore. Everything is just so screwed up." A shuddering breath eased from him. "*Beth.*"

He stared at Quinlan's slumped shoulders. They hadn't talked much since Quinlan had gotten out of the hospital. Every time he approached him, Quinlan seemed to withdraw. "Are you okay?"

Quinlan's head lifted, and his gaze met Max's. "I'm gettin' by." His lips twisted, and it was a sad sight. "Just when I think everything's gettin' back to normal." A harsh laugh. "But it'll never be normal again, will it?"

No. Max wouldn't lie to him.

"How did you do it?" Quinlan asked as he moved away from the cop car. Max caught the slight wince on his stepbrother's face and knew that the stitches must have been pulling at his skin. "After you killed that guy, how'd you stop the memory from driving you crazy?"

Max tensed. "What are you talking about?" He'd never told Quinlan. There'd never been a need. Frank had made sure his records were sealed. No one in this town—other than the Feds storming his stepfather's house—knew about his past.

Quinlan crept closer. "I know. I *know*. Frank told me about you years ago."

"He shouldn't have said anything."

"He thought you were a damn hero." Max glanced over and caught the narrowing of Quinlan's eyes. "You killed a man, and he thought you were a hero. Wonder what he'd think of me?"

Max just stared at him.

"No hero." Quinlan's hand bunched into a fist. "So what the hell kind of man am I?"

Max tried to figure out what to say.

"Max!" He turned at Samantha's voice. She ran toward him, her face pale. She dodged a few cops. Slipped past the line of cars.

He left Quinlan and hurried to her. Max caught Samantha's hands and held on tight. "What is it? What happened?"

Her gaze darted behind him. He glanced back. Quinlan was there and moving slowly toward them. "I'm sorry," she said, and the words were directed at Quinlan. "But Beth Dunlap is dead."

Quinlan froze. *"What?"*

Dead? "What happened?" Max asked. He hadn't heard any gunshots after the agents went inside.

"It appears that Beth went to your father's room and killed herself." Samantha paused. Her gaze was still on Quinlan. "She slit her wrists and died at the foot of his bed."

CHAPTER *Fifteen*

When the knock came at his apartment door, Max hurried forward, rubbing grainy eyes. He pulled open the door and found Nathan Donnelley waiting for him.

The doctor had a small black bag in his right hand. So damn typical. "I called you an hour ago," Max said.

Donnelley grunted as he came inside. "Do I need to remind you that I don't work for you or your family any longer?"

"Since when? Dammit, Donnelley, you were Frank's private doctor for years. And you just what—walked away?"

"Frank was dead." Donnelley shrugged. "Therefore I wasn't needed any longer."

Max grabbed the man's arm and dragged him over the threshold. "You're needed now." Max slammed the door shut behind him. "Beth's dead."

"I know." Flat. "I heard the report on the news."

Right. Hell, everyone knew. "I need you to check

on Quinlan, okay? He's too quiet. Shit, I'm worried about him."

Donnelley's green eyes raked him. "What is it you want me to do?"

"*Check him.* I don't know; go do whatever it is that doctors do when patients are about to break down." Helpless, yeah, that's what Max was, and he hated it. "Just make him better."

That cold, clinical stare pinned him. "You know as well as I do that sometimes, you can't make people better."

Because Donnelley had been there when Max's mother died.

"But I'll talk to him and see what I can do." Donnelley brushed by him. "Which room is he in?"

"Down the hall. Second door." Max exhaled. "Just so damn much," he muttered. "Every day, something new. I thought this mess was over."

"I'm sure it will be over," Donnelly said, not glancing back. "Soon."

A soft knock rapped on her office door. Sam glanced up, her mind still on the data that she'd retrieved, and mumbled, "Come in."

The door opened, and Kim Daniels stood there with her eyes glinting. "I need you to come with me, Sam."

Sam shut off the screen in front of her, automatically hiding the text. Her brow furrowed as she glanced at the clock: 8:12 p.m. "Okay, just let me finish up…" She'd hacked her way into Nathan Donnelley's personal bank account and found out that the man had barely a thousand dollars in his savings. Since the doc drove a top-of-the-line Benz and flashed a Rolex—yeah, she'd caught sight of that watch—the lack of money set off red flags in her mind.

"Hyde needs us all in his office. The ME finished working on Dunlap, and Hyde wants to go over the report."

Sam jumped up, and the knot of tension at the top of her spine tightened. She followed Kim down the hallway, turned a fast right, and then they were at Hyde's office.

Luke closed the door behind her. "Thanks," she whispered, pushing up the glasses that she'd put on earlier. She'd thought the glasses might help to ease the headache she had. No such luck.

Hyde sat on the edge of his desk. His fingers gripped a manila file. Monica Davenport was to his right. Figured. Ramirez wasn't there. He was still out shadowing Weatherly.

"We've got a problem," Hyde said, and his gaze zeroed in on her.

Her shoulders straightened. "Sir?"

"With the first slash of that glass, the veins and tendons in Beth Dunlap's wrist were cut, and they were cut too damn deep."

Sam could still see the blood soaking the wooden floor.

"Because Dunlap was right-handed, we must assume the initial cut was made to her left wrist," Hyde continued, "and according to the ME, her left hand would have been all but useless within seconds."

Sam's breath rushed out. "But her right was cut—"

Hyde shook his head. "The ME says there's no way Beth Dunlap could have done that on her own. And a tendon was severed there too."

Oh, hell. Sam rocked back, and her elbow slammed into the closed door.

"Sam?" Luke's murmur.

She shook her head. "We didn't see anyone else in the house."

"Because Beth Dunlap told the doctor—what was his name?" Hyde riffled through his papers. "Donnelley? According to him, she said that his services weren't needed any longer."

"And Quinlan told the maids not to come in," Luke said. "He told them he wanted some space to grieve." His lips twisted in a mirthless smile. "But during his grieving time, he was fucking Beth Dunlap. It seems Kerri Grace, one of the day maids, heard them upstairs before she was told to hit the road."

"Upstairs?" Sam asked.

"Kerri said they were in Frank's room this morning." His brows rose. "She told me the, ah, noise was louder than her vacuum."

Fucking and dying in the same place.

"Something else." Hyde's deep voice filled the entire room. "Crime scene techs found two drops of Beth Dunlap's blood in the hallway, right outside of Frank Malone's bedroom."

Sam swallowed. "Quinlan was there when we pulled up. He wasn't in his car, he was standing right beside it. He said—he said he'd just arrived." She should have touched the hood. Should have seen if he was telling the truth.

But she'd wanted to believe him. Wanted to think that he was a man who'd survived a nightmare. She *still* wanted to believe that. "We need to question the first responders from the bomb squad," she said quietly. "They would have touched Quinlan's car." They'd gone over every vehicle there. "They can tell us if his story is true."

"Where is Quinlan now?" Monica asked.

"I put a detail on him," Hyde said. "No way was I letting him just walk away." He inclined his head toward Sam. "He's at his brother's place, and that's where you're heading, Kennedy."

Like he could have kept her away right then.

"I want you to talk to Quinlan. I want you to get him to tell you every move he made this morning. Get him to talk about Beth. See if you can find something for me to use here."

When Hyde gave an order, you didn't refuse. But... "Did you find any evidence to tie Quinlan directly to Beth's death?" Circumstantial. He'd been outside, and Sam had seen his clothes—there'd been no visible blood.

And that crime scene had been full of blood.

So either Quinlan had managed to hide his clothes and get clean, real fast, or the guy was innocent.

When Hyde's lips compressed, she had her answer. But then he said, "You're getting the evidence. You'll wear a wire when you go in."

A wire?

"You have an in with Quinlan. His brother's not going to turn you away."

But what would Max do if he found out that she was wearing a wire in order to trap his brother? The brother who looked dead guilty. "I'm telling Max." She crossed her arms over her chest. "I'll wear the wire, but Max has to know." She wouldn't budge on this point.

"You trust him?" Hyde stalked toward her. "People are dying, left and right on a case that should have been over. Are you really sure you trust Ridgeway enough to risk this case?"

She stared into his dark, glittering eyes. *Hold your ground.* "I do."

He nodded. "All right. Then you tell him. But if this comes back on us..."

He didn't need to say the rest. She knew that it wouldn't look good on her already shaky performance record.

"Prove his innocence or prove his guilt," Hyde said. "Get him to talk."

"I will." She hesitated. "But Quinlan Malone isn't our only suspect here. I got access to Nathan Donnelley's bank records. His savings are nearly empty."

Luke whistled. "Money's always a motivator."

Even for murder.

"Where is Donnelley now?" Hyde wanted to know. "Find him and get the good doctor in here for another interview." He clapped his hands together. "Okay, let's get moving, people. And be ready for any damn thing."

Donnelley knocked lightly on the bedroom door, and after a moment he heard the gruff, "Come in."

He turned the knob and stepped inside, making sure that he had a big smile on his face. "Well, now, Quinlan..." His gaze swept the room, and he saw no one else. He shut the door behind him, and let the smile fade away. "What the hell have you done?" Because the kid was screwing with *his* plan.

"The bitch tried to kill Max. She *did* kill Jacobson." Quinlan swung his legs over the side of the bed. "What did you think I was going to do? Let her walk away? She screwed with *my* plan."

"*Our* plan." Nathan Donnelley snapped, pacing quickly

across the room. "Our damn plan. And she's not the one who fucked it up; *you* are."

Quinlan's eyes narrowed.

"Why did you kill them?" Nathan's hands fisted. "That wasn't the agreement. You said you were just going to hold the men, just going to make some money off them—"

Quinlan rose. "I would have, if their fathers hadn't been dicks." A little shrug lifted his shoulders. "I had to change my plan."

"I gave you the drugs because you promised you wouldn't kill those men!" It had all seemed so simple at first. Take the men. Don't ask for too much money. Get the cash that the rich bastards would have sitting in their banks. Then get out of town.

Quinlan laughed. The boy actually laughed in his face. "You gave me the drugs," Quinlan stalked closer and jabbed a finger into Donnelley's chest, "because you wanted your cut of the money. And you were a hard negotiator, Don. Forty percent." Quinlan smiled, and the sight chilled him. "Of course, I *had* to get rid of everybody else with you taking that much money."

Asshole. *He'll get rid of me, too.* Only a matter of time. He had to be careful with Quinlan.

But then, he'd been careful with Quinlan Malone for years, since the boy was fifteen. Donnelley hadn't been Frank Malone's doctor, not at first. He'd been there for Quinlan.

Because the boy had liked to hurt himself. Too much.

"Don't worry." Quinlan's jabbing finger finally left his chest. "The Feds think the bitch killed herself." His mouth hitched into a half-smile. "Another suicide."

"*How* did you kill her?" That part hadn't been on the news.

"I slit the whore's wrists." Quinlan turned toward the window and gazed below. "She killed for me." His head shook a bit. "Had to admire that. If she hadn't messed up my plans, I might've even let her live. Beth was always ready to do anything for me." He tossed a glance back at Donnelley. "You know what I mean. She fucked you quick enough when I told her to."

Donnelley swallowed. "When do I get my money?" This whole thing was about to blow up in their faces. He wanted to be long gone before the shit hit the fan. Far away from Quinlan and the bastard's blood-stained hands.

"I already transferred it to your account." Quinlan stared out the window. "It's in the Caymans, just like we agreed. You can get it anytime you want."

Donnelley's hands were sweating. "And what are you going to do?" Killing Frank hadn't been part of the plan. Never the plan. *Not for me.*

But he wondered now...had Quinlan been planning that all along? Was the bastard that smart? Maybe. Quinlan had hated Frank, and shit, now Frank was dead, and Quinlan only had one person standing between him and the Malone fortune.

Maybe the little prick had planned it all from the beginning...or maybe Quinlan had just started to enjoy the blood too much.

"I've got to take care of some final business."

"What you *need* to do is get out of town." Donnelley realized his voice was threatening to rise and sucked in a deep breath. "Those Feds are going to piece this shit together. Get out while you can." If that money really was waiting on him, he'd be running soon, too. As fast as he could go.

"Maybe they will." A shrug. Quinlan finally turned to face him. A shark's smile curved his lips. "Or maybe when you disappear, they'll think you're guilty. After all, they are going to find your semen on those sheets. Frank's sheets. And your fingerprints were all over his room."

"You kept the sheets?" *Bastard.*

"Why do you think I sent her to screw you?" A wink. "Always got to have a backup plan. When you cut out of the city, you'll start to look mighty guilty. That'll make those Feds shift their focus."

Nathan's fingers curled over the black bag. One last batch. He'd brought the drugs Quinlan demanded, and now the kick in his gut told him who they'd be used on.

"You want the account number, Don? Go give my brother a drink, and it's yours." Quinlan's smile flashed again, and the sight of it made bile rise in Donnelley's throat.

Only one person between Quinlan and the Malone fortune. And now Quinlan wanted him to dose Max. Donnelley tossed the bag at Quinlan. "You do it. I'm done." He had enough blood on his hands.

"Then you don't get a dime."

A tremble shook his body. Part rage. Part fear.

"I need your fingerprints on the glass, Don. Yours, not mine. When the Feds check, I need to be clean." He walked closer, nice and slow. "You'll be long gone. Hell, go jump a plane tonight. Doesn't matter what you leave behind because they won't be able to touch you."

Money. Finally, he wouldn't have to kiss some rich jerk's ass. Wouldn't have to watch while everyone else lived the good life while he stood on the fringes.

"I know why you stayed with dad. Your career was shot after that nurse found you using, wasn't it?"

He didn't speak. Why bother? Quinlan would know. The guy knew everything. Watched everyone.

"I had a PI do some research on you a couple of years back. That nurse—her name was Sheila, right?—she still remembered you."

Of course the bitch had. "My wife...she'd just left me."

Quinlan shook his head. "Do I really look like I give a shit? I don't need to know why. Save that crap for your shrink."

Donnelley glared at him. *Asshole.*

"I picked you to help me not because of the drugs. Hell, I could get those from anyone I wanted on the street." When had Quinlan's gaze become so mocking? "You're my fall guy, Donnelley. The man who takes the blame, but gets to walk away with a boatload of cash."

Only if the Feds didn't grab him first.

"Go back outside," Quinlan ordered. "Tell my brother I'm fine. Then have a drink with him." Quinlan's gaze dropped to the bag. "Just a drink. Then you walk away."

Max stopped pacing when Donnelley came out of Quinlan's room. "How is he?"

Donnelley stared at the floor, shaking his head. "He's not—he's not going to be the same, Max."

Donnelley walked across the room and headed straight for the bar. Max frowned. "Are you okay?"

Donnelley's hands shook as he reached for the bottle of whiskey. "Your stepfather was my friend." The back of Donnelley's hand swept out and sent a tumbler falling to the floor. It shattered, and glass flew everywhere. Donnelley stooped down to pick it up.

"No, careful! I'll get it!" Max bent and hurriedly scooped up the large chunks. He pushed them onto the top of the bar as worry filled him. Donnelley looked shaken. And the guy wasn't meeting his eyes. "What aren't you telling me?"

Donnelley's hands covered two glasses. "Beth was such a troubled woman."

Beth? "I didn't realize you two were close." Beth had barely seemed to tolerate the doctor.

Donnelley picked up one of the glasses and handed it to him. "You learn a lot just by watching people. Beth, she was so unhappy."

Max took the glass. "You knew she'd been screwing Frank when my mother was still alive, didn't you?"

Donnelley drained his glass in two gulps. "Doesn't really matter what she did now, does it?" A long sigh escaped him. "In the end, does it matter what any of us do? Death comes, no matter what."

Max took a sip of the whiskey. "That's one hell of a pessimistic view you've got there, doctor." This time, he took a longer pull from the drink.

"When you've seen all that I have, you tend to get pessimistic." Donnelley's glass hit the bar top with a soft clink. "Your brother—he needs to keep seeing that shrink. Maybe...maybe this one will even be able to help him."

The whiskey burned down Max's throat as he drained the glass. "Maybe." He could hope.

"The Feds aren't pressing charges against him?" Donnelley's eyes dipped to the empty glass that Max had just set on the bar.

"Frank's death was an-an accident." Max put his hand to his temple. That damn ache was back.

"If that's what you think."

What?

Donnelley came closer. The light glinted off the top of his balding head. "Sometimes people have blind spots."

The room seemed to dim a bit. "What are you talking about?"

Donnelley's hand slapped down on his shoulder. "I kind of liked you. Of all the assholes around Malone, you were the one who bothered me the least."

His knees gave way, and Max hit the floor, hard. "Wh-what the...f-fuck...d-did...?" *The drink.*

Donnelley crouched above him. "And I am sorry about your mother." Another sigh whispered from him. "Everything went downhill after her death."

Max's hands were numb. No, his *arms* were numb. A heavy weight seemed to settle over his entire body. He blinked, trying to keep his eyes open and on Donnelley. *The doctor Frank had trusted.*

"I hope it's quick," Donnelley said, but the words sounded funny. Distorted. "You shouldn't have to suffer."

• • •

It was a little after nine p.m. when Sam knocked on the door of Max's apartment. The doorman had let her through when she flashed her badge, and now she stood in the hallway, shifting from foot to foot. She was wired, a quick process, and she knew every sound that she made was being transmitted back to the team outside.

Sam took a deep breath and leaned forward slightly. The thick carpeting in the hallway muffled her movements. She knocked on the door again. Harder now. Louder.

She couldn't hear any sounds from inside the apartment. "Max?" She pounded again. "I need to talk to you. Let me in." The doorman had assured her that he was home.

The minutes ticked by. *Max was home, but not answering.* Shit.

She grabbed the door knob. Twisted it. *Locked.*

"Hyde, I don't like this." Her heart drummed even as her fist thudded into the door. "I don't like—"

Glass shattered inside.

Sam kicked at the door. Once, twice. The damn thing wasn't opening. The wood was too thick. "Hyde, something's wrong!" Max was in there. *Too quiet.* An image of Beth's blood-soaked body flashed in front of her eyes.

Sam kicked again, as hard as she could, and the lock shattered. The door opened with a groan, and Sam ran inside, her gun drawn.

The first thing that she noticed was the broken balcony door. Shards of sharp glass glittered on the floor. "*Max!*"

"S-Sam..."

She saw him in the shadows. Max lay face down on the

floor, and his outstretched arms were just inches from the broken glass.

"Hyde, Hyde, get up here! Max is hurt!" She ran to Max, knowing Hyde could hear every word. She put her gun down and flipped him over. "Max, what happened?"

But his eyes were closed and his mouth had gone slack. "*Max!*" Her fingers fumbled. She found his pulse. Slow. Her hands searched his body but she found no wounds. No blood. She eased back, and her foot brushed against something. A broken drinking glass. Understanding hit—*drugged*.

Just like the other victims. They'd been drugged, and they hadn't remembered…

She caught his face in her hands. "Max, I need you to hold on, do you hear me? Just hold on. Help's coming." Fear had her voice shaking because she didn't know what he'd been given. Something to knock him out, to immobilize him? Or something to kill him? "*Stay with me.*"

Sirens wailed in the distance. Their cry trickled through the broken door.

Check the apartment. She knew that she had to secure the scene, but she couldn't leave Max. *Wouldn't leave him.* Sam reached for her gun and held it tight. She kept her left hand on Max—her fingers were over his chest so she could feel the slow thud of his heart.

"I'm not leaving you," Sam whispered, her grip on the gun never easing. "And you're not leaving me."

Quinlan hurried down the street, hunching his shoulders as he sank deeper into his coat. Damn that bitch. He'd been so close…and then she'd come pounding at the door.

He turned left and slipped into the alley.

A police cruiser raced by. *Dammit*. Quinlan's breath blew out and a small cloud appeared in the cold air.

Somehow, Max had reached for that lamp. He'd grabbed it and sent the thing slamming into the fragile balcony door.

Then the bitch had started screaming.

He'd barely had time to hit the lights, plunging the apartment into darkness, before she'd gotten inside. *Knocked the door down.* Almost impressive.

She'd run for his brother. The agent hadn't even bothered to search the shadows, and Quinlan had just walked right out the front door. The door she'd left open.

The bitch hadn't seen him. But he'd seen her and her gun.

Wrong time.

He'd take care of her soon.

Since she'd been there, he figured some of the other FBI pricks had been around, too. He'd run down the service stairs and slipped out the back exit, making sure to duck and avoid the security cameras. No cars had been within sight, and it had only taken about ten seconds to jump the rear fence, even with his injuries.

He knew how to avoid the security at that building. He'd known that he'd have to take out big brother sooner or later, so Quinlan had made sure he could get in and out of Max's building any time he wanted.

Can't fucking catch me.

The chill night air bit into his skin. He wouldn't be able to stay out there long, not with the cops likely to search all the nearby streets. Good thing he knew exactly where he was heading.

• • •

"Clear!" Luke shouted as he strode back from the guest rooms. "No one else is here, sir."

Hyde nodded grimly. "Did you see anyone when you entered, Kennedy?"

"No, just...him." Her fingers were wrapped around Max's. He was still out. Not so much as a flicker of his eyelashes. The EMTs had him loaded on a stretcher. Kim had already bagged the glass on the bar and the shards left on the floor.

"The guy at the desk downstairs ID'd Nathan Donnelley," Ramirez told them as he stalked into the apartment. "Said Donnelly came in about an hour ago, and he never left."

"The doctor left all right. Just not through the front door." A muscle in Hyde's jaw flexed, then he said, "I want *all* the security footage from this place. I want to know when and how Donnelley and Quinlan Malone got out of this building."

The EMTs started to haul Max out.

"Kennedy . . ." Hyde's attention shifted to her. "Go start running the tapes. See what you can find for—"

"No." Her fingers tightened on Max's. So strong, but right then, so vulnerable. Out like that, anything could happen to him. *No way to fight back.* "I'm going with Max." Her voice came out, flat and certain, and she glanced up at Hyde. "*I'm going with him.*" Screw the case. *He* mattered to her.

Silence. She felt all eyes on her. Even the EMTs'. "Move!" she shouted at them. "He needs to get to the hospital!"

They moved.

"Get me an APB out on Quinlan Malone and Doctor Nathan Donnelley." Hyde's sharp orders followed her out the door.

Sam looked back, just for an instant, and found Hyde's glittering stare on her. Sam inclined her head but never eased her grip on Max.

I won't leave you.

CHAPTER *Sixteen*

Nathan Donnelley had gone back to his motel, the shithole he'd been staying in since he left the Malone house.

It took less than five minutes to toss his clothes into a bag. He grabbed his passport, shoved his wallet into his pants, and yanked out his phone.

On the second ring, Quinlan answered.

"Where's my money?" Donnelly asked. "I need the account number." He yanked open the motel room door. Juggling his bag and the phone, he hurried out. "Don't screw with me," he snapped when nothing but static crackled over the line. "I need—"

"I know what you need."

The voice hadn't come from the phone. Oh, fuck, no, it had—

Quinlan stood in front of him. A white-hot pain drove into Nathan's chest. Quinlan smiled and shoved the knife deeper.

Quinlan's left hand clamped around Nathan's shoulder,

and he pushed Donnelley back into the motel room. Donnelley's phone dropped and thudded onto the floor.

The knife left his chest with a long, slow *slosh*. Donnelley's breath wheezed out as the suitcase slipped from his fingers.

Quinlan smirked. "Missed your heart, didn't I?" He kicked the door closed. "Better try again." Then he lunged forward.

Donnelley opened his mouth to scream, but Quinlan's hand slapped over his lips and his knife thrust deep again.

"Did I miss this time, doc?"

When Max opened his eyes the next morning, he didn't know where he was.

White. The ceiling above him was white. The walls were white. The blinds—white. His arms jerked and something burned along his right hand.

His gaze flew over and found an IV. *What the hell?*

"It's okay," Samantha's voice. Samantha's hand touching his. His eyes met hers.

"Why the hell…" His voice rasped, "am I in a hospital?" He'd tried to remember, but everything seemed so foggy. He'd been at his place. He'd been pacing, waiting, and then—

Nothing.

Her eyes searched his. "You don't remember?"

"No, I don't." He turned his hand, caught her fingers with his, and held on tight. "Baby, tell me what's going on." The words came slow and rumbled out of his dry throat.

Instead of speaking, she leaned forward and kissed

him. Samantha pressed her sweet mouth over his and dipped her tongue past his lips.

He might have been in a hospital bed, but his body sure seemed to be in good shape. One part was *very* excited. His arms wrapped around her. Max ignored the burn of the IV. One kiss, one taste, and the hunger flared bright.

Fuck the hospital, it was a bed, they could—

Her mouth pulled away from his. A growl built in his throat. "Not fair to start what you aren't finishing."

That stopped her. Samantha blinked at him. Her head tilted to the side as she stared at him, and he realized that she had on glasses. Small, sexy glasses that made her eyes look even darker.

"Don't worry, I plan to finish." Her palm slid down his cheek, and her fingers scraped over the stubble. "Once you're out of here, you're mine, Ridgeway."

Promises. He yanked the IV out of his arm.

"Max! You can't—"

"I feel fine." He swung his legs over the bed.

"Trust me, you weren't *fine* a few hours ago. You were dead to the world. You couldn't talk. You didn't know me—" She broke off and drew in a deep shuddering breath. "For a time there, you were *gone*, Max."

Max saw the dark smudges under her eyes and finally noticed her rumpled clothes. "You've been here a while, haven't you?"

"All night." She shook her head. "I couldn't leave you."

"Samantha..." He stood, and she tilted her head back to stare up at him.

"When I found you," she stopped, swallowed, "you weren't moving. You were in your apartment, everything was dark, and, oh, damn, I was afraid I was too late."

His fingers curled under her chin, and he bent down to kiss her. A deep, open-mouthed kiss. A kiss to tell her that, hell, yeah, he was alive; she wasn't too late. *They* weren't too late. The need had his body tightening. A dull ache thudded behind his temples but he ignored it. Nothing would have made him release her then.

Nothing.

He drew her closer against him. Not like he could hide the arousal he felt in that paper-thin hospital gown, and not like he wanted to try either. When she was near, he *wanted.*

His hands settled against her hips, and his fingers touched the soft swell of her ass. He loved her ass. Loved touching her. Being with her.

She stayed with me all night.

When was the last time anyone had done that for him? When was the last time anyone had cared?

"Max..." She turned her head away. He pressed a kiss to her throat and heard the sigh of her breath. "Max, Nathan Donnelley is missing."

"Donnelley?" His hold on her tightened as he struggled to remember. "I...called him. Wanted him to come and see about Quinlan." Because his brother hadn't wanted to get checked out at the hospital. Quinlan's wounds had started to bleed again, and he'd been worried, and—

Nothing.

"The doorman remembers Donnelley coming up to your place, and video footage showed him sneaking out." Her voice seemed strained. "He took the stairs out, used the service exit."

"Why?"

"Because it looks like he drugged you." Her brown

eyes glinted with a steady fury. "His fingerprints were on the glasses in the den, and one of those glasses had trace amounts of Rohypnol in it."

His brows shot together. "Roofies? The bastard gave me roofies?"

"Only your prints and his were on the glass. We matched Donnelley's because he was in the system from his time in the military."

Samantha handed him a bag, one with fresh clothes inside. His clothes. Another agent must have brought them from his place.

"The SSD believes all of the victims were slipped drugs, possibly roofies, by their abductors."

He dressed quickly as he tugged on the jeans and shirt. "You're saying," he spun back to face her after he shoved on his socks and shoes, "what? That Donnelley was involved in the kidnappings? In Quinlan's kidnapping?"

Her gaze never faltered. "You tell me. The man drugged you, he's missing, and yesterday, he emptied out his bank accounts."

That bastard had been with his family for years. "He-he treated my mom. He-he found her...She'd taken too many pills..." Donnelley had been grief-stricken. Tears had coursed down the guy's face. *Tears.* And now the guy was screwing them all?

"Quinlan's missing, too."

That froze him.

"Hyde personally checked the videos. There was no sign of him leaving your building."

"He didn't just vanish!"

"No." Her shoulders squared. "But I saw the position

of those cameras, and if you wanted to get away without being seen, you'd just have to carefully time your movements."

His breath rushed out.

"You said you called Donnelley to come and take care of Quinlan. Did the two of them talk alone?" she asked.

The throbbing in his temples got worse.

"Did they, Max?"

"I can't remember." Oh, but he wanted to remember.

"I was coming to your place, and the reason I was there..." Her hands balled into fists. "Beth Dunlap didn't commit suicide. The ME said that both of her wrists were cut so deeply that the tendons were severed. She would've had no control over her fingers. That means she wouldn't have been able to hold the knife, much less manage to slice her other wrist open."

Someone else had slashed her.

"The room was staged to make it look like she'd gone crazy, wrecked the place, and then killed herself. But the wounds don't match with that scenario, and the techs found drops of her blood in the hallway."

No. He knew where this was going.

"The splatter angle indicates she was standing up, maybe trying to flee."

And someone had dragged her back into that room and killed her.

"Your brother was at the scene when we arrived."

His eyes closed for a moment.

"Max, your stepbrother told us that he'd just arrived back at the house, but two men from the bomb squad swear that when they checked out his car..."

Max opened his eyes and stared at her.

"His hood wasn't warm. If he'd just arrived, it would still have been hot."

Dammit.

"When Frank died," she continued, "Quinlan stood to gain a fortune."

Max shook his head. No, no, there *had* to be another explanation. All those other men, the wounds on Quinlan's body... "He was *cut*, slashed all over. His hand—"

"Sometimes, you'll do anything if the end reward is important enough." She gazed into his eyes, and a soft sigh escaped her. "There's something else you should know. We found unidentified blood in the alley where Veronica James was killed."

"And you think it's Quinlan's."

The faintest of nods. "Your brother refused to give us a DNA sample when he was in the FBI office."

Quinlan's words seemed to echo in his head. *What's it like to kill a man?* It was sure starting to look like little brother already knew.

"We have an APB out for him now, and for Donnelley. Until we find them," she exhaled, "you're under 24–7 FBI protection. You and the surviving victim, Curtis Weatherly."

"You really think they're going to come after me?" They—who were *they*? Some nameless assholes? Or his brother and Donnelley?

"I think we got lucky at your place. And I think we need to be ready for anything."

Guess "anything" included his stepbrother trying to kill him.

• • •

"Thanks for working with us on this one Lake," Hyde said, staring at the agent who'd left his job at the SSD just weeks before. Even before Kenton had turned in his request for a transfer, Hyde had known what the man planned. Kenton's heart hadn't been with the SSD any longer.

Special Agent Kenton Lake inclined his head toward Hyde. "Don't think I had a real choice."

Hyde let a brief lift curve his lips. "You didn't."

"Figured as much." Kenton paused. "What else do you need?" Kenton had already talked to the press more than a few times over the last couple of days.

"We've got a press conference scheduled in two hours. I need you to satisfy the reporters and keep them out of my way."

Kenton nodded. Hyde knew he had been thoroughly reviewing the case files. "You got a suspect?" Kenton asked.

"Two." He tossed him the files.

Kenton whistled when he saw the names. "You want me to say this on the air?"

"I want you to let the bastards know we're coming. Label them as people of interest, not suspects." Hyde knew how to play the game. He'd been doing it for years.

"People that should be approached with extreme caution, right?" Kenton asked.

Hyde nodded. "And we could use another man in the field on this one. Sam...she's protecting a witness." He saw the surprise on Kenton's face.

Kenton closed the files. "Then she's back to full duty?"

Hyde remembered the fierce glint that he'd seen in

Sam's eyes last night. He wouldn't have been able to drag her away from Ridgeway. Finally, that spine of steel. He'd been waiting for it to show. "She's back." And stronger than he'd ever seen her before.

"Talk to Monica. Get her to brief you on the profile she's worked up on the two suspects," he told Kenton, because they *were* suspects. Not damn "persons of interest." Sometimes covering your ass could be such a pain.

"Yes, sir."

Hyde hesitated. "And I hear...congratulations are in order."

A wide smile split Kenton's face. "They are."

"You work fast." The guy hadn't been married long, but... "You'll be a good father."

"Sir, I'm scared as all hell."

That brought a laugh from Hyde. "You should be."

Kenton rose. "That's not really what I was hoping to hear." But a grin softened his face as he hurried off to find Monica.

Hyde's gaze slipped to the frame on his desk. Such a beautiful smile there. One he only saw in pictures now. In memories that faded too fast. "You should be," he whispered again, the laughter gone.

Because Kenton knew, like he did, that there was evil in the world. Evil that waited to steal away the light and the moments of joy.

Hyde's fingers slid over the edge of the frame. They hadn't found Heather's body, and he knew they never would. His daughter would never be coming home.

Sam took Max to her place. Techs were still working at his apartment as they searched for evidence.

Two guards were stationed at her door—agents from the Violent Crimes Division who'd been sent over as backup. She knew a similar team was watching Weatherly. Ramirez had been relieved, and he was back to following leads on Donnelley.

The door shut behind them with a soft click. Sam cleared her throat. "You can make yourself at home." Max hadn't spoken on the ride over, just seemed lost in thought. "I've got plenty of food in the fridge, so I can make some lunch...."

"I'm not hungry for food."

She put her gun on the table and met his gaze. "Max."

He shook his head. "Everything's gone to hell, hasn't it?"

Yes.

"Quinlan's not answering his cell; the cops can't find him." He shook his head. "It's a waiting game, and it's driving me crazy."

The waiting was hell, but what was coming—it would be even worse. She took off her coat then walked toward him.

But his scorching look froze her mid-stride. "I'm not in an easy mood, baby," he warned.

Had she asked for easy? Ever?

"I need you," Max said gruffly, "so damn bad, but—"

She kept walking. When she reached him, Sam put her fingers against his lips. "I need you, too." More than she could say. Sam was desperate for him. She needed to feel him against her, in her, needed to be certain he was safe. Alive.

Hers again.

Because that was how she thought of him. *Mine.*

Her hands went to the top of his jeans. His eyes never left her face. She caught the button, popped it free, and lowered his zipper with a soft hiss.

"Samantha..."

His cock spilled into her hand. Long, thick, and heavy with arousal. Her fingers wrapped around him, then squeezed tight. She worked his flesh, one long, hard pump, from base to tip.

So warm and hard.

She eased onto her knees before him and took the head of his erection into her mouth.

"*Fuck!*" His shaft jerked at the touch of her tongue.

Salty. Rich. She licked the pre-cum on his cock. *Didn't think I'd have him again. So scared.*

Her mouth widened, and she took him in deeper. Her hand slid down her body and pressed against the hard ache of need between her legs.

Wanted him. Always want him.

His hands tangled in her hair. "*You're so... beautiful...*" He growled.

Her cheeks hollowed as she sucked him. She wanted to feel his control shatter as he came for her.

Her hand pressed harder against her sex. Her mouth tightened around him, and his cock swelled even more in her mouth.

"*No!*"

His growl had her pulling back. Max's eyes glittered down at her. "Told you, baby," his voice was so gravelly, so rough, "I wasn't feeling easy." His hands moved to her shoulders, and he pushed her back, down onto the thick carpet.

Max yanked off her jeans and panties, taking her shoes

with them, and he tossed everything into a pile in the corner. His hands—with slightly callused, rough fingers—closed around her thighs, and he spread her legs as he opened her wide to him.

"You're wet for me." Hunger and dark lust-flavored the words.

One touch, and she'd been wet. Just as he was hard for her. She twisted beneath him, needing more. "Come inside me *now.*"

"I get my turn first." His stubble pricked her thighs as he moved in closer. His breath blew against the light covering of hair that shielded her sex. Max's fingers slid up, parted her folds, and found her clit.

Her breath choked out. *There.*

Then his mouth was on her. Those lips, that tongue, licking, sucking, making the need tighten and the hunger flare so hot.

Her hips slammed up against his mouth, and her nails raked his back. She wasn't feeling easy, either.

Desperate.

Max's tongue drove into her sex. She came against his mouth. A hot, hard explosion. And he kept licking her.

Her eyes squeezed shut as the waves of release blasted her. So good, *so good*, but not enough. "Max…" Her lashes lifted.

His head rose at her throaty cry. His gaze—the pupils so big his eyes looked black—locked on her face. He licked his lips, and she knew he still tasted her.

He grabbed for his wallet and took out a condom. She rose onto her knees, wanting to help him, but he had his cock sheathed in seconds. Then he ordered, "Get on your knees."

The sensual command had her breath heaving out.

Not easy.

Sam's hands slapped against the floor. Her gaze hit the brown carpet as she brought her knees down, lifting her ass.

"You're fucking..." his fingers trailed over her ass and down to her cleft, "perfect."

No, she wasn't. Far from it.

His cock nudged at the entrance to her body. The head probed against her opening. Sam's fingers dug into the carpet.

Not easy.

The first hard plunge had her gasping, then driving her hips back against Max as she tried to take more of him. *More.*

His hand circled her hip, then slid over to push at the front of her sensitive flesh. His thumb rubbed her sex even as he retreated, then thrust deeper, harder, into her.

She arched, turning her head, and he was there, rising with her. His mouth took hers even as his hands and cock took her body. His tongue thrust deep, and his cock retreated. *Thrust, withdraw.* Again and again.

A second release swelled closer. Her hips rocked against him, the rhythm wild and too fast. She was so wet that her cream coated him.

Another thrust. One that rocked her entire body, and she came, exploding around him, on a wave of white-hot pleasure that stole her breath.

Max shuddered behind her, around her, in her. Her name tore from his lips, and his cock surged inside of her as he erupted.

When Sam's breathing slowed down, when her heart stopped racing, he still filled her.

Her knees ached. Her sex quivered, and her throat seemed bone-dry.

Not easy. But exactly what she'd wanted.

"*Mine.*" And when she heard the whisper, she wasn't sure if it had been hers, or his.

Sam and Max watched the press conference together. Max's arms were loose around her, but she felt the tension that hit his body when Kenton announced Quinlan's name.

"*Dammit.*"

Sam turned toward him, barely hearing Kenton's words now. She knew that Hyde had called Kenton back in on the case so the guy could soothe the reporters. When it came to the press, Kenton had a perfect touch.

Kenton had left the SSD after he'd fallen hard for Lora Spade, a firefighter he'd met during the hunt for a serial arsonist. They'd both almost died, but in the end, they'd come through hell, stronger. *Together.* Kenton had left the SSD to be with her.

What would it be like to have someone love you so much he'd sacrifice everything?

"How did this happen?" Max demanded. "Quinlan— shit, there has to be an explanation." He pushed away from her and shoved to his feet. "I'm not just going to sit here while he's hunted down."

"Max, wait!" But he was already heading for the door. Sam hurried after him. "You don't even know where to look!"

He glanced back at her. "*Everyone* is hunting him. If he did this—" a deep, gulping breath, "don't you think somebody might shoot first and question him later? *Don't you?*"

If Quinlan came out armed, yes.

"I can get him to turn himself in. Whatever's happened, whatever twisted mess he's involved in, *I can help him.*"

Sam could only shake her head. Max was willing to risk everything for Quinlan. Family—a bond that wouldn't break.

"What if you can't?" She grabbed his arm and held on tight. "They tried to *kill* you, don't you understand that? The dose they gave you—"

"*Donnelley* gave me—"

"Was too strong!" She nearly shouted at him, her fingers digging into his. "Your heart nearly stopped beating! Jesus, Max, you almost died! If I hadn't found you and got you to the hospital..." No, no, she wouldn't go there, *wouldn't*. "They left you to die."

His body stiffened. "All along, every damn step of the way, you've suspected him, haven't you?"

Not always. "He had a lot of debt. He knew all the victims."

"That doesn't mean—"

"No, it doesn't." *Circumstantial.* "But he was *there* when Donnelley drugged you. Right there, and he left you on the floor to die."

Their gazes held, and she saw the horrible struggle in his gaze. He didn't want to believe it, didn't want to think his stepbrother could be a killer. But she also saw that part of him—yes, part of him could see the darkness in Quinlan. Part of him suspected the truth, *had* suspected for a while now.

"The SSD *will* find him," she promised. They'd found her. "They're searching all of your stepfather's properties now and all of the properties linked to the victims. Any place you can think of, they've searched." Her shoulders straightened. This was the hard part. *Hell, it was all hard.* "And I can't let you get in the way of the investigation."

His eyes narrowed at that.

Sam wouldn't back down. Not even for him. "My assignment is to watch you, to protect you, and to make sure you don't hinder the investigation." *By tipping off your brother.*

"Is that why you brought me here?" he demanded, and there was a bite to his words that she hadn't heard before, at least not directed toward her. "To keep me *busy* so I wouldn't get in anyone's way?"

Anger boiled inside her. "I didn't make love with you because I needed to keep you distracted."

"Oh? Then why did you?" And then he was grabbing her, his hands hard on her arms as he lifted her up on her toes. "Why the first night? Why me?"

Because you'd been the most dangerous, go to hell-looking man in the room. "I needed you."

"You didn't know me."

And that had been one of the reasons why. Someone who didn't know her. Didn't know her past.

"You were running scared," he said, voice deeper, "and you ran to me."

Then. She didn't deny his words. Maybe that was answer enough for him.

"Why now, baby? I know your secrets." A rough smile twisted his lips. "Is it the case? Because Hyde orders you to—"

She wrenched away from him. "Hyde doesn't order me to screw anyone." *Stay close to him.*

"He said to stay close though, right? Dante gave that order to you the first day in my house. And you've been staying close…because you want to show 'em you can handle the job? Handle anything that comes at you when—"

"No, dammit!" Her voice tore across his. "I've been staying because I wanted to be with you!"

Time to stop being afraid. "Max, I'm not with you because of the case. I'm with you because you're the only man I want." A stranger to satisfy the dark need—*at first*. But then he'd become so much more.

"You know me," Sam told him. "Inside and out, you know me, like no one else ever has before." All the dark places, the fears. He knew it all, and still wanted her.

Not a victim. Not with him. And she'd be damned if she'd be one ever again.

His phone rang then, a low vibration. She wet her lips. "Max, I just…"

He yanked the phone out of his back pocket and glanced down at the screen. "*Donnelley*."

CHAPTER *Seventeen*

D o you want to see your brother again?" The voice was a rasp, surrounded by a crackle of static.

"Donnelley, you bastard, what do you want?" Max's fingers tightened around the phone.

A laugh. "Everything."

Samantha had her phone out. She'd moved away from him, and he heard her whispering urgently to someone.

"Where's Quinlan?"

Another husky laugh. "Your agents think he's a killer, don't they?"

Isn't he? "The two of you drugged me."

"Did we?"

"The FBI is after you, and you'd better pray they find you first!" Because Max wanted to rip the asshole's head off. Rage had his whole body tightening.

"If they find me, I promise..." still that low, rough whisper, "they'll never find Quinlan. Not until it's too late."

Another game. "Quinlan's been killing with you." That

was what Samantha thought and what he feared. *How? How had things gone so wrong? Could I have stopped this? Saved him?*

His mother's image flashed before him. *W-Watch him.*

Max's teeth clenched. Dammit. To just go back—

"I went to Quinlan's room *before* I dosed you..." Whispered. "And you don't remember me dragging him out, do you? The cameras saw what I wanted them to see... and no one saw him."

Samantha was back. She'd grabbed her gun and holstered it at her side.

"How much is he worth?" The voice taunted. "How much will you pay? What will you do? After all, you're the one who ruined everything—you and your whore."

"Don't you say—"

"You want to be the hero? The one who saves Quinlan? Then you'll fucking do exactly what I tell you to do."

Sonofabitch.

"Bring the bitch with you, get in the car, and I'll tell you where to go." A rush of static on the line. "You can trade your life for his. Quinlan can walk away."

Fucking liar.

"You're dead," Max said and meant it.

"One of us will be." More static crackled. "Now move. If you let that bitch bring in the Feds, Quinlan will be the one who is *dead*. I'll slice him apart, and his death will be on you, big brother."

"Sam called." Kim announced as she rushed into Hyde's office. "Donnelley's cell number just popped up on Max's phone. She said it sounded like he was making a demand, something about Quinlan."

Hyde leapt to his feet. Monica had been sitting across from him, but she jumped up too.

"Did you order a trace lock on Donnelley's phone?" Hyde asked.

"Yeah, we're triangulating the signal now. We should have the doctor's general location in just a few more minutes."

Monica fired a hard stare at Hyde. "If the doctor's on the line, then where's Quinlan?"

She'd just gone through her entire profile with Hyde. As far as Monica was concerned, Donnelley wasn't the key player. Too weak. Too disorganized.

Hyde's jaw clenched. "We're going to damn well find out."

The call ended with a soft *click*. Max swore and raced for the door, wrenching the knob.

"Max?"

Max didn't look back. "Don't come with me, baby."

But her steps hurried after him. Then her hand was on his arm as she tried to turn him back to face her. "What did he say? What's happening?"

Your life for his.

"I have to go alone." He shook his head. "He could be watching. *I have to go alone.*" Because he wasn't going to risk her.

"No, *you can't.*" Snapped out.

He faced her and saw the tears glistening in her eyes.

Samantha shook her head. "*No*, do you hear me? This is some kind of setup. You can't—"

"Give me your gun."

Her eyes widened. "I-I can't. You know I can't!"

He held out his hand. "How much is family worth?"

She flinched at that. "You know...you know what's going to happen."

He grabbed her and kissed her with the desperate rage that pumped through his veins. He kissed her even as his hands swept down her body and took her gun.

No, he took the gun because she *let* him have it. Max's head lifted, and he stepped back.

Sam stood before him, her lips trembling, red and swollen from his kiss. "Max, what did he say?"

"He wants me to come to him."

"Where? Just tell me—"

"I don't know." But the bastard wanted her. Max had put Samantha in his sights. *He won't touch her.* "He hasn't told me yet." *Hurry; no time to waste.* "Remember," he said, "he always knew every move we made." Just as he'd know now, because he was close.

Watching.

"Max."

There was no choice, not for either of them. "Some things are worth too much," he said quietly.

And he left her.

Sam stood for a moment with her shoulders hunched and her heart racing too fast. She watched Max leave because there was no other choice. If the kidnapper had told him to get into the car alone, then she'd make sure he went alone.

But I won't leave you alone.

She'd given him her weapon, but she had a backup. And *no way* would she let him face the hell that was coming on his own.

Sam reached for her phone. The other agents would

need to stand down and not interfere, yet. Max would take them right to their prey, and she'd be there to make sure he didn't end up like Frank.

I'm coming.

"We've got Donnelley." Excitement had Kim's voice rising. "The cell signal was traced to the four-hundred block of New Curtis." She looked up. "He's in a motel room."

"Get over there," Hyde ordered, crossing his arms over his chest. "You and Dante, *go*."

"Already going, sir," Dante called out as they ran for the door.

Monica stepped forward. Hyde saw the worry on her face. The attachment between her and Dante grew stronger every day. She'd told Hyde the news about their engagement, and while he was damn happy for Monica—*about time she had a life outside the SSD*—he couldn't have married agents working together in his unit.

Time for Monica to take that promotion.

"Stay on guard!" Monica called out as the agents slipped into the elevator. It was a warning they didn't need. But Dante looked back at Monica, and his green eyes softened.

"This isn't right," Monica whispered. "Donnelley doesn't fit the profile of our lead kidnapper."

Hyde agreed. He'd read Donnelley's file. *Drug use.* The guy was lucky to still have a medical license.

But Donnelley had been working privately for the Malones for years. You could learn a lot of secrets when you were that close to a family. Secrets worth killing for.

"Quinlan is the one we need," Monica said, her voice calm and certain, even if her hands had clenched into fists. "The links all circle back to him."

"Then we'll find him." The phone on Kim's desk rang, a long, low peal. *Sam.* He hurried forward and grabbed the phone. "Hyde."

"He's gone!" A rough edge hardened Sam's voice. "Max is going after Donnelly, and I'm not letting him go alone! I'm—"

"Sam, we've got Donnelley's location. He's in a motel on New Curtis. Dante and Daniels are on their way to apprehend him now."

"If Donnelley is there, then there's no way he's watching us now." Soft, muttered, almost as if she were talking to herself. "I'm going after him. I'm not letting Max get caught in the crossfire."

Hyde's fingers tightened around the phone. "Turn on the GPS in your car." Instinct and fear drove the demand. "In case we lose phone contact, make sure we can track you." Because he'd be damned if he ever lost her again.

"Yes, sir."

"And Kennedy?"

A door slammed in the background, and he knew she was already on the move. "Sir?"

"Keep him safe."

Max's rental car raced out of the garage. Good thing Samantha had gotten another agent to bring it by early that morning because he really hadn't been in the mood to steal a ride.

His phone vibrated before he'd even reached the street.

Swearing, he glanced down. Different number, one he didn't know. He picked up the phone.

"*Max . . .*"

"I'm *coming*, okay?"

"Put the bitch on the line."

Ice froze his blood. *Not watching, not yet, or he'd know—*

"She's not with you." Anger snapped in the whispered words.

"No, she's not, and you're not getting her." Max braked the car, heard the squeal of tires, and demanded, "Now tell me where the hell you are."

Silence.

"*Where are you?*"

"Get on the highway." A whisper. "Go West."

Max drove forward.

"Take the second exit ramp."

Max's teeth were clenched so tight that his jaw ached. *How had it come to this?*

"You'll pay for not bringing the whore."

His foot slammed on the gas. *No, you'll be the one who pays.*

Sam wrenched open her car door, jumped inside, and revved the VW's engine. In less than three seconds, she was out of the garage. Just in time to catch the flash of Max's taillights. *Hurry.*

Her heart thundered in her chest, and her sweaty palms gripped the steering wheel. She wouldn't lose Max.

The VW flew out onto the highway, and Sam realized they were heading the wrong way. New Curtis was toward the east, just a few moments away.

But Max was heading in the opposite direction.

"*Max.*" She fumbled with her phone. This was wrong. A setup. She had to warn the other agents.

His phone rang again a moment later. Max still had it gripped in his right hand. He punched the screen. "What?"

"4219 Willow Way."

His breath hissed out at the familiar address. The agents wouldn't have searched that old cabin because it wasn't Frank's; it was his. Left to him by his mother.

"Now roll down your window and throw your phone out."

He hesitated. It would be so easy to just call the Feds, to call Sam and tell her the address.

But if he did, would the guy be long gone before he arrived?

"I can see you . . . ."

His gaze swept around the highway. All he saw was a swirl of cars. Was the bastard watching now? Or lying again?

"Throw the phone out."

Max hit the button for the automatic window. It lowered with a whir of sound, and he tossed out his phone.

The maid was shaking as she unlocked room 203 at the Highline Motel. Luke grabbed her arm and pulled her back the second that the door squeaked open.

"Federal agents!" he yelled. "Nathan Donnelley, we're coming in!"

He kicked the door open the rest of the way and went in

with his gun drawn. Moving soundlessly, Kim was right at his back.

And Donnelley was waiting for them.

Sam's phone rang just as she was preparing to call the SSD. She grabbed the phone, not even looking at the screen as she kept her eyes on the rental car. "Hyde, did you get—"

Max was turning again. Her foot pressed harder on the accelerator.

"Throw your phone out the window, bitch." The rasp made her breath choke out.

Her gaze shot to the mirror. Sam caught sight of the dark truck with tinted windows that was closing in on her. *Following us.*

She glanced down at her phone. That wasn't the number she'd seen for Donnelley. *The asshole had switched phones.*

"Do you want him to die? It will be so easy to kill him."

Sam lowered her window. Wind whipped into the car and sent her hair flying.

The phone dropped onto the pavement. Shattered.

Luke stared at Donnelley's face. Pale and still. A red smile had been cut into his neck, a grin that stretched sickeningly from ear to ear. And the bastard's chest had been carved open.

Luke inhaled the stench of death and spun around, the phone already at his ear. "Hyde! We've got a problem. Yeah, yeah, we found the phone." Tossed next to the corpse. "And Donnelley."

"Get him in here. I want him to tell us—"

"Sir, he isn't going to be talking." Luke threw one more fast glance at the body. "Not to anyone."

So Donnelley damn well wasn't the one who'd made the call to Ridgeway. "Can you get Sam? She's got to know what's happening."

The pause on the line stretched too long, and Luke knew Hyde was trying to connect with Sam on one of the SSD's other lines. Then Hyde said, "She's not answering."

What? No, shit, she—

"But don't worry," Hyde continued, "she's showing us exactly where we need to go."

Sam's hands had a death grip on the steering wheel. The black truck had disappeared, veering away minutes before. Just a few miles down the road, she could see the trunk of Max's car in front of her. Had he seen her yet? She'd stayed back at first and tried to keep other cars between them.

The VW jolted when she hit a pothole. Woods surrounded her, and the old road had sure seen better days. Traffic had thinned quickly. No one else was traveling on this deserted stretch as she drove farther from the bustle of the city and into the thick woods of the countryside. No one else was there—Max *had* to see her. No place to hide now.

Virginia. They'd crossed the state line at some point. As the road snaked deeper into the woods, Sam wondered where this chase was leading them.

She lost sight of Max for a moment when she rounded a curve, and fear spiked her blood. The VW pushed forward, taking the sharp curve too fast, and Sam glimpsed the glittering water of a river. The river waited on the left, narrowing up ahead as it flowed hard and fast under a metal bridge. The sunlight hit the surface of the water, reflected back, and made the waves look gray, not black as—

Something slammed into the side of her car. Sam screamed, and her head whipped to the right. *The black truck.* It had shot out from a dirt road—a road almost completely hidden by the thick pine trees—and plowed right into her.

Glass shattered around her, and metal screeched. She slammed on the brakes as she fought to control her car. The VW was shaking, sagging, and the passenger side air bag had exploded out, blasting white and blocking her view of the truck as it reversed—

And then lunged forward, hitting her again. Metal screeched once more. She screamed, and the truck's motor revved as the horsepower kicked in. The truck started to push her car toward the edge of the road.

"No!" She fumbled, trying to unsnap her seatbelt. Glass rained down on her, cutting her hands, her face, and the blood made her fingers slick. The VW shuddered as the truck forced it closer to the water.

The seat belt popped free. Sam reached out to shove open her door.

Too late.

The VW rolled over the edge of the road and sent her tumbling inside the car. Her head slammed into the ceiling, and her body twisted. Her back rammed into the windshield, and her knee hit the gearshift. Sam felt something pop.

Roll. Roll. Roll.

Another loud screech filled her ears as the front of the car scraped past the edge of the bridge. Then the car crashed into the river. Water came flooding in through the shattered windows. The car filled up fast.

Cold. So cold. Holding her down. Killing her.

Sam opened her mouth and screamed as the water rose.

Max's gaze darted to the rearview mirror. He thought he'd caught a flash of red moments before. *Red... Samantha's car was red....*

Would she have followed him? *Hell yes.*

As he cleared the bridge, his gaze drifted to the river. After a moment, he glanced back in the mirror—and saw a nightmare.

A black truck plowed into the side of a red VW—*Samantha's car.* The truck rammed the car again, and the little vehicle rolled down into the river.

The water.

"Samantha!" His foot shoved the brake pedal all the way to the floorboard. He wrenched the wheel, spinning the car around in the road and sending up a cloud of dust. Then he flew hell fast back to her.

The drumming of his heartbeat filled his ears, and he whispered her name, again and again. *Be alive.* Oh, Christ. She had to be okay.

He jumped from his car even before it had come to a full stop. The black truck sat near the edge of the road, the engine idling, the door hanging open, swaying. But the driver's seat was empty.

Bastard's out there. Waiting.

Watching. He'd known Samantha was tailing Max.

He'd taken her out and deliberately brought Max into the open in order to attack.

Screw him.

Max ran for the river. He screamed Samantha's name because he didn't see her. The VW was sinking quickly in the deep water near the bridge. A fist squeezed his heart as he prepared to dive into that icy water—

A bullet tore through his shoulder. The blast of the gun echoed in his ears even as he fell. Max tumbled down the embankment and rolled toward the water. The fiery pain stole his breath, and when the damn world stopped spinning, he was in the water.

Samantha. He rose up, struggling to his feet.

Another gunshot—this one hit him in the back of the leg. He couldn't see the VW's tires anymore. The car had flipped, and it had sunk so fast, going completely under.

Max slid down again. "Bastard!"

Laughter echoed across the lake. "No . . . that would be you, *brother.*"

His head whipped around, and in that split second, Max found himself staring back at Quinlan. His stepbrother stood on the road, close to the black truck, with a gun in his hand. A gun pointed right at Max.

"Move toward her again," Quinlan said, "and I'll put a hole in your chest." And he smiled. *Smiled.*

The cold water lapped at Max with greedy, grasping hands.

I-I wanted to die. By the fifth time, I begged to die.

Hell, no, he wouldn't leave Samantha in that water. "Then shoot, asshole, *shoot!*" Max dove under the water, ignoring the pain in his shoulder and the agonizing throb in his leg.

Bullets blasted into the river, shooting around him. He struck out, swimming awkwardly because his leg was nearly useless. *Get to the car. Get her.*

His hand struck metal. The VW. He grabbed the door, wrenching it open more and—

Fingers touched his. Soft.

Samantha was there, kicking out of the car as bubbles rose from her lips. Max grabbed her. Pulling her close, he sealed his lips to hers, and gave her the last breath he'd taken.

Her body shuddered against his. He knew that she wanted to kick up. The surface was temptingly close.

But so was Quinlan. The brother he'd tried to protect. The one who wanted to kill him and his lover.

They couldn't swim straight up. They'd be perfect targets. *He'll take us out as fast as he can, and leave us in the water.*

An easy way to dispose of their bodies.

Samantha kicked against him, trying to rise, but he wrapped his arms around her, held tight, and pushed her down.

Her eyes opened, wide and panicked as she stared at him. He shook his head, needing her to understand. Desperate for her to see...

But there was fear on her face because he was shoving her farther down, farther...

A thick line of woods waited on the eastern side. If he could get them closer to the bank, they might have a chance to run for it. Better than nothing. He pushed her toward that side and kicked as best he could as they fought the current.

But Max had used all his strength to push her, and the

bullet wounds were taxing him, draining him fast. His lungs burned, and he knew they'd have to rise soon.

The fire in his lungs burned hotter. Samantha's eyes were on his. Wide. Dark.

So beautiful. Maybe the last thing that he'd ever see would be her pale face surrounded by the floating cloud of her hair.

Another bubble slipped past her lips.

They had to take a breath. Max kicked up. She kicked too, fast and desperate, and they drove up toward the surface.

Before he broke through the water, Max knew they weren't far enough away. Not even close. But maybe Quinlan would be looking the wrong way. Looking toward the spot where the car went down.

Just need a few moments.

The water lightened. He could see the bright rays of the sun. Close, so close.

They burst through the surface. They both sucked in deep gulps of air as hard as they could. Max spun around, shoving her behind him, because there wouldn't be much time.

His eyes found Quinlan. He saw his brother whirl toward them—saw him lift the gun and smile. Max braced himself as he got ready to take the third hit.

The thunder of the gun almost deafened him. But that hadn't been Quinlan's gun. It had been Samantha's. She'd lifted her arm out of the water and fired the small weapon he'd never even seen when he'd pulled her from the car. Quinlan staggered back with a look of utter shock on his face. Blood ballooned on his chest in a thick, wide circle, and he fell back into the water, slipping out of sight.

Samantha's hand was rock steady, and the gun stayed pointed at the spot where his brother had been standing seconds before.

Max's breath panted out, matching hers, and he looped his arm around her waist as he pulled her close.

"We've got to go," she whispered, her lips feathering against his neck. "We have to, Max. I-I don't think he's dead."

He started struggling for the shore.

"I...lost my glasses...couldn't see..." She choked a bit, sputtering water.

His feet hit the rocky bottom. "Go to my car," he ordered, aware that the liquid dripping down his body wasn't all water. "Go....I'll be..."

He fell, half in the water, half on the shore.

"Max?" Her hands were on him. "Max, you've been shot!"

He struggled to his knees. "*Go!*"

"Not without you." She tried to grab him, and he realized she was holding her gun with her left hand because the right hand hung limp. *Broken.*

And blood oozed from the cuts on her forehead and on her arms.

I'll kill him. The brother he'd tried so hard to protect. The monster hiding in plain sight.

They staggered together and managed to get up the damn slope. Samantha had her gun. She was ready, sweeping the area for Quinlan, but that little bastard wasn't anywhere to be seen.

"Need your phone," Samantha whispered.

"Fucker had me throw it out." He'd get her to his car, force her inside, then find Quinlan. *Get the gun.* The gun he'd taken from Samantha was inside the rental car. He'd get it, leave her with the weapon she had, and finish this nightmare.

Max pushed forward. His left leg dragged behind him and his arm lay across Samantha's shoulder. She shuddered against him. Wet, fragile. He had to bite back the rage that threatened to choke him. *Quinlan had gone after her.*

In the water. Fuck. Her worst nightmare.

The car waited just steps away. Max's gaze raked the area, left to right. Where was Quinlan? *Where?*

Max didn't speak. He shoved forward through the pain. Then he was at his car. Finally. He yanked open the door, pushed Samantha inside—

A loud, furious shout froze him. Max spun around and saw Quinlan running from behind the black truck. The gun wasn't in his hand anymore; maybe he'd lost it in the water. Quinlan held a knife. The edge gleamed, reflecting the light as Quinlan charged right at them.

Samantha pushed away from the car and lifted her gun. "Drop it!" Her own scream vibrated with rage. "Don't make me do it, Quinlan, don't make me—"

But he kept running toward her.

Samantha squeezed the trigger, but this time the gun just made a *snick*. Water droplets flew to the ground but the damn gun didn't fire.

Jammed. Shit. She'd been lucky the gun fired the first shot. The water—

Quinlan raised the knife high up into the air. Max shoved Samantha to the ground, and the knife caught him, slashing across the back of his arm.

"Always thought you were better..." Quinlan rasped at him. "Fucking show you...fucking show everyone..."

The knife swung again and sliced across Max's arm as he tried to hold off his brother.

Bile rose in his throat but Max managed to dodge the next blow. He grabbed Quinlan's wrist, holding tight, keeping the blade up and away from his face. "You need help! Don't you see that?"

Samantha rose to her feet behind Quinlan. She dove into the car, and Max knew that she was going for the other gun.

"You weren't always like this," Max whispered, wishing it had been different, wishing everything had just been different. "You weren't a killer—"

"But you were." The knife glinted. "And Frank thought you were perfect." The blade was inches from Max's face.

Max shoved up and managed to heave his brother back.

"You won't be perfect when I'm finished," Quinlan promised as he launched himself at Max. They slammed onto the earth.

Max tried to hold his brother tight but his hands were slick with blood, and Quinlan was twisting and fighting beneath him. Rolling, Quinlan rose with the blade.

Quinlan's gaze met Max's. Then his stepbrother smiled and thrust the knife into Max's stomach.

"*No!*" Samantha screamed.

Max slumped back on the ground, and a cold wind touched his skin.

"Max!" Samantha's desperate voice rose above Quinlan's laughter.

Max could have sworn that he heard the wail of sirens in the distance.

Quinlan licked his lips. "It's mine—every bit was mine... and I was sick of waiting for that bastard to die."

Max shook his head and gathered his strength. The blade would be coming at him again, and he had to be ready.

"Drop it," came Samantha's furious, shaking voice. "Drop it, Quinlan, or I swear I'll put a bullet through your heart."

CHAPTER *Eighteen*

Fear shook her body, but Sam held the gun rock steady. Max was barely moving. *So much blood.* And that prick with the knife wasn't going to hurt him again. He wasn't going to hurt anyone.

"It's over," Sam said, creeping closer.

"No..." Quinlan's voice was soft. "It's just beginning."

Not for you. Because this gun wouldn't jam. Sam took another cautious step forward. "You hear those sirens?"

And his head snapped up as he actually seemed to hear their wails for the first time.

"It's the SSD. They're coming for you."

Quinlan rose and faced her head on. *That's right. Step away from Max.* The sirens were so close. *Hurry.*

Max pushed up to his knees. She didn't let her gaze dart to him because Quinlan still had a knife, and he was edging closer to her. "It's over," Sam said again.

"*Bitch!*" Then Quinlan seemed to crack right before her eyes. He screamed and lunged at her with fingers tight around the knife.

"Samantha!" Max's shout. Her gaze flew to him. His eyes were full of terror and fury. As he struggled to his feet, Sam saw that his lips were moving but she couldn't clearly hear what he was yelling because the sirens were screeching so loudly now and Quinlan was screaming as he—

"It's over," she whispered and pulled the trigger. The bullet slammed into Quinlan—not his heart but his arm, the arm that held the knife. He howled in pain as the knife flew from his fingers and slid down the embankment.

"No!" he bellowed.

Sam watched as he wrapped his fingers around the wound.

Brakes squealed as the squad cars and unmarked SSD vehicles swarmed into the area. Backup had arrived.

She didn't lower her gun, though. She kept it aimed right at Quinlan. "It's not going to be that easy," she told him, her voice soft. No death by cop for him. He'd pay for his crimes.

"Sam!" Hyde's yell, and she'd never been so happy to hear that man's voice in her whole life.

"Get an ambulance," she called, trembling. The icy water had robbed her of every last bit of warmth, and each time she spoke, puffs of white appeared before her mouth.

Quinlan's head dropped. "Not ending like this! Not ending like—"

The agents closed in on him. "Quinlan Malone," Luke Dante's voice snapped out, "you're under arrest."

Sam's breath expelled in a hard rush. *Max.* She lowered the gun and tried to force her fingers to ease their too-tight grip on the weapon. *They hurt.* Every part of her hurt. And Max, oh, God, Max, all that blood—

"Easy." Hyde was there, standing right in front of her. He pried the gun from her fingers. "Agent Kennedy... Sam, are you all right?"

Her teeth were chattering. The bone-deep cold shook every part of her body. "M-Max..." He was the only thing that mattered to her right then. He'd gone into the water for her. He'd actually used his own body as a shield to protect her.

Been willing to die, for me.

And she'd been more than willing to kill for him.

She hurried over and fell to her knees beside him. His eyes were open. So blue.

She touched his cheek.

"Get the EMTs over here now!" Hyde barked.

"You can't do this!" Quinlan yelled. "I'm the victim, I'm—"

"You're a killer," Dante said, the words drifting to her.

Sam leaned in close to Max. His skin was so pale, and the same shudders that shook her body were shaking his. *Too cold.* "It's going to be okay," she whispered. "We're safe now."

Safe. But death had come so close.

Hands pulled at her, trying to tug her away from Max. The EMTs. She let him go even as tears tracked down her cheeks.

Then she was being guided to a stretcher. One of the EMTs started probing her wounds, and lights flashed in a red-and-blue whirl around her.

Voices droned on, but she could only clearly hear the chatter of her teeth and the fast beat of her heart.

They loaded her into the ambulance, covered her in blankets and secured her in the back. The EMTs pushed

Max in next to her. Max's head turned, and his gaze met hers.

Someone slammed the back doors.

Max's hand lifted and reached for her. She caught his fingers, held tight. When the ambulance lurched forward, she didn't let go.

She never wanted to let go.

"M-Max, I love you," she whispered, needing to say the words, desperate to say them. But his lashes had fallen shut, and she knew he hadn't heard her.

Patching Sam up was easy. The cuts on her face just needed cleaning and bandages. Her right wrist was set and put in a splint, and the docs put fifteen stitches in her left arm. They bundled her up, got her body temperature back on track, and she finally managed to stop shaking.

And started demanding to see Max.

But it wasn't as easy to patch him back up. Two hours later, Sam was still waiting to see him. Fear tightened her insides. *Be all right. You have to be—*

A knock rapped at her door.

"Come in!" If her visitor was a nurse then she could grill her for information about Max.

Special Agent Kenton Lake popped his dark head in the room. "Kenton?" she whispered. "What are you doing here?" Shouldn't he be off doing a news interview? Wrapping up this mess and making the SSD look good?

He flashed her a wide smile. It was the same smile that had—once upon a time—made her heart flutter.

"Couldn't leave without seeing you." Kenton ambled inside and pushed the door closed behind him. "Damn, woman, when I heard about the scene with Malone…"

Running a quick hand through his hair, he approached the bed.

When the Watchman had taken her and played his twisted game, Kenton had been there. When she'd opened her eyes, choking on water and struggling for breath, he'd been the first person she'd seen.

He'd also seen her, later, in the hospital. He'd seen her when she broke down, sobbing until the doctors had to drug her. He hadn't told anyone about that. Kenton was a man who knew how to keep secrets.

But he hadn't been the man to keep her heart. They'd dated, just casually, but he'd never made her need, never made her *feel*, like Max did.

His gaze raked her. "You look like hell."

Ah, Kenton, always the sweet talker. Actually, he usually *was* a sweet talker. "I feel like it." She tried to push up in the bed. Her wrist immediately protested, and a gasp broke from her lips. "They won't tell me *anything.*"

His eyes narrowed.

"Max," she sighed his name. "I need to know how he is."

Kenton's gaze was too watchful. "Malone's brother?"

She nodded.

"You care about him, don't you?"

Stop being afraid. "I'm in love with him." And she'd tell him as soon as he could hear her.

Kenton sucked in a deep breath. "They brought Quinlan down to the office. I, uh, think there's something you should know."

A nurse bustled in without knocking. "Ms. Kennedy? Max Ridgeway's out of surgery. Dr. Gretchen said I could take you to see him—just for a few minutes—if you felt up to it." She pulled a wheelchair into the room behind her.

Up to it? Nothing would keep her out of his room. Sam's left hand shoved back the covers, and she ignored the pain as she tried to get up.

Kenton leaned over her. "Wait."

No, there was no waiting. "I need to see him."

But he didn't move. "It's hard when you care, isn't it? When someone else's life matters more than your own."

No, it wasn't hard. It was freaking terrifying.

"But you have to be careful, Sam. Just because you love someone, it doesn't mean they're perfect."

What was he talking about? She knew Max wasn't perfect. She loved him because he wasn't. He was real, solid, strong, and ready to take on hell for her. A woman couldn't ask for more. Perfection could wait.

"Quinlan says…" Kenton leaned in even closer to her and dropped his voice so that the nurse couldn't overhear his words. "Quinlan is saying that Ridgeway was in on the kidnappings from the very beginning. He says they planned everything together and that Max only changed the plan because he fell for *you*."

She shook her head. "No, no, Max wouldn't do that—"

"Are you sure?"

"*Yes.*" She wasn't going to listen to any more. *I need Max.*

Kenton inclined his head in a grim nod. "You trust him that much?"

"I do." She'd seen the sick horror on Max's face. The fury when he realized just what his brother had done. No, Max hadn't been in on the crimes, no matter what crap his brother was spewing. Max wasn't like Quinlan.

Not evil.

She climbed carefully from the bed, but shook her head at the nurse. "I don't need that chair. Just tell me where he is." *I'm coming, Max.*

The nurse blinked. "Room...ah...212, just down the hallway."

Sam kept her head up and her spine straight as she walked.

"Sam!"

She glanced back at Kenton's cry.

"You did good on this one. Damn good."

"Thanks."

"I always knew you had a core of steel. You walked through hell, and it just made you stronger." His lips lifted the faintest bit. "You didn't break."

She knew he'd been through his own nightmare. The man had walked through fire on his last case with the SSD. She forced a smile to her lips. "Neither did you."

"And we're stronger for it. Remember that. You're not weak, Sam, and you never have been." Because he knew her well. "You beat that bastard before, and you beat this one, too."

Yes, she had. But she'd had help. A man who'd willingly stepped between her and a killer.

How was a woman supposed to walk away from a guy like that?

She wasn't. She was supposed to stay with him, screw what came, and fight like crazy for a future.

The machines surrounding Max beeped and whirred. His face was pale, and his lips were still tinged a bit blue. Bandages covered most of his upper body and mid-section.

"It took a long time to close those wounds," the young doctor beside her murmured. "Someone sure did a number on him."

Sam's hand reached for Max's. "How long until he's awake?"

"He'll drift in and out for a while, but he needs to sleep. After all that blood loss, he needs to rest." The doctor slanted her an assessing glance. "So do you."

She saw the redness in his eyes. Another long night for the doc. "There's a chair right here. I'll be fine."

His lips tightened but he gave a curt nod. "Anyone we need to notify? Family?"

Someone sure did a number on him. "His family knows."

He closed his clipboard. "All right then, when your boyfriend opens his eyes, let him know that he's lucky. *Very* lucky. The shot in his thigh nicked an artery but the cold water slowed down the bleeding. If the vessels hadn't constricted..." He trailed off and shook his head. "Going into the water saved his life."

"No." Her fingers tightened around Max's. "When he went into the water, he saved *my* life."

The door clicked shut behind the doctor. Sam used her foot to pull the chair closer to the bed, and then she sat, holding tight to Max's hand. The night stretched before her, long and dark.

The darkness didn't scare her. Never had. And even the cold embrace of the water hadn't stirred the terror. But the moment when she'd thought Max was lost to her, when Quinlan had closed in with that knife...

Fear choked me.

"Wake up," she whispered to him, leaning closer to the bed. "I need to tell—"

His lashes fluttered, and Sam stilled. "Max?"

The beeping grew faster. A groan escaped his lips.

Max. She squeezed his hand. "It's okay, you're safe. Do you hear me, Max? You're safe. You're in a hospital, everything's fine and—"

His lips moved. A soundless whisper.

"I couldn't—Max, I couldn't hear you."

His lashes cracked open. His eyes met hers. "Kill... him..."

Those words—they were the same words that he'd yelled to her when Quinlan had lunged at her with the knife. Her life versus Quinlan's. Max had chosen.

But she hadn't made the kill. "I didn't have to," she said, leaning in to press a quick kiss to his face. "The SSD came. They took him into custody."

His gaze looked so weak. She wasn't even sure if he could focus on her.

"He won't hurt anyone else," she promised him. "He'll be..."

"Cage..."

And she remembered the words she'd said to him so long ago. *They belong in cages, far away from innocent people.* She swallowed to ease the lump in her throat. "He's going to prison. The SSD will make sure he doesn't get out any time soon."

Max's eyes fluttered closed. "Over."

"For him." It hurt to see the pain on his face. The only remaining member of his family had been a psychotic bastard who'd tried to kill him. "Not for you though,

Max. You're going to be okay, do you hear me? The doctors patched you up, and you're going to be fine. For you, everything's just beginning."

Max woke up in a cold sweat, his body shuddering and Samantha's name on his lips.

"Shh...it's okay." Her whisper came to him in the darkness, and it took him a moment to understand....

Not in the hospital. After nearly seven days, he'd finally been released. He hadn't gone back to Frank's place—he couldn't stand the thought of that—and Samantha hadn't wanted him to be alone.

Her place. Her scent surrounded him, her soft bed cushioned him, and the feather-light weight of her hand pressed against his chest. "It's just a dream," she told him. "You're safe. It's over."

He'd been back at that river. Quinlan had been there, firing his gun, and Max hadn't been able to get to Samantha. Her body had floated to the surface. And he'd lost her.

He rolled, wrapping his arms around her and holding tight.

"Max, no, your stitches!"

Screw them. The pain just made him realize that he was alive. She was alive. And he'd be damned if he lost his chance with her.

His lips found hers in the darkness, and he kissed her with a desperate desire that fired his blood. A need only she could satisfy. She'd slipped past his guard, gotten under his skin, and he knew he'd never be the same without her.

But her hands were pushing against him, not holding him close, and the ache ripped through him.

"You'll hurt yourself," her husky whisper filled his ears.

"Not having you will hurt a lot more." Didn't she understand? Lust tightened his body. His cock was already hard and swollen, but the need for her was so much more. A hollow ache inside his chest.

Need her. Flesh to flesh. Want her. All that she is. Everything.

Her hands pushed him, and Max found himself flat on his back.

"I don't want to hurt you," she said, the words drifting in the dark, and a rough laugh built in his chest.

"You won't." Unless she left.

The sheets rustled, the cool air hit his legs, and then warm flesh was above him as she straddled his hips. Samantha was careful not to jostle his healing leg or to touch the wounds on his stomach.

She stared down at him, and in the faint moonlight, he could see the darkness of her eyes.

No panties. Her legs were spread, and his cock pushed against the hot core of her body. His hand slipped between them, found the center of her need, and his fingers stroked her. Max wanted her to be as ready, as desperate, as he was.

She arched against him, and a soft moan slipped past her lips. *Not good enough.*

His thumb pressed harder. Her hips pushed back against him. Max found the tight opening of her body and thrust two fingers inside. Proof of her arousal coated his fingers.

His fingers worked her body. Max touched her the way he knew she liked. Building the arousal. Pushing her to the edge. Her sex clamped around his fingers. The delicate muscles squeezed in a strong grip, and he wanted her around his cock. Wanted to be driving deep into her. So deep that she'd never be free of him. So deep that she'd know, always, that she was...

Mine.

"Max!" Need choked in the word, and then her fingers were on his cock, soft and delicate, touching and stroking, and he had to clench his back teeth.

She guided his cock, positioning it right at the entrance to her body. So wet and warm. Nothing between them, nothing—

Condom. "Samantha—"

"I'm safe," she managed, tossing back her hair.

So was he. And if she wanted skin to skin...

She eased down and took him inside her body.

And it was heaven. Hell. So good he lost his breath. So tight that he nearly came at the first hot glide of her body. He forgot the pain and only knew her.

Max worked the rhythm with her, lifting his hips up to meet her, holding tight, and keeping his eyes on her.

Samantha. The woman he'd nearly died for. The woman he would have killed for.

Her moans filled the air. His fingers dug too deeply into her hips, but he couldn't stop. *Need her too much.*

Her nails bit into his shoulders. Her sex rippled around him, and then she was coming, whispering his name and arching above him.

Beautiful.

Her climax shivered around his cock, and he exploded into her as a wave of hot pleasure pulsed through his body. Max wrapped his arms around her and held her close.

Because he wasn't letting her go. No matter what night-mares might come—for him, for her—he wasn't letting her go.

When the passion eased, she slid down to his side. Her hand lay over his chest, right over his heart. And he didn't speak because he knew what tomorrow would bring: the face-off with his stepbrother. The last round of questions. The future.

After a while her breathing eased, and he knew she slept beside him. But he didn't sleep because he didn't want to see her die again in his nightmares. So he held her in the darkness and wondered how a woman who fought killers could love one.

The next morning, Max walked with Samantha down the long, winding hallway. The clank of metal bars sounded behind them. He knew that sound well. For years, it had haunted his dreams. *The sound of freedom being ripped away.*

But this time, it wasn't his freedom. It was his stepbrother's.

Samantha's delicate fingers tightened around his. He was limping a bit, thanks to the bullet wound Quinlan had put in his thigh.

Then Monica Davenport was there, stepping forward with Ramirez by her side. They motioned toward the small conference room they'd been given. An empty table waited.

"You understand what's happening here today?" Monica murmured.

He rolled his shoulder and felt the pull of stitches. Last night, he hadn't even given a thought to his injuries. Sex and Samantha had made him forget. "Yeah, Quinlan's about to lie his ass off to try and cut down his prison term." *Or to make me look guilty.* Samantha had already told him about Quinlan's accusations.

Monica's gaze was assessing. "I've asked the DA to wait outside a bit. I want you to have the chance to talk to your brother first."

His brows climbed. "What good will that do?"

"I think you can make him confess. To everything." She offered a small, brittle smile. Ramirez watched them with guarded eyes.

"You're kidding me, right?" Max asked. Samantha's hand held tight to his.

"No, I'm not."

"The guy wants me *dead*. He's not gonna want to confess!"

"Your brother always wanted his father's attention, didn't he?" Monica mused. "The only son, at least for a long time, the one who never quite measured up."

Piss-poor excuse for a son...Frank's voice echoed in his mind. Max swallowed.

"The killings weren't about money. We looked at it all wrong. The money—that's just the surface," Monica said, with a wave of her hand. "He took the golden boys—the rich boys with doting dads—and he made the fathers prove how much they loved their sons."

Max shook his head. "That's fucked up."

"That's Quinlan." Finally Ramirez spoke. "He could have taken the money and run after the first two snatches, but instead he got to where the money couldn't compete with the pleasure he took from slicing open his victims."

"And himself." Monica reached for a file on the table. "I've got doctors' records—"

"Aren't those supposed to be confidential?" Max demanded. Beside him, Samantha leaned forward and peered at the files.

"About as confidential as your manslaughter conviction," Ramirez murmured, locking his gaze on Max.

"Screw off." Max wasn't in the mood for any agent bullshit.

"What do the records say?" Samantha wanted to know.

"That at age fourteen, Quinlan Malone was admitted to St. John's Hospital because he had lacerations on his upper chest." Monica raised a black brow. "He said he fell onto a fence, but the attending physician suspected otherwise and referred Frank Malone to a psychiatrist." Monica closed the folder and her gaze returned to Max. "Seems your stepbrother liked to injure himself."

Sliced off his own finger.

"Self-injuries like that can be triggered by depression, anxiety, an emotional stressor, or—"

"Frank met my mom when Quinlan was fourteen," Max gritted out from between clenched teeth.

Monica nodded. "Do you know why Nathan Donnelley was employed by your father?"

"He was my dad's doctor."

"Actually," now Monica's gaze turned to Samantha, "he wasn't."

Max glanced back at Samantha.

A little shrug lifted Samantha's shoulders. "I hacked into his computer and found some old files. When

Donnelly started working with Malone, he was there to take care of Quinlan." She paused, then said, "Frank was tired of the doctors at St. John's asking questions."

Max swallowed and felt the punch in his gut. "He's sick. Quinlan needs help." And it twisted his heart that he hadn't seen it sooner. *Could I have stopped this? Stopped him? Saved those—*

"If you believe that," Monica interjected smoothly, "if you really think he needs help, then we need you to help us. Get a confession out of him, and we'll make sure he gets psych treatments during his incarceration."

"For how long?" His temples pounded. "How long's he gonna be locked up?"

She didn't answer, but he already knew. *Forever.*

Ramirez glanced down at his watch. "They'll be here soon."

Max turned his head and gazed down into Samantha's eyes. He just wanted her, and, fucking miracle, she seemed to want him. Even with what his brother had done to her, she wanted *him*.

He would do anything to keep her by his side. Anything to keep her in his life. He bent and brushed his lips across hers.

"I'll talk to Quinlan." He released his hold on Samantha. "For all the damn good it will do."

Max didn't rise when Quinlan was led into the conference room.

Quinlan smirked at him. "Knew you'd be coming by, sooner or later."

"You *can't* talk to him." The tall, thin man in the suit next to Quinlan—the guy had to be his lawyer—shook his head. "This is highly irregular. We need to get the DA in here. You need to—"

"We need to talk," Max said, putting his hands flat on the table.

Quinlan laughed. "Yeah, yeah, we do." He jerked his thumb at the lawyer. "Get out of here."

The lawyer's eyes widened. "Don't you see what's happening here?" He waved toward the mirror. "They're watching you. Recording everything you say. It's just a—"

"When I want your opinion," Quinlan muttered, "I'll damn well tell you."

The lawyer's face slackened with surprise.

"Now get the hell out."

"You're making a mistake!" The man shook his head. "Fine. Your damn funeral, kid." Then he shoved past the two guards who'd brought Quinlan in.

Quinlan shuffled forward. A guard leaned down and cuffed one of Quinlan's hands to the side of the table.

"You good?" The guard asked Max.

Max nodded. *Not really.*

The guards left them alone. Probably the SSD's order. Max didn't speak at first. He just stared at Quinlan. His stepbrother was paler, and the orange prison garb was too bright.

"Don't!" Quinlan snapped. "Don't you dare pity me."

But part of Max did. And the other part wanted to jump across the table and rip the asshole in half. His palms pressed harder into the table. "I've got some questions for you."

Quinlan leaned back as far as the cuffs would let him. "Don't you mean your agent whore has some questions?"

He smirked. "I knew she was an FBI bitch the whole time. Kevin told me when she came into The Core, asking all her questions." His jaw hardened. "I warned you not to get the cops, but you were screwing her—"

"I've been thinking about you." Max bit back the rage as he cut through Quinlan's words. "The SSD called me in today. Said if I got you to confess, they'd give you therapy."

"I don't need fucking therapy! I'm not sick!"

"I don't give a shit if you are or not."

Quinlan blinked.

"I don't give a damn if they open up the cell, shove your ass in, and never pull you back out."

Quinlan shook his head. "No, you don't—"

Max's fists slammed into the table. "You killed Frank."

"The asshole needed to be put down."

"And then..." Max leaned forward. "You made your worst mistake. You came after *her.*"

Quinlan stilled.

"You're lucky she was the one with the gun, because I would have blown your head off and never hesitated." Disgust had his jaw tightening. "Therapy? They think you need *therapy?* Nothing's gonna fix you. You're broken, twisted. Hell, we never expected you to amount to much anyway. Dropped out of college, couldn't hold a job, and shit, now everyone knows that you're just a fucking psycho—"

"*Shut up!*" Quinlan was on his feet, the table jerking toward him as he yanked his arms up and the cuffs stretched taut. "Just shut the hell up! You sound *just like him!* Never fucking good enough! No matter what I did.

But I showed him! I showed every damn one! It was *me*. I did it. I planned it fucking all. I was king, I was *God*, I could do whatever I wanted—"

"And you wanted to kill." Softer, sadder, because Max had gotten what the agents needed. And he'd known just what to say.

He'd said what Frank would have told his son. So easy, really.

"I wanted to show those bastards that life wasn't perfect! Daddy couldn't always bail their asses out!" Quinlan's face reddened.

Couldn't or *wouldn't*?

"Did Beth beg?" Max asked because he had to. *They were watching*. He just wanted this over. Wanted it all over. Staring into Quinlan's eyes now...*I don't see the same man*. A stranger stared back at him with eyes that were too bright.

"Hell, yeah. She begged, she pleaded, and she promised me any damn thing I wanted." His lips twisted. "But I just wanted the bitch to die. This was my show, and she tried to screw with me—"

"A *show*?" Max's stomach tightened. "Is that all this was?" *A show to prove that he was the best*.

Quinlan's left hand slammed onto the table. "The cops couldn't catch me. The Feds couldn't stop me. Those assholes begged for their lives, but they weren't worth enough."

And how much was enough?

"What did you do with the money?" Max kept his eyes on Quinlan.

"I'll never tell." Quinlan slowly lowered back into the chair. Some of his rage seemed to have cooled just that fast. "I'm going to get out. The shrinks will say I'm crazy, and I'll get out." A wider grin spread on his face. "I'll get out, I'll get my money, and I'll be looking for you, *brother.*"

And he realized that Quinlan had a plan. Had always had his plan. "All those times you cut yourself..."

"Ah, good, they know about those already." Quinlan inclined his head toward the mirror. "I'm just a poor, sick boy, never given enough attention, always having to compete with the killer in my own home. A killer." He shook his head and pointed at Max. "Not a very good role model for a guy, huh? I wonder..." Quinlan licked his lips. "Do you think your kids will be as screwed up as me? I mean, with you as—"

The door flew open. "*Enough.*"

Samantha stood there, breath heaving and fire raging in her eyes. "We're done here."

Quinlan laughed. "Knew the bitch was there. I was hoping she'd come out to join us."

Max's vision went red. "*Don't even fucking look at her.*"

"I'll do more than that," Quinlan promised.

I'll get out....

"We've got everything we need, Max. It's over." She came toward him and took his hand. "It's time to go."

His fingers locked around hers. He rose, pulling her close. Her sweet scent filled his nose. Life. Hope.

So much more.

Love.

"Don't trust him, sweetheart," Quinlan taunted. "He's playing innocent, but he knew what I was doing. Why do you think he was at The Core that night? He was there to meet Veronica, to set up the next vic. He might have been screwing you, but it was just so he could cover his own ass. He didn't—"

Her fingers brushed Max's cheek. "He's not worth it," she said, and the words were clear, strong.

Silence.

Then Quinlan's face mottled, and he yelled, *"Fucking bitch! You fucking bitch, I'll slice you open! I'll make you beg, make you scream, and I'll make him watch!"* Spit flew from Quinlan's mouth.

Max took her hand and pressed a kiss to her knuckles. Then he looked back at Quinlan. Veins bulged from his brother's neck and his eyes were wide, wild. "You're not going to see daylight again," he told him.

Quinlan glared at him, hate twisting his face.

"They're going to throw you into a ten-by-eight room. They'll keep you locked up like a dog, and you won't get out." *He'll never touch her.* "But if you do somehow worm your way out of prison," and Max moved, deliberately shifting his body so that Quinlan couldn't see Samantha, "if by some stroke of the devil, you get out, I will find *you.* And trust me, Quinlan, you'll be the one who begs because I will *never* let you hurt anyone else I love."

Max held Quinlan's stare, needing to break through the madness and make sure his brother understood. "If I see you again," he said, "you're dead."

When Sam and Max walked outside, the wind blew her hair, tossing it around her face. She shoved it back and stared at Max, aware that her fingers were trembling. "Max, the case is over now. We've got enough evidence to keep Quinlan locked up for the rest of his life. You're clear; you don't have to worry."

Silence.

"Kenton's going to give a press conference with Hyde later today. They're planning to tie up the loose ends." She stepped closer. "*It's over.*"

"The case might be." He caught her left wrist and chained her to him. "We're not."

The knot in her stomach seemed to ease. "What do you want from me?" As direct as she could be.

Those blue eyes, so intense, searched her face. Then... "Forever. I want forever, baby."

And the fear melted away. Her lips lifted into a trembling smile. "So do I."

His mouth took hers. Desperate hunger, need, lust. Love.

Max.

Hers.

"Everything's been so screwed up," Max murmured against her lips. "Started it all wrong, then the case, Frank, *Quinlan*..."

Pain echoed in his voice. But she'd help him to deal with the pain, just as he'd helped her.

His head lifted, and he gazed down at her with gleaming eyes. "Can you be with me, knowing what he did, can you—"

"Try to stop me." Max *wasn't* Quinlan. "You saved me in that river. You came into the water and—"

"And I wouldn't have come out without you." Flat. "Don't you know yet, baby? Haven't you realized...?"

She waited, *waited.*

"I love you." Simple. Solid. His stare never wavered.

"I never thought I'd love a woman like this, but I swear, when I'm with you, I can't even think straight half the time. I want you, I need you, and I damn well love you more than anything in this world."

She put her left hand on his shoulder. "And I love you, Max Ridgeway." The stranger she'd taken to her bed. The lover who'd comforted her in the night. The man who'd pulled her from hell.

They'd started fast, started red-hot, and gone barreling through the darkness. More darkness might come—that was just part of life—but they'd be together.

She'd spent her whole life looking for a man like him. Someone to fight for her, someone to hold her, and someone to stir her desire. Someone who thought she was worth fighting for, worth dying for.

Someone...*Max*.

She stood on her toes and kissed him.

Worth the world. And more.

Epilogue

Six months later . . .

Quinlan Malone shuffled down the prison hallway. Cat-calls sounded around him. Loud whistles and taunts were hurled from the other inmates as he passed. The orange jumpsuit hung on his shoulders, and the shackles jingled a bit as he walked.

Keith Hyde watched Quinlan head to his new home, one that was a far cry from the mansion that could have been his. A mansion that Max Ridgeway had recently donated to the American Cancer Society. It would be a haven for recovering patients.

The guard opened cell door number 185. Quinlan walked inside. He turned back and offered up his bound hands to the guard. He knew the drill well by now.

Hyde stalked down the corridor. He glanced in the cell. A toilet. Two bunks. Quinlan would have company.

"Happy now, asshole?" Quinlan demanded. "You think this is the end of me? It's not! I'm gettin' out of here, you'll see. My lawyer's working on an appeal." He laughed, shaking his head. "Haven't you heard? I'm crazy! I should be in a mental institution, not jail."

"Your psych sessions will start soon." Because Hyde knew the truth.

Quinlan Malone *was* crazy. There'd been no remorse from him in the courtroom. No empathy for the victims. The guy didn't seem to get that he'd actually done something wrong.

And four days ago, they'd caught him in his cell cutting his upper arms with a shiv.

The guards would have to watch Malone. The longer he was in there, the more desperate he'd become.

"And if you ever do get out," Hyde said, watching as Quinlan shifted quickly from foot to foot. "You won't have a damn thing waiting on you." They'd recovered all the money from the kidnappings before the trial. Quinlan had kept the cash at one of Malone's rental houses, a little place on Sycamore Lane. A house that had smelled of bleach and death, but that had been stuffed with a fortune.

"My brother will be waiting!" Quinlan snarled.

Waiting to kill you. Hyde knew about that threat. There wasn't anything that happened in the SSD that he didn't know about. Hyde turned away.

"Peter and Jeremy were in on it," Quinlan's voice was nearly lost beneath the catcalls.

Hyde paused and glanced back.

"Didn't realize that, did you?" Quinlan's smile held a cocky edge. "Why do you think it was so easy to take them from the bars? Pete just walked right out with Veronica. He thought it was a great damn joke, and he couldn't wait to get his hands on some of his trust fund money."

Peter Hollings. He'd been sent back to his family in pieces. Hyde stared at Quinlan and kept his expression blank. "If Peter was in on the kidnapping, why'd you kill him?"

"Because his dumbass father wouldn't pay." Quinlan shrugged. "I told Pete that he'd die if the old man didn't pay. But, damn, you should've heard the way he started screaming when I pulled out my knife."

Because Peter hadn't realized just how deadly serious Quinlan had been. *Easy prey—he used his own friends.*

"And poor Jeremy," Quinlan shook his head. "He was so sure his father would pay for him. Jeremy already had that cash spent in his mind. He was heading back to Europe."

But he'd just gone to the grave. "And what about the others?"

Quinlan grinned. "Those assholes just pissed me off. I figured I'd give them a little payback."

Sick sonofabitch. "Guess you're the one getting that payback now." Life in Wallens Ridge State Prison. This time, Hyde let the icy façade melt, and he knew his disgust showed when Quinlan stiffened.

Then because there was no more to say, Hyde turned away.

He walked back toward the warden. Hyde didn't usually follow the criminals to their cells after conviction, but this time, he'd made an exception.

A man who should've had it all now had nothing.

One more killer off the streets. More victims buried in the ground. Not a fair score sheet. Not even close.

Not yet. But, God willing, soon.

We'll stop them.

Because he'd made a promise a long time ago. A promise to a girl that he hadn't seen in over thirty years.

The sunlight hit him when he walked out of the prison. So hot and clear. Hyde stopped just outside and pulled out his wallet. He glanced down and stared at the grainy photo.

Some promises time broke. Other promises, the soul kept.

I won't give up.

His daughter had been missing for so long, but one day, dammit, *one day,* he'd find the man who'd taken her away. And Hyde would make sure that the bastard paid.

Because he'd be damned if he let the monsters win.

Two brilliant agents.
One dream team.

———

Please turn this page
for an excerpt from
the sizzling first book in
the series

Deadly Fear

Available now.

CHAPTER *Two*

So...are we gonna talk about it?"

Monica froze at the deep voice. Her notes were spread in front of her, the shade on her window firmly closed—because she really hated to fly—and with only about ten minutes left on the private flight, it looked like Dante had decided to get chatty.

Great.

"I mean...we're gonna be working together, and we can't pretend the past didn't happen...."

Sure they could. She spent most of her days shoving the memories of her past away.

Carefully, Monica set down her pen. Then she lifted her gaze. Dante sat across from her, his long legs spread out, taking up too much room. He'd changed before they left, thankfully gotten rid of the blood, and now he wore loose khakis and a button-down shirt.

Over the years, she'd tried not to think about Dante. Tried to pretend the fling with him hadn't happened.

Tried and failed really, really well.

"Like what you see?" The words came out of his mouth sounding like some kind of sensual purr.

Asshole.

And, dammit, *yes*. Luke Dante was sex, he was power, and he was *temptation*.

A temptation she hadn't been able to resist when she was twenty-two. But one she *would* ignore now.

Tall, muscled, with bright emerald eyes and sun-streaked blond hair, Dante was a southern boy with charm and a dimple in his chin.

A long, thin scar marred his right cheek. She'd been there the day he got that scar. The mark didn't detract from Dante's looks. No, the scar just made him look all the more dangerous.

She stared at him, trying to be detached. A strong jaw, wide lips, slightly twisted nose—he *shouldn't* have been handsome.

But he was.

No, not handsome. Sexy.

Dammit.

Monica cleared her throat. "The past is over, Dante." They'd been over this before, when he'd made the mistake of tracking her down. *Serious mistake.* "We're professionals, we can—"

"Pretend we never had sex? Pretend we didn't nearly tear each other apart because we were so fucking hungry those nights?"

Her heart thumped hard enough to shake her chest.

He smiled at her, flashing his white teeth. "Don't know if I'm that good at pretending, *Ice*."

Her eyes narrowed. She *hated* that nickname. The jerks

she'd been in training with had tagged her with it. No one understood.

Control—control mattered. But she'd sure lost control with him.

Dante was her one mistake over the years. The one slip that had broken past the walls she'd worked so hard to erect.

Ice.

All the agents had been given names in their class.

Dante had been called Devil. The guy liked to take risks, to push boundaries. A devil who didn't care about being cautious. How were you supposed to resist the devil?

His name hadn't stuck, though. Hers had.

Monica sucked in a hard breath and deliberately relaxed her fingers. "Long time ago, Dante. And I don't deal in the past." *Wrong.* She'd spent years running from her past. "I focus on the present." As much as possible. She held his stare and knew that her face would be expressionless.

She'd practiced that. *Ice.*

So, okay, maybe she'd helped a little bit with that nickname. But being cold kept the others away, and it could be dangerous when someone got too close.

Straightening her shoulders, she said, "I'm the senior agent here, and I'm not looking to screw around." Too dangerous. "We're on a case. We work together because that's what we have to do in order to get the job done." Simple. Flat.

Dante didn't so much as blink.

"Now, are you going to have a problem with that? Because, if so, it won't be too hard to send your butt back to Atlanta." Total bullshit now. Like she had that kind of power.

Hyde wanted Dante on his team. He'd been adamant about him. He'd even overridden her objections, and the guy usually listened to her opinions about people. Not this time.

A muscle flexed along Dante's jaw. Perfectly shaven now, but she'd seen him at dawn, seen the rough stubble that—

"No problem, *ma'am*," the title was a sardonic taunt. "I can do my job just fine." A pause.

"Good."

"Can you?"

Monica ground her teeth together. "Trust me, Dante, it won't be an issue for me." *Liar, liar...*

She could still remember all too well what the man looked like naked.

And what he felt like.

She swallowed.

Leaving him before had nearly ripped her apart, but there hadn't been a choice. The man was a weakness, one she couldn't afford.

"Prepare for descent." A male voice broke over the intercom system. "Buckle your safety belts. We'll be arriving in Jasper..."

Monica caught the belt in her hands as the rest of the pilot's words washed right past her. *Snap.*

If Dante handled his first SSD case right, she'd be working with him, every day and all those nights, for a long time to come.

Shot down. Luke blew out a slow breath. He could handle it. A case waited. Victims. He could focus and get the job done.

THE DISH

Where authors give you the inside scoop!

From the desk of Hope Ramsay

Dear Reader,

Picture, if you will, a little girl in a polka-dot bathing suit, standing on a rough board jutting out over the waters of the Edisto River in South Carolina. She's about six years old, and standing below her in the chest-high, tea-colored water is a tall man with a deep, deep Southern drawl—the kind that comes right up out of the ground.

"Jump, little gal," the man says. "I'll catch you."

The little girl was me. And the man was my Uncle Ernest. And that memory is one of those touchstone moments that I go back to again and again. My uncle wanted me to face my fear of jumping into the water, but he was there, big hands outstretched, steady, sturdy, and sober as a judge. He was the model of a man I could trust.

I screwed up my courage and took that leap of faith. I jumped. He caught me. He taught me to love jumping into the river and swimming in those dark, mysterious waters, overhung with Spanish moss and sometimes visited by snakes and gators!

I loved Uncle Ernest. He was my favorite uncle. He's

been gone for quite a while now, but I think of him often, and he lives on in my heart.

There is even a little bit of him in Clay Rhodes, the hero of my debut novel, WELCOME TO LAST CHANCE. Jane, the heroine of the story, has to learn that Clay is the type of guy she can always trust. A guy she can take a leap of faith with. A guy who will always be there to catch her, even when she has to face her biggest fears.

And isn't love all about taking a leap of faith?

I had such fun writing WELCOME TO LAST CHANCE, because it afforded me the opportunity to go back in time and remember what it was like spending my summers in a little town in South Carolina with folks who were like Uncle Ernest—people who made up a village where a child could grow up safe and sound and learn what makes a life meaningful.

I hope you enjoy meeting the characters in Last Chance, South Carolina, as much as I enjoyed writing them.

Y'all take care now,

Hope Ramsay

www.hoperamsay.com

♥ ♥ ♥ ♥ ♥ ♥ ♥ ♥ ♥ ♥ ♥ ♥ ♥ ♥ ♥

From the desk of Cynthia Eden

Dear Reader,

Have you ever wondered how far you would go to protect someone you loved? What would you do if the person you loved was in danger?

Love can make people do wild, desperate things…and love can certainly push people to cross the thin line between good and evil.

When I wrote DEADLY LIES, I created characters who would be forced to blur the lines between good and evil. Desperate times can call for desperate measures.

The heroine of this book is a familiar face if you've read the other DEADLY books. Samantha "Sam" Kennedy was first introduced in DEADLY FEAR. Sam lived through hell, and she's now fighting to put her life back on track. She knows what evil looks like, and she knows that evil can hide behind the most innocent of faces. So when Sam is assigned to work on a serial kidnapping case, she understands that she has to be on her guard at all times.

But when the kidnapper hits too close to home and her lover's stepbrother is abducted, the rules of the game change. Soon Sam fully understands just how "desperate" the victims are feeling, and she vows to do anything in her power to help Max Ridgeway find his brother.

Anything. Yes, desperation can even push an FBI agent to the edge of the law. Lucky for Sam, she'll have backup ready to help her out—all of the other SSD agents are back to help track the kidnappers, and they won't stop until the case is closed.

I've had such a wonderful time revisiting my SSD agents in this book. And I hope you enjoying catching up with the characters too!

If you'd like to learn more about my books, please visit my website at www.cynthiaeden.com.

Happy reading!

Cynthia Eden

♥ ♥ ♥ ♥ ♥ ♥ ♥ ♥ ♥ ♥ ♥ ♥ ♥ ♥ ♥

From the desk of Robyn DeHart

Dear Reader,

There have always been certain things that fascinate me—the heinous crimes of Jack the Ripper; why cats get up, turn around, then settle back into the exact position they were just in; people who can eat only *one* Oreo cookie; and the ancient legend of the Loch Ness monster. Recorded sightings of the creature date all the way back to the seventh century, and not all of these sightings have been water-based—there are those who claim to have seen the monster walking on land.

Regardless of what you believe, it's interesting to think that there just might be some prehistoric animal hiding in a loch in the Highlands. It was this interest that compelled me to write TREASURE ME.

Another interesting tidbit about this book is that it was actually the first romance novel I ever wrote. Okay, that's not entirely true, but the concept of a couple who fall in love near Loch Ness, centered around adventure and action and danger, well, that was all in that first book—even the characters' names stayed the same. But I didn't keep anything else. When it came to the third book in my Legend Hunters trilogy, I took my basic concept and started from scratch.

If you've read SEDUCE ME and DESIRE ME (the first two books in the series), then you might remember meeting Graeme, the big, brooding Scotsman who looks and sounds remarkably like Gerard Butler. Graeme has been after the authentic Stone of Destiny for years, because he believes the one sitting in Westminster is a counterfeit. He's gone back to his family's home in the Highlands to do some research, and meets with trouble in the form of a delectable, self-proclaimed paleontologist named Vanessa. She's just run away from her own wedding and is determined to make a name for herself as a legitimate scientist.

Add in a marriage of convenience, a deadly nemesis,

and some buried treasure and you've got yourself a rollicking adventure full of intrigue and seduction that will leave you as breathless as the characters.

Dare to love a Legend Hunter . . .

Visit my website, www.RobynDeHart.com, for contests, excerpts, and more.

Enjoy!

Robyn DeHart

♥ ♥ ♥ ♥ ♥ ♥ ♥ ♥ ♥ ♥ ♥ ♥ ♥ ♥

From the desk of Kira Morgan

Dear Reader,

It's easy to write about a match made in heaven. Cinderella meets Prince Charming, they fall in love at first sight, and they live happily ever after.

But for my latest book, SEDUCED BY DESTINY, I wanted to take on the challenge of star-crossed lovers, characters like Romeo and Juliet—a man and a woman cursed by fate and thrown together by chance, who have to overcome their tragic history to find true love.

In SEDUCED BY DESTINY, set in the time of Mary, Queen of Scots, Josselin Ancrum and Andrew Armstrong each have a dark secret in their past and deadly peril looming in their future. They have little in common. They should avoid each other like the plague.

She's Scottish. He's English.

She likes to stir up trouble. He likes to fly under the radar.

She's a tavern wench who loves to play with swords. He's an expert swordsman who'd rather play golf.

Her mother was killed in battle.

His father was the one who killed her.

Talk about Fortune's foe . . .

All this would be fine if only they hadn't started falling in love. If they hadn't felt that initial spark of attraction . . . if they hadn't begun to enjoy one another's company . . . if they hadn't succumbed to that first kiss . . . their story might be a simple tale of revenge.

But Drew and Jossy, unaware of the fateful ties between them, are drawn to one another like iron to a magnet. And by the time they discover they've fallen in love with their mortal enemy, it's too late. Their hearts are already tangled in a hopeless knot.

This is where it gets even more interesting.

To make matters worse, outside forces are working to drive them apart. What began as a personal mission of vengeance now involves their friends, their families, and ultimately their queens. Suspected of treason, hunted by spies, they become targets for royal assassins.

The uneasy truce between Queen Elizabeth and Queen Mary is mirrored in the fragile relationship between Drew and Jossy. The lovers are swept into a raging battle bigger than the both of them—a battle that shakes the foundation of their union and threatens their very lives.

Only the strength of their fateful bond and the power of their love can save them now.

Of course, unlike Romeo and Juliet, Drew and Jossy will triumph. Nobody wants to read a historical romance with an unhappy ending! But just how they manage to overcome all odds, when their stars are crossed and the cards are stacked against them, is the stuff of nail-biting high adventure and a story that I hope will keep you up all night.

To read an excerpt from SEDUCED BY DESTINY, peruse my research photos, and enter my monthly sweepstakes, visit my website at www.glynnis.net/kiramorgan. If you'd like to read my daily posts and interact with other fans, become my friend at www.facebook.com/KiraMorganAuthor or follow me at www.twitter.com/kira_morgan.

Happy adventures!

Kira Morgan

Find out more about Forever Romance!

Visit us at
www.hachettebookgroup.com/publishing_forever.aspx

Find us on Facebook
http://www.facebook.com/ForeverRomance

Follow us on Twitter
http://twitter.com/ForeverRomance

NEW AND UPCOMING TITLES

Each month we feature our new titles
and reader favorites.

CONTESTS AND GIVEAWAYS

We give away galleys, autographed copies,
and all kinds of exclusive items.

AUTHOR INFO

You'll find bios, articles, and links to personal websites
for all your favorite authors—and so much more.

GET SOCIAL

Connect with your favorite authors, editors, and
other Forever fans, and share what's important to you.

THE BUZZ

Sign up for our monthly romance newsletter,
and be the first to read all about it.